Demonic Visions
50 Horror Tales
Book 4

Copyright © 2015 by various authors and Chris Robertson, *Demonic Visions*. All Rights Reserved.

No part of this publication may be reproduced, stored in a retrieval system, or transmitted, in any form or by any means, electronic, mechanical, photocopying, recording, or otherwise, without prior written permission from the authors.

This is a work of fiction. Names, characters, places and incidents either are the product of the author's imagination or are used fictitiously. And any resemblance to actual persons, living, dead (or in any other form), business establishments, events, or locales is entirely coincidental.

Demonic Visions 50 Horror Tales Book 4

© 2015

ISBN-13: 978-0-9861114-3-3

Foreword by the Editor

Welcome to the fourth installment of the Demonic Visions series. This new collection of macabre tales includes short fiction by all members of the Demonic Visions team. Every new book that we publish will take you deeper into the minds of these talented writers, and acquaint you with their various styles of prose. So enjoy, and I hope that you will join us for the entire Demonic Visions saga which is intended to last many, many years and span many, many volumes…

~Chris Robertson, author of *Death Dreams Deluxe*

Cover art by Grant Cross, artwork on Facebook: *Grant Cross Artwork*

Table of Contents:

Other Books by the Writers:

Matt Drabble – *Gated, Gated II: Ravenhill Academy, Asylum - 13 Tales of Terror, Abra-Cadaver, After Darkness Falls Volume One, After Darkness Falls Volume Two, The Travelling Man*

Peter Adam Salomon - *Henry Franks, All Those Broken Angels*

Marc Sorondo - *Aurora*

Marc Shapiro - *High Strangeness, Melancholy Baby* (Chubra Cabra House),

Robert Friedrich - *The Darkness Within: A Novella, Enlightened by Darkness - Vol.1 First Encounter, Enlightened by Darkness - Vol.2 The Invasion, Enlightened by Darkness - Vol.3 As Darkness Spreads, Enlightened by Darkness: Complete Trilogy, The Book of Metal Lyrics, Seed of Evil: An Ancient Evil Rises, Deathmongers: Where the Light Dies, Blessings from the Condemned: A Horror Legacy, Welcome to your Death: Part 1*

Christopher Conlon - *Savaging the Dark, He Is Legend: An Anthology Celebrating Richard Matheson, A Matrix of Angels, Midnight on Mourn Street, The Oblivion Room*

Ken MacGregor - *An Aberrant Mind*

Joe McKinney - *Dead City, Apocalypse of the Dead, Flesh Eaters, Mutated, The Savage Dead, The Red Empire and Other Stories, Inheritance, Dating in Dead World: The Collected Zombie Short Fiction of Joe McKinney, Dead in the Water, Lost Girl of the Lake* (with Michael McCarty), *Night Work and Grimoires, Deadman Wade* (with Sheldon Higdon), *Dog Days, Dodging Bullets, The Crossing, Crooked House, St Rage, Plague of the Undead*

Patrick Freivald - *Twice Shy, Special Dead, Blood List* (with Phil Freivald), *Jade Sky*

Mark Slade - *A Six Gun and the Queen of Light, Hellspeak: A Pete Chambers Book, Electric Funeral*

Naching T. Kassa - *The Venihi, Master of the Shade*

Julianne Snow - *Days with the Undead: Book One, Glimpses of the Undead, The Carnival 13* (collaborative novella for charity)

William Holden - *Words to Die By, Clothed in Flesh*

J. T. (Troy) Seate - Novels: *Valley of Tears, Tears for the Departed, And the Heavens Wept,* Novellas: *Something About Sara, Connor House, A Resting Place*

K. Trap Jones - *The Sinner, The Harvester, The Drunken Exorcist, One Bad Fur Day, The Crossroads*

Shenoa Carroll-Bradd - *The Minstrel Angel, The Widow's Painted Room*

Rick McQuiston - *Twelve Days of Christmas Horror, Giant Book of Nightmares, To See as a God Sees, Where Things Might Walk*

Rob Smales - *The Dead of Winter (Seasons of the Dead)*

James Pratt - *Cthelvis and Others, Horrible Stories for Terrible People, Vol. I: Monsters, Horrible Stories for Terrible People, Vol. II: Obscura*

Vince Liberato - *Redshifted: Martian Stories, After the Fall: Tales of the Apocalypse, What Has Two Heads, Ten Eyes, and Terrifying Table Manners?: An Anthology of Science Fiction Horror, Master Minds (Third Flatiron Anthologies Vol 3)*

Chris Leek - *Nevada Thunder* (Snubnose Press), *Smoke Em If You Got Em*

Justin Hunter - *Nostalgia, Chet & Floyd vs. the Apocalypse: Volumes 1 and 2*

S.C. Hayden - *Rusty Nails Broken Glass, American Idol*

Maggie Carroll - *Eurydice*

Ramsey Campbell - *The Face That Must Die, Midnight Sun, The Darkest Part of the Woods, The Grin of the Dark, Creatures of the Pool, The Seven Days of Cain, Ghosts Know* and *The Kind Folk. Needing Ghosts, The Last Revelation of Gla'aki* and *The Pretence* are novellas.

1. TWELVE VOLT EXISTENCE BY ADAM MILLARD

As The Doors once sang so many decades ago, people are strange. With all the progress we, as a species, have made, one would imagine that life – both as a level of material comfort and in terms of simplicity – would improve. However, as we approach the 22nd Century with an air of caution and uncertainty, the truth is that the world as we know it has gone – I believe the old adage goes – *to hell in a handbasket.*

I, Chester Walker, am one of those unfortunately targeted by the mindless drones of society that deem my – *our* – implants a heresy; a direct defiance of God. At the time of my operation, such procedures were all the rage. You were lucky if you could afford such expensive treatment, and even luckier if you could afford the system that *I* had had installed.

They called it an augmentation system; I called it a miracle. For people like me – those with a clear perception of their own mortality – it was almost too good to be true. I was terrified of dying, fully aware of the brevity of our existence upon this planet we call home.

This system changed everything for me. I am still going to die – as everything does, eventually – but my life should have ended years ago, and *would* have if I had decided against the implantation. You see, it is not some sort of immortality-device; such things are of science-fiction, and will remain so until our current abilities and sciences advance. It does, however, defer death for a later time.

Think, if you can, of the wasted hours spent sleeping, all the time growing older. Those periods of inactivity amount to something along the lines of twenty-six years. Can you *imagine*? A quarter of a century lying dormant, growing wrinkly and demented. Just thinking about it makes me queasy.

At the time of the system's arrival, I was a very successful multimedia producer. In other words, I had money to burn. A colleague of mine by the name of Walter Trent – dead now, as are most of my old friends – brought the implant to my attention on the week of its release. At first, I thought he was teasing. Old Wally knew how fearful I was of dying, and so I believed it to be some misbegotten prank.

Then, the system was everywhere. On the news, in the digital papers; you couldn't turn your head without finding yourself face-to-face with that silvery logo. To me it looked like two lower-case exes, in a font that suggested something far more futuristic than anything else on the market. It became almost a game, to see how many times during the day I stumbled across the logo. I kept count, and on an average day the final numbers were up in the high-hundreds. Once or twice, I reached a thousand.

That was the power of marketing, and the company behind the system had more money to burn than even *I*. Within a few weeks the system had been installed in more than twenty-thousand people, making it the fastest-selling implant ever. I knew it would only be a matter of time before I allowed myself to go under the knife.

An extension of life, the advertisements said, usually while some beautiful brunette held the tiny device between perfectly-manicured fingernails. I know how marketing works, and wasn't drawn in simply by the inclusion of some part-time tart with a salon loyalty-card.

I wanted the life.

No, I *needed* it. At the time I was almost fifty. Three decades of over-indulgence had probably taken a few years off the nationwide average life-expectancy, meaning I would live to perhaps eighty – ninety at a push. I was halfway and then some, and that was what decided it for me.

I booked into the hospital a week following my fiftieth birthday, and convinced myself it was merely an expensive treat, a gift from me…to *me*. Twenty-six extra years – at least – in which I could continue to enjoy life exactly as I had been. I would continue to age, as there was nothing they could do to change that, but in myself I would feel no older than those waking hours. As far as I was concerned, the system was the greatest thing ever created.

The implant was installed under minor supervision, and with very little in the way of pain. One port, somewhere between my first rib and my clavicle, was all I found on the left side of my body when I removed the bandages a few hours later. Modern surgery continued to astound me, even then. Now, of course, you can have a complete set of organs installed with nothing more than two tiny incisions beneath the nipples, but back then it was fascinating to me just what was possible.

The port, so I was told by the surgeon that same afternoon, led directly to the system, which was attached to the left ventricle of my heart. To me, it all sounded a little confusing. As long as it did what it promised, I wouldn't have minded if it was hooked up to my genitalia.

The doctor, whose name escapes me at this time, then proceeded to hand me a single charger. At one end was a connector matching the port embedded in my flesh; at the other was a battery, which was simply to be plugged into any available socket. Again, I thought I was having the proverbial piss taken out of me; it all looked a little dubious. The charger looked like something you would use to power one of those tiny, new-fangled cars.

"The lady on the advert never had one of these," I said to the doctor, watching closely for any hint of a smile. I patted the small black unit which, surprise-surprise, portrayed the futuristic double-exes upon its side. "So I just plug this thing in, and—"

"And the implant will do the rest," he said, rudely finishing my sentence for me. There was no sign of anything amiss with the doctor's countenance, which meant he was telling the truth, which in turn meant I had just installed countless extra years onto my life.

I thanked him, though words couldn't express how happy – how *relieved* – I was. I returned home with that magical little box and decided to celebrate with a bottle of something special.

Life was good – and *longer*, at least for me.

At night, just before closing my eyes, I would plug the charger into the port up near my shoulder. I would then sleep, the system taking over the duties usually tended to by my heart. In essence, my body lay in stasis until I unhooked the machine in the morning. I likened it to a credit-card. As I slept I was paying just the interest, and when awake I was using the balance of myself. In years to come, I would realise that it wasn't like that at all.

Those first months after implantation were the best of my life. I felt rejuvenated, reborn. There was no reason for it other than the peace of mind the system had afforded me. I was not going to start cartwheeling or marathon-running, and yet I felt like I *could*, if I tried. It's amazing what a little extension can do for you.

Things, however, soon turned sour. The system continued to sell – by the pallet-load – but certain religious groups had taken it upon themselves to set up permanent residence outside the manufacturer's headquarters, and also at some of London's most prominent landmarks. They protested diligently in an effort to have the system removed from the market. *The Devil Box* they were calling it, which was funny, to me, at the time. How could anything that offered people more life be considered evil? If anything, they should have been praising that little creation, praying to it. They should – and I honestly believed this at the time – have built churches and named them after the company responsible for its conception.

The Pope had a few choice words to say about the implant, none of them good. I was just grateful that people had stopped listening to what he had to say years before; the impact of his words might have been different if half the world didn't despise him.

It became shameful to talk about my implant to anyone – even friends. My own *sister* didn't know I had recently installed one; such was my reluctance to approach the topic. I should have been proud of it. That a man could artificially increase the length of his life with something so rudimentary was a miracle, and people were turning their back on it, and punishing those of us who had made the purchase.

At night, as I plugged the machine into my port, I would often try to convince myself that there was nothing wrong with it, that what I was doing was completely normal, and that those setting up protest across the country were merely jealous, or annoyed that their religion prevented them from installing an implant of their own. I'd fall asleep with the sounds of their incessant chanting ringing in my ears, but I didn't care.

I'd outlive most of them.

Which brings me to now, and the events leading to this missive. Last night, before I had a chance to insert the plug into my shoulder, I believe I suffered a heart-attack. It lasted no longer than ten minutes, but at the time I was terrified beyond anything I have ever experienced. The pain was so intense that I gnawed through my bottom lip. There is blood everywhere, and I can still taste its bitterness on my tongue.

So with this impossible agony wracking my body, I fought my way to the bed and the silvery box sitting upon my nightstand. After a few minutes of nervous fumbling – it's very difficult to concentrate when in pain – I managed to attach myself to the system. Whether I expected the pain to magically dissipate, I'm not sure, but I can tell you that I was a little surprised when I continued to feel the attack. I lay back on the bed, sweating and trying to regulate my breathing – which had become somewhat frantic – until the pain passed.

At some time between seven and eight this morning, the protestors returned to the front of my building and began to taunt me with their chants of disapproval. I haven't been able to respond, not that I would anyway; the way I see it, they have their reasons and we have ours.

If I knew then what I know now, would I do things differently? That's a difficult question. I'm almost one-hundred and thirty years-old, and I know that as soon as I unplug myself from this machine, this pathetic looking silvery box with its insignificant exes, I will succumb to whatever follows on from life. Time, it seems, gets the better of each of us. I have merely delayed the inevitable, continuing to rot and shrink into a shell of my former-self. The only thing I've succeeded in doing is extending my own agony.

In the beginning, it was almost a novelty. I would live beyond what was expected for a *homo sapien*. A decade following the implant's insertion, though, and I realised I had perhaps fifty years remaining, which soon became forty, then thirty. Before I even had time to realise it, I was thinking more and more about death, as I had before the operation. Instead of enjoying life, as I'd promised myself I would, I spent most of it still anticipating death. You see, the kind of people that jumped at the chance of installing the implant, all those years ago, were the type of people that feared death; the very same kind of people who believed that a glass was half empty when it was, in fact, half full.

The moral implications of the system have been questioned so many times across the years that I'm sick and tired of thinking about it. The augmentation device was removed from sale over a decade ago, with many surgeons and hospitals refusing to install it in any new patients. Last month, a document containing the names of those of us with the system still installed was leaked, which is why I can hear those zealots out front. They want me to unhook the machine, to die as God intended, but I'm still scared. I've lived half a century past my use-by-date, and yet death continues to terrify me.

Last night's heart-attack was the end, and the machine sitting on the table in front of me is my life-support. Those people I can hear in the street out front will have to break in and pull the cord from my flesh. I'm not sure I'll ever be able to accept death, though I'm slowly coming to realise why it's best not to spend the duration of one's life worrying about it.

Perhaps I will be fortunate and all options – as restricted as they are – will be removed.

If there is a God, I pray for a power-cut.

2. **TRIGGER WARNING** BY PATRICK FREIVALD

Tom slipped across the ruined plaza

> quad this is grass not pavement it's a quad

eyes down, hidden behind dark glasses polarized to reduce glare.
Automatic weapons crackled in the distance

> dammit just a motorcycle you used to ride one remember
> there's no threat here

 almost too far away to hear. He skirted the burned out tank,

> fountain look at it read the inscription it's a fountain

feet shuffling under the weight of the ALICE pack,

> books are heavy there's a math test tomorrow there is no threat
> here

straps cutting into his shoulders through the uniform.

> He took shelter in the mosque's

> library

entrance, letting the shadows pool around and hide him from the
midday sun. He closed his eyes and took a deep breath almost devoid
of gasoline and gunpowder and held it, savoring the hint of jasmine
and patchouli leftover from some pre-war bazaar.

> or the coed smoking three feet away

Fuck it. Orders are orders and

> my last order was a big mac there is no threat here

the squad needs cover.

Tom opened his eyes and scanned the burned-out husk

intact buildings

of the town—

campus

He squeezed them shut again and pressed his palms to his temples. Something had gone wrong, something terrible, and he couldn't keep his thoughts straight. He needed

pills like right now isn't soon enough it's been a week

to get upstairs before the squad got into position. If they tried to advance without cover the hajis would take them apart.

Three steps brought him inside the building, into an alcove gaudy with plaster scrollwork defiled by illegible graffiti under a broken bulb. An imam with a great gray beard looked up

she can't be more than twenty she's not a threat

and looked back down at the huge tome without reaction—his mistake. Tom slid left, toward the stairs, grunting in surprise at the flickering exit sign. *How do they have electricity*

come on man it's even in english it says "exit" not خروج why would it say that

with the whole grid bombed to shit?

The door opened without protest, revealing a black iron staircase leading up and down. He'd made it up two floors when a group burst onto the next landing, their raucous chatter

that's english not arabic they aren't threats

inappropriate for a place of quiet and introspection. He cut through the lower door into some kind of library, right into the path of a dark-skinned man in a red turban

the red sox don't make turbans that's a ball cap

and blue jeans.

Tom silenced him with a finger strike to the throat, then stepped in and swept the man's legs from under him, cradling him on the way down to muffle the noise. Eyes wide, he had no chance to struggle as Tom slit his throat with a k-bar. The angry red line bubbled and frothed as air escaped from lungs filling with blood. He tried to ignore the tears, put his knife above the heart and leaned in—even jihadis didn't deserve to suffer like that.

He dragged the corpse into the stacks, withdrew the knife. A spurt of blood, a last vestige of fading pressure, soaked into the flannel shirt

why would a mujahidin wear plaid flannel he was not a threat

in an angry, sad splotch. Tom fondled the steel watch on the man's wrist, somehow out of place, but noise from the stairwell pulled his attention that way.

He held his breath.

The group from above passed by in a wall of guttural chatter,

they're talking about the voice that's tv not jihad

then paused at the lower landing. Tom grimaced at the corpse's stench, iron and shit and body odor. He preferred the crow's nest, the recoil. The distance.

He looked down at the bloody mess

there's nothing there you need your meds there is no threat here

and frowned. If someone found it.... Too late. Done is done.

The door clicked shut below, muffling the conversation further. Tom peered out the tiny window, screened between the panes with wire mesh. *All clear.* He took the next four flights three stairs at a time, knees burning by the time he reached the top. Gasping soft, short breaths, he listened for any signs of movement.

In the distance a speaker blared, a crackling recording of a muezzin

two strokes it's afternoon it's a bell two strokes there is no threat here

calling the faithful to their prayers. *Is it Friday?* Dhuhr on Friday would mean dozens of hajis converging on the temple, everyone but the sentries and what few women remained in the war zone.

He realized he didn't know, and in the end it didn't matter. He had a job to do, and it wouldn't do itself.

He tried the knob. It rotated down a fraction of an inch, then stopped.

Dammit.

He wiggled the k-bar between the door and the frame. A twist, a slide, a fraction of an inch. He repeated the motion, again and again, cursing every lost moment. He exhaled in relief when the deadbolt slipped free, and yanked the door open.

No time to lose.

He kicked the door closed, locked it, and looked up. The ladder stretched another thirty feet, to the top of the minaret,

bell tower

ablaze under the midday sun. He pulled himself up, panting with worry. He'd taken too long. The gunfire

traffic

rose to a crescendo.

He shrugged out of the ALICE pack. He lifted the flap as it hit the plain concrete floor, a ledge just big enough to accommodate him. The black metal, cool to the touch, came together with brutal efficiency. Someone would see the .50 cal stick out the window. An RPG, or a well-placed shot, and that'd be it. But the unit needed him.

He tried the frosted window, but it had been sealed shut. He pried at it as precious seconds ticked by. *No time, no time.*

no threats there are no threats here

He drove the heel of his combat boot into the window. The glass budged. He did it again. Again. A crack appeared, blue sky and contrails. Again. The glass gave way and the view spread out before him. He swallowed. Hundreds of fighters swarmed the town,

afternoon classes it's two o'clock you have recitation now

well more than intel had predicted. A trap.

He pulled the Mk 323 ammunition from the bag, polymer-coated metal in a dozen ten-round box magazines. *Was it enough?*

too much there are no threats here

He lay still, took a breath, positioned the weapon, opened his eyes.

He looked through the scope and gasped, his calm shattered. Jennie lay on the grass, between a young man with a scraggly red beard and a cute brunette. His sister brushed back a lock of blonde hair and laughed at something he couldn't hear. He squeezed his eyes shut.

No, no, not this not now. He knew he was sick. He knew that. But he couldn't let that put his squad in danger. Sergeant Broud said he wasn't at home, had cleared him for action. He had a

math test tomorrow

duty. He took a breath and opened one eye.

The three sentries lounged in the open, the one in the middle a mass of scar tissue masquerading as man. *Bomber. Priority target.*

He put his finger on the trigger, centered the crosshairs below the neck, in the center of the white robe. Body armor couldn't stop this. He exhaled, long and slow.

there is no threat here

yes there is

Jennie rolled onto her stomach and the girl next to her swatted her shoulder. Playful.

The burned man

Jennie that's your sister she is not a threat

did pushups while his companions laughed, a fish in a barrel

she made breakfast this morning eggs and toast and coffee

unaware of the death that awaited her. *Her?*

Him.

Tom blinked. Shook his head. Blinked again. *What the—?*

He looked through the scope.

Jennie grinned,

That's not your sister, that's a target. Take him. Broud cleared you for duty.

rummaged in her bag and produced a pack of gum

Bomb. That's a man with a bomb and he's going to kill your friends.

gum dammit gum not bomb she's chewing it you can't chew a bomb you need your meds you have a test tomorrow there is no threat here

His finger tightened on the trigger.

Dr. Lange stopped the recorder and studied the man on the other side of the desk. Robert Hanover looked broken. He was wrecked with exhaustion, his lips purple, his skin a pasty gray and filmed with sweat, yet even still, he fought against the restraints that held his wrists to the chair.

Dr. Lange sighed.

Another session without answers.

Hanover unexpectedly rallied. With the blood vessels in his eyes cracked like a windshield and spit flying from his lips he looked like a madman fighting against the restraints. "God damn you!" he shouted. "You let me go. Let me help her. For God's sake, Gene, let me go!"

Dr. Lange's expression soured when Hanover addressed him by his first name, but he quickly forced his distaste down. Correcting the man would do little good. Hanover was a clinical narcissist – as close to a textbook case as Dr. Lange had ever seen, in fact – and refusing to address doctors by their proper titles was but one symptom of his inflated sense of entitlement and self-importance. Hanover also needed constant praise and reinforcement. He set unrealistic goals. Social clues went by him unnoticed. And, of course, his self-esteem was fragile as spun glass.

All of which was routine.

Just about everything about Robert Hanover was routine.

Only his delusions of power were exceptional.

More precisely, the nature of his delusions set him apart. For Robert Hanover believed he could see exactly seven minutes and twenty-two seconds into the future.

But not all the time.

That was the important part. When he was calm, he would always qualify his claim.

He couldn't do it on command. His premonitions came unbidden. They were violent and painful. And when they did come, they left Hanover exhausted and frantic.

Like now.

Dr. Lange studied the man, remembering when Hanover had told him about his supposed visions. He'd barely been able to contain his smile, in fact. The fantasy was thoroughly banal and absolutely unoriginal, straight out of a Stephen King novel and half a dozen episodes of *The Twilight Zone*. It was such a tired conceit that Dr. Lange was less intrigued by the delusion itself than by the very precise timing involved.

Seven minutes and twenty-two seconds.

Exactly.

But why that length of time?

Dr. Lange expected Hanover to have some pat answer. A fragile ego like Hanover's, one that believed itself superior to everyone else around it, should have had a ready retort to explain why that amount of time was important. But Hanover insisted he had no idea, and nothing in his history, and nothing in their sessions, offered any clues.

Still, Dr. Lange knew there was something there. If there was a key to unlocking Robert Hanover's condition, that odd length of time was it.

Dr. Lange began cataloging the events Hanover claimed to have predicted, hoping that he might shed some light on the problem that way. Most of Hanover's visions were insignificant, and ultimately unverifiable. His mother running over a cat in front of their house. A bird flying into the kitchen window. His dog killing a squirrel in the backyard. With no way to prove those claims, Dr. Lange was forced to dismiss them.

But there were some that could not be dismissed so easily.

When he was nineteen, Hanover saved a three-year-old little girl from getting hit by a taxi. Half of the lunch crowd gathered on Boston Common had been there to witness his heroism.

He'd once called 911 to report his elderly neighbor's heart attack, which seemed to have just started when the ambulance arrived.

He'd saved at least four people from drowning.

He'd once pulled a woman from a burning shop on Boylston Street.

Dr. Lange had the newspaper clippings for all of them. In fact, he'd been able to verify a total of forty-seven incidents where Robert Hanover had clearly saved another person's life.

For a time, the Boston *Herald* was calling him the Miracle Man.

20/20 even did a segment on him.

The man's record was nothing short of incredible, and personally, Dr. Lange believed the media would have fallen head over heels in love with Robert Hanover if he hadn't been such a self-absorbed prick. He was twenty-five, a good-looking guy, at least when he wasn't acting like a raving lunatic, and fairly well spoken. But he loved the adulation that came with saving lives.

No, Dr. Lange thought, love wasn't the right word.

Robert Hanover's motives were decidedly less pure than that.

He craved adulation and fame like a glutton. He swam in it. Wallowed in it like a pig in slop. There was something greedy and repellent in the way he begged for praise and recognition, and people had a tendency to back away from him, sensing instinctively that there was something wrong with him. Dr. Lange had even caught himself doing it a time or two.

The media, in an unusual example of discretion, marginalized him.

And just like that, the greatest American hero turned into a zero.

The predictable downward spiral of failed personal relationships and financial disasters that followed led Robert Hanover to the Paulsen Institute and to the ministrations of Dr. Lange. And Robert Hanover might have remained a pathetic, failed narcissist - at least to Dr. Lange - had he not made a fateful prediction during one of their sessions.

"The man's got poisonous shit!" Hanover had shouted as the orderlies dragged him away. "You have to listen to me!"

They were in the hallway outside of the common room. Patients were milling about, but they all stopped and stared after the raving Hanover. When he was gone, they turned back to Dr. Lange, questions lingering in their drugged expressions.

Dr. Lange smiled back at them, assured them it was all right. Then he'd smiled at Ms. Reynolds, the stunningly gorgeous young nurse on watch at the time. In fact, his gaze lingered for a long moment on Ms. Reynolds. It was easy for the eye to linger on Ms. Reynolds. Even in baggy scrubs, her body made Dr. Lange's mouth water.

Suddenly a patient stumbled out of the shadows. He was a middle-aged man in green pajamas, whose eyes rolled crazily from side to side in a psychotic fit of manic panic.

"My bowels," the man said. His voice had a tremulous quality, making him sound like some mad Baptist preacher calling forth hellfire and damnation. "It comes out of my bowels. My bowels!"

As Dr. Lange and the gorgeous young Nurse Reynolds stared at the man, he reached into the seat of his pants and rooted around in the crack of his ass like he was digging clams out of the mud.

Dr. Lange didn't understand what was happening until he saw the clod of shit in the man's hand.

Then he remembered what Robert Hanover had said. *The man has poisonous shit.* Hanover had raved that the man was going to throw his feces into Dr. Lange's mouth, and suddenly Dr. Lange knew what he had to do. Beside him was an autistic woman with an intense fear of being touched. He stepped behind the woman, who in her bovine-like stupor had no chance of reacting.

Bowel-Movement Man hurled his waste at the spot where Dr. Lange had just been standing. It splattered against the autistic woman's face, bits of it landing in her mouth, in her eyes, up her nose.

Shaken, but nonetheless convinced, he confronted Robert Hanover.

"Your premonitions," he'd said. "Everything you've told me indicates that they only concern life-threatening incidents. Having a handful of waste tossed in your face is disgusting, but it's not life-threatening."

"It is a life-threatening matter," Hanover had said. "That man is dying."

"But how do you know?"

Hanover just stared at him, angry and bitter, and yet poignantly sad.

Two days later, when a court-ordered test of Bowel-Movement Man's blood came back positive for HIV, Dr. Lange finally understood the bullet he had just dodged. He started keeping a separate file on Hanover's premonitions, one he nicknamed Cassandra, the young woman from *The Iliad*, who was destined to tell the future and cursed never to be believed.

For Robert Hanover was such a figure, a latter day Cassandra.

From the moment Bowel-Movement Man hurled his clod of shit, Dr. Lange was sure of that. He believed, without reservation, that Robert Hanover could foretell the future.

And yet Hanover was not credible, and never would be. His status as nutcase prohibited any sane man from believing in him.

It was a tough nut to crack.

Still Robert Hanover, the Miracle Man, had just saved his life.

What was he to make of that?

What would any sane man make of having his very own private oracle...and the intoxicating knowledge that he alone could control its fate?

Hanover's screams jarred Dr. Lange back into the moment. "For God's sake, Gene! You have to believe me!"

Dr. Lange smiled graciously. Then looked at his watch and was surprised that two full minutes had gone by. He had to hurry.

Orderlies were banging at the door.

Dr. Lange let them in.

"It's okay," Dr. Lange said. "Everything's fine. Just take him back to his room."

"Gene, please!"

The orderlies ignored his shouts, but were careful not to release the hold they had on him. "Any medications?" one of the orderlies asked.

"Alprazolam ought to do it. Let him sleep it off."

The orderlies dragged Robert Hanover out of Dr. Lange's office and down the hall, the man's screams echoing into the recesses of the Paulsen Institutes winding passageways. A lull settled over the patients in the common room. "It's okay, everyone," Dr. Lange said. He smiled and waved, and soon the patients went back to their routines, milling about as though nothing at all had happened.

A nurse came up to him.

"What is it?" Dr. Lange said.

"Doctor Pendergrass is on the phone for you, sir."

Dr. Lange grimaced. Wayne Pendergrass was the Paulsen Institute's director of operations, and, ostensibly, Dr. Lange's boss.

"Tell him I'll call him back," Dr. Lange said to the nurse.

"But sir, he said it was urgent."

"It always is Nurse" – he made a furtive glance towards the woman's name tag – "Cowell. Unfortunately, I have somewhere I have to be. Tell him I'll call him back."

And with that Dr. Lange walked toward the stairs.

He glanced at his watch. He had exactly three minutes and eighteen seconds to make it to the gorgeous Nurse Reynolds' new station on the second floor. Robert Hanover's latest premonition had been of her, and of the raving lunatic with the snapped off broom handle who was about to bludgeon her beautiful blonde head into a bloody mess.

Dr. Lange had a life to save.

He smiled, thinking how very appreciative the pretty young nurse was sure to be.

Afterwards.

4. LET THE CHILDREN COME TO ME BY JUSTIN HUNTER

Father Tavish felt his chest tighten in anticipation of the blessing of a new acolyte that would administer to his needs during mass. There were several services to attend to and new altar assistants were in high demand. Several boys had been rushed through the holy vetting process, which Tavish would never admit to and none of his congregation would dare question. It could be argued that none of the children really understood anything about the church to begin with. The impoverished nature of the city was conducive to a willingness of families to allow their boys to take the vows and serve the church. That way, at least, they could depend on them having enough food and receiving a good education. There was also some pride at having their young ones serving the most powerful man in the country.

Father Tavish swallowed dryly. His hands were sweating terribly as he held a small golden cup filled with oil. The boy was young, no more than ten. His hair was black and cut short, and he kept his eyes downcast. The boy could sense that the vicar was afraid. They were alone in the cavernous church sanctuary. The vaulted ceiling and gilded carvings dwarfed the priest and acolyte in both size and grandeur. Tavish felt small but he knew the boy felt even smaller than he.

Father Tavish walked over to the child and dipped his index finger in the oil, and drew the sign of the cross on the boy's forehead. It took utmost restraint for him not to caress the boy down the cheek. He swallowed again and put the golden cup on the altar. He wiped his finger on a white linen cloth and turned back to the boy and prayed aloud.

"God the father of Jesus, with the power of the holy spirit through baptism you saved your children from sin and blessed us with life everlasting. Send upon this child your holy spirit. Guide him in understanding. Give him wisdom, courage and judgment. Give him knowledge and with it reverence of you. Fill him with awe that only you, God, can give. We ask this in the name of Christ our Lord. Amen. Rise boy."

The child stood with the awkwardness that comes from one his age. Father Tavish ran his eyes up the boy's broadening shoulders. He saw his angelic and innocent face, and thought of the power he had over this child. He could ask anything of him and it would be done. Anything.

"You can relax," Father Tavish said. The boy stood easier. He ventured a quick glance at Tavish's face. "Do you know what 'Accipe signaculum doni Spiritus Sancti' means?"

"No," The child said.

"It means, 'Be sealed with the Gift of the Holy Spirit'. I gave you that gift when I anointed you with oil. It's the renewal of your baptism. The promise of your dedication to God that your parents made for you as a baby has just been reaffirmed by you as an adult. Do you know what that means?"

"It means...I'm saved?" The boy ventured.

"You have already been saved. You will experience everlasting life. When you die you will go to heaven. But what of your time here on earth? You can rely on God to save you from the clutches of death, but there is someone else who has saved you regarding your life here on Earth." Father Tavish put his hand on the boy's shoulder and the youngling flinched slightly. He squeezed the boy's shoulder lightly the patted his cheek. This time he allowed his fingers to linger on the boy's soft skin.

"I think you know who has saved you here. You know who you can thank for giving you food and a place to sleep. Where did you sleep last night and the night before that?"

"I slept in the streets near Dogtown," the boy said.

"Dogtown is a dangerous place. Anyone ever give you trouble there? Anyone ever make you do anything?" Father Tavish wanted to grab the child. He wanted to force his lust on that innocence. He could have had any women he wanted, but yearn for them he did not. They never drove him insane with their shy looks and impishly boyish smiles.

The priest bit his lower lip and tasted blood. He would have to take this slow. The boy would be his in the end. They always allowed him what he wanted. Tavish used his power, a little coaxing and a passive-aggressive reminder that without him they would be thrust back in the gutter from whence they came. He just had to be patient. It was all a matter of time.

"What do you mean by 'make me do anything?'" the boy asked.

"Did any boys make you do anything you didn't want to?"

"No."

"That's good." Father Tavish knew by the way the child turned his head with subtle shame that he was lying. The boy was worldlier than he had previously assumed. That would make this all the easier. "I want to remind you about some basic, yet very important, dogma of our faith. Jesus, having been raised up from earth and into heaven brings all people to himself. He rose from the dead and sent his spirit upon his disciples and established the church through them." Father Tavish spoke slightly above the boy's understanding. While the child tried to grasp the meaning of his words, he put an arm around his shoulder and led him back toward the door at the rear of the church which led to his personal office.

He continued his litany while leading the boy. "...universal sacrament of salvation... sitting at the right hand." The boy only heard half the message as he was being led out of the sanctuary. Something in his head warned him of danger. It was like a million voices were screaming at him to run. "He might make them partakers of his glorious life... nourishing them with his own body and blood."

Father Tavish opened the door and gently pushed the boy inside. "Christ is continually active in the world... this established body leads men to the church in second birth." He pulled off his priestly robes. The boy's eyes lifted to the closing door of the priest's chambers. The priest put his hands upon him. There was nowhere left to run. A sharp stroke of pain afflicted the boy, and then he felt nothing.

The millions of voices had stopped screaming for him to run and now seemed to hold him in their arms. He knew he wasn't dead, but his body had been left beneath him, his spirit departed. When he glanced down he could see it, but the brutal image was so ugly that he turned his head toward the sky. The million hands cradled him away from the pain that assaulted his form below. They spoke to him in soothing voices and abounded him with a love so pure that it filled him to bursting. One hand in particular, hard palmed but gentle, touched his forehead and he felt a peace which he had never before known.

The image broke and dissipated. The boy found himself alone in Tavish's chambers. His clothing was torn. Pain returned to his body and he cried out at the suddenness of it. He tried to stand but pain lanced through his limbs and he could not rise. The love was gone. There was no peace. He was back on the earth in the vicar's chambers, and he wondered if he was in hell.

5. THE ZOMBIFICATION OF LESTER NELSON BY
S.C. HAYDEN

"What the ever loving fuck?" said Doctor Stone, who was famous throughout All Saints for his colorful O.R. vernacular, a holdover from his Army days.

"He's having a seizure," a clearly frazzled young anesthesiologist said, "he's going to buck the tube."

"He's anesthetized," Doctor Stone, roared, "he shouldn't be doing a goddamn thing."

The patient, Lester Nelson, Les Nes to his friends, Big Les to himself, bit down on the endotracheal tube hard enough to crack his teeth.

"Fuck me in a snow globe," Doctor Stone yelled. "Hit him with two of Versed and bump up the Propofol."

Big Les, for his part, snapped his restraints as if they were dental floss, then reached up and tore the tube from his mouth.

"Jesus jumping Christ on a pogo stick!" Doctor Stone said, holding his gore slicked gloved hands in the air, still maintaining sterility through years of conditioning, despite the shock.

Big Les sat up, swung his legs off of the operating table, and spat a wad of bloody phlegm and broken teeth onto the floor.

"Twenty milligrams IV Valium, double the Propofol, grab some Succs and get ready for rapid sequence intubation," Doctor Stone shouted.

Big Les shimmied his butt forward and hopped off the edge of the table. When his feet hit the floor, he heard a splatting sound. He looked down and saw his guts hanging out of his abdomen. They were piled on the floor by his feet in a ropy mess. Reddish-black blood spread across the O.R.'s buffed linoleum in a stunningly beautiful sunburst.

Les took in his surroundings with a slow but mounting interest.

Three things occurred to him nearly simultaneously.

First, was that he must have been in the middle of some kind of surgery. He had a sudden recollection of driving himself to the Emergency Room with a searing pain in his gut, all too aware of the grapefruit sized time bomb he carried inside himself, his Abdominal Aortic Aneurysm. Triple A, they called it.

Second, was that he shouldn't, couldn't, possibly be alive.

Third, and perhaps the most immediately pressing, was that he was extraordinarily, ridiculously, freakishly hungry.

Les leaped at Doctor Stone, knocked him to the floor and bit into his neck. He nuzzled down through flesh and tendons until he found a fat juicy vein. His jagged broken teeth tore through Doctor Stone's jugular as if it were nothing more than liquorice. Hot blood filled his mouth. It was good; damn good.

Doctor Stone thrashed and bucked, then twitched and shuddered for a while but eventually he stopped moving and the blood stopped flowing. Once that happened, Les stood up. Doctor Stone was dead meat and Les wasn't interested in eating dead meat. Had he always preferred his meat alive and writhing? He couldn't remember.

Big Les stumbled out of the O.R., dragging his guts behind him. There was a lot of commotion in the hospital; a lot of running and shouting and other such nonsense. Les wasn't particularly interested in any of it. He wanted only to go outside. He tried to follow the red exit signs but he kept stepping on his guts and tripping. Big Les then grabbed hold of them and pulled. It wasn't easy, they were slippery, but eventually he managed to tear them away. He pushed through a door and found a staircase. He couldn't manage the stairs but it didn't matter. Once he tumbled to the bottom he stood up and pushed through another door.

Florescent light strips flickered along the hallway ceiling. Les stopped beneath one of the glowing rectangles. A fat housefly had found its way inside the light's plastic case and was banging around in there with a manic fury Les found fascinating. Had the fly lost its mind, ensconced in a prison of blinding white light? Perhaps it thought it had died and gone to fly heaven and was in the presence of some fiery wrath filled God. And who was to say that wasn't indeed the case? The nature of God is a mystery to flies and men alike.

Those were good thoughts, Les decided, thoughts he wanted to remember, thoughts he wanted to continue, but first he needed to get outside.

Finally, a glass door slid open and Les stumbled out into the street.

It was pandemonium. There were bodies everywhere. Some ran, some shuffled, others lay dead or dying. He heard people shouting and groaning and the echoing bark of gunfire.

Big Les closed his eyes. He found that he didn't need sight to tell the live meat from the dead meat. He could sense the live meat. He could sense where they were and where they were going. It was something akin to smell, but not quite.

Big Les stumbled off in the direction of what he hoped would be his next meal.

The words, "Welcome to Zompocalypse," sounded in his head. It reminded him of James Earl Jones saying, "Welcome to Verizon." That made him smile. Who was James Earl Jones again? He couldn't remember. And what was Verizon? Toothpaste? Shampoo? A football team? Something to do with computers?

And that was the last coherent thought Lester Nelson ever had.

Leonard Barrington fought for his life as the thing snapped its jaws perilously close to his face. He knew that one bite was all that it took and then he would be lost and mankind would fall with him.

He shoved his hand up under the thing's mouth and drove its head hard and upwards. He managed to get a knee planted on its chest and then rolled backwards, shoving his legs with every ounce of strength that he could muster. The thing flew over his head, its eyes flickering with pure rage and a subtle mix of confusion.

As soon as it crashed over the desk, Leonard rolled onto his feet and dragged himself wearily back to a standing position. He was no longer the young strong man that he had once been and now his muscles ached with the effort as his adrenaline levels started to fall.

They were in his small private office just off from his bedroom and he knew that there was no point in calling out for help as there was none to be had here anymore.

He turned to face the…, well the zombie. It was a ridiculous word and an even more ridiculous notion, yet the thing that was stalking him from across the room was a reality that cared little for his belief system.

The creature was dressed in the remnants of what looked like some kind of military uniform. The khaki shirt was torn in multiple places and the stone coloured trousers were filthy and soiled. The zombie's face was a mess of decaying flesh and flaps of skin hung loosely in places; the flesh was stripped completely away in other places. There was a gaping hole through one cheek and Leonard could see daylight through the opening.

His stomach churned violently at the sight but he steeled himself against the revulsion. This was no time to fall apart.

The zombie shot quickly to one side like a hungry predator. Leonard had been dismayed to find that these creatures were far from the shambling slow moving monsters of the silver screen. These things were fast and agile, running on pure animal instinct and caring little for their bodies, throwing themselves through glass windows and in front of vehicles without hesitation. The one thing from the movies that had held true was that you could shoot them all day in the torso without effect but one clean shot to the head put them down for good. Destroy the brain and you destroyed the monster.

The thing ran at him with its eyes burning with hate and hunger. Leonard took a deep breath and hooked his foot under a wheeled chair on the floor in front of him. As the creature tore towards him he kicked the chair into the thing's path and it stumbled forwards entangled. Leonard snatched the heavy lamp from the desk and swung it downwards without pity, ignoring the gnawing voice of humanity that still lived in his head. He hit the zombie squarely on its cranium with every bit of strength that he had left in his weary bones. The solid brass base of the lamp immediately caved in the thing's head and Leonard swallowed hard to stop himself from vomiting at the sight as the reverberations from the blow rang up his arm and he dropped the lamp onto the floor. The thing stirred again and he brought his foot down hard, feeling the squish of soft tissue and brains underfoot and wishing that he'd had time to put on a pair of shoes instead of the flimsy slippers that he wore.

He hopped backwards, gagging at the white and yellow mess that now encased his ankle, and managed to make it to the bathroom before puking into the sink. He sat on the edge of the bath and used the shower nozzle to clean his stinking foot.

Leonard Barrington had been elected Prime Minister of the UK some two years ago now on a wave of public anger at perceived border incursions and on a ticket of national pride. He had managed to garner enough support from those losing money to overseas companies and those who read the scare tactic headlines planted in his allies' newspapers. Leonard had promised a return to family values and a fair deal for those prepared to work. It seemed like a worthy sentiment, but in reality he had little interest in anything other than the election. The people were easily swayed, he had found, and everyone had a gripe about something; empty promises were always easy to offer.

The infection had spread so quickly and efficiently that no one had stood a chance. Either through design or pure luck, it had struck in the lower class ghettos first, rampaging through the working class residents before anyone had known what was happening. It was a shameful thing to admit but the time of delusion was far past now. His medical staff just simply hadn't picked up on the infection until it spread to those areas deemed more valuable and important. It was assumed by his advisers that there was some kind of disease on the march; perhaps a drug or alcohol related one, perhaps some kind of cheap food reaction. Whatever it was, it was deemed far too costly to start launching into any medical emergency investigation. It had only been when those of his own social standing had started to be affected that he had ordered a closer look be taken but, in retrospect, by then it had already been too late.

It was eventually deemed a contagious infection, spread only by direct contact through sharing blood or being bitten. The world seemed to be full of zombie experts in theory, but in reality most of them ran screaming from the infected and were soon run down by marauding packs. One bite was apparently all it took, and once a person was bitten, they were left alone in order for the infection to germinate. The horror genre wasn't exactly Leonard's preferred choice, but he had always wondered just how there were so many walking/hunting zombies on TV, when every time that the infected caught a person they ripped them to pieces not leaving enough left to become a walking member of the tribe.

The world outside was now a battle zone and the living were losing. The armed forces had failed in multiple areas as the brave young men and women were overwhelmed by the sheer force of numbers. His generals had told him that as soon as any of the soldiers were infected by the swarming zombies, they would quickly turn on their comrades. One person on a rooftop with a high powered rifle could make a difference but those on the streets were overrun by roaming hordes. The front line had fallen further and further back until London was all that was left. There were still some isolated pockets of resistance scattered around the country as people dug in to fight and defend but it soon became clear that running and hiding was all that truly worked.

He had his top medical people working around the clock but as yet no one had found anything close to a cure. The UK was an island and the only linked landmass was France via the Channel Tunnel. However, once the infection had threatened to spread into Europe, France had blown the tunnel from their side, collapsing the link under a ton of rubble and effectively cutting the UK off from any outside help. As the hordes ran rampant, the country fell apart. Widespread looting and fires raged out of control and the streets were soon a no-go area and the remaining survivors showed little of the wartime spirit that the country had once been so proud of. The modern generation had quickly descended into chaos and clambered over themselves with selfish pointless desires, destroying whatever the hordes did not.

Leonard still harboured bitterness towards his fellow Europeans but he understood their need to secure their own borders. As the country burned around them, some of his military advisers had suggested that they load a few of their remaining planes with the infected and fly over mainland Europe, dropping them onto those who had left them to rot. Whilst the idea was a little appealing, Leonard knew that if the UK was to fall then their last footnote in history could not be to take the rest of the world down with them.

He flicked the switch on the wall and found that the power was out. Number 10 Downing Street was the last remaining bastion where they had chosen to make their stand. In the beginning it had been important in Leonard's eyes to have a recognisable headquarters so that the people would be assured that the government was still operational and in charge. In hindsight it would have been far better to retreat to one of their locations out of the city but by the time they had realised just what they were dealing with it had been far too late to leave.

There were, of course, old nuclear drills and protocols from the 1940's onwards where Britain would have been split into 12 police states, each run by a Cabinet minister if the Cold War had led to nuclear conflict. A tiny elite would have been relocated into underground bunkers so government could continue safe from attack. All 'subversives' would be rounded up and the BBC censored to make way for state propaganda. The detailed plans showed the extreme measures deemed necessary if the Soviet Union had ever attacked Western Europe. Unfortunately, nobody had ever thought to consider a zombie attack and now they were all doomed.

There had been only a few of them left inside the heavily fortified building: a few key members of the government and military along with a handful of civilians trapped inside when it became too dangerous to leave. There were a few weapons but fewer bullets to fire. They had been besieged the last few weeks and everything from ammo to food and water was running low.

Leonard dressed quickly, feeling a little less vulnerable against his impending doom fully clothed. He grabbed a torch out of his bedside table and used it to look down at the mess on the floor in his office. He recognised the man as General Sir Nicholas Fotherskew who was the Chief of the Defence Staff and the British Armed Forces and the most senior uniformed military adviser to the Secretary of State for Defence. The officer had once been a formidable man of intellect and strategy but now his head was crushed and yellow juice leaked out onto the expensive carpet. If Sir Nicholas was lost, then the whole building must be overrun. He tried to fight the overwhelming crushing sense of loss; the infection had taken everything and everyone. His beautiful wife, Marjorie, had fallen early and he had thought that he wouldn't be able to continue but somehow he had found the strength, keeping her face in his heart and doing everything in her name. But now, as he looked down at the smashed face of his most trusted ally, all was surely lost.

He sank to his knees and waited for them to come for him. Soon, the hallways of Number 10 would be filled with their pounding footsteps as their drooling jaws slathered for his flesh. There were no sirens wailing and he could only think that no one had managed to set them off now that they were invaded and they had fallen. The generators had been running the power for the last couple of months or so but they were no longer functioning. There were emergency backup batteries that suddenly kicked into life and showered him in a red glow as he knelt on the floor and waited for the end.

He thought about his wife and their unborn child that had perished with her. He thought about the future that had been stolen from him and a small taste of anger fought through the malaise. The more that he thought about it all, the angrier he got. He was a good man. Maybe not great but certainly good. He was a proud patriot in a time where it was seen as unfashionable or even downright racist for some reason. He knew that this might be the end but was this really the way that he wanted to go out? Was this really a way that would make Marjorie proud?

He climbed to his feet on shaky legs as a seed of a plan started to grow in his mind. He moved to the door and eased it open a crack, risking a look out into the corridor beyond. The hallway was bathed in the same eerie red light and he tried to listen for any approaches. Once he was sure that nothing had been alerted to the noise of his struggle with the General, he stepped out. He suddenly stopped at the thought of the Armed Forces Adviser inside the room and he returned quickly to snatch up something important.

There was a nuclear bunker beneath number 10 Downing Street. It was deemed necessary in the case of an all out nuclear war. It was fully operational and it had been designated as their last fallback position; they had just never gotten the chance to use it.

He withdrew the Glock 17 Gen 4 side arm that he had taken, among other things, from the General. He vaguely remembered the fuss that replacing the traditional Browning with the Austrian weapon had caused in what seemed like a laughable lifetime ago. He had received multiple training lessons with the firearm and knew how to use it.

He stepped out into the deserted hallway and eased his way along with his back against the wall and the weapon out in front of him. Every couple of steps he turned his head in the opposite direction to check behind him.

He reached the end set of double doors and pushed them gently open. There was a staircase leading up and down that was barely visible in the dim lighting. He stepped out onto the landing and had to wipe the perspiration from his face with his sleeve. He moved as silently as he could, praying that nothing would hear him.

He swung the gun upwards and leaned around the metal railing. Once he was sure that there was no threat from above, he steeled himself for the trip downwards into further darkness.

He stepped slowly, one foot at a time, hoping that his shoes wouldn't announce his presence. He had made it three steps down when he started to feel a little more comfortable. The horde might move faster than the monsters on TV but they had still appeared to be disorganised and unintelligent. The idea that one might be skulking in the dark using some kind of strategy seemed rather farfetched. That was, of course, until a hand shot out of the darkness and grabbed his ankle.

He staggered forwards and in his shock dropped the gun. The Glock clattered on the metallic steps as it plunged downwards and out of sight. The hand that had shot out from between the railings was starting to shred his ankle as fingers bit deeply in the pink flesh.

Leonard stamped down hard on the hand once, twice, three times before the grip loosened enough for him to break free. He hobbled back against the wall and decided that there was nowhere left to run except down. He leapt to the next small platform as the shape emerged from the darkness. He recognised the zombie as one of his personal security detail, Jenkins he thought that the man had been called. He seemed to remember that he had been a good man, a reliable man, but now he was only in the way.

Leonard snatched up the fire extinguisher that was mounted on the wall behind him just as Jenkins came around the corner with one hand clasped to the railing. Leonard was horrified to see that his once bodyguard had a gun drawn in his hand and was raising it shakily. The idea that these monsters might possess any sort of residual intelligence or muscle memory was yet another shock upon a mountain of shocks.

The thing opened its mouth to moan or shriek but Leonard cared little and swung the extinguisher hard against the zombie's head. The bones crumbled under the swing of the metal canister and the figure slumped to the floor.

Leonard put his hands on his knees and fought to get his breath back as he stared down at his ankle which now ached monstrously.

He turned his head towards the corpse and for one horrible moment he thought that he was looking at an uninfected man, that Jenkins had actually been coming to save him. But when he blinked again, he saw that the bodyguard's face was predatory and possessed of the same madness as the horde. His eyes, or to be more accurate the one remaining eye, was pure white and devoid of colouring as was the way with the horde. Jenkins' mouth was stretched open wide and even in his second death Leonard still stepped around the man carefully.

He scanned the stairs but couldn't find the General's gun that he'd dropped. He was about to panic when he mentally kicked himself and stepped back to Jenkins. He gingerly bent down and pried the bodyguard's weapon from his fingers, ignoring the stench of the man.

Once he was armed again, he carefully checked over the gun and flicked the safety off. Now that he was sure that they had been overrun he wasn't about to take any more chances. He had a mission to fulfil and a promise to keep; a promise that he had made to Marjorie when he had been kneeling in his office upstairs. If they were all doomed then he had to make a last stand, one final act to save the rest of the world and make all of their deaths mean something.

He moved quicker this time, or at least as quickly as he could on one good ankle. He swung the gun out in front of him as he had been trained by the experts for an emergency. The scenarios were never quite like this; at least the training was all the same.

He reached the bottom of the stairs and pushed open the doors, stepping out into the lower level corridor. The same red lighting now seemed a little dimmer and he knew that it wouldn't be long before he was plunged into total darkness.

A figure lunged at him from a side hallway and he spun and squeezed the trigger, rather than jerked it, as he'd been shown. The Minister of Agriculture was flung back violently as the back of her head exploded against the stone walls, showering it in a crimson blast. He turned just in time to see The Chancellor of the Exchequer lunging towards him, his jowly mouth opening and closing in desperate hunger.

The Chancellor grabbed his arms and pinned him back against the wall with surprising strength and determination, driven by hunger and madness. Leonard fought to free his gun hand while keeping the gnashing jaws at bay. He thought of his wife and unborn child and used the rage to wrench his hand free and jam the gun up under the Chancellor's chin. Leonard felt a big twinge of regret, as the man had been a close and dear friend, and he felt a tear touch his eye as he squeezed the trigger, showering his own face in warm and sticky blood. He was grateful for the loud explosions as they kept his ears ringing and unable to hear his friend's tortured moans as the bullet ripped through his skull.

Leonard's ears started to clear as he limped his way along the hallway. He could hear running footsteps on the lower floor's stone ground. He raced forward as fast as he could manage but he had to turn and fire at more shapes emerging from the shadows behind. He hit several in the head, more through luck than good aim, and the bodies that fell soon entangled and slowed their fellow horde companions.

He tried to keep track of the bullets that he'd fired but soon realised that it was pointless as he had no idea. He scolded himself for not checking for extra clips on Jenkins when he'd taken the gun but what he had now was all that was left.

There was one last set of double doors at the end of the corridor and the shelter lay beyond that. He ran as quickly as he could manage, stumbling and shuffling. His ankle felt soft and spongy now and he felt lacerations on his arm where the Chancellor's nails had dug into his flesh deeply. He could feel a lump swelling on the back of his head where his old friend had pinned him against the wall. His vision wasn't the best but still he pressed forward, praying that he wasn't already infected.

He reached the doors and saw two silhouettes standing on the other side. The figures seemed to be standing in one spot but swaying back and forth as though listening to an internal beat. Leonard looked at the gun and tried to remember how to check the magazine to see how many bullets were still left, but he soon gave up; there wasn't the time.

He knelt by one of the doors and pushed it open slightly, just enough to look beyond. He could see that both figures wore military uniforms and had their backs to him. From his crouching position he eased the weapon up and took careful aim at the first man, narrowing his eyes and squinting as he lined up the man's skull.

He squeezed the trigger gently and grunted with satisfaction as the bullet struck home and the monster dropped. He swung the gun to the other man who was turning and barely had time to line up the shot. He squeezed the trigger gently when he was sure, but this time there was nothing but an empty clack as the gun ran dry.

He fought his panic as the thing reached for him. Leonard shoved one of the swing doors with his shoulder, catching the monster by surprise as the door hit it full and hard in the face. The figure dropped to the ground in front of him and Leonard reached out and grabbed the zombie by the hair, pulling its head through the doorway. He quickly scrabbled to his feet and placed his left foot against the bottom of the left hand door, taking hold of the handle and holding it firmly in place. With his right hand, he grabbed the right hand door and slammed it shut as hard as he could manage, sandwiching the monster's trapped head. He thrust open and slammed the door over and over again until his arm could take it no more. The thing lying beneath him now looked like a pumpkin that had been dropped from a great height onto solid concrete. Pulp and grey matter were splattered on the ground. Leonard's stomach wretched and he vomited violently to one side. Before he even had himself under control he could hear the footsteps echoing behind him and he walked through the mess on the floor, ignoring the sickly squelches beneath his feet.

He took the key from around his neck and opened up the shelter. It was an old solid structure built in the days of the Cold War. There was no other key apart from the one that he wore around his neck now. When the infection had started, it was decided that this place would be their final fallback, their last stand.

He unlocked the door and had to use his remaining strength to push open the heavy doors with his shoulder. The pounding footsteps were growing closer and the ensuing panic fuelled him to go the last inch. He stepped inside and strained every sinew to close the door behind him and seal it shut.

The lights flickered into life as the power kicked in. There was a large silver console that started to glow as banks of small lights sparkled and grew in strength. The science in here might have been old but it was all perfectly functional, enough to get the job done.

Leonard heaved himself into the central chair at the console and started to methodically go through the pre-launch checklist. It was all simple to him now; there was no more life left to save, only his to give. The UK had fallen and all he had left open to him now was to protect the rest of Europe from suffering their fate.

He started to punch in coordinates targeting all of the UK's major cities. The nuclear warheads would sink the island and destroy every last one of the horde in a blinding flash. He wasn't a scientist and he didn't know just how much fallout there would be onto the rest of mainland Europe, but he knew that saving most of them was better than losing all of them en masse.

He shook away the gnawing tiredness from his head and stamped his shattered ankle down on the floor hard, stifling the scream that rose to his lips as the sharp burst of intense pain woke him just enough to complete his task. Outside the door to the shelter, fists pounded helplessly against the solid metal bunker.

"What the hell is he doing in there?" the Deputy Prime Minister, James Burton, demanded. "I don't understand how the hell he got out of his private quarters. He was supposed to be under strict guard until the doctor arrived."

"It was Sir Nicholas; you know how close those two were," the Home Secretary answered sheepishly. "The General wanted to try and reason with Leonard, try and get through to him, try and reach the man before it was all too late."

James Burton had been the Prime Minister's right hand man throughout the campaign, and his Deputy since they had won the election. When Leonard's pregnant wife had died in a car crash two months ago, the man had slowly retreated into himself until no one was able to reach him anymore. They had done everything possible to keep his slipping state of mental health from the public right up until his total breakdown last night. James still found it hard to believe that the man ranting and raving about a zombie apocalypse was the same man that he had known for over 20 years. "When is the psychiatrist getting here?" he snapped at the senior ministers surrounding the old nuclear bunker.

"Any time now," an army officer stated coldly. "I want to know what we're going to do about that murdering bastard in there?"

"Watch your tone, Colonel," James warned him.

"Watch my tone?" The Colonel laughed incredulously. "That maniac has murdered several of my men including my commanding officer, not to mention several of your staff. I want that door busted down and I want that lunatic dragged out and shot!"

"No one is breaking into there," the Home Secretary interjected. "That's a nuclear bunker designed to withstand a full on nuclear war. You're not going to crack it open with a crowbar."

"He's right," the Deputy Prime Minister sighed heavily. "We just have to wait until the psychiatrist gets here and tries to talk him out."

"Excuse me?" a voice piped up from the back of the group.

James turned towards the voice and saw a young junior minister from somewhere like agriculture or pensions or something like that. "Yes?"

"I was just wondering…, I mean it is a nuclear bunker…, He couldn't do any damage from in there could he? Like launch any missiles?"

The group fell deathly silent as the words permeated until the Colonel spoke up. "No, don't worry. It takes two to launch any strike and he's all alone in there. The other man needed would be General Sir Nicholas Fotherskew, who's the head of the armed forces, and unfortunately he's lying dead upstairs."

The group let out a united nervous laugh as eyes flickered around. They were all wondering just what might have happened with a Prime Minister suffering a complete mental breakdown and the ability to launch a nuclear strike.

Leonard heard the horde continuing to pound and wail outside the bunker's solid door. He finished programming the console with all targets selected and acquired. He lifted the first of two small plastic scan pads and placed his eye on the scanner. He lifted the second pad and reached into his pocket.

When he'd returned back to his private quarters, he had not just taken the gun from his friend, General Sir Nicholas Fotherskew. He withdrew his hand and held the soft sticky eyeball over the second scanner as the automated system recognised the necessary authorisation for launch and sent the missiles flying.

7. THE PRIMA DONNAS BY VINCE LIBERATO

Carved in Latin, on the outside of the ice and stone circle, was written "Ubi finitur psalmus eorum, sic mundi."
When their song ends, so will the world.
Inside the ring, in the exact center of the forgotten cave, the Prima Donnas sang. Whiter than the snow that blanketed the frozen wastes above, stiff and uneven tentacle-like jagged appendages protruded from their asymmetrical forms, giving each of the creatures the appearance of a bouquet of dead trees. What they lacked in eyes, ears, and nostrils, they made up for with multiple mouths that crisscrossed their bodies; some of the tooth-lined cavities were silent and sucked in air, while the others made up the chorus of different voices that each of the creatures was unto itself. Despite each Prima Donna possessing dozens of voices, all of them seemed to only know one song, a chant that rang in organized chaos without interruption again and again and again.

There were objects laid at their altar, contributions left from bygone peoples and cultures. There were Grecian urns, mummified cats, Ottoman bronze lamps, terracotta statues, Renaissance busts, and countless spices, precious metals, gems, and coins from nearly all the civilizations that spanned human history. They all were in pristine shape, kept preserved and rooted in the same spot for centuries by a thin layer of frost and ice. For days I had passed the time by cataloging them as best I could, and while there were many objects I couldn't match with a place or period, there was a notable absence of anything dated past the sixteenth century.

The Latin glyphs made me fairly certain that the gifts were an offering to the Prima Donnas for the continuation of existence, a tradition that seemed to have been rooted in the consciousness of the gift-bearers. How people of antiquity had initially found this place at the roof of the world and had come to the conclusion that their survival predicated on the singing creatures within was something I had pondered since the accident that stranded me here days ago.

Thermal x-rays taken from our base showed no signs of wear on this section of the Arctic ice cap, but somehow missed the snow-buried fissure that my team and I fell through. I sustained no major damage in the fall, cushioned by the sled, provisions, and broken bodies of my dead colleagues. Technology seemed destined to fail here, as every safeguard we had in case of such an accident refused to work in the cave. My beacon would not transmit, my satellite phone refused to catch a signal, and the opening we had fallen though would be invisible unless a rescue party came right up to the cracked ice.

My ex-husband used to say that electronics were the greatest things except when they weren't, a mantra I had never repeated once until now. But why my fool-proof safety equipment failed was not the question that repeated itself inside my head as often as the song of the Prima Donnas did, outside of it. What bothered me was something I hoped I would not find out:

Would the world end if the song of the Prima Donnas did?

Their voices were being snuffed out, and like a timer counting down, mouths were disappearing in breather/singer pairs. Not just closing and going quiet, but disappearing from their bodies.

At the end of each full rendition of their melody, a rumbling loop of several notes bellowed and mewled in as many voices as the Prima Donna possessed, a liquid would sweat out from the perimeter of two of their closed orifices. It came like pus from a weeping wound; a glue that filled the tiny serrated teeth and mouth hole so completely that when the process finished, there were no visible signs remaining to indicate that a mouth had been there to begin with. At first I noticed it, I watched, not really sure what to make of the phenomenon.

Poking and prodding the creatures and otherwise trying to interact with them had yielded no results thus far, and they gave no hints that they could even perceive that I was there. For a while, I assumed that the gradual silencing was something that would eventually stop and that maybe new mouths would appear; all a part of the strange biology of these creatures.

But like a bomb's timer counting down, their mouths were closing at a steady pace and only a few remained. The song was reaching its end.

I had come this far north to study the ice, my team and I looking into it for hints of the planet's origins, and now I found myself attempting to put a halt on a possible apocalypse caused by things that defied logic and reason. I entertained no thoughts of rescue, not out of pessimism, but by the realism that I lived my life by. It was this mindset that kept me from fearing death.

Death… Death was inevitable, and because it could not be avoided, it was nothing to fear. Death could not be beaten, could not be stopped, and was to one such as me, as natural a state as life. Since

I do not fear life, I do not fear death. Failure, on the other hand, failure is the only thing I refuse to tolerate. This world is too unique, too amazing a place to let die, and even if I am about to cease to be a part of it, I do not want to die knowing that I let it down.

Perhaps nothing would happen if they stopped singing, perhaps the Prima Donnas were hallucinations brought about by the cold and some sort of subconscious reaction to knowing that I was going to die alone. Perhaps the Latin text meant something else entirely, but if there was even a small chance that their song either kept the world spinning or prevented its annihilation, I had to keep the Prima Donnas singing.

By now, I had tried everything I could think of, everything except the one thing I would only resign myself to do if everything else failed.

The idea came to me when I realized that the only dead human bodies here were those that died in my fall. People had come this far north, that much was certain, but the lack of frozen corpses was something that offered me a final clue for what the Prima Donnas could have wanted. Perhaps the gifts that I had spent days pouring over were only half of the offering to these strange gods, that they required another sort of sacrifice.

I had managed to keep warm from their clothes and fed from their provisions, and the cold had frozen their bodies to a brittle state. Breaking off pieces of my former colleagues was not that difficult, just a well-placed blow from an ice hammer and a twist and joints would pop off, accented with splinters of frozen flesh. The remaining mouths of the Prima Donnas were about twice the size of my fist, so limbs would be the best thing to try and use for this gamble.

I shoved the pieces into their singing mouths, moving from one to the next as fast as I could, only stopping to watch when they all had a piece of human flesh jammed inside. All of them paused on contact with the body parts, but held that note, a high pitched whine like a whale's call.

I watched the one in front of me and held my breath. It held the note while its jaws rotated like a drill, pulling the severed hand and arm inside slowly and holding that single sound while it ate. When the chunk had disappeared, the song continued. I counted down the notes and held my breath as the final one of the now familiar song was reached – a low rumble that crackled with every third second it was held.

And then…

Then the song restarted. On all the Prima Donnas, the glued areas melted away and the covered mouths reappeared one at a time, like flowers blooming and their rediscovered voices culminated into a crescendo even louder than how they had been when I had first laid eyes on them.

I listened to the song reach the peak it always did before it would begin again, the familiar low rumble, and readied myself for it to restart, content for I thought that I had saved the world.

Only instead, nothing happened. No new notes were hit. All of the mouths wilted, hundreds sealing shut simultaneously.

The final note echoed, and for a brief moment, I realized that I had failed. The song was over.

And then, I heard nothing.

8. DEVIL'S BREW BY JAMES PRATT

Sitting at the counter, Reynaldo watched the man in the corner booth. Not directly, of course. That would have defeated the point. To a casual passer-by, Reynaldo's attention was divided between a book and his phone. Each time he looked from one to the other, he stole a quick glance at his appointment. That was how Reynaldo did business; observe first and make sure things were on the up and up. Only when he was confident of walking away from the transaction would he make his presence known.

Well-groomed and dressed in a tailored suit, the man sitting alone in the corner booth looked safe enough. As far as Reynaldo, who was an expert at these things, could tell, the man hadn't broken any rules of their little get-together. The man was certainly a notch above the wide-eyed fanatics and tattooed freaks who made up the bulk of Reynaldo's clientele. That, unfortunately, couldn't be avoided. It was, after all, a highly specialized niche.

Hard as he tried to resist, something about the man put Reynaldo at ease. Handsome yet approachable, he had the sort of face one couldn't help but like. In a book of archetypes, that face would be the illustration for the 'best friend' entry. There was one thing though. Unless he was looking at the man, Reynaldo couldn't describe that wonderful face if his life depended on it. The instant he looked away, it simply vanished from his memory.

If the man's face did in fact reflect his character, Reynaldo couldn't help but wonder why they were about to do business. Sexual fetishes aside, nice, normal people living nice, normal lives tended to have nice, normal hobbies. The closest they came to dabbling in the supernatural was generally confined to church and the occasional horror movie. Partaking of the contents of Reynaldo's briefcase, which was in fact the purpose of their meeting, went far beyond dabbling.

Reynaldo checked his watch. The appointed time had arrived, as had the time to choose whether to proceed with the transaction. Reynaldo rose, laid a twenty dollar bill on the countertop, crossed the room, and slid into the booth across from the man.

The man studied Reynaldo for a moment then flashed a nervous grin. "Are you…?"

Reynaldo nodded. "I'm him. You came here alone as agreed, right?"

The man nodded. "I followed all your instructions. I wasn't sure why you wanted to meet in a diner on the south side of town, but I guess a public place is safer for-"

"Did you bring it?" Reynaldo interrupted.

The man reached into his coat pocket, produced an unmarked envelope, and laid it on the table. "A cashier's check for one million dollars as we-"

"Keep your voice down," Reynaldo hissed. "You never know who's listening."

The man winced. "Sorry. I'm just a little nervous. So…" His eyes drifted toward Reynaldo's briefcase. "Is that it?"

"That's *them*, yes. Here's how it's going to go down. I show you the goods, and you make your choice. Afterward, you hand over that envelope then we go our separate ways. Clear?"

"Crystal clear. Simple and straightforward, just how I like them."

Reynaldo wondered if that was a reference to whatever the man did for a living, but he didn't ask. Only asking and answering questions related to the transaction was one of his rules. Knowledge was power, and even the most innocuous scrap of information could be forged into a potent weapon. He knew that from experience.

"No time like the present," Reynaldo said, reaching for the briefcase clasps.

"Wait," the man said. "How… how do I know they're real?"

Reynaldo's eyes narrowed but only for a moment. Displaying emotions hinted at what was going on in one's head, which in turn put one at a disadvantage. Besides, the question was related to the transaction and therefore allowed.

"That's why you don't hand over that envelope till afterward," Reynaldo explained.

"How do I know they're not, I don't know, poison or something? That you'll just kill me and take my money?"

"If I wanted to do that, we probably wouldn't be sitting in a diner. Plus, killing clients tends to be bad for business."

The man considered that for a moment. "Okay, fair point. So… where did you get them?"

"From my boss," Reynaldo replied in a brusque voice. At that point, most people took the hint.

"And where did he get them?" the man continued. "I'm sure it's an interesting story."

"I don't know," Reynaldo admitted. "He has a gift for finding these sorts of things."

"How did you meet your boss?"

"That's not important. The sooner we-"

"I'm about to give you a check for one million dollars," the man interrupted. "Humor me."

Phrased that way, the request seemed almost reasonable. But it went beyond the scope of the transaction and therefore wasn't subject to the rules. "It doesn't really-"

"Humor me," the man politely insisted. Sans the nervousness, his smile remained intact.

Reynaldo sighed. The fact of the matter was he hadn't had a real conversation with another human being in years. Loneliness was the ever-growing chink in his armor, and the warm, open face of the man sitting across from him struck true. "There's a lot I don't know about my boss. I just know that I owe him."

"How so?"

"He saved me from a bad situation. It's my dad's fault, really. He was into some pretty strange stuff. In exchange for one hour's access to a book that isn't supposed to exist, he promised me to a cult before I was even born."

The man leaned forward. "Devil worshippers?" he asked in a hushed tone.

Reynaldo shook his head. "They worshipped something a lot older than the Christian Devil."

"'The Devil' is just a name," the man agreed. "It's a disguise for something much older than Christianity, or Judaism or the gods of Sumeria and Babylon for that matter. Shaitan, Ahriman, Baal; it has enough names to fill a phone book."

"If you say so. Anyway, when they came to collect me, my future boss showed up and got me out of there before they could do their thing.

"What was 'their thing'?" the man asked.

"I don't know, but it probably wasn't good. I remember seeing a lot of knives."

"How did your future boss know all this was happening, or who you were for that matter?"

Reynaldo shrugged. "I don't know. He never told me. He never talks about himself. I don't even know his name."

"That's understandable. There's power in names."

"Right," Reynaldo agreed, and it was true. Names were symbols, and symbols were the interface between magic and the mundane.

"Well, it was nice of him to rescue you."

"Not really. He did it because he's not a people person. He needed a delivery boy and go-between."

Grinning, the man shook his head. "He always was an opportunistic bastard."

Reynaldo leaned forward a bit. "Do you know him?"

"No, of course not. He just sounds like an opportunist. All in all, it still sounds like a fair arrangement."

Reynaldo grunted. "Sure, if you're not interested in getting a real job, starting a family, or anything like that."

"Those things aren't meant for everyone," the man said. He was no longer smiling.

"Maybe not. Anyway, he showed me how to hide myself from the cult, and the signs to watch for that show they're near. They have ways of finding people that you wouldn't believe."

"Oh, I believe it," the man assured him.

Reynaldo glanced at his briefcase. "Considering the circumstances, maybe you do."

"Thank you for indulging me," the man said. "That was very considerate of you, especially considering you probably don't like to stay in one place for too long."

"Why do you say that?'

"The cult. They're still after you, aren't they?"

Reynaldo glanced at the plate glass window to his left. Outside, a scrap of paper tumbled down a deserted street, painted a bleak, foreboding shade of grey by an overcast sky. "Yeah."

"Well then, what say we get down to business so you can be on your way?"

Reynaldo opened the briefcase and removed its contents: two unadorned glass bottles, one filled with a watery black liquid and the other with something a bit thicker and colored a startling shade of red. Rough-hewn cork stoppers kept their contents in place.

"So there they are," the man said.

Reynaldo nodded. "The Devil's black blood in one bottle, the blood of Christ the Redeemer in the other."

"Any idea how the blood was collected?"

"I asked my boss that. All he said was 'Waste not, want not'."

The man studied the dark bottle. "The Devil's own brew."

"You might say that. You know the deal. One million dollars for one sip from either bottle, you choose which."

"And whoever spilled that blood, I'll see through their eyes and know what they were thinking as the blood was being spilled. Is that correct?"

Reynaldo nodded. "That's how it works."

The man's gaze shifted to Reynaldo. "Have you drunk from them?"

"My boss had me drink from one of them. For some reason he wanted me to know they were the real thing. But he did let me choose."

"Which did you choose?"

"The Devil's blood. I figured drinking the blood of Christ would be sacrilegious."

"And yet churches across the country eat his flesh and drink his blood on a regular basis."

Reynaldo couldn't help but smile at that. "Yeah, I suppose they do."

"So what did you see?"

"It's hard to describe. At first just a…a bright light, so bright it hurt. It was like looking into the sun. There were all these crazy shapes everywhere, but I couldn't get a good look at any of them because of the blinding light. I could just see fuzzy silhouettes, all sorts of shapes and sizes…some were tiny and some were big as buildings, and they were all moving. Every one of them, even the ones that looked mechanical or spun through the air like flying saucers, were alive. Then the light flared and I really did go blind. The next thing I saw were clouds rushing at me, like I was flying. But when I hit the clouds and broke through, I knew I wasn't flying after all. I was falling. I could see for miles and miles…a raw, prehistoric landscape with big, leafy plants and giant, lumbering monsters…I only got a glimpse because I was shooting toward the ground like a falling star-"

"Falling star," the man murmured from across the booth.

"-but I think they were dinosaurs. The…vision, or whatever you want to call it, ended just as I was about to slam into the ground. I think…"

"What do you think?" the man prompted.

"You know how they say a meteor wiped out the dinosaurs? What if it wasn't a meteor? What if it was something else?"

"Something like…the Devil's giant, smoking corpse?"

Reynaldo had waited years to share that theory with someone, and immediately regretted doing so. "Sounds pretty stupid, doesn't it?"

The man's eyes strayed toward the window then up to the sky. "Burning, they fell. Some screamed in horror at what they had done; others begged forgiveness, plunging through the sky like falling stars as the earth rushed up to greet them. Only the one who had led them to ruin remained defiant, for his wrath was vast as the heavens and deep as the bottomless sea."

"Who said that?"

The man looked at Reynaldo. "What?"

"Who said that? Who were you quoting?"

Smiling, the man shook his head. "I wasn't quoting anyone."

"Oh. I just thought it sounded like a quote, like Milton or *Dante's Inferno* or something."

The man nodded toward the red bottle. "I believe I'll have a sip of that."

Reynaldo slid the bottle across the table. "I'm not supposed to ask this, but-"

"Why choose that one? I want to know what he was thinking there at the end."

The man raised the bottle to his lips, gave Reynaldo a wink, and took a drink. Eyes closed, his brow knotted and his fists clenched. Trembling, he seemed to bite back a moan. Sweat tricked down the man's cheeks, staining the starched collar of his pressed shirt. His body jerked as if from a blow, then the vision passed and his body relaxed. Opening his eyes, the man sighed and dabbed at his forehead with a napkin.

"What did you see?" Reynaldo asked, retrieving the bottle.

"I tried to warn him but he wouldn't listen," the man said, shaking his head. "He was a good kid but way too trusting. Oh, he knew how to handle the locals but he couldn't believe his own father would forsake him."

Reynaldo swallowed. "Who are you?"

The man slid the unmarked envelope across the table. "A cashier's check for one million dollars as agreed."

As Reynaldo reached for the check, the man reached out and touched him on the forehead. Reynaldo shuddered as a wave of nausea swept through his body.

"What... what was that?" Reynaldo demanded. "What did you just do?"

"Your father's debt is forgiven," the man said, sliding from the booth. "Get a real job, start a family, and have a nice, normal life."

"Who are you?" Reynaldo repeated as the man headed for the door.

The man looked back from the doorway, gave Reynaldo a wink, and was gone.

9. FALLING LIKE FLIES BY MAGGIE CARROLL

3:34pm.

Chelsea eyed the clock over the door, blew her bangs out of her eyes, and returned her attention to her work. Sick butterflies crawled in her gut as she bent her head to the microscope. She couldn't remember what slide she'd loaded, but it didn't matter. She couldn't concentrate on it anyway.

Her gaze went up again. 3:37.

She squeezed her eyes shut. *Get it together.*

Other doctors, her co-workers, moved around the lab. Chelsea was hyperaware of each and every single one of them, tensed and primed for one of them to notice something was wrong. Her eyes flicked to her lab coat, slung carelessly over her desk chair, but she dragged them away. *Don't draw attention, don't draw attention.* It was a steady mantra in her head. The back of her neck was cold. Her face was hot. Her hands were clammy.

Don't draw any attention…

At 3:52, she couldn't stand it anymore, and made a beeline for the bathroom. She huddled in one of the stalls, hunched over her knees, and did her level best to keep her lunch down. She forced herself to draw deep, steady breaths through her nose. They hissed out between her teeth. Cold sweat soaked her hair, trickling uncomfortably to pool on her collarbone.

Oh god, was she really going to do this?

She raised her head, stared blankly at the stall door for a moment, then jerked her gaze down to the lab coat at her feet. She reached a shaky hand down and fumbled in the pocket for the vial she'd snuck out of cold storage.

It was an innocuous little thing, a glass vial in a hard plastic tube. The liquid in the vial was clear, looked as harmless as water. She popped the lid off the plastic tube and carefully slid the vial into her palm, twisting it with her fingers until she could see the white label. CDCP logo, string of letters and numbers and dashes. The important ones were at the end.

H1N1/1918

It wasn't too late. She could go back to cold storage, sneak it in just like she had sneaked it out, forget the whole thing, call it all off. But staring at the little glass vial, one crack, one chip, one scratch away from the deadliest flu in history, Chelsea knew it was already far too late.

She took one deep, centering breath, slid the vial back into the plastic case, and stuffed it into her bra. It fit under the curve of her left breast, nestled against the underwire. Random pocket and bag searches were common at security checkpoints, but she'd never heard of security groping a woman's breast. It was the safest place.

She could do this. She *had* to do this.

She took one final breath and let it out slowly. She straightened her hair, smoothed out her skirt, flushed the toilet for good measure, and left the ladies' room.

***

The back of the limousine was much warmer than the parking lot had been. Chelsea sat back against the upholstery, hands on her knees, doing her level best to present a cool, collected front to the man sitting across from her. She knew him only as Mr. Chin, a bland-face Asian of indeterminate ancestry, her first and only contact with the consortium that promised her the world.

"Were there any troubles?" His English was very good, with no trace accent Chelsea could detect.

She shook her head, tucked falling locks of hair behind her ears. "No," she said, and cleared her throat. Her voice sounded strangled. "They checked my bags and pockets, but I had it hidden elsewhere." Absently, she rubbed the underside of her breast with the back of a hand.

Mr. Chin's lips curved faintly. "Clever girl. You have it with you?"

"Yes." She reached into the pocket of her skirt and pulled the plastic case out. Or, at least she tried to; her hand, clenched around the tube, refused to come out of her pocket. The absurdity of it all struck her. She was sitting in the back of a black limo with a man she didn't know, preparing to hand over a deadly virus with no idea of where it would end up or what it would be used for.

Her breath caught in her lungs, black spots swam before her eyes. Hysteria bubbled up in her throat until she thought she might start laughing uncontrollably. *What am I doing? This isn't me!*

Mr. Chin watched her with his dark, dead eyes. His face didn't shift once. "Ms. Bourne, if you are entertaining second thoughts, I might remind you of what is at stake."

53

The first laugh died in a hiccup. Yes, the stakes were very high. She closed her eyes and pulled her hand out of her pocket. Eerie calm settled over her, the fatalism of knowing she could only do what she was going to do. It was too late to do anything else.

"It's a reconstituted virus," she heard herself saying, clinical tones like she was presenting a lecture. "As I told you before, the original virus went extinct shortly after the end of the 1918 epidemic. This is an accurate re-creation, based on tissue samples and historical research."

"I assume it was tested?"

She nodded. "The macaques exhibited the classic symptoms. Their autopsies revealed they died from cytokine storms, massive overreactions from the immune system. This tracks with what we know. It's as close as we can make it."

"And this particular vial?"

Chelsea swallowed, feeling that chill in her bones again. "Is live."

"Very good." Mr. Chin held out his hand. Chelsea stared at it for a moment, then put the vial in his fingers. He whisked it away, snapping open the briefcase beside him. He carefully slotted the vial into a slot carved in the foam interior, and closed the case. There was a hiss of gas, and a digital readout lit up. Temperature control. As he worked, he spoke. "Under your seat, you will find a briefcase. It contains your payment. Two million dollars, the bills both unmarked and non-sequential. This concludes our business, Mr. Bourne. Have a nice day."

Chelsea knew a dismissal when she heard one, but that was fine with her. She wanted out of this limo. She reached awkwardly between her legs, feeling around with her fingers before finding the handle of a briefcase. She pulled it out, opened the door and stepped back out of the vehicle.

She hurried back to her car, heels clicking against the pavement. Behind her, she heard the limousine engine turn over, and the sound of wheels crunching across rock-strewn asphalt. She didn't look back. If she looked back, the enormity of what she had done might hit her, and there would be no recovery from that.

***

Chelsea drummed her fingers on her knee, leg bouncing nervously as she waited for the hospital administrator to return. She was so tired of this office, tired of visiting it, tired of fighting in it, tired of the bland peach walls and lacy yellow curtains. But this was the last time she would have to come here, the last time she would have this conversation. That alone might have been worth—

No, can't think about it. Just forget it happened.

The door opened, and she turned in her chair. She was quick enough to catch the consternation and impatience on Hugo Reyes' face as he recognized her. His expression quickly smoothed out to a smile as bland as the walls, and he shut the door. "Chelsea," he said, and his tone was just condescending enough to make her want to scream. "What can I do for you?"

She watched him walk around the desk. Her eyes felt hot and dry, burning in her head. "I'm here to talk about the treatment plan," she said, and twisted her fingers together in her lap.

Mr. Reyes' smile faltered, and he sighed. "Chelsea, we've been over this. The HMO coverage has run out, and—"

"I can pay." Her hands were so tight, she might never get circulation back.

He hesitated, then shook his head. "It's an expensive procedure. You're a doctor, you know what's involved."

"I can pay," she insisted, leaning forward. She was so close, *so close...*

Reyes sat back in her chair, swiped a hand down his face. "Okay," he said slowly. "How much can you pay up front?"

Chelsea reached into her pocket, pulled out the brand new checkbook the bank had issued her that morning. Euphoria, triumph, surged and pulled at her body. "All of it," she said, and started writing. "Start the treatment. Right now."

***

Chelsea stuck her head in the room, mindful of the sleeping woman tucked in on the bed. Nancy, the regular nurse, bustled quietly around the room, clearing away dinner trays and checking the readouts on the machines near the head of the bed. She paused, then glanced over her shoulder and offered Chelsea a genuine, welcoming smile.

Chelsea waited at the door for Nancy to finish what she was doing, then stepped into the hall outside with her. "Hey," Chelsea said, glancing through the door. She could barely believe how much color and life the woman had regained. "How's she doing?"

Nancy's smile brightened. "Really well," she said. "She's responding beautifully to the protocols. She's regaining cognitive function, motor control. There are more good days than bad lately. She's even reading again. *Wuthering Heights*. She says it was your favorite."

It was the best news Chelsea had all week, and she had to swallow past the lump in her throat, the tears in her eyes. "It is," she said. "We read it when I was home sick from school. Is she plateauing at all?"

"Some," Nancy admitted, "but that's expected. Chances are, she's got a lot more healing to do before she hits the final one." Nancy put a hand on Chelsea's shoulder, rubbing her bicep comfortingly. "The treatment is working. I prayed for you, asked Jesus to send you a miracle. I guess He was listening."

Chelsea had a flash of Mr. Chin's face, half-shadowed in the back of that limo, and a cold chill shuddered through her. Jesus never had eyes so dead. She forced a smile. "Yeah," she said, with cheer she no longer felt, "I guess He did."

***

Chelsea stared at the internal memo in her email, and her blood turned to ice. All week, she had been overhearing snippets of conversations, concerns about some new outbreak in India and Asia. She hadn't paid it much mind; outbreaks happened all the time. It was a conversational hazard of working where she worked.

But this…

Chelsea couldn't process it. Her brain refused to see more than two-word phrases at a time: *overseas travel, China and Thailand, fever, myalgia, sore throat, respiratory distress, morbidity, mortality, cytokine storm, rapid spread, Spanish flu, quarantine protocols, masks and gloves, avoid infected…*

Oh god. Oh *god*. Bile swirled in her gut and stars swirled in her head. Her vision went grey, then white, then spotty. She pulled the wastepaper basket to her in time to vomit her lunch into it.

She straightened up, dragging the back of her hand over her mouth, the cold, shaky post-puke sensation trembling through her. Clammy sweat beaded her forehead, and her stomach lurched again. She scrabbled for a bottle of water, and lost the cap somewhere under her desk as it bounced away from her leaden fingers. She drained it in one continuous swallow, and sagged back in her chair.

The entire office stared at her. Some were reaching for masks, faces filled with fear and worry. On the monitors around her, the same memo was open. Her eyes burned with tears, but she gulped them back and reached for a mask in the emergency stash in her drawer.

When it was secured behind her ears, shaped against her nose, she reached for her purse and stood up. "I'm going home," she said faintly, and her co-workers nodded encouragement.

***

The facility was in lockdown. Chelsea had been trying for three days to get in, but staff was adamant. Quarantine protocols were enacted; there were no visitors allowed in or out. Chelsea didn't stop trying, though. The news was full of outbreak stories, talking heads shrieking that the end of the world was here. Ninety percent morbidity. Forty-three percent mortality.

The young and old and already sick were falling like flies.

***

The church down the street from Chelsea's townhouse was filled past capacity every day. The faithful prayed for a miracle, for God and Jesus and the Virgin Mary to save them from the devil. Chelsea never went in. She knew that God wouldn't save her, because the face of the devil was the one she saw in her mirror.

***

"Please," Chelsea begged, near tears and clinging to the doorknob. "Please just let me see her."

Nancy's forehead creased above the mask, and her eyes shimmered with sudden tears. "I'm so sorry, Chelsea." The bottom dropped out of Chelsea's stomach. "Your mother passed yesterday. This flu was just too much for her compromised system."

***

Chelsea stepped to the edge of the building and looked down, tucking her wind-whipped hair back behind her ears. The pavement was eighteen stories straight down, peppered with bodies. Plague

57

victims or suicides, Chelsea didn't know. The world was filling up with the corpses of both, stinking in the streets, piled in parking lots.

Every one of them was her fault.

It wasn't Chin, or the shadowy group he represented. They had manipulated and tricked her, played off her desperate need to pay for her mother's treatment, but it wasn't their fault. She had let them. She had made the choice, and these were the consequences.

She had thought about pills, thought about slipping away from life wrapped in slumber, but she didn't deserve peace. She deserved screaming terror, and violent pain.

She spread her arms, tilted her head back. Slid her foot forward. Open air beneath. Leaned forward. Gravity tugging at her. Tipping over, falling to death.

A hand closed on her wrist and jerked her back. Confused, Chelsea stared at it without comprehension. It was enormous, wrapping halfway down to her elbow. "No," she breathed, and the hand lifted her, twisted her snapping and snarling, and she howled and clawed at it. "Let me die! Let me die!"

"You will not," said the man holding her. He dropped her into the gravel on the rooftop, and she gaped up at him. He was massive, scarred, scary and looming. His two companions were smaller, but no less terrifying. As Chelsea stared at them, stark realization sank in. It was impossible, insane, but she knew it in the marrow of her bones it was true.

"Let me die," she whispered, broken.

"I will never reap you," said Death. He was bland, with the kind of hair and bottle-lens glasses that made Chelsea think of the 1940s. "You're not done."

"It's your fault we're short a Rider," Famine said. Chelsea couldn't look at her. Nobody could be that skeletal and still live. Her voice was incongruously rich, with the light lilt of Ireland.

"My fault?" Chelsea squeaked.

"Your virus killed Pestilence," War rumbled.

They stepped apart, showing Chelsea the other side of the rooftop.

"You will take his place," Death said, with finality.

Chelsea couldn't think, couldn't move. Her stomach churned, her mind whirled. Her eyes locked onto the horses. Red, brown, pale. The white one, the one buzzing with flies, turned an eye to watch her, and Chelsea fell to her knees.

Come, it said in a voice like thunder. The first fly landed on her cheek.

10. FINDERS KEEPERS BY ROB SMALES

"Quit picking at that! You'll mess up the shape!"

Jonah started, pulling guilty fingers away from the tape crisscrossing the lens of the headlamp. He looked up at Elijah, but saw nothing but the "E" shape of his older brother's own lamp, shining out of the dark.

"I ain't gonna wreck it none!"

The 'E' shape slid from side to side as Elijah slowly shook his head.

"Don't mess with your pattern. You wanna be a Finder, that ain't the kinda thing Finders do."

Jonah put the helmet on and looked down the tunnel, his eyes following the metal rails through the pools of dim yellow light cast by the emergency lamps. The padding Pa had added kept it from floating too loosely, but the chin-strap was necessary. He flipped on the lamp and faced the wall. His identification pattern, the one Pa had helped him create by covering parts of the lens with thick black tape, splashed against the stone.

A smiley face.

"I can be a Finder. Pa said so."

"Pa was being nice to you 'cuz your birthday was coming. Just 'cuz Pa's a great Finder don't mean you are."

Elijah moved to where Jonah could see him better, never shining his light in Jonah's eyes. You didn't blind one another down here in Blacksville #2. Even at seven, Jonah habitually avoided the eyes of others with his light. His gaze left the wall, wandering down the tunnel again.

"You hear something?"

Elijah snorted.

"You can't hear the jenny from here. The hoist neither. You're awful jumpy for someone who's gonna be such a great Finder."

"But Pa said . . ."

"I don't care what Pa said. You're a scaredy," Elijah said with all the derision of a sibling three years older.

"I ain't."

"You are. You're down here safe and jumping' at shadows. Whatcha gonna do up under the Big Sky, with all the Deaders?"

Jonah stared at the tunnel bend 40 yards away, listening.

"You see a Deader, you'll crap your pants."

"Will not!"

He could not see Elijah's face in the darkness beneath the 'E', but the smile was clear in his brother's voice.

"Deaders won't even have to catch you out. You'll crap yourself to death, an' then they'll eat ya."

Jonah tried not to let Elijah see his shudder. Truth be told, the Deaders terrified him. He'd seen pictures, they'd all seen pictures. A Finder, not Pa, but a man named McMillan, found a camera a few months ago. One of those with film . . . a Kodak. He took pictures of Deaders in Wadestown, and made sure all the kids got a good look. Jonah hadn't wanted to look, not really. Especially after hearing some grown-ups going on about "their eyes," But the eyes in the grainy pictures had not bothered him.

"You're just mad 'cuz you ain't never found nothing."

"Well, you ain't neither!"

"Found this," Jonah pointed to the lamp on his forehead.

"You didn't Find that! T'werent Finding, you just saw something folks had overlooked."

"Was too Finding!"

"Finding," said Elijah, coming to stand directly in front of Jonah, "ain't just opening a drawer. Finding is going where most daren't go, like up with the Deaders. It's facing danger in order to get what we need to survive. It ain't," he was shaking his head again, "just opening a desk drawer."

Jonah's face felt hot at the lecture; his dry mouth could barely answer.

"'Tis when it's in a Pulled area."

Elijah's expression was invisible beneath his lamp, but it took him a few seconds to respond. When he did he was leaning back, not forward as he had been, his voice as raspy as Jonah's.

"You went in a Pulled area? For real?"

Jonah nodded.

"No wonder Pa let you keep that pattern."

Only Finders and the like were allowed to use creative designs for their patterns. Others, like Elijah, used the initial of their first name. Pa, though his name was Abner, was identified by a blazing sun design, shining from his brow like noonday. He said it was to remind his sons of what was above ground; the good things, not just the

Deaders and the leftovers. Jonah unconsciously reached up and straightened the helmet on his head.

"So. Is it Finding?"

"Yeah . . . I guess it is."

Jonah shuffled his feet. No reason for Elijah to know he hadn't meant to go in the Pulled area. He had been wandering, not paying attention, and had seen the office in a dark corner. He'd found the helmet in the desk and was carrying it back when he saw the timbers. When the old miners had put up wooden supports and pulled the pillars out, taking that coal as well, they had started a slow motion collapse that no timbers could halt. No one was allowed in the Pulled areas; if a Pulled area hadn't collapsed yet, then it was going to. It could be caused by anything, even a sound. You just never knew when.

"Pa knows?"

Jonah nodded." 'Course."

"Huh. That's why the puppy?"

Jonah nodded again. "I guess."

Reminded of their purpose in waiting near the hoist up to Wana, closer to the surface than they usually ventured, Jonah looked down the tunnel once more.

"Think he'll make it?"

"He always does. Pa always keeps his word."

"He said he'd be back by my birthday, and that's today. He ain't back."

"Today ain't over." Elijah sounded more like his old self. "He'll make it. Maybe it's just harder carrying a puppy."

"I hope so. He ain't never been gone a whole week before."

Jonah couldn't help it. Though he tried not to think about those pictures, he couldn't help it. The eyes had not bothered him. It was the Deaders' sense of purpose. Of determination. In every picture, all the Deaders were coming toward the camera. Every one. They all had the same snarling, hateful expression on their faces. He knew the Deaders had been trying to get at McMillan, but it had felt like they were trying to get at Jonah. He hadn't reacted to the pictures, not in front of everyone, but it had been the hardest thing he'd ever done. Especially that last one. He could not stop thinking about that last one.

"Why a puppy anyway?"

Jonah glanced at Elijah so quickly his helmet did not keep up, and he had to straighten it again.

"Huh?"

Elijah was sitting on one of the rails, looking up at him. His lamp cast a huge 'E' on the ceiling that danced as he spoke.

"What made you decide to ask for a puppy? You know it'll be work; Pa ain't going to keep after it, and I sure ain't. And there ain't a lot of food down here as it is . . . so why a dog?"

Jonah shrugged.

"Couple reasons. Someone to play with, maybe help me be a Finder. Dogs can sniff things out, bark at strangers, stuff like that."

It was the barking, when he thought about it. In stories sometimes there was a guard dog or two, barking at intruders, protecting their masters. That was the thing, protecting their masters. Those pictures . . .

"Okay, that might just be some good thinking," Elijah said in a tone of grudging respect. "Specially with them up there always trying to get down here."

Jonah spun away from his brother, looking down the tunnel again. With only one emergency bulb every ten yards or so, there were four pools of light before the turning, and most of the tunnel was shrouded in darkness.

"You sure you didn't hear nothing?"

He didn't want to think about the Deaders trying to get in. He was trying not to think about the picture of the lady. That one had bothered him.

"Relax," Elijah said. "Pa will be here. Quit your worrying."

But Pa was up there with the lady. She was a Deader. She would always be up there. In the picture the woman was in a blue dress. Dark hair matted, eyes glazed, face twisted into a snarl, she had been lunging, hands out-thrust like claws. Her side had been burst open, like an apple stored too long. When the skin split, letting the overripe fruit leak out. The lady had . . . stuff . . . hanging out of the split in her side. A thick rope of something gray and pink had hooked on the doorknob as she passed. She had not stopped, or even glanced down, but was still coming. So determined.

"Think Pa will have some meat?"

Jonah groaned inside. He had meant to change the subject.

"I dunno. Why? You hankering for some venison? You want some rabbit for your birthday?"

Jonah's stomach churned at the thought. Sometimes there was no time to dress the meat up topside, not if the Deaders were after you. Pa had showed them what happened to rabbit, opossum and one time a deer. Evisceration, he called it. Cleaning out the cavity. Jonah had never had a problem with it. It was something they had to do to survive.

She was eviscerating herself . . .

Jonah swallowed the lump in his throat. "No, not venison, I guess. I could go for an apple, though. Fresh one. I'm thinking that would be nice."

"Yeah . . . Apple would be nice, but I been wanting a taste of banana for a long time."

"Banana?"

"Yeah. You're too young to remember bananas. They don't grow hereabouts, so Finders ain't gonna be Finding 'em, not after all this time. But I used to love bananas, and Ma–"

He stopped abruptly. Jonah strained not to turn toward Elijah. Why had he gone and mentioned her? They never mentioned her anymore. They all thought he was too young to remember her. He wasn't. But even if he was, there were pictures. Not McMillan's pictures, but Pa's pictures, from long-ago days, before the Deaders. Three old pictures Pa kept in their quarters. One of the family, with Jonah just a babe in her arms. One of just she and Pa, his arms around her. One just of her, wearing what Jonah knew was her favorite blue dress; a simple, pretty dress, as yet un-split like an overripe fruit.

Elijah suddenly stepped up next to him facing down the tunnel toward the hoist, head thrust forward and turned slightly, offering up an ear.

"Okay, you might be getting to me, but did you hear something?"

Jonah reached up to dash the tears from his eyes. They couldn't be seen in the darkness that dwelt in Blacksville #2, but it was a reflex. He thrust his head forward and cocked an ear, unconsciously imitating his older brother.

" 'Dunno. Before you thought I was jumping at–"

There was a metal-on-metal squeal that ended with a thump, and both boys jumped.

"Guess you heard something earlier after all. Good ears, little brother."

Elijah was speaking quietly. He flipped off his lamp, gesturing for Jonah to do the same.

"But–"

Elijah's extended finger came to rest sharply across his own lips. With the headlamp off Jonah could make out Elijah's face, and it held a deadly serious expression.

"You know the rules," he murmured behind the silencing finger. "This close to the hoist, someone entering the mine, we got to find out who it is first. Before they see us." The finger left Elijah's lips and flipped the switch on Jonah's helmet, dousing his light.

"But it's Pa," Jonah whispered.

"I ain't seen no ID light yet. Now heshup."

Two boys stood in the dark, four eyes fixed on the turn ahead. The metallic squeal came again; the accordion gate at the bottom of the hoist. There was a shuffling. A thump. A tall figure shuffled to the edge of the light cast by a dim emergency bulb. One hand held something against its chest, while the other reached up, fumbling a helmet onto its head. As the helmet settled, a bright pattern of light splashed against the dark stone wall across from it.

A blazing sun.

"Pa!"

Next to him Elijah was quiet, not telling him to be quiet. The figure turned to face them, the sun seeming to leave the tunnel wall and come to rest on his forehead, blazing like the noonday. He squatted awkwardly, and something leapt from his arms and began to scramble toward them. Something small and four-legged, making happy little growling sounds as it raced along between the old cart rails.

"A puppy!"

Not bothering with his headlamp, Jonah ran out to meet his birthday present, also running between the rails where he knew the floor was clear. He raced through a pool of light while the puppy did the same further down the tunnel. *Finder, I'll name him Finder,* he thought as he entered the darkness again. Behind him Elijah was shouting now, calling a greeting to their Pa. There was one pool of light remaining between him and the puppy, and being bigger, and faster, he reached it first. He knelt in the dim circle and spread his arms wide.

"C'mere boy! C'mere Finder!"

"Jonah, no!"

Elijah wasn't shouting Pa's name, but Jonah's. He glanced back to see his brother running in the pool of light he himself had crossed just seconds ago. Elijah was running, screaming his name and pointing.

Jonah turned back toward the far end of the hall in time to see the blazing sun fall off the figure's head as he rose, the helmet landing upside down and spinning on its domed top. In that jouncing, spinning, flickering light he could see that the figure was not alone. There were others with it, figures shambling around the corner into the dim light. In the spinning light he could see them in flashes. There, among the others in the light, a blue dress.

"Ma?"

Jonah was distracted from the figures by the scrabbling, whimpering, grunting arrival of his puppy. Without stopping, it launched itself in one long leap toward his outstretched arms.

"Jonah no!"

As the squirming little body flew through the air, entering the pool of light he knelt in, Jonah caught a quick clear view of his present. The missing eye, the exposed bone, the gray, mostly hairless skin that sloughed off the face, exposing the long, sharp, extremely white teeth snapping shut.

11. THE VIGIL BY J. T. SEATE

Martha lay in the hospital bed of a private room, in some nether region between life and death. Her eyes were often open, but it didn't mean much, or so the caregivers told me. I was able to stay as long as I chose, and I wanted to be present if or when she regained consciousness. I sat in a chair near her bed watching and waiting, myself half in and half out of consciousness most of the time.

The first time it happened was during the still of the night. I sat in the chair and was dosing when I sensed a change in the room. I opened my eyes and looked toward the bed. Martha was sitting up. Her head slowly twisted toward me like a mechanical object. There was just enough light to see her face. A wide clownish grin stretched her features out of shape, a leering, evil expression that was no less than demonic. Her eyes were wide and glaring and seemed to burn a hole into my soul.

Rattled by her appearance and too creeped out to speak, I bolted from the chair and went looking for a nurse. When she and I returned, Martha was, of course, back in her usual state of repose, oblivious to the outside world. I revealed nothing more than the fact that she had sat up.

"Vegetative patients don't just sit up, especially with a broken neck. You must have been dreaming," the nurse said.

A couple of nights passed and my vigil had become increasingly uncomfortable, my attempts to rest more fretful. Each time I dosed off, I awoke with a jolt expecting a repeat performance from Martha.

Then it happened. From the familiar bedside chair, I was terrified by a sense of foreboding, not knowing at first where I was at first. Finally, I focused on the hospital bed. The machine to which Martha was attached emitted an irritating whine. She was up again. Her leer had grown into an abominable grimace with an accompanying loathing I'd only seen in movies dealing with possession. Her eyes had turned into the bulging black orbs of a hungry shark, vibrant with menace. Her long hair hung limply on either side of her face while her torso rested over the palms of her hands like a winged demon about to take its revenge; a hideous form changing before my eyes from a comatose woman into something else ready to spring from the bed and pounce on me.

Had she become some kind of demon monster, or an avenging angel? I had enough to worry about without bringing either manifestation into the mix. The sight of her was enough to freeze the blood running through my veins. Every nerve in my body tingled with a premonition of imminent peril. "Stop it, Martha," I stupidly said. "Stop it now." This time, I didn't call for help.

"You shouldn't be alive. The fall down the stairs broke your neck."

As if on cue, her head canted to one side revealing eyes that were now buried in dark and ruined sockets, and appeared to be incalculably ancient. Her jaw distended to an unnatural distance from her skull. An elongated tongue slithered around inside the maw as a flat humming sound accompanied her stretched features. The sight was exorbitantly more terrifying and inhuman than before.

"And YOU pushed me," she growled.

I had dreaded the moment she might emerge from whatever dark hole her mind had fallen into and utter this very thing to someone. A nightmare image of leathern wings unfurling to reveal a scaly torso lunged into my mind. Rather than succumb to my body that shook from head to toe and run from the room in horror, I had no choice but to silence this hideous thing before being overwhelmed by whatever Martha had become.

I grabbed the pillow I'd been using and rushed the bed forcing the creature down onto her back. I straddled the abomination and held the pillow over that lurid face with all the force I could muster. What I had witnessed drove a fear so deep inside me I could feel it in my blood, eating away at my soul. Unbelievably, I could hear her mockingly giggling underneath. I pressed even harder, trying to snuff her out once and for all.

"You're supposed to be dead," I breathed, holding the pillow fast.

An overhead light lit the room. An attendant stood at the door- I was still on top of Martha, pressing powerfully, trying to stop the infernal laughter beneath my hands, but came suddenly to my senses, and cast the pillow aside. They would see the abomination I was attempting to kill before it infected all of us.

What lay beneath was the face of my finally dead wife, her eyes open, blood red with burst capillaries, and that slight-but-evil grin of censure that I'd seen so often in life. But her appearance was otherwise normal. Had this event merely been a mirror in my imagination, an illusion reflective of what I had attempted to do, and at first, failed?

Then it hit me like the proverbial ton of bricks. That whining noise. It was the machine showing a flat line; the sound that had brought staff on the run. Martha *was* finally dead, a woman whose corpse must have been momentarily inhabited by a demon to taunt me into committing yet another criminal act. My hands tingled as the attendant pulled me away. I was no longer keeping vigil, but felt certain some unknown entity was. The corpse of my wife lay still as I was led from the room, but some animating force had passed from her to me, something alien that would have the power to drive me mad. It was then that this new presence inside me made itself known. I could feel it begin to grin.

My vigil was over, but not my freedom from something unmistakably more terrifying than Martha.

"Mama…mama…"

Mike opens his eyes but the bedroom is black. The shades are down; the TV is off. The green glow of the digital display on his alarm clock dusts the edges of the objects in the room. The darkness is all but complete.

"Mama…"

His wife stirs beside him. She turns over and begins to sit up.

"I'll get him," Mike says in a whisper. His voice is thick, not completely awake.

She mumbles half a thank you, slumps onto her side, and is asleep again before Mike can sit up.

He fumbles on the nightstand, bumping his glasses away twice before grabbing them. He puts them on and looks at the clock.

"Mama…"

It is 3:07.

He gets up and heads for the door connecting their bedroom to the nursery. He can make out the vague shape of his son standing at the side of the crib, his little arms thrown over the side and already reaching out to be lifted up.

Mike shushes and whispers, "I'm coming, bud." Then he bumps against the footboard of the bed, his thigh slamming into the sharp corner. He mutters whispered cursing, rubbing the throbbing, aching lump on his leg as he limps toward the nursery.

"Mama…"

"It's okay. It's okay. I'm coming."

"Mama…"

"Stop, buddy," Mike says as he slips his hands under his son's armpits. He hushes once more as he lifts the little boy up and cradles him against his chest.

"Mama…" His small voice is growing quieter, the word now said through a yawn. He lays his head on Mike's shoulder.

His wife throws back the blankets as he approaches. She is still partially asleep—the half-conscious slumber of a parent with young children.

Mike puts the baby down beside her, and she covers him up to his little chin with the blankets before pulling him close.

Mother and child snore in unison.

Mike shakes his head and grabs the alarm clock from his nightstand. He heads out to the living room yet again.

Through the windows of their second floor apartment the treetops are black silhouettes against the night sky. They sway slightly in a breeze that isn't strong enough to rattle the old windows in their frames; a breeze that Mike thinks looks quite pleasant.

He puts the alarm clock down on the end table and unlocks the middle window; the one over the center of the couch. He opens it just a crack, just enough to let the weak gusts of that cool breeze pass over him while he sleeps. He takes off his glasses and puts them down beside the clock. Then he lays down, pulls the quilt off the back of the couch, and rolls onto his side so that he faces into the brown cushions…

He knows he's been asleep but isn't sure for how long. It's still dark, so it couldn't have been more than an hour or two.

Then there is a noise over him; a mucusy snuffle, like a bloodhound with a bad cold trying to get a fix on a scent.

Mike looks up. There is a shape at the window, a black silhouette against the darkness.

He freezes.

Without his glasses he can't hope to make out what the thing is. It's too dark and his eyes are too bad.

There's that wet snuffling again, then a few light thuds against the windowpanes as the dark shape adjusts itself.

Mike reaches up for his glasses, careful to move only his arm and to do so as slowly as possible. He isn't sure, if he spooks whatever the thing is, it will take off or come bursting through the window. Either way he'd rather not find out.

His fingertips hit the surface of the end table. He slides them to where he thinks his glasses should be and instead hits the alarm clock. It slides back, goes over the edge of the table, and falls onto a pile of plastic toys with a clatter.

The shape at the window inhales sharply. There is a moment of silence in which Mike does not move. Then that snuffling at the open window resumes.

Mike slides his hand sideways across the tabletop until his fingers hit the base of the lamp, then moves it back the other way until he reaches the edge of the table. He scoots himself up a bit to reach further back.

The sound at the window falls silent again.

Mike slides his hand to the back of the table and bumps against his glasses with the tip of his ring finger.

The shape in the window changes—grows taller and unfolds, like an eagle spreading it wings.

Mike inhales, a gasp that he holds. He seeks the lamp with his hand, never taking his eyes from that amorphous darkness in the window, from that thing that was only separated from him by about a foot and a half of air and a pane of glass. He finds it, slides his hand up the base until he encounters the black knob just beneath the bulb, and turns it so hard that it clicks three times in quick succession. The bulb flares into brilliance and then grows brighter and then brighter still with each click.

In the light, the thing in the window isn't black, but a dusty brown. It screeches, a shrill sound like the click of a dolphin or the scream of some bird of prey. It flaps its wings a single time—strong enough to rattle the glass of the windows like a gale—and shoots off into the night sky.

Mike hears soft footsteps behind him. They are hurried, panicked.

"What the hell was that sound?" his wife asks.

Mike sits there, looking at the blurry world outside. "I don't know." He reaches over, feels around for his glasses, and finally finds them. He slides them on and looks at the windowsill. There are faint scrapes in the paint, as if something with claws had gripped it. He sees smears of mucus on the pane over the middle of the couch.

"You didn't see anything?"

Mike shakes his head and stares at the cloudy yellow swirl on the glass. "It was too dark… didn't have my glasses on."

He is struck by a sense of relief, one that overpowers any curiosity he feels about the thing at the window. He silently says a short prayer, one in which he thanks God for not letting him get his glasses on before the thing had left. He'd seen far too much without them… even through the lenses of his all but useless eyes, he'd seen too much.

"Whatever." His wife turns and pads back into the bedroom, all the hurry out of her stride now.

He reaches up, closes the window and locks it. Then he checks to make sure the others are all locked as well. He reaches over and touches the knob on the lamp but pulls his hand away without turning it.

Mike stands and heads back into the bedroom.

His wife is already back asleep. Her soft snoring is once again synchronized with the baby's.

He turns on the bedside lamp.

His son's face scrunches up for an instant when the light hits him, but then relaxes.

His wife's eyes open, and she squints at him in annoyance. "What are you doing?"

"Sleeping with the light on."

13. THE BUS DRIVER BY JODY NEIL RUTH

I hate people.

I hate the people who get on my bus, mumbling their destination as they slap their coins in my tray, snatching their change and ticket without so much as a 'thank you' or a smile.

I hate the school kids who scream and shout and throw food and fight and squirt drinks on the windows. I gave up shouting at them a long time ago. They never listened anyway.

I hate the motorists who can't muster the energy to wave a hand at me in gratitude when I grant them leave at junctions or side-roads.

I hate the council princesses I shout at who smoke on my bus. They spit at me as they clip their cheap cigarettes and put them back into their fake handbags; screaming at their spiteful offspring as they charge up-and-down the aisle.

I hate the idiots who step out in front of my bus, looking at me like *I'm* the one in the wrong; like it was *my* fault that they didn't have the fucking brains to wait on the pavement a moment longer to let me and my ten tonnes of rolling rubber and metal pass.

I hate the drunks who board late at night; giving me pity stories about how they have no money to pay their fare as they drop burger and chips down their hideously-expensive shirts.

I hate the police who I call to escort the cheap-burger-eaters off. They Old Bill sneer at me for 'wasting their time' and suggest that if it happens again I take a stronger stance and kick them off myself, ignorant of the fact that the burger-eaters have now made me several minutes late on my run.

I hate my manager; the fat jumped-up prick who always picks my bus for a routine 'cleanliness check' when I pull in at the end of my shift in the early hours of the morning after the burger-eaters have dropped food everywhere.

I hate the cleaners who sigh as they board my bus, casting me sideways glances to make me feel like all the food, spillages, and shit on my bus came from my own tired ass.

If I had a wife I would hate her.

I hate myself more than I hate anyone. No one's forcing me to do this job, yet I clock in day-after-day, the disgust within me writhing as I paint my face with a fake smile, greeting the *general public* as they get on my bus, forgetting me the instant I am gone from their sight.

But today is going to be different. Today I am going to stop hating. I am going to be constructive.

I am going to cut these cancers from my life.

My shift starts at 4 a.m. It's a Friday morning, and - without fail - an old drunk who delivers newspapers has just finished his round and awaits me at the first stop. He sits beneath the canopy of the plastic-walled bus-stop, slouched on the bench, hands folded over his whiskey-filled belly. The old bastard won't even get to his feet until the bus is parked before him; the 'kneeling' mechanism dropping the left-hand side of the vehicle to the curb, asking his highness if he would be so kind to grace my vehicle and I with his presence.

He is a little surprised when I pop the doors and walk out, smiling at him.

"Morning Dave, you miserable fucking drunkard," I say to him, beaming a smile that no longer feels fake on my face.

"Wha--" the whiskey on his breath is cheaper than the clothes he wears. Barely. "Ger back o' da fu-fu-fuckin' bus and drive, ye cont."

"I intend to," I say, and ram a kitchen knife so hard into the underside of his chin that only the hilt of the handle catching his jaw stops it from going all the way through his skull. He tries to open his mouth but the pressure from my hand on the blade keeps it closed. As his eyes bulge and his hands flail I cannot help but wonder if the tongue within that trapped-mouth has been severed in half.

I withdraw the blade to find out, and the git slumps backwards on the bench, fingers pressing the underside of his mouth to try and stem the blood that colours his clothes. He chokes on blood and opens his mouth to suck in air, and I can see the blade has indeed sliced his tongue, the end of it slipping out and falling to the pavement between us. I pierce him again, in the same spot, severing one of his intervening fingers. I experiment with the knife as I push it up-and-down into his skull, toying with him like a child's first interaction with a ventriloquist's doll.

Blood soaks my hand and reaches my watch, and I glance at the time, seeing that I should have set off two minutes ago.

Leaving the sodden sod dead on his bench, I wipe my hands on my trousers, and board my bus.

I feel calmer as I drive, knowing that I will never again have to tolerate the drunken prick and his bad temper. This lightens my mood. I should have done this a long time ago.

The next stop is moments away, and my headlights reveal a lad in a greasy boiler suit, carrying a tool box. He is not rude, but he does fail to thank me for providing him a service. I mull over what to do. If he does not learn manners now, then he probably never will.

I pull away from the stop, allowing the bus to drive a few yards before flicking off the ignition and we roll to a halt.

"Oi, mate," the lad says, getting to his feet. "Why 'ave we stopped?"

I shrug, looking at him over my shoulder. "I'm not sure," I say. "Something's gone wrong with my dash. Care to come up and take a look?"

The kid huffs as he steps forward. He stands next to me, bent over as he looks at the lights behind the steering wheel. He starts to mutter something, but his words halt as his neck opens on my blade. He falls to his knees, hands clutching the open wound, blood spraying the floor as rain starts to spray my windscreen.

He doesn't struggle as I slide him down the aisle to the back seats. I sit him in a corner as he covers us both in scarlet. He's dead before I retake my seat.

The rain comes heavier, but the unhappiness in my chest lightens.

The early hours mean the next two stops are empty, but the third contains a couple sheltering underneath an umbrella. I have picked them up many times; they both have long black hair, and both wear eye-liner. It makes my shit itch.

"Be a fucking man," I say to him as he pays and boards - looking at me as angrily as a man with a vagina can - before his girlfriend's screams alert him to the dead mechanic on the back seat. I step from my own seat and pierce the bottom of his spine with my knife. I'm upon the girl as her boyfriend hits the floor.

She is a pretty, delicate thing. She weighs no more than my thighs put together as I stab her under her chest-bone and lift her clear off the ground. Her hands grab my neck, and I feel her nails bite as I shake her back-and-forth, impaled on my knife.

I sit the now-dead girl next to the already-dead mechanic. Surprisingly, her boyfriend is still alive. He is unable to move or talk, yet his darting eyes show me the hell he is in.

I sit him opposite his girlfriend, and then I play 'dolls' with her and the mechanic. I drape one of her dead arms around the mechanic's dead shoulders, and then unzip his boiler suit and place her other hand within the confines of his groin.

I wink at the living-dead boyfriend with the long hair and head back to my post.

My next passenger is exactly who I was looking for. It's just after 5 a.m. and the clubs have all kicked out. The prick is eating a burger with all the devotion of a Cambodian hooker on a cock. I pull up, open the door, let him get on, and even allow him to start his 'I have no money' speech before I gut him where he stands. His eyes widen, and he drops his food.

This infuriates me and I lose my temper; stabbing him in a rage until his shit-shirt is in tatters. He is very dead. I think he was a while ago, but the sight of the dropped-burger really pissed on my chips. No, not *his* chips. They're scattered on the floor, covered in ketchup or blood. Or both.

I consider not allowing him on my bus, like I did not let the drunk at the first stop on because of his poor hygiene. I end up dragging him to the back and seating him the other side of the dead girlfriend. The state of the drunken prick's stomach prevents me from sitting him upright; he tends to fold easily in the midriff. I lay his head on dead girlfriend's stomach. The living-dead boyfriend stares at the threesome in front of him.

"Keep an eye on them for me," I say, patting him on the cheek, leaving blood on it.

A crowd of eight or nine people are waiting at the next stop, and I feel that requires too much work on my part. That and I really should do something about the blood covering the decking next to me. I drive on some more before pulling over and using my bottled water and mop from a small cabinet to push the majority of the blood out onto the rain-covered road. A young man jogs up to the bus to ask if he can get on, jacket pulled up over his head to keep him dry. He stares quizzically at the reddened-mop. I push it toward him and he catches it, bafflement on his face at the sudden move. He looks even more confused as I pull the knife from the back of my belt.

I add him to the back seat gang.

They are joined by a man who is banned from driving because of drink-driving offences and has to resort to 'fucking scummy public transport'. Then there is another couple - the guy putting up a real fight and blackening my eye - and one of those council-estate princess sluts who I really go to town on. I cut her ponytail off to see if her face falls back to normal, having been released of the tresses that contort it into stupidity.

It does.

This amuses the fuck out of me.

I jam her ponytail in her mouth and seat her just in front of the fully-laden back seat.

An old lady boards at the next stop. She is all smiles and manners as she pays me, and even gives me a cupcake, patting my blood-stained hand as she squints behind her glasses at the people at the back of the bus.

She sits in one of the seats nearest me, chatting away as I drive, completely unaware of the blood slowly flowing from the back of the bus towards her.

We reach her stop. She thanks me, dropping a small coin of appreciation on my money-tray as she hobbles off, wishing me a good morning.

I wave a red hand at her as blue lights appear behind me.

Late as ever.

The living-dead boyfriend slips from his seat and hits the floor, and I can see his wide-eyes staring at me as I pull over just as more lights flash ahead of us. I go back to check on the living-dead boyfriend, and find that he is now the dead-boyfriend.

I sit him back on his seat, resting his head on the shoulder of the lad who gave me a black eye. I quickly take one of his eyes. I feel it a fair exchange. 'Eye for an eye'. Ha.

The lights are all around us, and I can hear shouting. I wipe my hands on my trousers and head for the front of the bus. Opening the doors I turn to my passengers.

"Sit tight," I say, slipping the knife from my belt.

They stare at me without a word of thanks.

I hate people.

14. THE CASTAVAL TRAVELLING CIRCUS BY
JULIANNE SNOW

It wasn't the greatest show on Earth. In fact it didn't even deserve to be in the rankings…

The Castaval Travelling Circus was little more than a troupe of clowns and freaks who travelled the back roads of North America for pocket change. In some circles, they were revered, but none of those circles involved the mainstreams of society. Fronted by Roderigo Castaval, it was a place where many could hide from the taunting and the stares that had filled their lives up to a certain point.

Under the umbrella of the dilapidated Big Top, the freaks were held in awe, and the lighting of the exhibits helped to conceal the fear and disgust that warped a few of the patron's faces. They were a tightly knit family, willing to do whatever it took to protect their own. But sometimes protection wasn't the only thing they offered. Sometimes they dealt in retribution and it was in those moments The Castaval Travelling Circus truly thrived.

***

"Welcome one and all to The Castaval Travelling Circus!" He waited for the applause to come and go before starting up again. Opening his arms wide, he continued, "My name is Roderigo Castaval and I have assembled the world's greatest attractions just for *your* viewing pleasure tonight!"

He paused for more applause and was disappointed when only a few of the younger children clapped earnestly. It was going to be a tough crowd tonight from the looks of it.

Settling his hands on the lapels of his roughly hewn and threadbare tweed suit, he spoke to the crowd again. "We have clowns to entertain you, feats of strength and agility to amaze you, as well as a few freakishly delightful displays of pure fantasy! So let's not waste any more of your time and introduce you all to the Farrallee Brothers!"

The brightly painted faces of the clown troupe burst from the dusty curtain behind the makeshift stage. Their antics amused the children and some of the adults, but the applause was less than desired. Until the fighting began.

Renowned for their inability to remain sober, the Farrallee Brothers barely made it through an act without dissolving into punching or kicking each other. Luckily all three were amnesiatic drunks so they never remembered what had occurred during the previous performance. It suited Roderigo just fine as he never had to find a replacement for a dying art.

Coming back on stage, he shooed the quarrelling brothers off and waited until the crowd had calmed, and he no longer heard the angry shouts of the clowns. "Well folks, that was the Farrallee Brothers! Let's give them another round of applause, shall we?"

Again he waited for the unenthusiastic response to fade. Surreptitiously he glanced at his pocket watch, wondering how much time he actually had to wait before he could announce the end of the show. Only a few minutes had passed during the parody of a clown act and he realized he was going to have to make the time up elsewhere lest the patrons demand their admission back.

"Straight from Copenhagen, I have a special treat for you! Meet Melvin, the Strong Man!"

There was a smattering of applause as Melvin took the stage, pumping his fists and showing off his massive biceps. The crowd oohed and aahed in appreciation at his display while his assistants struggled to wheel his weights onto the stage. Seeing their effort, Melvin walked over and pulled the trolley into place.

It was all part of the act. The assembled weights weren't actually heavy enough to necessitate the fanfare, but the audience didn't need to know that.

Setting himself squarely in front of the first barbell, his voice thick with a German accent, he proclaimed, "I will show you just how strong I am. 300 pounds I will lift with no problem."

He placed his hands equidistant on the bar and pulled upward. The weights did not lift from the trolley. Looking up, Melvin smiled slyly then heaved the weight-laden barbell into the air high above his head.

The crowd erupted at the feat of strength and the classic fake-out. A thunderous sound followed as Melvin let the barbell drop to the wooden floor of the stage. It was the part of the act Roderigo hated; the stage was old and at some point, those barbells were going to plummet through it to the ground.

As Melvin continued his act, Roderigo checked on his next performer. Tatiana was a small slip of a girl who had been born with very flexible joints. In her youth, she'd been a gymnast, but an injury had forced her into another creative outlet. That's where he'd found her—drugged up to numb the pain of her years spent in pornography.

Giving her a second chance was the only thing he could do to help her. It didn't hurt that she showed her appreciation in other ways either.

"Are you ready to go on Tatiana? Melvin's almost done."

Breaking her contortion, Tatiana turned her face up to meet his. Smiling sexily at him, "Sure thing boss. Maybe later I can show you this move in private?"

Roderigo smiled back at her, brushing his hand over her sequined clad breast. "Absolutely. You know how I love to devour my little pretzel. But I must go for the moment, I hear my cue!"

He rushed back to the stage, barely missing a beat, "And that my dear friends was Melvin! Let's give our strong man a healthy dose of applause! Trust me, you don't want him coming after you!"

The crowd reacted with a hearty showing of appreciation as Melvin left the stage. Roderigo turned to them again and spoke, "And now, straight from Russia, may I present to you Tatiana, the Human Pretzel!"

Tatiana strode on stage confidently, the meager lighting playing off the sequined gown dully. She flashed a beautiful smile full of perfectly straight white teeth as she lifted her left leg and placed her foot behind her head. The crowd gasped and some of the children looked at their parents for confirmation that they had actually seen something that should be impossible. Applause followed as Tatiana launched into her routine of varying poses.

Standing on the sidelines, Roderigo felt the stirring in his pants as he was reminded of what her flexibility allowed him to experience. Knowing he couldn't give into his lust at the moment, he disappeared behind the curtain to get himself under control.

Coming face to face with Virgil helped. "You're up next, you ready?"

"Yes sir."

"Do you still have that cold?"

"Yeah, but it's getting better." As if on cue, Virgil coughed. Roderigo swerved as the fire belched from his open mouth.

"Watch where you point that thing!"

"Sorry Roderigo."

"Not to worry my good man, just make sure you don't set the curtains on fire today, okay?" Not waiting for a response, he turned to go back on stage. "And that folks was the lovely and talented Tatiana! Let's give her a round of applause as she untwists those limbs of hers!"

As Tatiana expertly unravelled herself, Roderigo caught the tail end of a few comments from the crowd. Peering into the semi-darkness he could just make out the trio of young men who sat high on the bleachers. They were laughing and whispering loudly to each other, but Roderigo couldn't make out what they were saying over the din of the crowd's applause.

Watching them, he continued, "Have you ever wanted to meet a Dragon?"

The crowd gasped in pleasure and excitement and Roderigo fed off their heightened interest. "Exclusive to The Castaval Travelling Circus is Virgil, *the* Dragon Man! Born of normal parents, his body is covered in thick scales with a set of wings on him that would make any angel jealous! Oh and his tail—that's just marvelous when it's not hidden away. You'd better not make him angry though, he just might barbeque you to a crisp! Come out here Virgil and meet your newest fans!"

The crowd erupted in excitement, but Virgil failed to appear. Roderigo tried again, "Virgil, your newest fans are waiting…"

A thunderous flapping filled the air and the crowd looked up into the canopy of the tent, mesmerized with fear. It sounded as though hundreds of birds were about to descend upon the gathered group, but what they saw instead was both terrifying and awe-inspiring.

Virgil hung in the air, his wings flapping gracefully. His tail whipped gently through the air, the act spinning him slowly so the crowd could get their fill. Coming to rest on the stage, he furled his wings and let them rest against his back. Loving the attention, Virgil drank in all the gasps of delight and whispers of wonder. In this moment, he was the star.

Inclining his head, he bowed for them, earning more applause from the assembly before him. "Thank you very much. Your applause means the world to me!"

"That's fake!" The remark came from the back of the crowd, high upon the bleachers.

"I can attest to you sir that I am no fake." Taking to flight again, Virgil performed a number of aerial feats before settling down onto the stage once again.

"Fake! There's no way any man can do that!" There was an insistence in the voice that cut through the applause.

"But I'm not really a man, am I?" Virgil silently fumed at the pissant who dared to interrupt his show and the attempt to besmirch his birthright. The crowd responded to Virgil positively, clapping to show their support. He rewarded them with a display of fire from deep within his primal belly.

The applause grew, but so did the voice of the dissenter, fueled by his friends and too much alcohol. "See? Fake! There's no way a man can breathe fire. Fake! Fake! Fake!"

As his chanting continued, his friends joined in, trying to rile the crowd against Virgil. Roderigo rushed to the stage, his eyes immediately drawn to the three young men sitting in the bleachers. "Gentlemen, that will be enough."

They laughed at him while continuing to make a scene. Anger bubbled up, but he hid it from his voice as he continued. "Ladies and gentlemen, a great big round of applause for Virgil who luckily has kept his cool in the face of such disrespect."

As the clapping drowned out the heckling for the briefest of moments, Roderigo leaned and spoke to Virgil, devising their plan of attack. As the Dragon Man left the stage, the applause dwindled to reveal the three hecklers still intent on disrupting the show. "And now I invite you to view all of our freaks of fantasy where you'll meet Philomena, Brenda and many, many more!"

Gesticulating to his left, Roderigo invited their guests to enter the exhibits that lay beyond the thick curtains. The crowd rose en masse and began to move in the proffered direction. The hecklers continued to cause a ruckus as they stood, staggering over each other to climb down the stairs of the stacked seating. Roderigo kept his eyes on them the entire time, his anger focussing him. He couldn't believe their stupidity—didn't they know anything about the ferocious loyalty of the circus?

Guessing the answer was a solid and irrefutable no, he disappeared behind the curtain again, knowing he only had a few moments to get into position. Running into Melvin, he drew him through the labyrinthine corridors made of curtains toward the entrance of the freak show where they would wait for the offenders.

Peeking through the slit, Roderigo saw the last of the appreciative crowd pass through the plush curtain and pushed the secret panel into place. It was something he'd had built a long time ago for occasions such as this one. A way to funnel the rude, the mean, the disgusted, and the overly critical into another part of the circus normally left unseen. The part where retribution could be swiftly dealt, or drawn out, depending on his mood. He had a feeling that today's session would be an extended event.

Entering the area behind the curtain, the young men continued to denigrate the acts they had seen; getting lewd about Tatiana and then indignant concerning Virgil. Letting them come deeper and deeper into the maze that existed under the big top, Roderigo soon found himself almost giddy with excitement. He wanted to hurt those men and he wanted to do it now!

The corridors opened into a room that housed a number of chairs, and a table in the corner draped with a thick cloth. Virgil stood in one of the corners, his wings furled as he smoked a cigarette slowly.

"What's this? You're the only freak? I want my money back!" The words came out somewhat slurred and were soon echoed by the pair who'd come with him.

Roderigo collected his thoughts before he spoke, attempting to harness the anger coursing through him. "You're not at the public freak show. This one's just for the three of you. Perhaps you'd like to take a seat?"

The drunks tried to focus their attention on the chairs in front of them, laughing as they fell into them. Roderigo made a gesture the three couldn't see and from the shadows a troupe of midgets came forward with short lengths of ropes, scurrying to bind the hands of the reprobates before their faculties came back to them.

"Hey, what's going on here?" The inebriated voice flashed a bit of righteous indignation for a moment before dissolving into laughter. It was contagious and soon all three of them were giggling like schoolgirls.

"The Castaval Travelling Circus doesn't look too kindly upon you at the moment." It was meant to sound threatening, but Roderigo was having trouble keeping his cool. His anger leaked into his next remark, "It's time you pay for your transgressions."

"Trans-what?"

"Do you think you can sit and mock us without paying a price? Do you think you can act like assholes just for fun? You—"

"Well yeah! That's what's fun about it!"

The retort earned the young man a backhanded slap that split his lip. The sting of pain and the taste of blood sobered him up enough to say, "Hang on a second here!"

"Silence!" Roderigo had heard enough. It was his turn to talk and he wasn't going to give the stage to anyone else. "This is my family and you have no right to say anything about any of them. How dare you open your mouth and speak such lascivious things about my wife! How dare you insinuate that the Dragon Man is a fraud! You insignificant little shits will pay for your ugly words!"

With a flourish reserved for only those in the circus, Melvin removed the sheet from the table to reveal an arsenal of weaponry. Roderigo let the men view the table's contents for a moment before continuing. He could read the fear sobering them up and felt delight when they started to struggle against their bindings.

"Hey man, we're sorry. We never meant to insult anyone. We just had a few too many and let that make us stupid." The ringleader focussed his attention on Roderigo, not wanting to look at the table for any length of time. "Why don't we just agree to let bygones be bygones and you let us go? I swear none of us will tell a soul what happened here."

Roderigo laughed, gaining a perverse pleasure as he begged for his life. "C'mon, is that all you have? There's no way I would believe you with a performance like that. If you want to survive, put a little something into it. Some pageantry or something!"

The young man stared at him, dumbfounded. Accustomed to getting his way, he retorted, "Don't you know who I am?"

"Yeah, you're the little fuck I'm going to kill." Roderigo let that sink in and found true joy as the meaning of the words overcame them. Struggling ensued, but there was no way they would break from the bindings. Little people had superior knotting skills.

Roderigo turned to Virgil, his face deeply creased with a smile, "Which one do you want?"

"I'll take the one who's slobbering through his tears." Virgil strode forward to jerk the head of the man on the far right back, staring deep into his eyes. "You're not going to like me much after this…"

Roderigo and Melvin both chuckled as the Dragon Man ran a taloned finger across the quivering throat, drawing a bead of blood along its length. Virgil chuckled as the bound man lost his bladder. He coughed as a result and singed the eyebrows from his captive's face. The scream of pain and panic ignited a reaction in the other two and they fought to get free even harder.

Melvin walked to the table and hefted his favourite wooden mallet. Walking over to the troublemaker on the left, he swung the heavy weapon over his head and down onto the knee of the seated man. The scream of pain echoed in the confined space, causing the drunken ringleader to hop frantically in an effort to move his chair across the room away from the line of fire.

"Not so fast, you're mine…"

Brown eyes as wide as saucers rose to meet his. The fear in them fed his anger and Roderigo knew just what punishment he would dole out. Going to the table, he picked up a pair of pliers. Turning around, he presented his choice to his waiting captive and smiled.

A whimper escaped the lips of the bound man as he fought to maintain control. His nose ran freely and the thumping of his heart made him lightheaded. He could only pray it was all over soon.

The first fingernail came off easily, but the others held tight to their beds. Roderigo wasn't going to be deterred and when he realized all eyes were on him, he casually said, "Gentlemen, we can all view each other's handiwork when we're done. Each of you has tasks to achieve before the dinner hour."

The screams were muffled by the music that played in the other exhibits and the crowd had no idea what was occurring under the big top with them. As they left for the evening, getting into their cars and driving away, each of the three men suffered at the hands of their torturer until death seemed as though it could not be staved off any longer.

"I could let this be a lesson to you, but none of you will remember it." Roderigo slicked back his hair with the blood of the inebriated ringleader on his hands and grinned. He took in the work of his brothers and was pleased they both held such fondness for pain.

The prisoners couldn't hold up a head between them so Roderigo signalled the end of the session, a silent command to kill. He looked at Virgil and Melvin in turn and saw the hunger in their eyes. Knowing the other members of the circus had gathered in the shadows around them while they worked, he proclaimed, "Tonight we eat meat!"

A round of applause fitting of any performance echoed against the curtains as Roderigo strode from the room to ready the barbeque, looking back for a moment before saying, "Virgil, can you give me a light?"

15. A CALMING BREEZE OF DEATH BY K. TRAP JONES

It was only a matter of time. I realized early on that I could not carry on my sadistic ways forever, but it certainly was a good ride while it lasted. The mountain that I call home was a safe haven for me. It didn't belong to any of the people that crossed my path or who turned down my dirt road looking for directions. They had no rights to venture where they did. For centuries, my family lived on the mountain and made their way the best that they could. The media had a shit storm and called me an insane killer, but they didn't understand the methodology behind my acts.

Like I said, it was only a matter of time before someone came a knocking. There were just too many deaths occurring on the mountain. From the numerous wrong turns on my property to my nightly stalking of prey on the twisted roads, the mountain seemed to feast upon the weak. But it wasn't the bodies that first rang the alarm; it was the sheer amount of displaced vehicles. Bodies were very capable of being fed back into the life cycle of nature, but the cars proved to be more difficult. When the tourists took a wrong turn and traveled up the mountain, my porch light guided them to me through the darkness. I never had a problem discarding flesh. Most were left to erode naturally or feed the bellies of the wild boars. The bones could either be hidden or altered into tools that no one ever questioned. I even constructed a fence that aligned the northeastern portion of my property. Even though the fence alone should have been a deterrent, I still put a *No Trespassing* sign on there.

Much like a vulture stalking its prey, I too had urges to survive. The mountain was my labyrinth and the tourists were my rats. I was not a complete monster like the media made me out to be. I did not enjoy the act of killing; I more so enjoyed the act of survival. Killing was a resource that the mountain provided for my family in order for us to prosper. I learned the act of cleansing bones from my mother and the method of creative survival from my father.

The ravine where the cars were hidden would be my downfall. Although, I believed that the valley was well hidden, nature always had a way of allowing the sky to see everything. I remember the sound that the rotating blades of the helicopter made. The cracking of the limbs as the trees struggled to stay upright. Hovering over the ravine, the helicopter witnessed the wonderful spectacle of the twisted metal and rusty car frames. Concern was not what was flowing through my mind at that moment. I was more curious about what the murderous junk yard looked like from above. I could only admire the contents of the ravine from the ledge. Some nights, I would sit on that ledge and watch as the moonlight danced between the different metal colors. The intertwining vines seemed to connect each story that the individual cars were telling. It served as my trophy pit, but would ultimately take me from the mountain.

The next morning came quick as I sat on my front porch watching the sun rise above the mountain. Their black cars swerved up the dirt road producing a dust cloud that tightened my veins with disgust. The spikes concealed in the dirt shredded every single one of their tires, forcing them to weave to the side of the road. Sipping on hot coffee, I merely watched as the doors opened. They were all dressed the same with no individuality. Their black suits stood out against the green of nature. The spikes stopped their cars several yards from my porch. I could sense each set of their eyes staring at me, even though they were well hidden behind darkened sunglasses. With no other choice, they had to leave their cars behind and walk the rest of the way up the road. Shouting words that I could not hear, they had their guns drawn and appeared hesitant. Unfortunately, their attention was solely on me and with only a coffee mug in my hand, I was not the threat they needed to worry about.

The two men in front of the pack both fell at the same time within the pit that was barely covered by a thin piece of plywood with dirt on top. When building a pit of that kind, it was always difficult to determine how much weight it would take in order for it to collapse. I found the answer when the two men splintered the wood and disappeared from the road. A few well-placed sharpened bones from previous victims at the bottom would halt their fall and screams. I wish I could have looked down into the pit along with the others. I'm sure seeing a man skewered by bones of another was quite a display of art. Unfortunately, I chose to remain on the porch and enjoy the rest of my coffee.

There were a total of five more men remaining, but their nerves were shot to hell. One of them vomited after peering into that pit. Much to my pleasure, they stuck to their training and kept coming up the road. I always admired triggering mechanisms; the impulsiveness behind the mechanics of the contraption. Testing them always seemed to work, but when placed out in the open with unpredictable people;

that was when shit got chaotic. There was nothing worse than spending many days on a trigger and the damn thing didn't work. However, everything seemed to be going my way as the feet of the next two men triggered the rope that fired up the shotguns. The weapons were buried at such an angle in the dirt that the tips of the double barrels were barely exposed. Two buried wooden boxes held the guns. That particular mechanism caused me a lot of grief and never worked when tested, but I didn't have enough time to create something different. I was very excited to see that under the pressure, they both functioned. The shotgun blasts tore through the upper legs of both men and splattered those behind with blood. For some reason, after those two triggers worked, my coffee tasted even better.

The last three men became very cautious in their approach. Their movements were chaotic to say the least. I don't blame them; they were out of their element. They were used to concrete and streets, not dirt and trees. I almost felt pity for them as their suit coats and neck ties flapped in the wind. With their feet inching towards the section of the road where ten bear traps were buried, I leaned forward to get a better view. Nature seemed to quiet down as the grinding sound of the traps constricting against ankle bones echoed up to the porch. They each became a victim to the rusty traps. One of them fell forward where his face triggered another. My dirt road was tattooed with death and highlighted with the blistering screams of those still alive. All I saw was a bloody mess that I would eventually have to clean up. Patience was always a strong asset of mine, so I continued to drink my coffee.

The mountain air siphoned through the trees and rustled my beard as I lit up a cigar. A good, molten hot cherry was perfection in my eyes. As the men bled out, the screams lessened and nature once again took center stage on the mountain. The sound of the rocking chair against the wooden planks of the porch always calmed me down after a kill. It's the little things that kept me going.

The peaceful tranquility that I found myself in would not last long. Everything was interrupted when I heard a small squeaking sound of a floor board being compressed. To the right and left of me were two more men; both in black, both wearing sunglasses. I underestimate the enemy and put them in the same category as regular tourists. If my father were still alive, he would have been very disappointed in me. Flanked from either side, the barrels of their guns were pointed directly at me, but I chose to stare straight ahead to my dirt road. I swallowed the last of my coffee and took another toke from my cigar. Without any more triggering mechanisms at my disposal, I was successfully caught within a trap that I did not create. I knew it was only a matter of time before I was caught. I just didn't want to believe it.

16. MR. PARKER GOES TO SANGRIA by Mark Slade

The town was nothing but black clouds and dust swirling around in an angry wind.

Eddie Parker had just rode into the small sleepy town of Sangria, north of Mexico City. His black Cadillac broke down just as he crossed the town line, luckily right in front of the bar and hotel. Across the street was a shop that sold antiques, the police dept. and a restaurant that was actually a rundown trailer. He noticed a statue that stood in front of the bar. A strange looking man, small, with a fat face, tiny eyes, goat-like legs, baring his teeth, grasping at the air with its claws.

Parker was bothered by the image. Definitely.

Parker was tired. He took a shower and fell on the bed, a mattress made of stone, and found lucid dreams.

He was there in a strange town to do a job. A job for the Ganger family, tire kings in the automotive industry, and notorious family of thieves and murderers.

Parker met with the head of the family, Rudolf and his younger cousins, Spiro and Haskell. They met at one of the tire centers in Pittsburgh. Outside he could hear guys talking, and engines starting up and tires being removed.

"God, I hate coming to these shitholes," Rudolf said.

Parker thought that was funny. Considering the old man owned about two hundred of these "shitholes" all over the U.S.

Rudolf shrugged, gestured to his cousins. "But what are you gonna do?" The old man was dressed to the nines, a homburg on his head and glasses kept the bright sunlight out of his eyes. Every few seconds he would tap a white cane on the concrete where their metal chairs sat in an empty garage.

"Mr. Parker," Rudolf said. "You have been a trusted associate of mine for many years, now. I have a job for you in Mexico. I want you to even an old score. The details are in this." He took the manila envelope from Haskell and handed it to Parker. Parker unhooked the metal button and peaked inside. There was a picture of an old man in a white suit.

"Along with your usual fee," Rudolf shrugged again. "Of course you get a bonus if the job is done quickly and without public response. This man... owes me a life. My son, Domi, God rest his soul, went missing when I sent him to sangria to do business with this scum. He owes me his life. It took me thirty years to build the empire I have now, and thirty years to make reason with those that stand to gain nothing by his death. Do this for the family, me, and Domi."

Parker smiled. He placed the envelope under his arm. "The job will be done with respect for the family, Boss."

He jerked awake, arms flailing. Then there was the terrible stinging pain on his abdomen. Parker screamed, saw steam rising from claw marks across the inflamed skin. Markings of some kind. A symbol and Latin phrases. He pulled himself off the cot and barely made it to the mirror. Parker ran a finger across the fresh wound.

"Damn it. How did this happen?"

He searched the room, his Walther held tight in his hands. He found no sign of any one, or entry of any kind. But on the table beside the cot, he found a peso with those same markings on his midsection.

Parker sat wearily on his cot, the springs creaking underneath him. He ran a hand over his tired face. He looked at the alarm clock and saw two hours had passed by.

He was late. He was supposed to meet his guide in the bar downstairs at nine. The guide was to take him into the village of Peros a few miles from the town square in Sangria.

Parker quickly dressed. The blue suit, gray shirt, no tie. It was his death suit. He used it many times.

Suddenly.

Out of the corner of his eye, Parker saw something. A blur of a small dark figure passing by him, racing by him. He turned, saw nothing.

His mind was fucking with him.

Parker saw his hands were shaking. His heart was racing. Everything felt intense. This was an odd feeling before a job. He hadn't felt that since the first kill.

His first job was on a wife of a senator that was probing the gambling syndicate in Jersey. He followed her to a bar. She was meeting a guy there that was not her husband. Parker had watched them closely. An argument ensued. The man left.

So Parker picked up the Senator's wife. He slept with her. Hours later, he'd strangled her with her own stockings. That mysterious man in the bar went to jail for her murder. Turned out, he was the senator's campaign manager.

Funny how things work.

He left his room, stepped out on the red carpet. He glided down the hallway as if he were floating on air. His eyes were transfixed on happenings in front of him. A woman and her sickly poodle sitting in the lounge. She broke off pieces of molded bread on her stained slip and the poodle was eating them off her plump belly. A little boy was standing in a corner of the lounge holding hands with an old man who was an older version. A bellhop walked by, grimacing, showing Parker his rotting teeth and black gums.

He was gliding past it all, right through the doorway of the bar.

Parker stood there, feeling the cool coming from the central air from a vent in the ceiling. The bar was nicer than the hotel. Everything was shiny and glimmered in the florescent lights. Five people were in the bar. The bartender spit into a spittoon compulsively, wiped down the counter.

A fat man with no shirt on lay dead drunk across one of the tables. And a couple who were mooning over each other, holding hands. They looked intently into each other's eyes, mouthing words no one could hear. In the back, sitting at one of the tables, sipping a beer, was a young dark haired woman in a bright green dress. Her hair was in her face. She was caressing that beer glass.

Parker watched her. He felt his temperature rise, his hands wet with perspiration.

The bartender said something in Spanish. Parker walked over, sat at the bar. He clucked his tongue, rolled his eyes. Parker pointed at a sign for Tecate beer. The bartender nodded.

Parker took a piece of paper from his breast pocket and handed it to the bartender when his beer was brought to him. The bartender chuckled. He pointed to the man passed out on the table behind him. The bartender shook his head and gave the paper back. He walked away, chuckling.

"Great," Parker said. "All I want is a guide and they set me up me with a guy that will end up choking on his own vomit."

"I can take you where you need to go," a voice said from behind Parker. It was the young woman from the back of the room. She was smiled, showing how poorly she'd put on her red lipstick. Parker noticed her hair was still covering the left side of her face.

"I don't know," Parker said. "The firm I work for set me up with this guy. How do I know I can trust you? You won't roll me, steal my wallet?"

"And you think something like that wouldn't happen with him?" She pointed to the drunk who lay in dreamland. "I know Cucho. He couldn't find his dick if he needed to pee."

Something about a woman who used phrases like that, turned Parker on. He laughed and nodded. "Okay, chickie. I'll give a hundred when we get to the village of Peros."

"You buy me a meal for starters. Then we start out. And my name's not Chickie. It's Teresa."

"Hey!" Parker yelled to the bartender. "Bring us something to eat!"

The bartender looked at Parker quizzically. Teresa sighed. "Nos trae unas enchiladas," She said.

The bartender smiled, "Si," he said as he walked away.

"Look," Parker stood. "I gotta go to the toilet, okay? Be back."

"I'll be here when you get back," Teresa gave him a smile.

Parker flashed her a quick smile.

The bathroom was not a high priority, Parker could see that. The two stalls were missing doors. The last toilet looked like somebody dumped a case of Van Camps beans in the bowl. Parker thought he was going to puke at the smell. But he held on.

He went to the urinal. There was no water and all signs pointed that it had been bone dry for eons. Parker sighed. He decided that this was just as good as any place to take a piss, and not flush. God knows, that damn thing would overflow and no way in hell was Parker going to get his new alligator shoes wet.

He unzipped his fly. Out of the corner of his eye, he saw a blur of something dash behind him. He turned quickly. Nothing. Parker closed his eyes. Shit, he thought. I'm getting jumpy. He relieved himself in a hurry, dribbling on his trousers. He cursed out loud.

Parker heard breathing from behind. He drew his gun from the holster and turned. Again, there wasn't anyone there. "Get a hold of yourself---"

That was the moment he felt the sharp pain in his back. He had heard something that sounded like paper being ripped. Parker felt a warm sensation. And when he fell to the linoleum floors, he saw the blood slowly run from his left side.

He tried to make himself stand, he just kept falling. Out of nowhere, a peso coin fell to the floor beside his body. Soon he gave up on the idea of walking out of the bathroom. A black veil fell over Parker and his consciousness.

When Parker awoke, he was in a bed in a different room in the hotel. He saw Teresa standing by the open window, smoking, and a slither of light from the streetlamp engulfed the features of her face. He tried to sit up, the sheets under him made a rustling noise.

Teresa jerked her head around nervously. She flicked her butt out the window. There was sparks from the lit end striking the window ledge. "Please don't move," She said.

In three quick steps, she was at his side, helping Parker to settle down. He grabbed Teresa and forced her to kiss him. It wasn't much of a struggle. He unzipped her dress and moved his hands inside to her breasts. She removed his hands, made him lay down. She stood and let the dress fall to the floor, stepped out of it. Slowly she stalked the bed. Parker waited in heightened anticipation.

*****

"Geez...I feel like shit. Somebody knifed me." Parker stated. "Man, I haven't been laid up like this since the Pinter family war a few years ago. Never been knifed."

"You should rest," Teresa eased him back on the pillows. "The bleeding may start again."

Parker turned over on his right side. He saw the marks through the bandages. Three long claw marks. He gasped, sat up. "What the hell? Did I get attacked by a tiger?"

Teresa touched his shoulder, "Please...you'll hurt yourself worse."

Parker saw the peso on the night table. He winced. "This is the second time I have been attacked." He licked his lips. "I'm not even sure...."

"What?" Teresa was curious. She sat on the bed beside Parker. "What aren't you not sure about?"

"No. I don't know... I'm not sure what I saw... but... in my room a while ago... I saw a flash of something.... I was lying down the first time....woke up and my stomach had these weird markings!" Parker showed her.

"I saw them. Very strange. I could read them... in Spanish... it is a warning," Teresa rose from the bed. She went over to the night table and retrieved a cigarette from her handbag. She walked to the open window, lit it. "Were you half asleep?"

"Maybe. No. I woke up from the pain from those markings. Then I saw one of those pesos. In the bathroom I heard breathing. Sounded like a winded animal. Whatever it was, it was fast." He thought a second. Then said, "a warning, huh?"

"You saw another Peso." Teresa threw her head back and blew smoke from her tiny nostrils. The smoke curled, lingered in the air, and then moved on through the window.

"Yeah," Parker thought. He forced himself to a standing position.

"What are you doing?" Teresa scolded him.

"I need to get to Peros. Finish that job. Get me my shirt."

"No...."

"You want that hundred? Earn it. Guide me to Peros," Parker said.

"It would be my pleasure." Teresa tossed her cigarette out the window.

The car driven twenty miles north of Sangria was a model Parker did not recognize. It was boxy, an early 1980's model, and the paint rusted to its primary color. But it ran good. Better than any car in recent memory.

"The man who sold it to me said it was made in Brazil," Teresa told Parker. "The factory made fifteen of them before going bankrupt. Or so he said. For all I know it could be a Russian vehicle. I bought it cheap."

They drove through a few miles of desert before they ended up in Peros. In the village, on the streets and around buildings, Parker noticed there were more of those statues like the one he saw in Sangria. He felt uneasy, weak.

"Are you okay?" Teresa put a hand on his clammy forehead. "My God, you are very sick...burning up!"

"I'm okay," Parker pushed her hand away. "Keep driving."

"We're here," Teresa said.

The car pulled into a duty driveway of a huge stucco villa. It looked empty. Vines grew over the outside walls and over the roof. The grass was the beginning of an Amazonian jungle.

"I see he still lives alone," Parker said.

"What are you going to do?"

Parker lowered his eyebrows. His small black eyes darted back and forth. "That's my business. Understand?"

Teresa breathed deeply. She nodded her head nervously.

"Stay in the car. Be out in a few," Parker commanded.

He got out of the car gingerly, ambled toward the villa. It felt like a million miles away. Parker stopped at the front door, looked back at the car. Teresa was watching, but only casually. Parker smiled, saluted with a finger at his forehead. She scowled, waved back.

Parker turned the knob, the front door creaked open too easy. Way too easy. What's waiting for me on the other side? He eased it partially open. Peeking in, Parker only saw an old man sitting in a wheel chair, half-asleep. It was the man he was looking for. Parker drew his Walther from his holster and pushed the door completely open.

"I told him not to sleep with that witch," the old man blabbered. "Malo ... muy malo ... el hombre de piedra, ahora." The old man shook his head.

Parker put his finger on the trigger. "This is for Rudolf Ganger!"

It all happened in a flash. Just as Parker pulled the trigger, he heard a loud growl, and out of nowhere a small hairy man leaped upon him, pulled him to the floor. The Walther fired, the bullet roared above the old man's head and struck the ceiling. Wood particles rained on the old man. The small man was strong. The creature pinned Parker down with its claws dug deep into Parker's skin, bearing its sharp teeth. Parker screamed as the small man ripped flesh from his left cheek.

The old man babbled away as the small man devoured Parker.

Teresa walked in. She had a blanket in her hands. She watched for a minute as the small man finished his feeding. She walked over, covered the old man. "Keep this on you, Amapola."

She collected the third Peso by the body of Parker, added it to the other two coins. She handed them to the old man.

"I told him not to lie with you...very bad...sleeping with a witch," the old man said.

"Domi," Teresa called to the small man. He came running, jumped in her arms and immediately turned to stone. "But Amapola, he's such a good servant."

17. EMPTY HOLLOW BY MEGAN N. WATSON

Located in a remote area in New York state, just outside of the Finger Lakes region, sits one hundred acres of isolated forest on a small mountain top. Directly in the middle of that forest is a perfect circle, devoid of all but plant life. No insects, no deer, no bears, no anything. Just a mossy ground cover surrounded by forest that can only be accessed by one little road.

Known as Empty Hollow, the locals' tales are of the sort often told around late night camp fires or at sleep over parties, the scary but true legends meant to terrify captivated listeners into a state of panic and nervous laughter. "Factual" stories of the horrors of Empty Hollow number in the hundreds, maybe more. Everyone in the small valley town of Laurel Village knows someone who is related to someone who had been a victim of Empty Hollow. Even the indigenous people of the region had long declared that Empty Hollow was cursed. However, unlike most typical urban legends, Empty Hollow had no distinguishable villain. No mad man with an axe, no weird creatures, no ghosts, not even a beginning to the terrors. Just a long history of strange events and devastated families, always left with a hole too deep to ever be filled. Empty Hollow has long been abandoned, but historical records show that three families tried to make the land their home. Empty Hollow had other ideas.

The first was the McGeins family, who moved there in 1820. Newly married and wanting to start a family, the couple built a small homestead in the circle. Mrs. McGeins immediately went to work starting the family gardens while Mr. McGeins tended to the animals. The circle provided a perfect grazing area for the dairy cows, while leaving ample room for the chicken coop, gardens, and Mr. McGeins' workshop. A carpenter by trade, he would sit out there for hours, lost in his art. By all accounts, it appeared the couple had created a nice, simple life together in their wooded oasis.

The trouble began about two months later when Mrs. McGeins started complaining of strange dreams and an unrelenting feeling of being watched from the woods. Her husband paid her no mind, thinking it was just stress. One morning, she went out to get some fresh eggs for breakfast and found the chickens were all gone. Confused, she called out for her husband and the two tried to figure out what happened. There was no sign of an intruder, animal or

otherwise. Aside from a few feathers, the coop held no clues to why
the chickens vanished. The couple searched the entire circle, some
twenty acres, but found nothing out of the ordinary. They resigned
themselves to the fact that this was a mystery that would not get solved
and moved on with their life. Mr. McGeins acquired a couple chickens
from a family in the village, who told him the missing chickens were
just a warning, there would be worse to come. He merely smirked,
thanked them and headed home. A week later, the McGeins awoke to
find the cows dead, or what was left of them. The animals were
mutilated, as if several miniscule eruptions had occurred all over the
body. Death by a thousand cuts. Since an early but light snowfall had
dusted the area the day before, Mr. McGeins was able to see that there
were no prints, except his own, anywhere near or leading up to the
mutilated carcasses. Baffled, he and his wife stayed inside the house
the rest of the day, feeling frustrated and scared. What a shame the
snow had covered up a small clue because two days later, they found
the goat dead, missing both eyes. That was the final straw. The
McGeins abandoned their dream, never to be heard from again, and it
was rumored that Mrs. McGeins never spoke another word for the rest
of her life.

The Wallace family moved onto the property in 1941. They had
two children, three year old Sara and six year old James. Coming from
a long history of farmers in Laurel Village, Tom and Ellen Wallace
were well aware of the legends of Empty Hollow. They simply never
believed a word. When the opportunity arose, they decided to try to
turn Empty Hollow into a small working farm and perhaps dispel some
of the rumors. The buildings were run down but still sturdy,
considering they were built over a hundred years ago. Once the crops
were planted the family only had to wait a week to see the surprising
results of vegetation, the equivalent of a month's growth in their
former fields. Feeling this was a good omen, they invested all their
money into fixing up the house, buying a few head of dairy cattle and
some chickens, along with a couple horses to ride through Empty
Hollow's lush forest. The chickens lasted one night, the family finding
a scene similar to the McGeins' chicken coop. Then Ellen started
noticing how little Sara often looked over her shoulder when playing
outside, a concerned expression on her tiny face. Soon James
complained of bad dreams. Several days after they lost the chickens,
they were awakened by the screams of their six year old son. Thinking
it was just bad dreams, Ellen went to calm him but found his bed

empty. James had woken up early after hearing strange whimpering sounds from the family dog. Fearing his canine friend was lonely, he set out to bring the dog inside to sleep in his room. Instead he found the dog dead, missing both eyes, just like the McGeins' goat. The canine looked as if someone had stretched white cotton candy over it, like a sticky, translucent shroud. That was end of the Wallace family farm.

By 1964, Empty Hollow was considered forbidden territory by the residents of Laurel Village. Anytime an inquiry was made about the property, the first response was to inform them of the bizarre history. Usually that was enough to scare off potential buyers. That is until the Tinner family bought the property as a vacation home. No matter what the realtor or the locals told them, they just brushed it off as silly superstition. Of the three families, the Tinners owned Empty Hollow the longest. Having bought it during the height of winter, they didn't step foot on the property until well into the following spring. They tried hiring local contractors to fix up the old farm house, but were refused by every last one. Mr. Tinner finally gave up and hired contractors from the city to come out. Eager to use their new place, work began as soon as the paperwork was signed and, just as quickly, the renovations abruptly halted. One of the workmen had been badly injured and another was found dead, but the Tinners were never told any details. Unable to get anyone else to do the work, the family finally gave up on the remote vacation home in the woods. At least that was the assumption, as no one ever saw them actually leave the property. The family was reported missing several months later, but was never found.

And so Empty Hollow sat, unused and unoccupied for decades. That is until Simone Roberts came along.

***

For most of her life, nature was Simone's passion. She spent every moment she could outdoors, even in the rain and snow. Her dream was to live in a tree house in the middle of nowhere. Six months ago, that dream came true.

She met a man, fell in love, fell out of love, and left him. Her mother passed away around the same time, causing a sad but much needed windfall for Simone. That money took her to the mountains of upstate New York, where she found the hundred acres of undisturbed forest. In the middle of what was now her woods, was the perfect clearing with the perfect tree for her dream house. Simone was the

100

happiest she had ever been in her life, building that tree house herself. Everything was better, she could see better, smell better, her senses were heightened and she felt joy on levels never imagined.

Though Simone too had been warned of the history of Empty Hollow, she didn't care. She had finally found her peace, her own forest where no one could find her and no one could hurt her. Pain was all too familiar for Simone and Empty Hollow was her escape, where she could live alone, in peace. The tree house had retractable staircases and ladders so that once home, no one could get in her house unless she wanted company. Which was never.

Simone had been living there about two months, when she first had to run into town for supplies. While in the store, a man came up to her empty car and waited. Simone sauntered over, not caring or feeling any fear, and hopped in without a second glance. As she started her engine, the man tapped on her window. It was then she noticed the bump on his cheek. It was about the size of a pea and she swore it was pulsing. The sight repulsed her to the point of gagging. Trying not to be rude, she took a breath and rolled the window down.

"Can I help you?"

"Yeah, you seen any dogs in those woods of yours? A lot of the townsfolk been complaining that their pets have gone missing."

"No, sorry. Good luck."

She started to roll up her window when his hand smacked the glass.

"What? What do want?"

"Move the hell out of those woods. You don't know what's waiting for you."

"I've heard the rumors and you can go to hell if you think I'm moving. If that's all, goodbye." Simone was trying not to gag in front of the man, afraid to piss him off even more.

"I'm trying to help you. You will regret ignoring me!" the man yelled at Simone's moving car.

She tore out of there, not caring what his so called warning was and wanting nothing more than to get away from his disgusting pulsing bump that looked like it would explode at any moment. Once back on her tiny dirt road, she opened all the windows, taking in all the sounds and smells of her woods, her peace. She deserved this, after everything, she deserved her happy ending.

The crickets had started their serenade early this evening. Still a little shaky from her encounter with zit-gone-wild man, she let out a huge sigh of relief at the sight of her tree house. Among the supplies she bought was a bottle of Chianti to go with a baguette, smoked gouda and freshly roasted peppers for her evening picnic menu. She laid out a blanket on the second story balcony of the house, the one that faced west, so she could watch the sunset while she enjoyed her simple feast.

Half the bottle was gone by the time the stars made their first appearance in the sky. Her cheeks flushed from wine, her belly full and happy, she laid on her back and stared at the stars. The sounds of her woods lulled her to sleep faster than anticipated, despite the unsettling encounter earlier. Simone woke up early the next morning, rain drops slapping against her face, with an ever increasing rapidity. Groggily she gathered her stuff and retreated indoors. But not before she thought she saw movement along the tree line. She gazed out, surveying her land. Finding nothing out of the ordinary, she proceeded inside.

Simone didn't notice her cheek was swollen until that evening, when preparing to shower. Looking in the mirror, she thought it might be a small bug bite or pimple, nothing to cause concern. Showered and relaxed, Simone strolled out to one of her balconies and took a deep breath. It was then the silence hit her. The woods weren't just quiet, there literally was not a sound. Not a cricket or a frog or an owl. Nothing. Her gut was nagging that something was wrong, that she was being watched. Her hand went up to her cheek without her knowledge as the strange man's words started to echo through her head. Simone shivered but shook off the feeling and went to bed. After all, Empty Hollow was feared by the people of Laurel Village, that's why she wanted to live on a cursed property. Call it her version of a security system.

By morning her cheek was throbbing and a growth had formed. The pain had gotten worse. Worry didn't set in until she went outside and, again, noticed the uneasy stillness that had taken over. It was as if the whole forest was holding its breath, trying to hide from something. Some of the shrubs near the base of the tree house had a strange sheer covering, almost invisible except for the dew reflecting a few rays of light. An uneasiness set in, along with a lot of pain in her cheek. Simone was overcome with the feeling she was being watched. After a cup of tea and some breakfast, her apprehensions had calmed, reduced to anxious background noise in her brain.

A few days later the pain had gotten so bad she had no choice but to see the doctor. Driving down the remote dirt road towards the bottom of the mountain, she felt something begin to move. Simone slammed on the breaks, bringing the Jeep to a jostling stop. She grabbed her rearview mirror and pulled it towards her face. Her eyes filled with a terror that had yet to reach her vocal chords as she realized the growth looked like the bump on that peculiar man's face, only larger. And it *was* pulsing. She could see and feel multiple areas of movement, her skin gently stretching and contracting, ever so slightly. Simone's mind went into complete denial mode, focused solely on the pain.

She pondered what would happen if she just popped it, thinking that would relieve pressure and at least reduce the pain a little. Simone sat back and sighed. She could feel it increasing in size, pushing against the inside of her mouth, her cheek almost forcing her teeth backwards. Her hand, involuntarily but gently, raised itself to her cheek. She squeezed until, POP! A thick, viscous fluid, greenish yellow in color, splattered all over the mirror and windshield. Simone felt such sweet relief, until a new sensation snapped her mind out of denial. She touched her cheek, feeling a bit of a cavity where the blemish had been. Trembling, Simone slowly adjusted the mirror once more, afraid to look. Her eyes met her reflection, allowing her to view the full horror that used to be her face. Hundreds of tiny, almost miniscule fur covered legs were crawling up out of the hole in her cheek. In a matter seconds, she was covered in brightly colored, baby spiders, seemingly very proud of their bright hues. Specks of brilliant blues and reds and yellows and greens, were marching all over her and the car. She frantically slapped at her face and chest as her foot slipped off the break. The car immediately rolled down the small mountain road, coming to rest against a tree.

As if on cue, a truck approached, coming up the road from the opposite direction and stopped at her car. It was the strange man from the store accompanied by his father. Both calmly walked up to her car and peered in. Simone was out cold.

"I told you she was in trouble, Dad. What do we do now?"

"The evil only steals what it needs. You're lucky we got to you in time or your face would look like that. Maybe now you'll stop going into those damned woods."

"I was worried! She was all alone up there!"

"You're an idiot. Well nothing we can do now but wait 'til those things retreat into the hollow. She should survive."

The two waited in their truck until morning. The baby spiders, now about the size of a small wolf spider, had vacated Simone's car leaving it covered in that sheer, sticky substance, like a cocoon. Just like little James Wallace's dog.

***

Simone's cheek had to be reconstructed and though the surgeons were able to reduce the exposure, her two back teeth were still visible through her otherwise milky white skin. After smashing any mirrors she came near, the nurses were ordered to cover all reflective surfaces in Simone's room.

She spent several months in the hospital, most of that time spent trying to stop the screaming to little avail. Then one day, the screaming stopped. With an unnerving calm, she left the hospital to return to her tree house in her woods. Simone's first and final words since the incident were, "They were just the messengers but I received it. I have to go back to my woods now, the hollow isn't empty anymore."

Laurel Village residents never saw or heard from her after that. Though, thanks to the two men who rescued her, Simone Roberts' story eventually was woven into the labyrinth of legends about Empty Hollow. Now it was the mention of Simone, more than Empty Hollow itself, that caused fearful giggles from the village children. Warning each other in the dark of night not to mess with the woods of Empty Hollow for fear of the disfigured ghost of Simone, whose screams will swallow your soul.

18. THE RAVEN 2 BY CHRISTOPHER CONLON

I had been writing in my chamber—a small, ill-lit, melancholy room whose main feature is a huge painting of my lost love, a beautiful young female whose name is untranslatable into the present tongue but which means something along the lines of "swift graceful huntress"—when there came a tiny rapping at my window. Pulling myself from my oppressive mood of sadness, I hopped over to the ledge and discovered a very small human standing outside.

Angling my beak just so, I pulled open the window and stood staring at the little man. He was perhaps three inches high. He wore a silver suit which covered his entire body, neck to feet.

Once upon a time, in the years before the Great Light, we ravens feared and loathed human beings for their guns, their stones, their shouted voices—and their sheer *size:* if one of us was hapless enough to fall into their hands, lo! all hope was lost. They were vastly bigger than we and capable of utterly destroying us. Our only means of survival came through our sheer slippery cunning.

How things changed after the Great Light. Whence it came we know not. But one morning it was there, obliterating almost all it washed over: and after it passed away virtually everything was dead. Horses, dogs. Most vegetation died and then grew again in new shapes and colors. Happily, rats and mice and other such tasty prey survived, though many in the raven community agree that they tasted somehow indefinably *different*—not without savor, but different.

The humans all perished—or we thought they did—and their carcasses were a pleasure to devour for weeks to come. That was the great period for the ravens. We ate our fill without fear. We circled the skies and cried out to each other in joy.

And we grew. Perhaps in reaction to the sudden cornucopia of food available, we rapidly became enormous—I myself, once about eighteen inches tall in the way man formerly measured such things, am now nearly four feet high.

I said earlier that we thought man had utterly perished. We were soon proved wrong by some of the mightiest hunters of our clan, who began bringing back strange little creatures with arms and legs, creatures the likes of which we had never seen before. One of our greatest and profoundest thinkers pondered the problem for some time before coming to the conclusion that, as we ravens had grown, the humans had shrunk. Millions of them had died, yes—but the ones that hadn't perished had shrunk, as this one before me now, to a height of around three inches. The Great Light certainly moved in mysterious ways.

And now here was this man before me. I could easily have grabbed him with my lightning-quick beak and devoured him, but I am not particularly partial to the taste of these new miniature humans. Anyway, I was curious about this one, and taken aback by its boldness. I decided to discover what the little animal wanted.

It was waving to me and saying something. Its voice was very small and low, but it was audible. Happily I am well-versed in the language of humans as it was once spoken in this land.

What the human said was, "Filthy bird!"

Now this was even more surprising. Surely the creature understood that it could be assassinated at any instant by the simple application of my own rock-hard beak to its soft, tender man-flesh. I was tempted to laugh, but laughter was not an indulgence in which I had engaged for many moons. Something about the miniature being instead made me take pity. I leaned close to it and spoke its language—my ability to speak human is limited because a raven's vocal apparatus is completely different from that of a man, but I can manage a few words of the barbaric tongue.

"O Man," I said, "wherefore dost thou come to me in my hour of sorrow?"

For I had indeed been sorrowing, staring at the picture of my lost Swift Graceful Huntress and attempting to peck out a poem to her blessed memory.

Quoth the man, "Filthy bird!"

This was most strange. Perhaps, I thought, the poor creature was demented. After all, in addition to the aforementioned fact that I could kill the thing at any moment I chose, there was the additional truth that ravens, myself included, are very clean birds. We bathe assiduously and work constantly to keep our feathers free of fleas and mites. I myself had had a lovely bath in a pond not far from my chamber only a few hours before. Afterwards I had preened for some time, wanting to feel as clean and pure as I possibly could in order to compose my poem to my lost love. Therefore, while I was admittedly and proudly a bird, I was most certainly *not* filthy.

"O Man," I said, working my way around the unnatural sounds and syllables as best I could, "thou art confounded. No doubt the new order of the world hath baffled and bewildered thee. Perhaps thou art frustrated that we ravens hath overtaken everything that was once Man's. Perhaps thou once lived in this chamber, or one like it, long ago, before the Great Light. I feel sorrow for thee, O Man."

Quoth the man, "Filthy bird!"

"What I suggest," I continued, ignoring the poor thing's feeble insult, "is that thou stayest here with me. I will care for thee as a beloved pet. I will feed thee and bathe thee and give thee a place to sleep thou shalt find comfortable. Thou mayest ride upon my head or seated atop my feet as I go about my daily duties. I will protect thee, O Man, and guide thee, and love thee."

Quoth the man, "Filthy bird!"

I confess: at that point I grew enraged. Already overcome with my feelings of loss for my Swift Graceful Huntress, I reached with my great beak to silence the minuscule vulgarian forevermore.

To my astonishment, however, my beak snapped closed on nothing.

Looking up I saw that the human was *flying about the room.* Flying, as a raven would fly—though of course with none of a raven's grace. There was some sort of device strapped to its back that emitted two little flames which seemed to grant the human the means of this aerial locomotion. The human swooped this way and that through the air and, although I cannot be sure, I believe that I heard the ill-mannered thing laughing.

This was an outrage I would not stand. The impertinence! Man in flight! It is true that in the days before the Great Light Man did have its mechanical contraptions which flew with great noise among the clouds, but *this* was different. This man was flying—himself!

I resolved to pursue him and bring this blasphemous farce to its conclusion by snapping the wretched animal in half. Yet, try as I might, I could not seem to catch the creature. It was so small that it could dart like a sprite and hide in small cracks and crevices I could not penetrate. Chasing the thing in that small, enclosed space, I was at a disadvantage—I was too big, too clumsy.

At last I was winded and, in despair, flapped back to my desk, with my incomplete poem under my feet.

The little man had taken refuge atop the bust of Polly which stood above my chamber door. Polly the parrot, the first bird, according to our tradition, ever to speak. Just below his bust was the smaller statue of the cracker Polly is said to have requested with those initial words.

Quoth the man, "Filthy bird!"

But now, to my surprise, the man continued speaking.

"It won't be long now!" said he. "Mankind is coming back! There are pockets of us everywhere around this city! We've developed technology, like my Jet Pack here! We've developed weapons—deadly weapons! Weapons a size we can use! Weapons that will destroy you and your kind! The reign of the raven will soon come to an end!"

The pitiful little human raved on insensibly about its mad fantasies regarding its technology, its weapons, its glorious future. It all made me sad, almost as sad as when I looked up and beheld the image of my Swift Graceful Huntress.

"O Man," I answered, inspired to metaphor, "take thy beak from out my heart!"

The man merely laughed. It obviously had no understanding of the compliment I had (admittedly insincerely) attempted to pay it, suggesting that Man too might contain the power and beauty of a bird's beak, if only metaphorically. Nor did it comprehend how melancholy I had been made by its meaningless babblings, which truly did hurt my heart.

The strange thing is that the human still is sitting on the bust of Polly above my chamber door. It watches me day and night. Occasionally I hear it laughing, though for what reason I know not. Yet something within me whispers that a time of great change may be coming, a change possibly as tremendous as that brought on by the Great Light. But such things are too large, too foreboding, to think about. Instead I return my beak to the paper, slowly pecking out my sorrowful ode to She whom I shall meet again—nevermore!

19. THE EMPTY ONES BY JAMES PRATT

The man in the muddy overcoat was the first living person I'd seen in months. Living bodies were scarce by then, dead ones not so much. When he saw me, he yelped, actually yelped, and came running. I didn't know what his intentions were. Maybe he was overcome with joy at the sight of another living person. Maybe he was a cannibal and wanted to eat me alive. It didn't really matter. I'd spent over a year making preparations; tracking down rumors, compiling information, and staying one step ahead of *them*. I was finally ready; all I needed was a living human and now I had that too. No matter what the man's intentions, things would have ended the same.

I waited till the last second to act. Almost within touching distance, the man spread his arms wide. As he closed in, I thrust my knife. The blade slid through his ribs and bit deep. Frozen in shock, he simply watched as I withdrew the knife and struck again. This time, I angled the blade upward so it pierced his heart. As he sunk to his knees and toppled forward, I caught him and gently laid him on the ground. I didn't want him to suffer. I just wanted it to be over with. His labored breathing became a phlegmy gurgle then he died. I was alone again, but not for long.

I didn't have much time. One of *them* would show up soon. Somehow they knew when a living human died. Maybe our deaths were like ripples in…whatever it is that separates our world from theirs. Maybe we emitted some sort of psychic death cry that echoed across the unknown gulfs, drawing them to us. Whatever the case, every human death created a vacancy. As we moved on, they moved right in.

I traced a circle in the dirt around the corpse then a second circle outside the first. In the space between the two circles, I inscribed the proper formulas. I learned them from books once kept under lock and key, but now no one was left to guard them. Whatever apocalypse their keepers vainly hoped to avert had come about, or been replaced with a different apocalypse altogether. The formulas looked less like mystic symbols than mathematical equations. For all I knew, that's exactly what they were. Like physics equations, they were the symbolic representations of literal forces. The difference was they represented forces so potent even their symbols had the power to influence the physical world.

The soon-to-be host's bowels evacuated at the moment of death. The air reeked of human waste, but I was used to bad smells. The world had become a dead place, *their* place, and even the possessed continued to rot. Ignoring the smell, I squatted down just outside the perimeter of the outer circle. The formulas were useless against flesh but would contain the thing inside the flesh. That's what the books said, and that's assuming I did everything correctly. It was an experiment, and I didn't have long to wait.

The corpse shuddered once, twice, and the eyes fluttered opened. As expected, one of *them* had come through and taken possession of the body. Sensing my presence, it turned its head and looked at me. The host's eyes were now covered by a red film. That's how *they* saw the world; through a red haze. We were just meat to them. And of course, hosts.

Moving awkwardly, the ageless, newborn thing clambered to an upright position. It sat staring at me for a moment then reached forward, testing its newly acquired limbs. The instant the thing's hand came into contact with the invisible wall of force born of the formulas scribed in the dirt, the corpse jerked as if from an electric shock and fell back. For a moment, the section of the force-wall it touched became visible. Tiny rune-shapes scrolled through the air then faded back to transparency and vanished.

Breathing a sigh of relief, I looked at the thing trapped in the circle. Eyes filled with the primal rage of a caged animal, it simply stared back. No, I realized after a moment, that wasn't right. It wasn't rage. It was hunger.

It was the first time I'd ever had a chance to study one of them up close. Filtered through the force-wall, I could see a hint of the puppet-master hidden within the fleshy sheath. Hovering around the possessed corpse's head was a vague shimmer, a seething disturbance in the air not unlike a heat mirage. I wondered how its true form looked then remembered it didn't have one. That's why they inhabited our dead, I reasoned. Whatever powers they commanded were no replacement for a good, solid pair of hands.

The force-wall worked. Now it was time to finish things. I removed the quarter-sized disc of polished quartz from my satchel; strung on a thin leather strip, I hung it around my neck. The stone was one of the artifacts I found at the abandoned military research station where my search for answers came to an end. Like the other artifacts, the stone operated on no known scientific principles. It just worked.

"Can you understand me?" I asked, knowing it could. That was the power of the stone.

The thing's stolen eyes narrowed then it nodded.

"Where do you come from?"

Outside, it replied in a voice as devoid of life as the cold lips through which it spoke.

"Outside what?"

Everything.

"How did you get here? Into my world, I mean."

Always here, but not here. All around you but unseeing and unseen. Then a hole opened and we saw. We saw and we came through.

I thought of the other thing I found at that military research station, the jagged rip in the fabric of space somebody opened and couldn't shut. According to the scientists' logs, it's where the artifacts came from, and maybe something else.

"Why do you possess the dead?" I asked.

To take what we need.

"Flesh?"

Dead flesh is only a vessel. What we need dwells in living flesh. We cannot enter the living, or feed on the dead. To take what we need, we need hands…and teeth. We use the hands and teeth of the dead.

"What are you? Demons?"

The thing paused, searching through its host's mind like a dictionary.

No.

"Alien parasites?"

No.

'Then what?"

The inevitable.

A thought occurred to me. "Are you entropy?"

We are…empty. We eat thoughts and memories. We eat moments in time.

"What will you do when nothing is left?"

Move on to the next world until nothing is left.

"Then what?"

Move on.

And on and on. It would never end. Now that they were here, they wouldn't stop. They would devour the human race, not through its flesh but through its history. Every momentous occasion, every sacred event stored in the collective psyche would be chewed and swallowed till only bones, literal and figurative, remained. There was only one thing left to do. I brushed a clear spot in the dirt, disrupting the force-wall. The thing rose up and, crossing over the circles, approached. It laid its hands on my shoulders and pulled me close. At the first bite, I bit back a scream. At the second bite, I felt its true fangs sink into my mind. Using dead flesh as a conduit, it had entered and infected me with the virus that was itself.

Soon I will be gone. Maybe my body will live on as a shell, mindlessly wandering the ruins of the old world. Maybe I'll die and one of those nameless things will use my corpse as a vessel. No matter how long my flesh lingers, the thoughts and memories that made me *me* will be lost forever. I want to call it a tragedy, but that sounds too pretentious. Isn't it really the fate awaiting us all, to be forgotten and rejoin the dust? Maybe that's why the thing called itself inevitable. There's no such thing as hope or tragedy. There's only the inevitable.

20. DRINKS AND A SHOW BY KEN MACGREGOR

"I just want to do something *normal* for once," Amanda yelled at her mother.

"Don't be so dramatic," Gina said. "You know why I don't want you to go. We both know what could happen."

"Oh, Mom," Amanda sighed, "don't you trust me?"

"Of course I do, honey. I just don't trust, I don't know how to put it, circumstances, I guess. Who knows what the other kids will do."

"Technically," Amanda said, "we're all adults. Please? When am I gonna get another chance like this? Free tickets, free hotel, free *food*. Please, Mom. Please?"

"That's another thing," Gina said. She put her hands on her hips. "Just why is Scott paying for everything? What does he expect to get for his money?"

"Mom!" Amanda's jaw dropped. "Scott was supposed to go with Vince, but Vince broke his leg two weeks ago. Scott and I are just friends. I don't even like him like that. And, he's a good guy; he's not going to try anything."

Gina looked at her daughter for a long time before speaking. Her little girl was all grown up. Gina closed her eyes and took a deep breath. She let her hands fall to her sides.

"You'll be careful?" Gina asked. Amanda nodded several times fast, holding back a grin. "Okay. You can go." Amanda shrieked and hugged her mother. Gina hugged her daughter back, frowning; she didn't think this was going to end well.

***

The water below the plane looked like glass. Below the endless window, pink and orange coral abounded; a school of silvery fish swooped under the surface. She turned around and flashed Scott a big smile.

"Have I thanked you yet?" She asked. He nodded, rolling his eyes. That was about the thirtieth time she'd asked since they left. This on top of at least ten actual 'thank yous' between Amanda's house and the airport. In Scott's car, between the *thank yous* he glanced over at Amanda's lap - her faded jeans hugged her thighs. A flush crept up his neck to his cheeks and Scott put his gaze back on the road.

The plane descended toward the ground with effort. When the wheels touched down, they bounced and the plane shuddered. Scott gripped his armrests, knuckles white and jaw clenched. His eyes locked onto the chair back in front of him. Amanda put a hand over his and he looked her way with wide brown eyes.

"You're not gonna die today," she said. Scott nodded. The plane leveled out, slowed with the squeal of brakes and taxied to the terminal. The airport consisted of one small building and a mile of cracked blacktop; on the tarmac were prop planes and fuel trucks. Beyond the fence, five unshaven men huddled in a group and smoked thin cigars outside their taxis.

Two airport crewmen wearing coveralls pushed a stairway into place and locked the wheels. The flight attendant opened the door and invited everyone to disembark. Amanda pulled her bag down from the overhead compartment; she caught Scott looking at her exposed midriff. A steel ring looped through the skin of her bellybutton, the skin around it still red from piercing.

"That's cool," Scott said, frowning.

"I like it," she said. "And, if I get sick of it, I can always take it out. It's not a tattoo or anything." Scott, who had gotten a tattoo of a skull on his shoulder on his 18th birthday stuck out his tongue. She smiled to show she was kidding and pulled down her shirt. They descended the stairs, carrying one bag apiece; she and Scott were only on this tiny island for four days. The ocean breeze, with its sharp, salty fish smell blew back Amanda's hair.

Their hotel room was clean; that was its only real selling point. Otherwise, it looked like every other mid-range hotel Amanda had seen back in the States. The mirror over the sink boasted a *not potable* sign with one corner peeling up. A handwritten sign taped next to it said there was water in the fridge. Opening it, Amanda found four of them. There was a bifold *complimentary* note on the top shelf. Amanda snagged two plastic bottles, handing one to Scott. He was sitting on one of the twin beds. They were covered in southwest-style quilts and dominated the room. Amanda put away her things while Scott thumbed through a brochure of local restaurants and clubs.

"There's a place by the beach called Reef's where well shots are fifty cents," he said. "Says 'live entertainment' too. Probably a local band. Might be good though. Drinks and a show. That sound good?" Amanda shrugged without turning around. Scott read the other options to her; they were pretty similar to the first. Cheap drinks and live entertainment were the order of the day. What else did people do on spring break but get drunk and get loud? The brochure assured them that the legal drinking age here was 18. This message was sponsored by Coors and Captain Morgan. Since the nightlife here all looked the same, Scott and Amanda opted for the first place on the list. Also, it was the closest to their hotel, down the street from the beach.

"How did you afford this trip?" Amanda asked out of the blue. Scott shrugged.

"My family does all right," he said. "Mom travels for business a lot and had a ton of frequent flyer miles. I didn't have to pay for the tickets. Vince already paid for the hotel, so all I had to do was budget for food and drink. Vince told me not to worry about it, but I'll pay him back in a few months."

"My dad used to travel for business," Amanda said. "One time, he went out of town and never came back." Scott looked out the window and tapped his fingers on his leg. Amanda blushed. "Sorry. I don't know why I told you that."

"No," Scott said. "Don't worry about it. You gotta get that kind of thing off your chest, right?"

"Yeah," Amanda said. "Listen, I'm gonna grab a quick shower and change. After, we should go drink ourselves unconscious." She grinned at Scott.

"Deal," he said, and they shook on it. Amanda brought her things into the bathroom, turned the tiny lock on the doorknob and put her toiletry kit on the counter by the single sink. She brushed the mossy feeling off her teeth, making sure not to swallow any of the water. She showered in trickles of tepid water. When Amanda was dry, she dressed in a yellow skirt, black blouse and low-top, and high-heeled boots over fishnet thigh-highs. She brushed out her hair and put on make-up. She winked at her reflection and blew herself a kiss. Scott knocked on the door.

"Hey," he said, "are you almost done? I drank a whole bottle of water and I think I'm about to explode."

"Thanks for sharing," Amanda said from the bathroom, then opened the door.

"Wow," Scott said when he saw her. Amanda grinned at him and tossed her hair over her shoulder. She moved aside so he could get in the tiny bathroom.

Amanda and Scott arrived at Reef's just before nine. Fifteen to twenty people, late teens to early twenties sat at the bar or at tables for two along the wall. Neon beer ads reflected off dark-stained wood in electric candlelight. A stage, ten feet across was built into one end of the bar. A man wearing sunglasses sat in a DJ booth next to the stage, sipping a cocktail. His skin was so tan it looked like cracked leather, his hair so blonde it was almost white. The man's face was pointed in Amanda's direction, though his eyes could have been on anything. Ignoring him, she stood at the bar with Scott. They ordered tequila shots with Corona chasers; with tip, it was only five bucks for everything. They took their drinks to a small table.

Twenty dollars later, Mr. Sunglasses sidled up to Amanda. The neon flicker-reflected in his hair. The DJ nodded to Scott, who nodded back and raised an eyebrow.

"How's it going?" Mr. Sunglasses asked over the music. Amanda tossed back her tequila shot, gave him a sloppy grin and a thumbs-up.

"Havin' fun so far," Scott said. His voice had a defensive edge.

"I'm Brad," Mr. Sunglasses said. He focused on Amanda. "I run the DJ booth, and I was wondering if you'd like to be part of tonight's entertainment. There's a pretty big cash prize for the winner."

"What would I have to do?" Amanda asked. The booze sloshed in her belly and the man in the shades swam in and out of focus. Brad held out small white cotton pieces that were roughly bikini-shaped.

"Wear these," Brad said. "Dance. Get wet. Give the crowd a thrill. The more you do, the better the payout."

"A wet T-shirt contest?" Scott asked. "Guess it's not a band." Amanda looked at Scott, who shrugged and half-smiled at her.

"How much money are we talking about?" she asked. Brad grinned like a cat.

"Twenty-five just for getting wet; fifty if you take off your top; a hundred if you take off your bottoms; more if you get really crazy."

"Buy us another round, and I'll do it," Amanda said. Brad signaled the bartender and paid for another two shots and beers for Amanda and Scott. She made short work of the shot, drank half the beer and belched. They all laughed and Amanda took the skimpy cotton bits from Brad. She changed in the ladies room with four other young women, all of whom were pretty, fit and looked caught between nervous and excited.

They all stripped to their skin and changed into the tiny cotton outfits, stuffing their normal clothes into purses or folding them neatly in stacks. Each of them took a moment to touch up her make-up, using the slow careful strokes of the alcohol impaired.

"Are we crazy?" one of them, a blonde woman with big green eyes asked. Amanda shrugged.

"Does it matter?" another asked. "I'm only doing it for the money." All the women nodded at that. They filed out of the bathroom, each dropping their stuff off at their respective tables. They mounted the stage to the DJ's enthusiastic introductions. Amanda was chilly with only thin cotton between her and the bar's air conditioning. She stood in a line of barely shivering women and waited. The music blared from the speakers, heavy on the bass; it wasn't a tune Amanda recognized, but it was danceable. Her hips swayed to the rhythm and she waited to be called.

The first one up was the green-eyed blonde. She danced for a few seconds, and the DJ dumped a bucket of water down her front, rendering the thin cotton transparent. The crowd cheered, mostly men, but some women, too. Amanda wolf-whistled at the blonde, caught up in the fun.

"Make some noise, fellas," the DJ said. "Let Cindy know you want to see more." The crowd got loud, and Cindy took off her top. Amanda thought, *easiest fifty bucks she ever made.* A chorus of *take it off* assaulted Cindy, but she balked and held the wet top to her chest.

"That's all right," Brad said into the microphone. "Give Cindy a hand guys. She gave us a little thrill and we appreciate it, don't we?" The men in the crowd clapped without much enthusiasm.

The next woman, Gina - a name that startled Amanda, as it also belonged to her own mother - took off her bottoms too, and let them sail into the crowd. They landed on a table and the guy sitting there put them in his mouth. The guy next to him laughed so hard he fell off his chair. Gina did some things with her fingers that were illegal in public in the U.S. and that probably earned her more than a hundred. She stepped to the edge of the stage, clearly comfortable in her nakedness. It was Amanda's turn.

When the water hit her, it was quite cold. Amanda's nipples popped up, almost painfully hard against the cotton. She tore it off, to the happy yells of the crowd. *Fifty,* she thought. Amanda danced around the stage in only wet, sagging cotton that was already falling off her hips. She hooked her thumbs in the edges and pulled them down. *Hundred,* Amanda thought. The men in the crowd were whistling and bellowing; Amanda caught Scott's eye and grinned at him. He gave her a thumbs-up.

"Who wants to see Amanda go really crazy?" the DJ asked. The men got very loud and the other women on the stage stomped their feet, keeping beat with the music. Someone shouted *do it* and soon it was a chant. Amanda grabbed a full shot of some dark liquor from the bar and slammed it. She ran her hands down her body, cupping her breasts and then sliding one hand between her legs.

"Show us what you got, Amanda," the DJ said, his voice in the speakers hitting the low, sexy register Amanda could feel in her groin.

"Okay," she whispered. "You got it." Amanda grabbed the skin of her upper thighs and pulled. It came away in sheets, blood splashed onto the stage and the mostly naked women behind her. Someone screamed.

Amanda peeled the skin from her shoulders down across her torso on both sides. She yanked hard on one arm, then the other, stripping the skin off one at a time. Last, Amanda pulled off her face and hair, letting them fall in the pile of discarded flesh on the stage.

The music pumped out of the speakers, but there was no other sound now. One man had fainted dead away, and the rest were shocked into silence.

Amanda stood, naked and free for the first time in years. She flexed her limbs, testing the joints of her exoskeleton. Amanda flicked the blood off her claws and opened her beaked mouth.

"Ahhh," she said, her normal human voice coming out of the alien mouth, "that's better."

Amanda whirled on the DJ, severing his head with one swipe of her claws. The other women on the stage fell to her seconds later. Amanda leaped from the stage, slaughtering the screaming audience, the bartender, everyone but Scott. Five people made it to the door and escaped. The rest were toast.

Amanda stopped, carapace glistening in the neon. She looked at Scott, who cowered under his table, wide eyes staring at her.

"Amanda?" he stammered.

"Yes?"

"You told me I wouldn't die today," he managed. Amanda cocked her head to one side, considering this. She glanced at the clock on the wall: 12:07.

"That," she said, "was yesterday." Amanda eviscerated Scott with her claws. He gurgled and his back hit the floor. She was the only living thing in the bar, though the music still played. Amanda swayed to the beat for a moment, then she put her hands on hips annoyed.

"Damn it," she said. "Mom was right."

21. THAT SOUND OF A HOOK TO THE CAR BY

JOHANNES PINTER

"Here it is! *TURN!*"

Linnea's sudden shout makes Roger slam on the brakes. Although they don't keep more than twenty-four miles per hour, the rain-soaked road makes the red Toyota skid for almost twenty yards before stopping.

"*Jesus!* Did you have to yell like that?"

Linnea taps the map, perched on top of the brochure from the cabin rental in her lap.

"I'm sorry. But the sign said *Järna*. That's where we're heading."

Roger mutters a curse as he stares in the rearview mirror, ensuring that no headlights approach from behind before he backs up so they can read the sign. It says *Järna, 4 km.*

"Do we need milk?"

"Huh?"

Linnea points at a gas station a hundred meters further along the main road. Besides the gigantic numbers that proclaim today's gas prices, a Seven-Eleven logo is seen on the huge sign by the entrance.

"Should we buy milk?"

"There's no fridge! This will be a week with black coffee."

Roger turns the wheel. They leave the main road and slowly begin moving into no man's land.

Linnea alternately watches the map and the road, trying to read the landscape outside the car. But it's raining so hard that the world is a haze behind the curtain of water. She glances discreetly at Roger's tense bottom lip, his knitted brow and strained profile. This is probably a stupid idea, she thinks; that some higher power probably doesn't want it to work. This vacation, which she thought would be a fresh start, seems to be more like one last pathetic attempt to fix something that is broken beyond help.

The gravel road is bumpy, the red Toyota wobbles through puddles at walking pace.

"What happens if we meet another car?" Linnea asks to break the awkward silence.

Roger gazes along the narrow road which is only a couple of ruts wide. It's flanked by overflowing ditches on both sides.

"We'll just have to keep our fingers crossed that we won't, won't we?"

They pass fenced fields, where small herds of ruminating cows stare at the car from the shelter of birch groves. The surroundings soon goes from open countryside to dark and dense spruce forest, and the road shifts from gravel to neglected natural surfaces. The Toyota sometimes skids on the slippery surface.

"How far have we come?" Linnea asks, staring at the map.

"No idea. Hard to tell at this speed." Roger nods to the mileage. "I don't know what that said when we turned."

"We should drive towards Järna for about two miles, and then turn right onto a smaller road."

"Even smaller *than this?*"

Linnea nods.

Roger sighs and follows the road that cuts through the dark forest like a crack through black ice. The dense rain and the light from above give the haze an intense luster. Linnea watches the map.

"I think we're close to the next turn. Either we are at this curve, or this one. Just keep driving-"

"What the hell do you think I'm doing? I'm going as fast as I can in this gruel."

He floors the gas pedal when the road straightens, but the car responds by slipping in the mud. Roger parries and brakes to avoid sliding into the ditch. A second later they stand still. Roger shifts down and carefully presses the gas, but all that happens is that the rear tires spin and dig even deeper.

"Try the third gear," Linnea suggests.

Roger does and the engine roars, but the car is stuck with its wheels sunk into the muddy forest road. He turns off the ignition and hits the steering wheel a couple of times, swearing. The rain patters against the roof, making the hood steam. Linnea wipes the moisture off the window and looks out at the woods. It's dark and dense and lush, with a saturated glow from the intense wetness.

Roger takes a newspaper from the car door pocket.

"I have to check. One and two and ..."

On three, he pushes the door open and quickly steps into the pouring rain with the newspaper over his head. His feet sink deep into the mud.

"Damn it!"

Linnea watches as he painstakingly squelches around to the car's rear end. A few seconds later he's back, lands in the seat, kicks the mud from the sneakers and closes the door. He runs his hand through his soaking wet hair and shakes his shirt sleeves.

"The rear wheels are half sunk", he says.

"Can we push it?"

"No chance."

"What do we do then?" Linnea asks. "Can we walk to the cabin?"

Roger picks up his cell phone.

"We don't know how far it is. And we can't just leave the car. I'll see if I can find the number to the gas station we saw out by the main road."

He launches the mobile browser and taps a few words. Then holds up the smartphone, watching the display as he moves it in different directions.

"No signal. Of course there's no mast out here where nobody lives. Shit!"

Linnea looks down the road.

"Maybe someone will pass?"

Roger gives her an incredulous look.

"Yeah right. In, like, a week, when the next resident arrives."

"What should we do, then?"

"One of us will have to walk back to the gas station. And I guess I know who that'll be."

Linnea puts her hand on his arm.

"I can do it."

Roger pulls his arm away and grips the steering wheel.

"No. I'll do it. I've already ruined my sneakers. Did we bring an umbrella?"

Linnea produces a folded umbrella from the back seat.

"Hopefully, someone at the gas station can pull us," Roger says and opens the door. Outside, the whispering sound of rain resonates through the forest. The massive clouds above them make the atmosphere dim and haunted.

"Please, hurry," Linnea begs.

"Look at the weather. I'll hurry as much as I can."

He unfolds the umbrella with an irritated gesture. Gets up and shuts the door with a bang. Linnea watches Roger's shape disappear down the road in the direction they came from, until it fades away completely, swallowed by the rain.

She holds up her mobile phone. Still no signal. She unfolds the map and tries to deduce how far it might be to the cabin. What a stupid idea. What was she trying to do, persuading Roger to rent a cabin in the middle of nowhere? No TV, no internet, not even any electricity. Her plan was that they would get a chance to be all by themselves. Talk. Find their way back to what they had. Now they were stuck, literally, more than ever.

After twenty minutes, the rain seems to have intensified further. It rumbles against the roof, fumes when hitting the hood, and the whole forest looks covered in translucent plastic sheeting.

Linnea is about to dig out a newspaper from a bag in the back seat when she hears the sound.

It is low and almost concealed by the clattering of the rain. The first time, her brain doesn't even register it as something to pay attention to. The second time she lifts her head and listens. The third time, she locates the sound: it's the sound of something hard against the car's exterior. A low thud followed by a short scraping.

Linnea straightens in the seat, all senses focused on the sound. She worriedly lets her eyes sweep the surroundings, but nothing is visible outside the car. Frightening thoughts flash through her brain, the kind of thoughts you get when you're all alone in the middle of a forest, hearing something unknown. The thought that shines the brightest is that story of the insane killer with a hook for hand, that the scout leaders told Linnea and the other terrified ten-year-olds around the campfire during a camping trip. How long ago, twenty years? She tries to shake off the memory, she is a grown up and can't let her imagination run away with her as if she was a little girl. Nevertheless: the sound is here. Now. For real. And this time more persistent. It's not coming from the roof (as it did in that stupid campfire story about the hook) and not from any of the sides.

It's coming from below.

Linnea cranes her neck, trying to see as much as possible outside the car. Could Roger be back with help? Can it be them trying to attach a cable to tow the car? But there's nothing on either side. She gets up on her knees and tries to look behind the car. Nope, no towing truck and no people. She's alone out here in the woods. Alone with the sound under the car.

Thud. Scrape. Thud. Scraaape. Could it be an animal? Maybe they ran over an animal, and now the poor thing's trying to get loose. Yes, that could be it.

Linnea prepares to stick her head out in the rain to look under the car, when the sound changes: something just got attached to the car's underside. She freezes. Listens frantically.

But it's all quiet. No movement, and no more thuds or scrapings. Complete silence, except for the muffled roar of the rain against the car roof and Linnea's heartbeat in her throat. She looks at her watch - how long has it been since Roger left?

The car jerks. The movement startles Linnea, who screams as the vehicle veers in the mud. Another jerk, and this time Linnea feels the car sinking an inch into the mud. She hugs her knees as she tries to understand; who on earth pulls the car from *underneath*? There must be some kind of device in the ground. But what man would build a device in the middle of the dark forest that pulls down cars? How is the hook attached? Who could dwell down there in the mud to begin with? Maybe the hook is not a hook, but a claw...

Another tug and Linnea screams again. It's a forceful jolt that gets the car to drop another few inches. And worse: it's as if the whole car was bent slightly in the middle. Linnea pulls the door handle to get out. But it only opens an inch, the edge of the hole blocks it. She is trapped.

Frightened, she looks around, hoping to see Roger come walking down the road. But all she sees is the dense forest beyond the curtain of rain.

Once again the car is tugged, and now the squeak of metal proves that the vehicle really is bending in half. She grabs her cell phone. Still no signal. With a hard shove, she manages to open the car door a few inches. She presses her face against the narrow opening, droplets of rain hitting her face.

"HELP!" She screams into the woods. *"HEEELP!"* But the only answer she gets is the faint echo of her own voice.

A new jolt, and the car sinks further into the ground.

What is down there? What does it want from her? How could it possibly know that a car - *their* car - would stop here? Or maybe it didn't. Maybe the thing down there has been waiting for a very, very long time for someone to end up right here, at this very spot. Just like a moray she once saw on TV. The ugly fish was quietly hiding in a crevice on the ocean floor, waiting until a smaller fish was unfortunate enough to swim by. Then the moray struck, devouring the prey in seconds.

Now the *whatever-it-is* steadily pulls at the car, making it slowly descend, first one side, then the other in a steady rhythm. The folded angle of the vehicle is now even more prominent, with the rear and front seats tilting toward each other.

Linnea lies down and tries to kick the door open, but it is firmly blocked by the edge of the hole. She aims for the window instead; with as much power as she dares, she throws a couple of kicks at it.

It's as if *whatever-it-is* pulling the car realizes that the prey is trying to escape. A few violent jerks from below, and the car sinks even faster. The mud now reaches the windows. Linnea gasps in terror, then assembles every scrap of strength left in her body. There's no time to hold back, it's time to go all in, her ankles might snap from the blow, but she must break the window. *Must get out!* With a rush of adrenaline she kicks full force with both feet. But nothing happens. The window, as well as her feet, is still intact. Screaming, she furiously kicks again, and again. But it remains whole. She's too thin and weak.

She sits up, tears of fear and frustration running down her face as she feverishly scans the interior for something hard to break the window with. She only has a few seconds left now. The car tilts to the left so that the mud reaches halfway up the left window, but the right side inclines upwards. The right side of the windshield is still clear. But she finds nothing to hit with. Bags and beddings, and a cooler made of hard plastic won't do it against a car window.

The car starts to tremble, as if the force from below prepares itself for one last decisive haul. Linnea lies down again, taking aim with her feet. One last fucking kick! Before it's too late. One last hard kick, even though she knows it's useless.

That's when the window explodes, and she's suddenly in the midst of a roaring chaos of glass and heavy rain, when a large stone hits the steering wheel next to her head.

"LINNEA! *TAKE MY HAND!*"

She sees Roger's face up there in the opening that was covered with unbreakable glass a second ago. Roger's hand is reaching for her, and she instinctively grabs it. As she feels the car beginning to fall it is as if the muddy ground gives away; she doesn't fall with it, but is pulled up to the light and to the solid ground and to the safety of Roger, and a stranger in a rain coat.

They all fall into a struggling pile of waving limbs in the water-filled ditch next to the road. In the corner of her eye, Linnea sees the red roof of the Toyota disappear in the mud and is gone. She's not sure, as the rain bellows around them, but what she hears next could be the vibrant, booming, disappointed roar of an ancient being that just lost its prey. Maybe it's just the way it sounds when a car is swallowed by the earth.

***

Later, Linnea is sitting in the back room of the gas station with a blanket over her shoulders. She's showered and holds a cup of coffee – with milk –from the vending machine in her hands, already doubting what she's been through. The only thing she understands, with some effort, is that she was not swallowed alive. She survived it, whatever it was.

She touches the patch on her right calf. It covers the wound she got from the broken window when she was pulled out of the car. Other than that she feels okay, at least physically.

"I got hold of Joseph. He'll come and pick us up in about half an hour."

Roger stands in the doorway. For a few seconds the buzzing, whispering atmosphere from the gas station slips in before he closes the door and the room is silent once again.

"You almost disappeared from me back there," he says.

Linnea doesn't look at him. She just sips the lukewarm coffee – in her emotional state she had forgotten to drink it.

"That was horrible!" Roger continues.

Linnea nods wearily.

"Yes."

Roger squats down beside her. Tucks a wet lock of hair behind her ear and tries to make eye-contact.

"I mean... it was horrible to almost lose you."

Linnea looks up. Meets Roger's dark blue eyes. Tries to process what he's saying.

"When I saw the car... saw you disappearing," he says, "I knew that I don't want you to."

His smile is tentative, searching. Linnea doesn't respond. But somewhere inside her something grows that will eventually become a smile.

125

The narrow windows were set high in the wall, too high for me to see out. Thin bars of sunlight squeezed through them to lay crooked patterns of light and shadow on the whitewashed plaster. Everything in this place was white; the walls, the sheets, the nurse's uniforms, my own gown, even the kooky slippers they put on my feet. It was as if all the color had been scrubbed away from the place leaving an antiseptic void that smelt faintly of sick people and strongly of pine disinfectant.

Clyde whistled tunelessly through his teeth as he pushed me along the hallway, the wheelchair gliding over the smooth tiles—white tiles. I liked Clyde, he was one of the good guys; a gentle giant with hands like bunches of bananas and an easy smile. Although I couldn't help worrying that he liked me too. Once or twice I had caught him looking at me when the nurses helped me undress. I've got nothing against gay men; it takes all sorts, right? But I don't go that way and those looks made me feel uncomfortable. That is, when the meds allowed me to feel anything at all.

"I could have walked, man." I told him as we pulled up by a set of double doors and he punched in the key code.

"The doc says you gotta ride, so just sit back and enjoy it."

"But I'm fine now. Good as new," I said and patted my knees.

My naked legs looked pale and oddly slender dangling out from of the bottom of my hospital gown. I had probably lost some muscle tone from being laid up in here, but I knew I could walk, if they'd let me.

"Did my wife say she'd be visiting today?" I asked.

"Err, I don't think so," he said.

"I could have walked you know. It's not far."

"I'm just an orderly, I don't make the rules."

"I know, man, but can't you help a brother out, you know put a word in with the doc. Tell him I'm good to go?"

I twisted in the chair and saw that he wore that big easy smile of his. "You can tell him yourself," he said and spun the wheelchair around flicking on the brake with his foot. Clyde handed a clipboard to a nurse with pervasive gray hair and a face that would stop a runaway truck. I couldn't call up her name, but I knew she wasn't one of the good guys. She signed the clipboard and thrust it back at Clyde. "I'll be back for you later, when they're done," he said.

"Oh hey, Clyde, did my wife say she'd be by today?"

His smile faltered a little. "Well, you see, Mrs. J—" The nurse gave him a hard stare. "Look, you just hang tough, okay?" He held out his hand and we fist bumped. His huge knuckles dwarfing mine.

"Sure," I said and shrugged.

No doubt, this was going to be another round of the same old bullshit. I'd be poked and prodded by some specialist and then maybe the color of my pills would change. Nothing else ever seemed to change though. The days in here just bled into one another. Yesterday faded on waking like a dream, a jumble of disjointed images that hung tantalizingly at the edge of my memory before they were carried away like a kite on the wind by the rattle of the pill cart making its morning rounds.

I tried to remember exactly how long I'd been here and found that I couldn't. Time was a slippery thing in this place. Sometimes it seemed as if I had only just got up and then it would suddenly be dark again. I guessed it must have been a couple of weeks since the accident. I looked up at sunlight streaming through the windows high above me. It had been snowing hard the night we wrecked, that was why Helen lost it on the bend.

I could remember the accident just fine. The one thing I wanted more than anything to forget and I could recall every damn detail: the soft whump of the blow-out, the scream of metal on metal as we plowed along the guard rail and then the whole world slamming sideways when the car flipped, the dashboard lighting up like a slot machine that was about to pay out. There was a scream that suddenly vanished, as if somebody had hit the mute button, and there was blood—too much blood—dark and syrupy in the staccato flashes of red and blue lights, dripping from the shattered glass of the rearview mirror and reflected a dozen times over in the spider-webbed fissures of the busted windshield. It was all brutally fresh in my mind. I could even smell the acrid stench of hot oil seeping out from the cracked engine casing. I knew it couldn't have happened more than two weeks ago, three tops.

I wondered why Helen hadn't been to visit. Was she still mad at me? We had been in the middle of a blazing fire-fight when we crashed, I don't recollect what we were arguing about, but surely it didn't matter now. I ran a hand over my chin, surprised by how smooth my skin felt. I couldn't remember shaving this morning, but there wasn't even a ghost of stubble lurking there. Maybe I did shave, could I have forgotten that? I worked back through my day and got as far as Clyde helping me into the wheelchair, everything before that was kind of hazy. Maybe Helen had visited me and I'd forgotten that too. I would have to talk to the doc about these damn pills they had me on.

The nurse came around behind me and kicked off the brake. "Doctor Halliburton will see you now," she said and backed me in through an open door.

The room was small, white and smelt like Band-Aids. The nurse parked the chair in front of a metal desk with a lamp at one end of it and an unruly pile of papers at the other. A man I didn't recognize was seated behind it, his bald head giving way to a flat, moon shaped face, which seemed to be at odds with the precise angles of his wire framed glasses. I thought I knew all the doctors here, at least by sight. This guy must have been new.

He pulled a thick file from the top of the stack on his desk and began thumbing through it. "How are we feeling today?" he asked.

"Well, I don't know about you, doc, but I'm just peachy. When do I get out of here?"

He pushed his glasses up his nose and glanced over at the nurse who was loitering somewhere behind me, ignoring my question. "On a scale of one to ten how much pain are you in right now?"

I hadn't noticed any at all until he mentioned it, but now there was a cruel throbbing in my lower back. It felt like a five or maybe a six to me, but I knew any number higher than a three would probably get me shot full of something and then I would wake up back in bed again, an hour, or maybe a day later, feeling lost and alone like a jilted lover.

"Not much, hardly any at all, maybe a two." I allowed.

"Good, good," he said and went back to his notes.

"Look doc. I know you're new around here, so let me bring you up to speed. I was in a wreck a couple of weeks back. I guess I got busted up some. But I'm okay now. If you can just sign me off, I'll get out of your hair… so to speak."

"Can you tell me your name, please?" He asked without looking up.

I examined the top of his bald head and wondered what kind of trick he was playing on me. "Why? Don't you have it written down on one of those bits of paper?"

"Please, just answer the question."

"What is this some kind of test?"

He looked up, his flat face completely unreadable. "Just tell me your name, if you would be so kind."

"Jones, Kevin Jones," I said at length.

He took off his glasses, dropped them on top of the file and studied me like I was a puzzling stain he'd found on his tie. "Are you sure about that?"

I glanced at my legs and saw that they were prickled with gooses flesh, but I couldn't feel a draft. "Of course I'm sure. My name is Kevin David Jones. I'm 34 and married. My wife's name is Helen. We live at 225 Wiltshire Drive and we have a black Labrador called Dozer. Does that about cover it or do you want my shoe size as well?"

I wished Helen was here, she would straighten this guy out. The pain in my spine suddenly felt worse, a shower of yellow sparks vaulted across my field of vision, just like the ones the cutting equipment made as the fire crew fought to free me from the wreck. I screwed up my eyes and I was back there again, snow falling heavily outside the busted windows, my breath coming in short painful gasps, fogging out in front of my face, snaking through the chill air like a living thing. I looked around expecting to see Helen, but there was only a dark stain on the seat beside me, the blood showing up black in the dancing beam of a paramedic's torch.

When I opened my eyes again the newbie doctor was still staring at me. "Where's Helen, where's my wife?" I asked him.

He jotted something down in his file. "And you've been here for two weeks, you say?"

"Why won't you answer me, dammit?"

He turned to the nurse and said. "We'll try increasing the Risperdal to 600 milligrams a day and continue with the ECT for another month."

"Hey, I'm talking to you, don't fucking ignore me."

"Please, try to remain calm. We'll have you back in your room in just a couple of minutes."

"To hell with calm, what's going on here? Where's Helen?"

"Now, now, if you'll just—"

I swung my arm at the stack of papers on his desk and sent them tumbling to the floor. "Fuck you, I'm out of here," I gripped the sides of the wheelchair and pushed myself up, my arms shaking under my own weight. I couldn't understand it. I used to bench press 200lbs. I tried to make my feet move, but they just lolled around uselessly at the end of my legs. A bolt of hot agony shot up my spine and bright colors exploded behind my eyes like 4th of July fireworks. My arms gave out and I collapsed breathless back into the chair.

"What have you done to me?"

"Nurse, would you give the patient something for the pain, please."

I sensed the nurse moving behind me. She came around the wheelchair and pushed up my sleeve, drops of clear liquid falling from the tip of her needle as she tapped it. It must be the drugs that had made me so weak. They were keeping me like this so I was easier to control. I bet they put them in the damn food too. The nurse bent toward me and I slapped the syringe from her hand, sending it clattering across the tiles. I made to slap her too, but she caught hold of my wrist and held me easily in a vice-like grip.

"There's no need for that, please let her go," the doctor said.

"Tell her, not me. She's the one holding on," I yelled at him.

The nurse released my wrist and I rubbed away the angry red marks her fingers left on my skin. The doctor sighed and reached into his desk drawer. "I'm sorry we need to do this again," he said leaning over and holding out what looked like a small picture frame. "I thought we were making progress." He held the frame face down so I couldn't see what the picture was. I just stared at him and made no move to take it. "Please, you need to see this."

I grabbed the picture from him and turned it over. It was a photograph of Helen. She looked pale and drawn. She was dressed in a hospital gown; her fluffy blonde hair pulled back from her face with an Alice band, revealing a long scar in her hairline.

"Jesus, when was this taken, is she all right?" I reached out and touched the picture. Helen did the same mimicking my moves exactly. I snatched my fingers away as if I'd just touched a hot stove, my mind screamed for me to drop the picture, but my hand clung stubbornly to it, refusing to let Helen go. "W—what the hell is this, some kind of trick photography?"

"Mrs. Jones, you need to accept that your husband, Kevin is dead. Until you do we can't move forward."

I looked from the doctor to Helen and she looked right back, her eyes anxiously flitting over me. She looked as if she was in pain. I raised a hand to my face, watching Helen do likewise. I could feel the bumpy scar tissue under my fingertips as she traced the old wound on my forehead.

"Do you remember now, Mrs. Jones?"

The picture of Helen started to cry, tears running down her gaunt cheeks and plopping onto the mirror I held in my hand. I remembered, I remembered it all. The wet cracking noise like an egg breaking on the rim of a bowl as Kevin's head slammed into the windshield and the blood gushing over the seat as he slumped back down. I remembered the surgeries on my back and the doctor in green scrubs, who told me I would never walk again. But most of all I remembered the guilt; it was like somebody kneeling on my chest, a suffocating weight that made it difficult for me to breathe.

We had argued. Kevin was mad at me, saying how it was my fault. I was shouting at him and he was shouting back. Harsh, angry words that neither of us meant, but now it was too late to take them back, and god, how I wanted to take them back. I was driving much too fast; taking my anger out on the gas pedal. The guard rail came out of nowhere. Kevin was right. It had been my fault.

"You are a patient at a secure psychiatric care facility, Mrs. Jones, do you understand that?"

I nodded dumbly, understanding completely. I had killed my husband and this was my punishment.

"I'm sorry. I know it always comes as a terrible shock to you, but perhaps this time you won't forget."

I handed the mirror back to Doctor Halliburton, the man who had been treating me here for the last two years.

He smiled, dimples appearing in his cheeks, making craters on his moon face. "Try and get some rest, Mrs. Jones. I'll come by and see you later. "

"Thank you, doctor," I said wiping my eyes on the sleeve of my hospital gown.

***

"You okay?" Clyde asked as he wheeled me back up the corridor. "Was they rough on you again?"

"It wasn't so bad. I can remember things now."

"That's good, right? You got to remember if you're going to get better," he said. "And a pretty lady like you deserves to get better."

I allowed myself to smile. Clyde really was one of the good guys, but even he must have realized, there was no hope of getting better; only the hope it would end. And it would, today. The next time the med cart came around I would swipe the biggest bottle of pills I could and swallow the damn lot, or perhaps I could steal something sharp

131

from the nurse's station and open a vein. I didn't think bleeding out would hurt all that much, at least, not as much as remembering did.

I wondered if I would get to see Kevin again. I wasn't sure if it worked like that once you were dead, but I thought that maybe it did. I didn't know how to apologize to him for what I'd done, but eternity is a long time, I would figure it out.

The sun had dipped below the level of the windows, leaving the hallway in the gloom of a premature twilight. I watched the milky tiles slip beneath the wheelchair and wondered what happened to all the other colors. Clyde started whistling.

"You know, I could have walked this, if they'd let me, Clyde."

"I know, Mrs. J, I know."

Four in the morning and the building slept while Sarah kept herself awake. She didn't sleep anymore.

Her computer hummed, spurring its internal gears till the thing was near searing hot to the touch. Sarah poured herself another mug of coffee but by the time she took a second sip, it was cold. Her fingers felt so icy-cold on the keyboard. No matter how many layers she wore there was this pervasive coldness deep down in her bones.

I lay in the wide bed, watching her. She was icy to the touch now, growing colder each night till I thought she might freeze over. Words and figures and indecipherable strings of characters played across the screen with that blinking line at the end; she didn't know I was there when she was writing code.

I pulled the sheets up to my neck, curling up into the fetal position. The place where she used to lie felt cold like it'd been sitting in front of an air conditioner.

I curled up tighter and tried to sleep but the clacking of her keyboard kept me awake. I don't think she knew I wasn't sleeping because every once in a while she'd start muttering gibberish to herself.

Sounded like gibberish, anyways.

I was about to drift off despite the persistent noise when she dropped the mug and it clattered to the floor, shattering on impact and spilling cold coffee over the worn floorboards. I jumped up instinctively with the sheets tangled about me and she was standing before the desk with the coffee pooling at her feet, black and undiluted.

"Jesus Christ," I said before I noticed what she was staring at. The monitor. It was covered over with a film of brittle ice, blue and flickering behind the clear crystal sheet. The keyboard had gone pale and shiny like an ice sculpture, hazy with snow crystals below the smooth surface.

"Jesus," I said again. She turned around on the ball of her foot to look at me. Her eyes went wide.

"You saw that, didn't you?" she said.

"'Course I did. What the fuck happened?"

"Nothing." She snatched one of the old towels from the top of her dresser and draped it over the computer tower and monitor so it billowed down softly. "You didn't see anything. Now go back to sleep."

"I can't sleep."

She came over to our bed and perched on the edge of the mattress, gripping the rumpled bedclothes so tightly that her knuckles went white. Up close, I could see she was trembling.

I disentangled myself from the treacherous sheets and crawled over to the other side of the mattress where she was sitting, grinding her teeth together. I could hear my heartbeat behind my ears. Jesus Christ.

I wrapped my arm around her waist, snuggled up close to her and burrowed my head under her chin like I knew she liked. She was like ice. "It's okay," I said. "Don't worry about it. You'll be okay."

Sarah cringed away from me, tightening and pulling away into herself. Her eyes had gone impossibly dark till they looked like inky pools hidden in shadow. I could see death lurking beneath her pale skin, the skull waiting for its emergence out of darkness, gleaming white. I held her close despite the ice that lingered inside. Like a corpse she gave off no body heat. If you left her lying on an icy lawn she wouldn't have melted the frost.

I held her tight and squeezed my eyes shut so I couldn't see that distant, sorrowful expression on her face. I pressed my lips to the underside of her jaw like kissing a granite monument. "Let me go," she said finally. She squirmed away from me, disentangling herself from my arms till I relented. The places where I'd touched her were white, shining with crystalline frost, transparent.

"Sorry," I said, rubbing my hands quick on my arms to get back the warmth. "I didn't mean to offend you. It's just that I'm scared, okay? Aren't you scared, too?"

"No," she said. Sarah wouldn't look at me. She hunched up on the far side of the bed with her knees drawn up and her feet curled up around the frame. Ice shone over the places on her throat and arms where I'd touched her. She wore a pained expression. I was careful not to touch her but I perched on the mattress beside her, close enough to see her breath billowing white with each shuddering exhale.

I scooted away from her when I saw the ice splintering all down her arms. I didn't want to know how this'd feel inside, this freezing from the inside out. I lay back down when she didn't move. I pulled up the sheets again and drew my knees up to my chest underneath the blanket.

When I woke up in the morning she was gone and she'd left a crust of frost on the bed where I lay, with an icy hand-print beside my head. I looked through the whole apartment, every single room, and I went down into the lobby to wait for her but she never showed up. Every single time I saw a car pulling up from our apartment windows, I thought it might be her. I got my hopes up.

But she didn't come home that day or the next. I worried she'd left the city entirely or that she'd come into an accident. I tried calling her cell about sixty times a day but she never answered, though it went on ringing so I knew she hadn't turned it off.

On the third day, I found the phone lying underneath the sofa, turned onto silent mode. Ice was melting off the keys. Sixty-one missed calls. I kept the phone and wrapped it up in the pillowcases off our bed, lay down and snuggled up with her favorite sweater. I could call the police and report her as a missing person, but I wasn't sure if they'd think I was wasting their time.

She couldn't have wanted to stay here anymore.

She didn't want to see me anymore.

On the fourth night a storm came up from the coast, howling around and snarling at the spindly apartment house. I'd kept myself awake with Dr.

. Pepper while midnight came and went again. Now four o'clock was approaching again. I could almost feel the dawn light bristling the hair on the back of my neck.

This crazy storm raged on till the whole building rattled its steel-reinforced bones. I'd stayed up reading and already gone through two books, working close to the third. In the past few days I'd worked my way through nearly half my insubstantial bookcase. They kept my mind occupied whenever I didn't come across a passage to remind me of Sarah.

Don't know what it is about the name Sarah but it doesn't feel like an icy name. She's not a cold person and she never was till that night a few weeks before her disappearance, the first time I felt the ice inside her like a brilliant core. She wouldn't listen to my questions about that sudden chill that'd taken her heart and twisted it.

I'd learned quickly not to piss her off; I still had bruises on my arm from her fingerprints and a slow-healing cut on my lip from where she'd knocked me in the face with a toaster. So even when she'd left I had these reminders of her. I touched the bruises on my arm where they'd gone lurid purple and green. Something twisted deep inside me where the ice had touched her.

Sarah came back that night.

Four o'clock.

The windows rattled with the storm; that, at least, I'd grown used to. But the chill that blew through the apartment a moment later definitely surprised me. I shot up out of bed with the sheet tangled around my ankle. One of the floorboards in the hallway creaked, outside the bathroom door. Almost here. I gripped the blanket edge so tight that my fingernails cut into my palms through the fabric.

"Sarah?" I said. My voice sounded too high and weak in my ears. "Is that you?"

No response but another creaking floorboard and naked, splatting footsteps in the hall.

"Talk to me," I said.

A shadow passed on the other side of the door and ice splintered on the floorboards, glinting in the skewed moonlight that shot through the parted window blinds. Shit. Cold set into my mind. I wouldn't want to face whatever stood on the other side of that door. "H-hey," I stammered. "Come on in. Door's unlocked. Go ahead."

Doorknob twisted.

An ice sculpture looked back at me when the door creaked open. I swallowed hard. Something in its face reminded me of Sarah but everything else had shifted or morphed into this new thing. The fingers were like twisted skeleton-bones, sharp as knives on the ends. They could pierce flesh easily.

It left a path of sparkling frost in its wake; I thought the old floorboards would buckle for sure. Alright. Okay. I stood up trying to look calm but my face went pale when she stepped into the room and came up before me in a blink. I didn't flinch.

It opened its mouth to speak but the words didn't come out, only a plume of ice droplets. Nothing but the swift screaming wind and rain broke the silence between us. Silence made up of a million unsaid prayers or curses.

I broke the stillness and took her in my arms. Let myself fall into her cutting flesh, a little knife of heat cutting through the ice inside her bones. I burrowed my head under her chin and embraced her tightly, running the tips of my fingers through her thin white hair. It used to be dark, almost black, but now it felt insubstantial as pulled sugar. I kissed her throat. No fluttery pulse underneath, only granite cold. Her razor fingernails dug into the flesh of my upper arms, piercing the skin to draw bright healthy blood that flowed down over her hands.

She let go of my right arm and her frozen claws gripped my chin, lifted up my mouth to meet hers; kissing her was like kissing a winter storm and the cold sank down into me, cutting through into my bones. I pulled away but she gripped me tight and drew me toward her while her tongue explored the inside of my mouth. I couldn't fight anymore.

I opened my eyes and looked into her face but there wasn't anything left of Sarah there but the familiar sneer, broken by a slanted mark that cut down the middle of her face. Her claws traced patterns on my naked arms, slicing deeper when I struggled. I gave in when the blood started trickling down my arms to pool in the hollows of my inner elbows.

I met her eyes. Cold blue fire burned deep inside her skull, blistering in my mind. My heart pounded so loud it filled my ears; I wondered she couldn't hear it going. Somehow I felt her reach inside me with her mind. Skeletal claws tore into my shoulders and back, drawing blood that froze on contact with her crystalline skin.

I pulled away from her kiss and murmured, "It's okay, you're back now, everything's okay," into the hollow of her neck while she tore her fingers out of my back and ran them through my hair, clotting it with red gore.

I kissed the frost on her throat, wondering what lay beneath these layers upon layers of hazy ice. There must have been something left of my Sarah somewhere inside. She tangled her fingers in my hair and drew my head back so she could look directly into my eyes.

Something twisted and tightened deep inside of me so I blushed and looked away. She kissed me and something loosened in my innards. Her tongue was both pliant and icy at once. "I love you," she murmured into my mouth. I knew. This storm could take away the visage of Sarah and it could inject her heart with ice, but it couldn't take away our bond.

The blood on my back froze against my skin and I felt strange inside as if my body were fighting someone without my consent. My head swam but my vision kept steady aside from a slight blurriness around the edges; I kept my eyes fixed on hers and finally noticed the severe difference there.

Her eyes used to be a deep jade green but now they'd paled to an icy blue, nearly transparent. She pinned my wrists together at the small of my back and took her mouth away from mine to run her lips along the line of my jaw, where they left a thin wet trail that froze over immediately. I exhaled long and slow and saw my breath plume out beside her head.

Something had changed outside; the rain which had rattled the windows and pushed at the building now was silenced, replaced by the soft patter of snowfall on cement.

In this city we rarely found snowfall on our streets. The river had never frozen over for so long as I'd been in this place but now I felt we might see an end to our eternal lack of wintry snow.

Her grip on my scalp tightened till I nearly screamed but I dared not anger her further with an outburst; I still remembered the violence she could inflict on me without regrets. I kept quiet and still, hoping to quell the fright building up inside me while the snow outside pummeled the apartment windows.

Though I knew she might not hurt me without provocation, the chill which was now setting into my bones sent an icy fear straight to my heart.

"Let me go okay?" I said but she didn't answer, only tore back the hair from my scalp so hard I couldn't help but let out a whimper; tears stung my eyes.

I struggled away from her and had to break a layer of frost and ice which had been gradually overtaking me. Shards of ice came off my arms and neck, shattering when they hit the ground.

The heat from my body started to melt the frost off my back and the frozen blood went slick and wet on my arms. She shuddered with disgust and pried her fingers out of my flesh, out of my hair, out of me. I kept my eyes fixed on her white-blue ones while the snowstorm raged on outside, growing stronger and quicker by the millisecond.

I got away from her but in a moment she had my wrists pinned again; she swept me into her arms and turned around so my back was to her. An icy shiver whispered up my spine when her lips pressed against the base of my neck.

Fuck.

Then she had both my wrists in one hand and the other was on my belly, lifting up my t-shirt to bare my stomach, tracing the ridge of bone of my lower ribs, moving down my body terribly slow; I shuddered against her and my heartbeat sped, breathing getting more unsteady.

Sarah's fingers were ice; her mouth left trails of spit on my neck and upper back that froze on contact with the icy air hovering around both of us. I couldn't keep from reacting with a low whimper when her fingers undid the zipper on my jeans and started to explore below the waistband, brushing against my bony hip. Fuck.

"Sarah," I whispered, "stop, please," but her bitter-cold fingers like shards of ice were moving down there, steadily. I suddenly tore away from her or tried to at any rate, catching her off-guard. I twisted my neck around to knock her head away but she went on unfazed while I fought against her. I dug my elbow into her ribs and she bit hard into the back of my neck, hard enough to draw fresh blood that immediately froze over.

Sarah - or this thing that used to be Sarah - muttered something but I didn't quite catch what she said before she flexed her ice-razor fingers and they tore into my belly.

I screamed but she silenced me with a shot of ice over my mouth and throat. At least I wouldn't bleed out; all my wounds were frozen over but it wasn't normal ice. Felt harder than ice - more like diamonds - and didn't break when I moved, despite how thin and crusty it looked.

I couldn't move and she was digging her razor nails into my gut, parting the flesh and spilling quickly-frozen blood but not doing more than surface damage. I closed my eyes and prayed it would be over quickly.

She murmured incomprehensible phrases into my upper back, my neck, the crust of icy blood making my neck stiff. I squeezed my eyes closed tight, praying. Something about this felt so familiar and strange both at once.

Felt both lovely and frightening, twisting deep in my guts, in my mind, in my heart. I'd missed her for so long and now we'd be together once more, forever. In the last moments before the ice drove into my heart, my mouth collided with her jaw.

24. HOLE CARD by Devlin Giroux

There are people and there are cards. Given the two, I'd take the cards any time. Flip a king, you know its worth. Same with a two. Black or red, didn't matter. The only damn ones that could step outside the law were the aces. Romanticized, those single bastards. Like assassins. Turn up an ace and it could change the course of the game, or it could slink away, keeping low pro and only worth a whisper. Then there's what I became. No word I know for it. Figured there were a lot more like me. That mortuary reject Mr. Gone had hinted as much. Never expected an invite to a company picnic, but a newsletter might have done the First-of-Mays some good.

"This one is mine, Suicide King," the woman said.

Some real damn good since I hadn't the first clue if the word *woman* was accurate as a way of describing the thing talking to me in that moment. Man, woman, or other, it inspired my gag reflex to new levels of ferocity.

She was rot and sickness, pus and bile pooling at her skeletal feet. What skin she did have either roiled with maggots or was stretched tight to cracking. Fever and pestilence wafted on the air around her. Worst of all, not a scrap of cloth covered her, hence landing on the woman side of what it might have been. The things dropping off the arm she pointed at me were vile, but it was fuck all compared to the hate coming from her eyes of piss and green ichor.

If Mr. Gone was a storm of malice, this woman was the slow, lingering death everyone fears; the incurable virus, the phage that consumes until the painful, maddening end.

"Not been at this long," I said, gathering my own brand of hoodoo to me, "but I don't remember hearing anyone shouting dibs."

"Recognize your betters, novice," she said. Congealed blood thickened her voice and ran down her chin. "I have taken mortals for centuries."

"Really? That long?" I bolted on the best winning smile I had, the one I often used when I knew someone at my table was on tilt… just to push 'em that little bit more over the edge. "Been at it that long and I still beat you to the Take."

Sometimes I'm just the dumbest sonuvabitch walking.

She hit without so much as batting an eye, not that I wanted to see her version of Jeannie, no telling what else would slop off. Lips puckered by open sores spread into a smile, twin worms parting to show me jagged teeth black with ruin. I no longer needed to wonder what the mother fucker of all hangovers with a bubonic chaser would feel like.

I shot a glance at the Take that Princess Pox and I were negotiating over. Almost pitied the bastard. Would have if not for what made him so popular with the otherworld killer brigade. The shore rat had been charming his way up and down the East Coast, a wake of Rohypnol comas and HIV infections behind him.

Piece of shit actually looked worse than I felt, which was something since Molly Meningitis couldn't kill me. Did mean she could dose me with everything cooking up in that moldy brain case of hers.

"How long should you suffer for your insolence, Suicide King?" she asked. "Only a few moments before Mr. Santora is mine. You? I can play with you for much, much longer."

I cleared my throat and spat out something tumorous, which I wasn't too certain I didn't see it moving, before making sure I kept my feet under me through the sheer power of being a right asshole. "You sure about that centuries thing?"

More broken teeth as her smile widened.

"They not have gravity back then, bitch?"

The loose flesh dangling from her face whipped around a little slower than her head, breaking glass drawing her attention away from me. Damn near laughed when she flinched at the wet splat of the Take's sudden stop.

Her power fell away as easily as dirt in a nice, hot shower.

"Mine," I said.

Then I was alone.

I stood at the window's edge, kicking some of the glass and watching its ten story fall to cold cement. There lay the bloody, diseased street pizza formerly known as L. to the J. Santora.

"Too far, lady," I said. Maybe she heard me. Maybe not. I was still learning the rules. "All I had to do was tell him how to end the pain."

I knew he was there before his hands came together.

"I do so love when she gets put in her place," said Mr. Gone. "Remind me to tell you what I did to her at the leper colony in Romania. So many interesting holes she has."

I waved him off and let my own power sweep me away someplace… out.

25. ONE WITH NATURE by Marc Shapiro

The world could be a beautiful place. Especially at 7 a.m. Especially at 7,000 feet.

Clouds flitting through the contours of a mountain range like an atmospheric coat and tie were a delightful vision. So was the dusting of snow that lapped the crags and slopes as it crept toward the dense foliage and thick forest below. On a good day the sun stood full and swollen, hanging in the sky, radiating out on the horizon.

Andrew began his day this way more often than not. The view had brought him here some twenty years ago. The solitude and peace of this heaven on earth was why he stayed.

Andrew stepped out of his cabin and took a few crunching steps into the new fallen snow. He looked up, momentarily blinded by the glare. He tugged at a ragged but sturdy fur lined parka. His pants bloused above the tightness of his old boots; they had survived many winters but had hung on.

Andrew was a true mountain man. But this had not always been so.

When he had disappeared into the night and come here, he had been just another cog in a big corporate machine, destined for long hours, unhealthy habits and an early grave. Andrew had quite simply upped and left it all in the middle of the night: the trophy wife, the BMW, the ungrateful children and the notion that life was absolutely worthless.

He had come here on a whim. He did not even know where here was. But Andrew knew that this outpost of isolation near the base of a meandering mountain range was where he wanted to be. He had spent the beginning of the first winter in a tent, moving by instinct and piecing together a log cabin using Boy Scout training from his distant past.

In the beginning Andrew had no idea how he was going to survive in the middle of nowhere. But he was a quick learner. He learned to build a fire the old fashioned way. Melting snow made water for drinking and boiling. And it was not only the bears who shit in the woods. He did right by his waste and buried it deep in the nearly frozen soil, watching as the days past and bits of grass and plant life would inevitably fill the black circles, and return the fresh earth to obscurity amidst the tundra.

Andrew took a few more steps into the fresh snowy powder, took a long drag on some unusually bitter coffee and walked somewhat unsteadily into the woods. Behind him the door to his cabin stood wide open and, yes, inviting. As he moved through a gully and into the first layer of trees, the sound of early morning was interrupted by howls, chirps, bellows and the skittering of small animals in the trees and on the ground.

Andrew came by hunting out of necessity alone. He was as anti-gun as one could be. But the reality was that, once the food he had brought with him was gone and his stomach cried out its anguish with regularity, he knew he would have to take life to beget his own.

That he would not consider using a gun temporarily put a crimp in his food choices. But there was a river nearby and he was a fair to middlin' fisherman. Exotic fruits, nuts and plant life did not kill him and also became a part of his menu. It was only during the rarest of times that he would set a primitive trap for a ground squirrel. And on those rare occasions, he had to admit that squirrel tasted a lot like chicken.

Andrew's boot came down hard on a downed branch, snapping it with a crack that brought him back to reality. The fact that the sounds of the day and night, the rustlings of the wind, the footfalls and chance encounters with the forest dwellers had been his only companions for several years was not lost on him. This was a hard place for a woman.

In the beginning he had used the contacts of his former life to periodically order in a high class call girl for a week or two. Each time he had hoped that one of them would take a liking to the great outdoors and stick around. But ultimately they were too city for his extreme lifestyle, and would leave hastily when the term of the arrangement had ended.

However on one of his infrequent trips to the nearest town for supplies that nature could not provide, he made the acquaintance of a waitress. She was much younger, had spunk and also, in his estimation, was a bit bipolar. When Andrew jokingly suggested she join him up in the mountains for a while, she did not think twice about immediately quitting her job, jumping into his all-terrain puddle jumper and heading off with him. It had all been great for about a month. But then things got funny. She got funny. He got funny. Nary a word was said on the ride back down the mountain. She had hoped to get her job back, and he was simply glad to be alone again.

A call in the distance, echoing through the trees and seemingly dancing madly over the horizon, snapped Andrew out of his thoughts, his eyes staring off in the distance. Ahead stood a break in the trees and underbrush, a circular plot of flat ground, more dirt than grass and snow. Andrew stopped in his tracks, his eyes reflecting something unknown. Part of him wanted to turn around and head back to the cabin. Part of him knew it was way past the point of no return.

Andrew had learned how to live with nature and to respect its unwritten rules. Which in his world meant share and share alike. When he had scraps or parts of his larder were on the verge of going bad, he would take his leftovers out to a patch of ground some fifty yards from the cabin and leave them there. Invariably he would return to the spot to find his offerings had been devoured or dragged off into the forest. He sensed that it must be wolves, or perhaps bears out of hibernation or even raccoons. He had never seen mountain lions but he was convinced they were there. All he knew for certain was that there were always tracks around the drag marks and a pile or scat or a fresh puddle of urine. Andrew surmised that it was a calling card of sorts.

A way of saying thanks.

Andrew moved into the circle. He was not so much afraid as he was awed by the majesty of the moment, his surroundings and how the world welcomed him on this day. A relaxed, content smile spread across his face. He looked across the circle and saw a sturdy oak. It would do. Andrew moved to its base and sat down. The wood was firm yet accommodating. It would certainly do. His thoughts returned to reality as he remembered the time.

Andrew had not needed a doctor to tell him that he was getting old. He knew he had found a new life and many wonderful summers at 7000 feet. But he also knew that nature was taking its course and that he was about to discover first hand if there really was a heaven. Or a hell. He spent his last months, weeks and days in quiet contemplation, all the while marveling at how the body quite naturally and deliberately begins to break down. When Andrew finally awoke this morning he knew in his heart and soul that the end was truly near.

And he also knew that as he had lived by nature's code; that was also how he would die.

Andrew peeled off his parka, reached into his shirt pocket and pulled out the stub of a crudely carved pipe. Through trial and error he had discovered a mixture of fine twigs and brush oil, something he called 'Mellow' and had easily succumbed to the quite gauzy blanket it put on things. He lit up and took a couple of deep drags. The desired effect was not long in coming. Andrew was feeling no pain.

He rolled up his flannel shirt sleeve and reached around to the sheath that contained his hunting knife.

It was his old reliable, a double sided, ever sharp blade that had sawed its way through many fish and had set the table for many a meal. Andrew pulled the knife out and moved it to his now exposed arm. The blade was poised precariously over his arm as Andrew sought out a nice soft spot that contained a pulsating vein. As almost an afterthought, Andrew moved the knife blade to his skin…

…And dug it in deep.

The blood revealed itself immediately and began to drip down in slow but steady rivulets that crisscrossed his arm. Andrew gazed at his work for what seemed like minutes. A rustling in the woods caught his attention. It was a deliberate, yet cautious scratching and footfall. Something was out there.

Watching.

Andrew mentally took it in before opening his shirt and exposing his chest. Once again the knife was set to its bloody work. In another life the symbol that broke through skin and bled would have been a cross. But Andrew had long since passed on Jesus in favor of the wind, the sun and all things that ran and flew free. So what appeared bloody and splayed was a mixture of Indian Shaman and his personal favorite, a very sixties' Peace Symbol.

Andrew was feeling weak at the blood loss. His eyesight blurred as he gazed off into the forest and was met by the head of a wolf breaking softly through the underbrush, sniffing the ground and eyeing Andrew with a sense of curiosity and caution. The wolf stepped forward and revealed itself as a large male, the silver-hued hide speckled with brown, and a body that was muscular and youthful. The look in its piercing dark eyes was that of an experienced creature of the wild.

Instinctively Andrew tensed but quickly returned to a state of bliss. As the wolf moved ever closer, Andrew spied others emerging from the woods behind him. Of varying ages and sexes, they were an obedient tribe, waiting for a signal from their leader.

Andrew tossed the hunting knife as far as he could. The leader of the pack flinched, but did not hesitate to move closer and closer…

And closer.

The wolf came to within a foot of Andrew and stopped, its snout almost touching his face. It stared into Andrew's eyes, the classic showdown of spirit and soul. The bridge between man and nature was complete.

Andrew looked skyward. He opened his shirt wide to display the blood and flesh. The wolf's head moved to the wound, sniffing and nuzzling the blood. Then it looked skyward and howled, a long, lingering ironic and remorseful howl.

Nature was saying thank you.

26. COMMUNICATION BREAKDOWN BY WINIFRED BURNISTON

The crushing fire inside her skull had surpassed the jaw-dropping agony crippling her body. The fluorescent lighting's incessant humming had transformed into an electric buzz saw between her eyes. None of this kept her from dragging her nearly rigid form to the communications terminal.

How long had she struggled at this? Minutes? Hours? Days? She had no idea but it felt like an eternity.

The distance to the chair in front of the console had shortened, but the light from the buzzing bulbs reflecting off the white walls and tile floor was blinding her. It was as if she were standing in the midst of an arctic snowfield at high noon.

She knew she was alone, sealed in this space by her own doing. She glanced back at the door, only to confirm once again that she'd managed to shut it. Her eyes shifted from the room's only entrance or exit to the brown-black streak zigzagging behind her. The blood trail was definitely old and congealed. She refused to look at her right leg. The image of its shattered ruin would be right there, tattooed on her mind's eye for the rest of her life.

Closing her eyes against the fierce whiteness, images flashed through her mind: strobing lights, alarms, and the sounds of screaming all pulsed in conjunction with the throbbing pain which threatened to squeeze her brain as if in the grip of an errant blood pressure cuff. Faces also danced behind her closed eyelids. People she was supposed to know, and yet, somehow she couldn't quite place, whose individual smiles and laughter were slowly melting down into an agonized rictus before disappearing from view.

And running. She remembered running. The breath tearing from her lungs as something, some THING that simply shouldn't be able to move at such breakneck speed, but did nevertheless.

She'd been trapped behind a workstation in the adjacent room. She'd picked up a tool, a heavy wrench of some kind, and had bolted towards the door. A sickly sweet stench had enveloped her. Then something more solid had struck her, sending her tumbling to the cold, hard tile. She recalled screaming and beating against some physical thing, while being engulfed in a nauseating aroma. Kicking, punching, slamming it in the back with the wrench, she managed to wriggle out of its grasp. Her elation evaporated as she felt and heard her leg snap. Blood from her split bottom lip ran into her mouth as the scream had erupted from her body. Writhing with lava-veined agony, she had twisted just enough to see what had once been her husband chomp down on the bone protruding from her leg. Only then, swimming against the waves of pain and fear did she manage to gather enough reserves to rain blow after blow with the wrench upon his skull.

Somehow, after some unknown length of time, she'd managed to push out from under his mercifully motionless form and drag herself into the laboratory control center and shut the door. Then, at some point or perhaps several times between then and now, she'd passed out. She lay trembling on the blood soaked floor, realizing time was losing all meaning.

Part of her mind understood that she was now a corpse; a living horror. She tried to hold it together, to stay lucid enough to make whatever message she could relay clear enough to be perceived. She hoped, prayed, that someone was still alive on one of the floors above, watching the cameras.

Her hand brushed against the leg of the chair and she opened her eyes. Slowly, agonizingly, she pulled herself closer and began the pain-filled process of getting her body into the chair. When she finally plopped into the hard wooden seat, she was shaking and sweating. She was also eternally grateful that it hadn't been a chair on casters, which would have slipped away and made her assent impossible.

Through ragged breaths she tried to focus on the control panel's dials and knobs in front of her. She didn't remember there being so many. A low, eerie moan escaped her lips as she tried to recall which one powered the microphone jutting out towards her.

The big, red one attached to the base finally seemed plausible. She took a deep breath and tried to concentrate on making sensible words come out of her mouth as she reached for that button. Her body didn't want to cooperate and it took her a half a dozen tries to finally crash her limp fist down on the button. Her hand trembled as she tried to force it to stay in place. The words refused to form. Her body was beginning to betray her and would soon be operating with a primal will of its own.

At last she got her mouth to open with a willpower she never realized she had; her mind fixed on what had to be done, and the words came tumbling out.

"Is there anybody still left up there? I don't know how long I've been in here, but I don't have much time left. There are no weapons in here, other than a big wrench, but I doubt I'd be able to use it even if I tried. I can feel myself changing and I won't be able to communicate for very long. It's difficult to concentrate and I hope I'm making sense."

"What I really need to say is, I can't be saved. None of us down here can be saved. If the biohazard has escaped this level, none of you can be saved, either. Those of you with arms… I mean armed and coherent, need to kill those exposed at once, including yourselves…"

"You can't stop it and you can't control it. If there is anyone still alive in the control booth or watching me from the security panel, turn off the generators."

"Stop the air circulation. This little gift from our lab is traveling through the ducks… uh, ducts…up to you!"

"Don't try to get in here to shoot me. Don't even think about using me for another perverted experiment. If the toxin in the air doesn't infect you, I surely will. No matter how long you watched me take to get to this spot, it was because I was in control and in pain. Once the virus takes over, which should be any moment now, then everything changes."

Trembling all over, she took a deep breath and continued.

"I watched my husband transform. I know that this body will move a hell of a lot faster than you think when it smells living flesh. When it hears the pounding of your heart, the delicious pulsing of your blood through your veins, which will quicken sharply if you see me face-to-face… Dear, sweet Jesus, I'm salivating at the thought!"

"Shit! I can't see! Can you hear me? Hello? Hello! Oh, God, I need… This is not a test, a test, a test of the emergency broadcast system is shutting, mine is, shutting down, peas, peas and carrots, please help me!"

I heard you sing. I listened. Truly listened. That first time, I stayed in the shadows. Watching.
They adored you. You closed your eyes, absorbing their applause. I never clapped. I never wanted to be part of their adoration. My applause was silent, for you alone. I was the only one who truly listened. Who heard the artist and not just the song.
I heard you sing. I listened.
But I also watched. Always watching.

I watched the way the sun crept across the floor of your bedroom, cutting through the tiny breach between the curtains until it reached the foot of your bed. Then up, over the sheets, the sun crawled over your skin. Finally, it reached your face and you'd blink. You'd stretch.
I lived every day for that stretch.
Then I'd slink back into the shadows before you put your glasses on and could focus on the parted curtains allowing the sun access.

I watched at night, as you sang to yourself. My applause, as always, was silent. I listened. Always listening.
The space between the curtains breathed with your song, humming as you crossed to the bath. A towel, the color of your eyes, draped across your shoulders. That was all you wore.

You sang, soft. Sweet. For no one but me to hear. Mine, alone. As it should always be.

Then you disappeared, sliding into the tub. Your song continued, not even words any more, just a whisper of melody.

The window slid up silently, no noise to interrupt your song, louder now without the glass in between. One shadow broke free from the rest as I crawled through. I couldn't see, but I could hear.

Soft splashes of water, softer sigh of song. I closed my eyes, applauding in silence as you stopped singing long enough to drain the water. Then you walked into the bedroom.

Your song skipped like someone had bumped the record player as I reached for you. Your song turned into a scream for a single heartbeat until I covered your mouth with cloth. You inhaled, once. Twice. Then fell limp in my arms.

Without the song, your lips seemed duller than they should. Quiet never did suit your face. Silence disfigured you. You were built to sing, your mouth open in song, holding a note almost forever before it slid into the next. It was too difficult to look at you like this, unnatural.

I shivered, covering your face with the chemical laden cloth so I wouldn't have to see you mute.

Then I zip-tied your hands and threw you over my shoulders, the way you'd worn the towel the color of your eyes. It was better, without being able to see you. I listened to the soft sigh of my shoes on your floor as I carried you out of the house. There was a music to the wind that reminded me of you as I tossed you into the back of my car.

At home, I pushed play after making sure you were comfortable. My favorite Pastorale by Scarlatti, Tocco la prima sorte a voi, pastori, started. Your voice filled the space, soaring to the ceiling, as I walked around the table you were tied to.

Drool puddled in the corner of your mouth, a trickle falling to the pillow. I wiped you clean and your eyes, the color of your towel, opened at my touch. You screamed, lips open wider than the longest note had ever forced them. So many teeth, so white. Such a soft tongue, so pink, caught in the forceps as your screaming faded away into the harmonies of the Pastorale.

"Shhh," I whispered. "Listen." I closed my eyes, following the rhythm with my hands, tugging on your tongue with each movement.

Tears joined the drool and I wiped you clean again.

I always heard you, even in the silence I was listening.

The song faded out, until all that remained was the soft melody of your scream around your captured tongue.

My tongue, now.

"Shhh," I whispered. "Listen."

You screamed when I let go of your tongue. Screamed again when I rested the tip of the scalpel at the base of your throat. Screamed once more when it slipped through the skin, stopping only when it rested on your sternum.
You screamed when I peeled back your flesh. Screamed again when I left your side to bring the Finochietto Retractor over. Screamed once more when I spread your ribs.

I pushed play. Your voice filled the room, soaring to the ceiling. I closed my eyes, listening to you. When I opened them, it was impossible to see anything but your lungs. The source and power of your song. The fountain of youth. The holiest of grails. Soft, so soft as I ran my fingers over them. Caressed them. Kissed them.

The music soared.

"Shh," I whispered. "Listen."

Then the screaming stopped.

Gently, I placed each piece aside. Lungs. Diaphragm. Vocal cords. Larynx. Throat. Trachea.

I started the song as I attached your lungs to the bellows. I pushed play each time you stopped singing. Rivets stitched it all together, gears waiting for the bellows to pump and make them turn. I pushed play. Finally, I sewed your mouth on at the top, held there with pulleys and the finest silver chains curling around your tongue like a necklace.

The music faded into silence. I closed my eyes, trying to capture each fading note until the silence was complete.

"Shh," I whispered. "Listen."

Then I pushed down on the pedal. The gears turned, a touch rusty, like the orchestra tuning up. The bellows pumped. Air filled your lungs.

Soft, so soft as I ran my fingers over them. Caressed them. Kissed them.

Gears turned, your lips opened. Your teeth, so white, came into view. Your tongue, so pink.

"Shh," I whispered. "Listen."

You sang for me at last.

I closed my eyes, finally applauding as you screamed our song.

"I'm sorry… I've got what?"

"Grant, I know this is hard for you to hear, but you have stage four colon cancer. It's inoperable. Had we found it sooner, you may have had a chance, but it's in the first stages of metastasis and fairly soon it will have spread throughout your body. We can try an aggressive round of chemotherapy, but all that's likely to do is make you sicker. You need to think long and hard about how you want to spend your last weeks."

The cool detachment of the oncologist chaffed Grant. He could feel the anger boiling from within at news of his diagnosis and the demeanour of the person delivering his fatal news. He lashed out verbally at the doctor—the only concrete thing in his path.

"Are you fucking kidding me? I have cancer? Me?"

The doctor could only stare at him, used to the gamut of emotions that came from those who'd been recently diagnosed. No one wanted to believe it could happen to them and, based on past experiences, he just sat there, waiting for the storm to pass.

"This isn't supposed to happen to me. I help people! It's my job to keep people healthy…" Grant trailed off as his mind exploded with the treachery of his body. He looked up at the doctor and saw a charlatan; a man who spent years in school just so he could watch people die. The air around him felt foreign. All he wanted to do was leave the claustrophobic atmosphere of the office and drown himself in a drink.

Grabbing his coat and hat, he stood while giving the doctor one last parting look of disdain, "There will be no aggressive rounds of chemotherapy for me. If God has decided I must die of this disease, then that is my lot in life. It's simply too bad the world will be robbed of all of my future discoveries in the process."

Turning on his heel, Grant stalked out the office and into the chill of the early autumn air. Soon it would be flu season and the paranoia surrounding the illness would hit the streets. What superbug was coming our way this year? An H1N1 variant? Perhaps a less virulent strain of SARS would make an appearance. There was no telling what strain of influenza would strike and what mutation it would undergo while replicating in its hosts.

Grant Mazra turned up his collar and hunkered into the warmth of his jacket, his mind still spinning with the news of his diagnosis. He wondered what it all meant as he walked the six blocks to his office at Hubertson Pharmaceuticals, the drink forgotten for the moment.

As the biochemist in charge of new drug development, Grant had the rewarding job of helping millions of people. With his hands and mind behind so many of the recent discoveries, he was lauded as one of the most brilliant biochemists in the field.

None of that seemed to matter to his own cells however, and he cursed how they had betrayed him. Sitting behind his oaken desk, he could almost feel how they mutated and multiplied. He could see them in his mind's eye, turned black with cancer, tiny pieces breaking off and entering his blood stream in search of healthy tissue to infect.

His head dropped to the blotter on his desk, tears causing darker blotches to blossom on the paper. Grant's shoulders shook as he allowed himself the moment of self-pity.

As quickly as it started, it was over, and the fist slamming down on the desk rattled the picture frames that covered the top left corner. Grant looked up to see his secretary eyeing him warily over the cubicle wall surrounding her desk. He shook his head and smiled haphazardly. Not wanting his colleagues to know just yet, Grant decided to do the best he could to hide his cancer from them.

Figuring it was the best way to drown his sorrows enough to forget them, he dove into his work. Pulling up the newest data from the preparation of this year's flu shots, he concentrated on the molecular formulas and recumbent DNA curled into them. His mind began to spin and within a few hours, he knew he was well on his way to creating his legacy. One last discovery to bring the collective world to its knees in awe of his brilliance…

***

"Damn! Why won't this work?" Grant spoke, thinking he had the lab to himself. He jumped when the voice answered him.

"What are you working on, Dr. Mazra?" It was Lucille, a very talented PhD candidate who interned at the lab while using their facilities to research her doctoral thesis.

Grant's head snapped up at the sound of her soft voice so close to him. Shuffling his papers and angling his body in front of his computer's screen, he turned to give her his full attention, nervous at what she might have seen before revealing her presence behind him. "Ahh, Lucille, hello! I didn't realize you'd be working today… thought maybe you'd be off doing what young women get up to these days." He smiled in an effort to reassure himself he hadn't let her see his lack of composure.

Lucille smiled back before answering, always a little stilted and nervous when speaking to the senior biochemist, "I had to check on the samples for the Bovine Spongiform Encephalopathy study. Results need to be documented each day or we might miss something important. You know how it is." Her shoulder rose in a tiny shrug before falling back down.

"I certainly do, Lucille. Do you need any assistance?"

"No, Dr. Mazra, I'm fine. Just a few Petri dishes under the microscope, some notes about growth, and I'm good to go. Thank you, though, I always appreciate anyone's help when I need it." She smiled before moving away to a different corner of the lab.

Grant watched her put on a white lab coat before collecting her specimens from their labelled shelves in the lock-up. Observing her walk carefully to her workstation, Grant was struck by how self-assured she was in the lab setting and knew she would make a brilliant biochemist. She might even be the one to cure cancer…

He snorted at the thought, drawing a strange look from Lucille. "Sorry, was thinking about something I'm working on. I think the answer just hit me while watching you. Isn't it odd where we get our inspiration from?"

"Yes, I think that sometimes myself, Dr. Mazra. I can be driving to the lab and something in the traffic patterns can spark an idea. Or even the song on the radio can make me think of a process in a new way. I love how the mind can always be working on those little things even while it's concentrating on a different task."

"So true, Lucille. And on that note, I must get back to what I was working on. Please let me know when you leave."

Grant turned back to his workstation, and while keeping a wary eye on Lucille, he got back to work. He witnessed the cancer cells he'd harvested attacking the healthy cells through the lens of his microscope and frowned. Had he made them *too* aggressive? His legacy rested delicately on the aggressiveness of the cancer cells he was working with; if they were too aggressive, they may end up killing themselves. And that certainly wasn't in Grant's plans.

Having come from his own body, he now knew more than he ever wanted to know about them, but in experimenting with them, he was struck by their aberrant perfection. They had one simple job—the infection of other cells—and they carried out that job in absolute simplicity. Mutate, replicate and infect. Over and over and over again.

Could he revolutionize the way the world saw the cancer cell before he died? Grant believed he could, and on that cool October day, he made his breakthrough.

A cancer cell that behaved like a cancer for other cancer cells.

He was confident his research would be the cure for cancer everyone was looking for, but his motives were not completely altruistic. No one would ever see his work for what it was: his cancer would kill him, but it would kill the rest of the world as well. For, while he'd created a lethal cancer for cancer, he'd also devised a way to make his cancer virulent. Grant thought of it as a necessary side effect, but in truth, it was his way of evening the odds. It was too late for him though, his body too far ravaged to be repaired.

Gathering his data, he shut down the computer at his workstation, erasing the files from it, and left for the day. Grant's mind was consumed with what he planned to do and he wondered if his resolve would withstand his conscience. In his heart he knew his plan was immoral and depraved, but his head didn't seem to care either way.

Grant gave himself the night to sleep on his decision, deciding he would know what to do when he awoke. For the first night in a long, long time, he drifted peacefully into sleep.

Waking with his alarm on Sunday morning, he showered and dressed, grabbing a quick cup of coffee on his way back to the lab. He had work to do and a new virus to synthesize; luckily he had no shortage of replicated cancer cells to work with.

The lab was empty, just as he knew it would be, and he set to work immediately, knowing it would take him days to synthesize enough of his new virus for what he was planning to do with it. Just as he was setting the DNA synthesis machine to begin, Lucille walked into the lab to check her samples.

"Hello, Dr. Mazra, I wasn't expecting to see you here today."

"Hello, Lucille, just working on a little something I think I've figured out. Sometimes the brain doesn't let you rest until you've started your next big project." With a smile, he turned back to what he was doing, unaware that Lucille was crossing the room toward him.

"What are you working on?"

Grant jumped at the sound of her voice in such close proximity. Whirling around, he closed his notebook and said, "Nothing for you to concern yourself with."

Said in such an authoritative tone, Lucille immediately backed away. "Sorry, Dr. Mazra, I didn't mean to pry."

"Not to worry, Lucille, I just don't want to share what I think I've discovered until the time is right. Check and double check—you know the drill…"

"Understandable, Dr. Mazra," she replied as she retrieved her samples and brought them to her workstation.

The two worked in silence at opposite ends of the lab until Lucille left for the day. Once Grant was alone, he relaxed and worked through the night. For the next week, he barely left the lab, stopping only for a few hours to sleep in his office in the middle of the night. He couldn't risk leaving his work unattended and open to prying eyes while the other scientists were working in the lab during the day. Plus, he needed to be there when each step of the preparation was complete. He only had a short window of time.

It was 3:47 a.m. when it was finally complete. In total, Grant had synthesized over three litres of a highly virulent and continually self-replicating strain of his cancer. It was his crowning achievement and would affect the medical community in a profound way. He just needed to do one more thing with it.

Hefting the container into his arms, Grant walked the distance to the manufacturing area of the compound. He had only a small window of time to add his discovery to the newest run of flu shots that would be packaged over the next few days. While the three litres did not seem like a lot in terms of the volume of vaccination vials they would package in the coming days, he knew his addition would use the dead strains of influenza virus to continue its replication, infecting the entire batch. In fact, the virus he had created would likely withstand the sterilization procedures performed between batches. There was no way of knowing just how far this could spread.

Pouring the contents into the vaccine reservoir, Grant felt no remorse. He was simply completing his life's work. If he must die of cancer, so shall the rest of the world; Grant was just a little disheartened to realize he would not be around to witness the fruits of his labour.

Closing the lid on the reservoir, he made his way back to the lab and gathered up all of his notes. He erased the hard drives in both the lab and his office, then used a program he'd purchased from the internet to fry the mainframes completely. It wouldn't keep them out of his computer, but it would buy him some time. After that he'd be dead and unlikely to care which fingers they pointed at him.

As an extra level of security, he uploaded the program onto the server and let it run rampant through the databases. All of data from countless experiments scrambled and disappeared. It would take someone quite some time to reveal even the smallest of fragments. Careful not to disrupt the production side of things, Grant brought the development side of Hubertson Pharmaceuticals to its proverbial knees.

Taking one last look around the lab, he gathered his notes, donned his jacket and left for the night. Looking back at the structure of iron and glass, he let a small smile curl his lips. He would burn his notes at home and call in sick the next day. His co-workers would understand when he revealed the news of the cancer consuming his body.

***

Three weeks later, Grant Mazra was dead, the cancer having eaten more healthy tissue than his body could sustain. He was laid to rest in a simple ceremony attended by many of his colleagues and close friends. His eulogy outlined a legacy that started with his first synthesized drug for diabetes control and ended with his work to create a more comprehensive flu shot. None of them knew of his last discovery; his parting contribution to the world.

How could they have? Hubertson Pharmaceuticals was still trying to dig their way out from under a catastrophic computer failure in their development department. Production of flu shots continued uninterrupted and the demand this year exceeded their initial supply. More people were getting their preventative shot than in previous years and more pharmacies were holding clinics to help inoculate the public.

Shipments of the flu vaccine were dispatched across the country, even around the globe as the demand rose along with stock prices in Hubertson Pharmaceuticals. All of those shipments were tainted with Grant's legacy as he had correctly predicted his new virus would be resistant to sterilization.

It didn't take long for the world to see the effects of that legacy either. The rates of aggressive cancer rose exponentially, but no one could figure out why, and no one connected it to the influenza vaccine. There was no reason to suspect anything.

Anyone who received the tainted inoculation died within a few short months of its introduction into their bodies. With many of the doctors and nurses knocked out of commission in the early stages, the world's remaining medical community could barely cope with the steep rise in cases. No one knew what was going on; they just knew it was an event unlike anything they had ever seen. Like an apocalyptic culling of the population.

And the engineered virus didn't stop there. It continued to do what it was made to do. Mutate, replicate and infect…

29. THE LONGRIDER by Michael Schomaker

As the sun set on the small western mining town of Churchill New Mexico, a calming but short lived quiet fell over it and its occupants. A sign stood, or kind of stood, half broken at the side of the main road leading through town. The sign read "Churchill don't want no trouble, don't make no trouble" - an ominous message to travelers or a well-meaning note to live and let live?

No one really knew, for all of the town's original descendants were long gone since the gold mines dried up years ago. The town consisted of five major businesses: Sully's saloon, Don Broodmeyer's general store, Katie O'Hara's Inn, Boone Hays' Livery, and of course Sheriff P. Madsen took care of the jail. What was an old miner's town without a jailhouse? And lastly; a white church that sat quietly atop a hill overlooking the entire spread - gently rubbing its fingers together in shame at the debauchery that took place almost every night in the shadows of the once prosperous settlement.

Sheriff Madsen stood outside Don Broodmeyer's shop leaning against a wood column. He pulled a pinch of tobacco from a small leather pouch and began to roll a cigarette. "Evening Sheriff," Don Broodmeyer said aloud as he locked the shop door for the night.

"Evening," Sheriff Madsen replied.

Don joined Sheriff Madsen and gazed down the one and only road through town. "Something wrong Sheriff?" Don asked.

Sheriff Madsen took a long draw on his cigarette and paused a moment. "Don't rightly know, but looks like we got some weather coming." The Sheriff gestured toward the western sky where lightning had begun to strike.

"Yea" Don answered, "Been stormin' out thata way the last couple nights."

"Yup, seems a bit odd if ya ask me," the Sheriff said as he took in another draw from his hand rolled cigarette.

"But, nobody does," Madsen mumbled under his breath. "Well, 'night Sheriff." Don started to walk down the old wood planked walkway.

"'Night Don."

A strong wind began to tunnel down the road from the west like a wild river torrent; the buildings lining the road like boulders splashing the whitewater back onto itself. Sheriff Madsen reached for his hat as it was almost blown from his head. Dust like sandpaper blew into his old glaucoma stricken eyes and he closed them tightly.

When he opened his eyes now watery and red, a vague figure on horseback stood in front of him. Madsen startled, and reached up to rub the debris from his eyes when a lightning strike set the sky afire in blue flames behind the stranger. Madsen could see the chiseled and grisly features of a man who had rode too long and seen too much.

"Sheriff," the man atop the giant horse said.

Sheriff Madsen tried to compose himself. "H- howdy Longrider," he stammered, and then in a more authoritative voice, "Hope you're not lookin' fer trouble."

In a large and raspy voice, that of a man who didn't shy from a whiskey or a smoke, the stranger answered. "No sir, I read the sign and I don't plan to make trouble."

"What's your name Longrider?"

"The name given to me by my mother is Efrain, but if it's all the same Sheriff you can call me Longrider."

***

The next day in Churchill was business as usual. Travelers passed through but no one stayed in the dilapidated town. As a result Katie O'Hara's Inn clientele mostly consisted of locals, drunks and cowboys with their whores. But on this morning the town's normal hustle and bustle was shattered by the front door of the Inn banging open.

Katie O'Hara came running out hands clasped over her mouth, "Help! Help! Sheriff, someone help, Tom is dead!"

Sheriff Madsen heard the commotion while taking breakfast in the saloon and ran out to the street. "Calm down Katie, what's going on darling?" The Sheriff held her shoulders consolingly.

Through her clasped fingers she mumbled in terror "He's dead. Tom Dalton is dead, murdered, he he...," she trailed off in tears.

Sheriff Madsen drew his revolver from his holster fumbling his way to its grip like a greenie at his first shootout, and made his way into the inn.

***

That night Efrain sat in the corner of Sully's saloon playing poker and drinking whiskey shooters. But more importantly listening to the gossip and chinwag of the saloon's patrons. His stone cold eyes never leaving the table and never missing a trick of the game.

"They said he was drained of his blood," came a whisper from one corner of the room. "Boone Hays said he's been missing some stock

162

too, a couple horses dead of apparently no reason." Then the other murmurs commenced, "This all started when that stranger showed up in town, and I'd wager he had something to do with Tom's death. Did you hear? Drained of blood."

Efrain's attention snapped quickly back to the game when the dealer asked, "What's your name stranger?"

"My name is of no importance," the stranger replied. "Just deal, thank ya."

"Now listen here son, you come to our town, drink our whiskey and take our money at the card table. I'd at least like to know what your name is."

Efrain leaned toward the dealer as if to whisper a secret, and simultaneously the dealer leaned toward him. "My name is Efrain De Dios."

The dealer leaned back in a jolly laughter. "You don't look like no spic." Efrain's eyes glazed over, and hatred stretched across his face. He reached to his hip. By the time the dealer leaned back down in his chair and opened his eyes the barrel of Efrain's Colt single action army revolver was squarely between his eyes. "Now listen partner, I didn't mean anything by it."

Efrain gently pulled the hammer back on the old revolver. "I'd watch your words boy, my mother named me and it is a name that runs deep in my family. And if you have a problem with that, then I guess we have a problem here don't we?"

The legs of the dealer's pants slowly wet from the urine soaking through them. The entire saloon was quiet and everyone's attention was directed upon the two of them.

The hand of a woman slowly came down on the hand that held Efrain's gun to the dealer's head, pushing is ever so gently to the table. Then a voice came from the stranger's right, his eyes having not yet left the dealer's. "Come now you two," she spoke, "we don't need any more killin' tonight." "My name's Katie and what is yours stranger?"

Efrain finally looked toward her. "You can call me Longrider."

"Well Longrider, due to unforeseen circumstances I have an open bed at the inn. Would you like to take up rest there?"

Efrain holstered his pistol. "I guess I would," he almost reluctantly replied.

When the sun rose again on the dust stricken town, a crowd had begun to gather around the little white church. By nine in the morning the entire town stood outside the church, with the exception of Efrain that is. Three men had been strewn across the few gravestones in the yard of the church. Their hazy eyes and colorless skin accentuated the two puncture wounds on each of their necks.

An elderly man spoke up from the crowd. "The stranger done this. This all started when that Longrider came to town." The rest of the townspeople 'hurrahed' in agreement.

"Hold on people I'll be the one to do the investigating," Sheriff Madsen barked.

"Besides," Katie O'Hara called out, "he was in a bed at my inn all night."

More arguing and yelling began. Another called out from the crowd. "Well then let's go see for ourselves." A moan of agreement from the newly formed posse called out to concur. The entire crowd stampeded toward Katie's Inn, but discovered Efrain's bed empty and his belongings gone.

After the crowd had cleared the inn Sheriff Madsen walked slowly through the room the stranger had occupied. Everything seemed to be in its place; *had someone even slept in this room*, he thought to himself. He reached for his tobacco pouch at his hip and noticed a glimmer of brass on the floor beneath the bed. Sheriff Madsen bent over and picked up the unspent round and rolled it between his fingers. He felt a rough slash upon the lead projectile and when he pulled it closer to his weak eyes he could see what it was. A cross; a cross had been carved deeply into the soft lead of the bullet. Sheriff Madsen slipped the shell into his pocket and strolled out of the room to finish his cigarette.

By the time darkness had fallen the townsfolk had all gathered around the small white church. Torches lit the small area and cast demonic shadows of the building and headstones across the dusty desert floor. This was a lynch mob out for blood the angry cries of *vampire* and *demon* filled the night air. The town holy man, Father Dante was leading the pack. "The Devil has entered our little piece of the desert. This is God's punishment for the sins of man." *Hallelujahs* and *praise the Lord Jesus* bounced off the cool night air.

Lightning once again lit the sky to the west of town, and a rumble of thunder cracked. The whole mass of people now moving as one jumped at this boom and turned toward the western sky. The outline of the Longrider on horseback at the edge of town glowed against the blue background of the lightning strikes.

"There he is!" and cries of "Vampire! Get him!" peeled from the mob. The sea of people started toward Efrain with torches, pitchforks and various weapons in hand.

At the next lightning flash and thunder crack the Longrider started his gallop toward the crowd. For a moment the crowd which moved as one stopped advancing. Struck initially by a sort of confusion they started to stammer forward again. Efrain's gallop turned into an all-out run as he pulled his pistols from their respective holsters. Lightning flashed blue hues from the barrels of the Colt army revolvers.

Now the mob stopped moving forward once again. Efrain's hat blew upward from the wind in his face, revealing his grimace of pure concentration. His eyes glimmered with intent and madness. As he drew closer to the crowd some of the people began to peel off and meander out of his path.

Lightning struck again and Efrain's tightly drawn face shone two teeth like daggers from each side of his mouth. Screams emitted from the people; "Vampire run!", and "He'll kill us all!" Saliva gathered at the points of his knife-like k-9's. As Efrain drew closer and closer to the diminishing mob he pulled the hammers back on each pistol. People scattered and lay out prone in the dust of the desert floor. Only Katie O'Hara and Sheriff Madsen stood near the church, mouths agape in utter shock, unable to move a single muscle.

"Get down! Get out of my way!" Efrain bellowed, his teeth seeming to enhance his excitement. Efrain pointed his pistols toward the top of the church bell tower. What was now left of the assembly of townsfolk watched him in horror.

A large black mass was then seen, standing atop the church roof - evil and dark and seeming to screech at Efrain. "You half breed, I will end you!" echoed a voice from the rooftop. Efrain aimed both pistols with an eerie calm. Six cross inscribed rounds sat in the chamber of his left pistol and five ready to fire within the other. When the shooting started it didn't stop until both pistols were empty.

The dark body tumbled from the darkness of the rooftop above. Efrain leaped from his horseback and all at once pulled a knife from the scabbard on his belt. It looked like a blade of metal but did not shine; its color was a dull brown.

It was a twelve inch knife made of pure black ash, sharpened to a deadly edge and point. In midair, knife now extended, Efrain collided with the creature and drove the wooden dagger into its heart. Before the two hit the ground the black vampire was gone; burned to an ash cloud and taken by the wind.

Efrain lay motionless at the foundation of the church. Katie O'Hara and Sheriff Madsen rushed to Longrider's side. A fatal wound had been drawn across Efrain's throat in the struggle. Gasps of air and blood seeped from the wound.

"What just happened?" Katie sobbed. Sheriff Madsen stood puzzled. In front of their eyes the wound across the Longrider's neck began to close and heal within seconds.

Efrain spoke in a garbled and quiet, but firm voice. "I am Efrain De Dios, born not of man and I am a vampire hunter."

The Longrider pulled himself into a sitting position and Katie O'Hara rested on her knees beside him. "What just happened? What are you?" she questioned as she took a choppy breath inward. "What was that thing?"

"That," Efrain began to explain, "was a dark vampire. They feed on misery, death and the sweet blood of the innocent. I have sworn to avenge the curse of my slain mother." The Longrider lowered his head and continued. "A curse that that took half of my human soul while still in the womb…"

30. TOGETHER FOREVER BY MICHELE TALLARITA

This is Tabitha's chance, maybe her last chance, to make things right with her sister.

She and Rachel didn't always have such a poisonous relationship. Once upon a time, things were great between them. Since they were teenagers, though, they've never gotten along.

Now they're in their twenties, and Tabitha is getting married next week, and all she wants is for she and Rachel to be on good terms for the wedding.

Is that so much to ask?

Tabitha gets the tea ready, using expensive leaves and loading the sugar into a delicate porcelain bowl. But who knows if Rachel will even show?

There's a knock on the front door.

"You came," Tabitha says, opening it quickly.

Looking at her sister is almost like looking in the mirror—almost. Tabitha and Rachel are identical twins, but Rachel has always been the sickly one. Both women have hair the color of sand, slightly wavy, kept just above the shoulder, and both have the family nose, but while Tabitha's skin glows from her suntan, Rachel is so pale she seems covered in chalk dust. While Tabitha's arms are slim and muscular, Rachel's are sticks.

Even now, Rachel's eyes bore into Tabitha from deep hollows, the color of her skin slightly yellowish.

Jealousy, Tabitha thinks. The root of their problems has always been jealousy.

"Please, come in," Tabitha says.

Silently, Rachel follows her into the living room and settles herself carefully onto the edge of the couch. With a slight frown, she eyes the kettle and teacups.

Tabitha sits down across from her. "Do you want some?"

"No," Rachel snaps.

Tabitha swallows hard. Rachel's voice is exactly like her own, but hard and cruel.

"What did you want?" Rachel says.

"To talk." Tabitha keeps her eyes on her lap. "Maybe to…make things right."

Rachel laughs, and the sound is terrible: like choking. "You can never make things *right*."

"It…wasn't my fault, Rachel."

Rachel stands. She's wearing a faded yellow sundress that does nothing more than emphasize her blade-thin limbs, her knobby knees. Since they were teenagers, when things went bad between them, Rachel has been ruining her life. The terrible things Rachel would say to her: *You don't deserve happiness. You don't deserve friends.* The way Rachel terrorized anyone who showed the slightest interest in Tabitha.

Tabitha told their parents, time and again. She was never believed.

"Of course it was your fault, Tab."

Tab. The name Rachel used to call her when they were still little, still friends. Those times when they would sit together and have tea parties, just like this, and Tabitha could tell Rachel all of her secrets.

"Look," Tabitha says, standing. "We don't have to be friends."

Rachel lets out a choked laughed.

"All I'm asking is that you don't touch him," Tabitha says. "Please."

Because Rachel *could* touch him. Rachel can get away with anything. That girl in high school who was nice to Tabitha: found dead at the bottom of a staircase. Tabitha's college roommate: found hanging in a closet.

When Tabitha met Mark, it was a miracle. For two whole years, Tabitha was with him in peace. She'd just begun to think that maybe Rachel had moved on—until a few weeks ago, when she began to see her sister lurking around corners; began to have the nightmares again…

And knew, suddenly, that Rachel had merely been biding her time.

Rachel laughs.

"Rachel, *please*."

"You're hilarious. You really think I'll let you be happy?"

"Rachel, I was a toddler, for Christ's sake."

Tabitha thinks about the funeral, the tiny coffin being lowered into the ground. She thinks about the first time she saw Rachel again, afterwards, the way she just appeared in their bedroom as if nothing had happened. She thinks about how Rachel grew up with her, always by her side, aging as Tabitha aged, but getting increasingly pale and sickly looking, as if her spirit was decomposing along with her body.

And Tabitha thinks about when Rachel began to turn on her, as she realized that Tabitha would get to have a life—a job, a family, a house of her own—while Rachel would never have any of those things.

You really think I'll let you be happy?

Tabitha speaks slowly, her breath coming fast. "I didn't mean for you to die."

"Of course you meant it."

"I didn't know what I was doing!"

"And yet."

With a smile, Rachel vanishes, and Tabitha collapses onto the couch, sobbing. She can't help remembering that afternoon when they were three—was it raining? Were they stuck inside all day, bored?—when she and Rachel were playing in the bedroom, playing with the pillows, and she'd held Rachel under until her legs stopped kicking. Held her there because she hated being one of two.

No, she hadn't meant to. She hadn't noticed Rachel couldn't breathe. It had been a game.

Rachel hovers in the room, unseen. Until Tabitha admits she's a murderer, Rachel will never, ever leave her side.

31. THE HIGHWAY BY JEFF MCFARLAND

Author's Note: This story appeared originally in Issue #10 of Sirens Call Publications' e-zine, "The Sirens Call." It has been revised for its inclusion in Demonic Visions.

***

To this day, I refuse to take US-385 when I travel. Especially at night.

I know, I know, it's a *long* stretch of highway, but I'm never taking the chance again. It used to be a route that I would take two to three times a month: to Rapid City, South Dakota from Chadron, Nebraska and back again along 385. I'm sure some of you have taken it, too. Even if you didn't realize it at the time.

If you know the Midwest, you know it's flat-as-hell, and it's always a boring drive. There's absolutely nothing on either side of the road to take in. After four hours of constant noise, lights, and booze, though, the senses can use the break. This time, I was on the way back from playing a gig in Rapid, counting the reflectors and struggling not to zone out. The highway at night, man, it's mesmerizing. Almost hypnotic. There's nothing but miles of black enveloping you, the prairie is flatter than a pancake, and it makes it easy to get lost in your own head.

The highway is dangerous, too. All sorts of critters find the middle of the road comfortable for whatever reason, especially in pitch darkness, so you need to stay alert. When your eyes start to droop and your brain struggles to deal with the monotony, your mind will start to play tricks on you. Reflectors become eyes, two lanes become one, other cars start to dwindle, and eventually you'll feel like the only living thing out in the middle of the wasteland.

You're not.

About a half hour into my drive, my body began to mimic the car's cruise control. The radio was on, but only up loud enough to serve as a dull hum in the background. My eyelids were beginning to feel heavy right about the time I heard my phone buzz.

I snapped out of my stupor and gave my usual greeting, "What's happenin'?"

"Dude," a voice slurred out, though it sounded more like *dooOOooOOood*, "did you leave town yet?" It was our guitar player, Ray, obviously hammered.

"Yeah?" I said, somewhat irritated. I had told those guys that I had to work back in Chadron the next morning. "I've been on the road for like half an hour. What's up?"

"Aw man, we're about to head to some dude's party. We were gonna see if you wanted to come."

"Too little, too late bro. Where did you guys go after you stopped for food, anyway?"

"We were.. uhhhh... oh! We were gonna get gas on the way out of town, and another guy at the pump recognized us from the show. I guess a bunch'eve people are headed to his house to get liquored up. I'm already about halfway gone, m'self, so Steve's drivin'."

"I hear that. Don't let any of those fuckin' frat boys near the van, Ray. We don't make enough to replace that gear."

"Yeah, yeah, I hear you. Well, drive safe dude. Looks like there's a storm brewin' over your way. We'll see you tomorrow?"

"Yeah, for sure. Later." With that, I dropped my phone back in the cup holder. Oblivious as Ray usually was, I couldn't be mad at him for forgetting that I was leaving. It was only about 11:45 anyway, so I wasn't too worried about the time.

Still, not being able to be with my friends bugged me, so I turned the radio up to try and curb my moodiness a bit. As the smooth sound of a saxophone flowed through the car, my nerves started to relax, and I settled in to enjoy the rest of the drive. A ripple of light off in the distance and the rolling thunder that followed put a smile on my face. Ray the weatherman had been right about the storm. The soft pitter-patter on the top of the car began slowly enough, but soon it would be pouring down.

Summer storms in Nebraska always start slow. A lot of drivers are intimidated by the rain at night, but I have always welcomed it as an old friend of sorts. I absolutely loved driving through storms. I mean, being on stage is cool and everything, but if you want tranquility, nothing can quite match up to the light show out in the Sandhills.

Another half hour passed, and naturally my wipers were going full-throttle. I was trying to focus on not riding the rumble bars when suddenly the car bounced with a heavy *THUD*. A spray of red completely blocked my windshield for only a second before the rain and my wipers cut through it. Between the beating of the rain against the car, the tires screeching, and my heart pounding in my ears, I could barely hear the static that was now pouring from the radio. My hands, knuckles all bone white, clutched the steering wheel like a pair of vices. I had instinctively stomped on the brake and thrown the car into park. *Jesus Christ. What the hell was that? Did I just kill some hitchhiker or a vagrant or something?* I wasn't going to take any chances, I immediately began fumbling trying to grab my phone from the cup holder, and, in defiance of all expectations, I had one bar of service. As I dialed 911, my hands trembled. After a few deep breaths, I held the phone up to my ear and listened for the dial tone.

"911, what is your emergency?"

"Oh thank Christ, um, I'm on 385, about thirty miles outside of Chadron, and I just hit something, or someone, it might have been a person, I don't know, I can't see shit. It's raining too hard."

"Sir, I need you to relax. It'll be alright. Where did you say you were? Are you injured?"

"I'm fine, on Highway 385, about an hour away from Rapid City, just send someone out here god dammit!"

"I'm sorry, sir, yo-*hiss*-reaking up."

"What? Oh, fuck, not now. I said I'm on 385, I need help out here!"

"Si-*hiss*-e can't u-*hiss*-and yo-*hiss*-,"

"Hello? Hello?!" I cried. I glanced at my phone, and felt my gut sink when I read the words *Call Failed* on the screen. All I was left with was some static laden jazz from the radio and the rain, now slamming into the roof of the car.

I obviously couldn't just leave. I wasn't totally sure I had hit a person... but what if I had? If I just drove away, there's no way I would be able to live with myself. And would the police really believe I just plowed right into some stranger on total accident? I could see it now: my name under 'Vehicular Manslaughter' in the newspaper. I had no choice but to cross my fingers, brave the weather, and assess the damage. I sat there for what felt like forever, watching the blood trickle down the parts of the windshield the wipers couldn't reach. With a groan, I flipped my hood up and opened the door, deciding to use my phone's flashlight to guide my way. Seeing any more than five feet in front of me was a struggle.

"Hello?!" I called out, my voice barely reaching through the roar of the rain. From the light of my phone, I could just barely make out the skid marks my tires had left. I glanced off to the side at the surrounding fields, but between the rain and the dark, it was almost impossible to see anything. Only the occasional lightning flash allowed me to see some cow-shaped silhouettes off in the distance. I continued up the road a ways before noticing a crimson trail flowing down by my feet. Trying to prepare myself for the worst, I continued to follow the trail back down the road, stopping the phone's light at what looked to be a quickly diluting pool of blood. I took several quick breaths, stepped closer, and recited every kind of prayer I could think of in my head.

I let out another groan when I saw it. Gnarled, mangled flesh lay in a broken heap on the asphalt. The chest had been imploded by my tires. Not a single rib was left in one piece. The limbs were all sprawled out, and the fur sticking to the blood was matted down by dirt. *Wait. Fur? What the hell?* Puzzled, I inched my light up a little further, and noticed that the gnarled, mangled mess of flesh had antlers.

I let out a huge gasp of relief and busted out laughing right there in the middle of the road. I had only run over a buck. No hitchhiker or homeless wanderer, but only a deer. I was so happy I could have kissed the ground beneath my feet were it not still pouring rain or soaked in blood. Messy as the scene was, I decided I should probably try moving the buck off to the side of the road, lest someone else go through the same shock I just had. The clean-up crew wouldn't be able to make it until the storm cleared up, so I grabbed a hold of the antlers and did my best to drag the heavy bastard off to the highway's shoulder. Satisfied, relieved, and soaking wet, I started to head back to the car, but a quick glance back at the deer made me pause. Why had the buck just been lying in the middle of the road in the first place? It didn't seem to have been struck by any other car; there had been no skid marks on the road besides my own. I didn't find any pieces of glass or metal on the road. I supposed that stuff all could have gotten washed away, but who would have just hit and killed this thing and then not bothered to move it? Wouldn't they have at least gotten out to check the damage? My questions changed completely when another flash in the sky revealed gruesome details the light of my phone had missed.

The deer was completely missing its jaw, and along with it, its tongue. The left eye had been gouged out by what looked to be a trio of claw marks. Zoning out or not, I had for sure ran over the deer's chest. It being relatively flat was evidence of that. A quick sweep from my phone's light didn't turn up a jaw or a tongue (again assuming the rain didn't take them). Even if I had somehow removed the jaw, where could it have gone?

I was sure I hadn't dealt the damage to the deer's head. The fact that it had claw marks on it made me uneasy, and the missing jaw downright freaked me out. There had been mountain lion sightings out in these parts before, and I had no desire to see if they were true. I turned and started to walk back towards my car.

That's when I saw it.

Off in the distance, as another ripple lit up the fields, I noticed a figure. One distinctly different from the cows. It was hunched over on all fours, but it was far too gangly and too large to be a dog. I thought for a minute that it might have been a person, so I shined my phone's light toward it and called out. "Hello?"

Its head snapped up.

Slowly, inch by inch, it turned its gaze towards me. Even armed with nothing but my phone's tiny flashlight, I could see the glassy shine of its eyes through the dark. Like a deer's in headlights. Before I could turn to run, the eyes disappeared, and I froze. A few moments later, they reappeared, seemingly bigger than before. In the dark, I couldn't see anything, but the timing of the lightning was making this thing's movement look like some creature out of a stop-motion flick. When the eyes disappeared once again, my blood went cold. I realized the truth. The eyes weren't getting bigger.

They were coming closer.

Panic washed over me like a tidal wave. My trip back to the car began as a slow tiptoe and quickly turned into a mad dash. True to form, I slipped trying to maneuver around the back of the car and crashed my right knee into the bumper. Pain exploded up my leg, but I didn't have the time to care. I could hear it coming now: the pounding of feet against dirt, and a heavy, grinding sound, like a lawnmower that doesn't want to start mixed with heavy breathing. I ripped the car door open and jumped in, locking it behind me out of pure instinct. Without thinking to take the car out of park, I slammed my foot down on the gas, revving the engine but not moving at all. I could hear the noise over the rain now, even over my engine, inching closer with each set of heavy, galloping footsteps. The tires struggled to grip the rain-slick highway, peeling out as I threw the car into drive. Just as I managed to get some traction, a loud *CRUNCH* of twisted metal screeched in my ears and the car started to tip onto its right side.

The lawnmower sound had become a chainsaw. Glass shattered into the backseat, and the car fishtailed wildly in its attempt to grip the road with only two right wheels. For the second time that night I gripped the steering wheel for dear life, and this time, I screamed. I did everything I could think of to try and startle or distract the thing long enough for the car to pull away: flashed the brights, honked the horn, hell, I even popped the trunk. I don't know why, but that must have been what did it. I felt the car's two left wheels hit the road, hard, and didn't wait to find out what happened. I took off as fast as the car would take me.

For a little while, I heard the galloping footsteps trailing after me, keeping up until I hit about 45 miles per hour. I heard them over the rain, pouring in through my broken window. I heard them over the static blasting through the radio that had gotten turned up in the frenzy. I didn't slow down until I was sure I didn't hear them anymore. It wasn't until the footsteps had completely faded away that I sat back and struggled not to cry. I have no idea why, but I decided to glance in the rear view mirror for a quick minute to assess the damage done to the backseat.

They were a ways off, but even through the rain and through the dark, I know what I saw. I saw them clear as day.

A pair of eyes, shining, in the middle of the highway.

32. THE DITCH by Naching T. Kassa

Lily fumed down the country road, gravel crunching beneath her rubber soles. It was Greg's fault that she was in this predicament. She had, rather innocently, brought up his unhealthy obsession with a fellow co-worker and he had denied it. The argument had escalated from there and, in the end; she had walked out on him. She had left him, parked up on Lover's Lane, shouting out the window. Her ears were still ringing with, "You've just kicked our relationship through the goal post!" Greg brought sports into everything.

That argument had been twenty minutes ago and Greg hadn't even come looking for her. She rubbed her arms and watched as the sun dropped behind the hills. It left a bloody sky and a slight chill in its wake.

Lily slowed, suddenly aware of her surroundings. She'd been so focused on Greg's short comings; she'd left the main road. An owl hooted in the trees ahead and she jumped. She despised owls.

The dirt road was lonely and sloped down into ditches on either side. Lily turned back the way she had come, her eyes searching the trees for the elusive owl. It sounded again, a few feet ahead of her and on the right. At last, it burst into flight gliding effortlessly over the ditch.

A strange shape, lying within that shallow trench caught Lily's eye. It was a black garbage bag, torn asunder by the elements. Inside were the bleached bones of what had once been a dog, a very large dog. Staring at the skeleton, she wondered who could relegate a pet to such a dismal fate. As she studied the ditch further, a frown spread over her pretty face. Bag upon bag lay upon the recessed ground.

The skeletons and their shredded, plastic shrouds extended from the edge of the road to the tree line. It was a dumping ground, probably used by city people who were either too poor or too lazy to dispose of their pets properly. Lily shook her head as her eyes roved over the mess.

Her gaze fell upon a newer bag lying at the base of a large pine. It was tied at the top with blue plastic draw-strings and something had pushed through it; something with four fingers and a thumb.

Lily stared in horror, unable to break away from that pale hand and its black-varnished fingernails. It was, perhaps, the worst thing she had ever seen. She blinked with the hope that it would disappear, but it did not. In fact, it did something much worse. It moved.

The hand twitched and clenched as if pleading for aid. Lily, slow to interpret, stood frozen to the spot. Finally, a small voice within her mind shouted to her, calling on her to run forward. She did, nearly tripping over one skull and crushing another in her haste.

The first thing she realized, when she reached the bag, was that it was small. She couldn't imagine how anyone could fit inside. This thought was pushed to the back of her mind, as the hand grasped hold of her arm. Spurred on by the desperation in that grip, Lily tore the sack open.

And screamed…

A headless torso lay confined within, pale and bloodless; it raised another arm toward Lily. She fell backward, trying to wrench her own arm out of its left hand. The black fingernails dug in deep, drawing blood. Lily screamed again as the right hand caught hold of her sweater and pulled.

Lily, empowered by adrenalin, broke free. She scrambled away as the torso turned and began to drag itself toward her. Bones crunched under Lily's hands and feet as she fled toward the road. She could still hear the thing skittering through the ditch when she reached the top.

Blinding headlights and the roar of an engine announced the arrival of an approaching vehicle. Lily rose to her feet, waving her arms in the air. Brakes squealed and gravel sprayed. The car halted and the driver's side door flew open.

"Are you alright?" a male voice called out. Lily shielded her eyes against the glare of blue-white LED lights and tried to stave off her panic. She failed when the hand appeared at the edge of the ditch and pulled the torso into view.

"It's coming!" Lily screamed. She ran toward the driver. His face was ashen above his dark jacket and his eyes were fixed on the torso.

"No…," he said under his breath. "No! She's dead!"

Lily didn't wait for an invitation. She pushed past the man and crawled over to the passenger side of the car. Pressing the lever on the door, she locked it.

Her savior shook off the shock and quickly closed the open door. He disappeared around the rear of the vehicle and emerged seconds later, bearing a long-handled shovel. Advancing upon the torso, he raised the implement above his head and chopped at the dismembered body. The thing writhed under his frenzied attack and retreated back into the darkness. He followed.

Lily turned away, her gorge rising, a sickening taste filling her mouth. She would have vomited had she not heard the sound emanating from the back seat. Something was moving. She stared into the blackness that filled the seat behind her. No one seemed to be there.

Rustle! Rustle!

"Who's there!"

To Lily's horror, she received an answer to her question. A raspy whisper filled the stifling interior of the car.

"Help me!"

"W-what?"

"Help me! I can't move!"

"Why can't you move?"

No answer.

Lily reached out into the gloom. "Are you tied up? What's-"

Her fingers came into contact with something soft, something like hair. When she reached out to touch the rest of the body, she found nothing.

Lily snatched her hand away a moment too late. Jaws clamped onto it just below the thumb. Sharp teeth drew hot blood. Lily screeched.

She shook her hand, trying to dislodge the horror and finally grabbed hold of it by the hair. She ripped a clump out by the roots, but the jaws failed to release her.

As Lily fought, she saw snatches of the thing which held her. Furious black eyes and streaks of her own blood smeared across pale skin, appeared before her eyes in strobe-like flashes. In desperation, she slammed it against the bucket seat. The grip on her hand relaxed and the head fell to the floor with a soft *thud*.

Lily struggled with the car door, forgetting that she had locked it earlier. Finally, she released the latch and escaped the vehicle.

"He's mine!" the whisper cried. "You can't have him!"

A voice spoke behind Lily, startling her. She whirled and stared into the confused eyes of her savior. He leaned on the shovel, gazing into the car.

"I can't kill her," he said his voice thick with disbelief. "I cut her up and she still won't die. Why won't she die?"

Lily began to back away, her heart in her throat.

“Mine!” the voice rasped.

Lily ran. She ran until her lungs were on the verge of bursting.

Smooth asphalt lay before her, releasing the heat it had collected during the day. Lily’s hand throbbed. She wrapped it up in her sweater and cradled it against her chest.

Headlights appeared behind her, bathing the road in cold white light. A chill sped through Lily’s body. She glanced back, poised to run.

The car slowed and crept up beside her. She heard the swish of power windows and a man spoke to her.

“You gonna walk home?”

Lily stopped. She looked at the man within.

“I lost my way,” she replied.

“I thought I’d lost you.”

Lily opened the door of Greg’s car and slipped inside.

“Jesus! What happened? Are you alright?”

“Long story,” Lily sighed.

“I’ve got time.”

“I just witnessed the undead version of *Fatal Attraction* and…a disembodied head bit me.”

“Damn! You’ve had a bad night!”

“I’m serious!”

“I know.”

Lily grew silent. At last, she said, “My life flashed before my eyes.”

“Was I in it?” He didn’t look at her.

“You were.”

“Was I old and grey?”

Lily grinned. “Yes.”

“Did…did I need Viagra?”

Lily laughed.

Greg turned to her, eyes wide. “Was that a yes?”

“No.”

Greg mopped his brow in mock relief.

“Do you know what I would have done to that head?” he asked.

“Kicked it through the goal post.”

“Damn straight.”

Lily smiled and shook her head.

33. THE DECEPTIVE SECURITY OF EVERYDAY NORMALITY BY RICK MCQUISTON

Green flames sprouted out of the engorged fissures like fireworks haphazardly lit by mischievous boys. A slurry of airborne spores erupted from the fetid ranks of the roiling landscape, smearing themselves across the diseased sky. And cyclopean peaks rose and swelled to immeasurable proportions. Each bordered a swarming wasteland of burning flesh and nebulous silhouettes, bringing even more gelatinous forms that swayed in hazy, rutting dances unfit for the eyes of anyone or anything even remotely sane.

A solitary form, sinuous and rubbery, undulated through the primordial soup that pooled near the center of a seething cauldron of dense mauve and angry red. The creature, a bizarre cross between an elongated spider and an amorphous blob of jelly, seemed to have a distinct destination in mind. Unlike the other horrors aimlessly milling about in the wasteland, it made its way in slow, steady increments of movement.

It saw him.

****

Jerry snapped awake. His neck was stiff from the angle (a penalty for falling asleep in class), and his vision was blurry. He rubbed his eyes with the back of his hands.

"Mr. Costello? How nice of you to join us."

Jerry looked up, past the leering and giggling faces of his classmates, and into the hardened visage of Mr. Warner. Warner the Warden was the popular nickname unceremoniously bestowed on the History teacher.

"I ... I'm sorry, Mr. Warner."

"You're sorry? Please, Mr. Costello, if you're not interested in the Industrial Revolution do us both a favor and drop out of my class."

"It won't happen again, Mr. Warner."

Jerry had been suffering from the nightmare for three days. At first, it was only during the nighttime hours. And then it started happening every time he dozed off. Now it seemed that whenever he was in darkness he would be transported to that same hellish landscape populated by all those horrors and terrible green flames. And to make matters worse, he had no one to talk to about it. His dad had left right after he was born, and his mother seemed always to be either working or sleeping. He had no siblings, and even fewer friends. He was the epitome of a loner.

But this episode was by far the worst. This time when he visited that hideous place something was different. Something *noticed* him instead of him just being an objective bystander. This time he was part of his nightmare.

****

"Hey Costello," Aaron Bulkep called out. "Did you have a good nap?" He positioned his oversized body between Jerry and the bathroom's door. "Did you have a nightmare?"

Jerry tried to ignore the bully, but with two other kids flanking him, it was nearly impossible. He finished washing his hands and stepped over to the hand dryer. He tapped the silver button on the box and waited for the blast of hot air.

Nothing happened.

"Now he broke the dryer," one of Aaron's minions said.

"Let's get outta here before we get blamed for it," the other kid said.

Aaron reluctantly nodded and gave Jerry a threatening gesture with his fist. "Next time, loser," he scowled, and then left the bathroom.

Jerry stood there, alone, confused, and afraid. He tapped on the hand dryer a few more times before giving up, and finished drying his hands on his pants.

The door wouldn't budge.

Jerry gripped the handle with both hands and pulled even harder. Still, it wouldn't open. He braced his foot against the jamb and pulled with all his might. Outside, he heard the tardy bell ring through the halls.

Backing away from the door, Jerry felt an unusual sensation gradually overcome him, one that was not rooted in fear. Instead, it was one of belonging. He couldn't deny to himself that it felt good. For the first time in his lonely life he felt as if he were a part of something.

The green light crept through the opening around the door. It seeped down to the floor of the bathroom and pooled into a disgusting puddle. Tiny things began to squirm within the quagmire.

Jerry stood perfectly still. He closed his eyes and felt the darkness envelope him. He was going to release himself to a better place, a place where he would belong.

The walls of the bathroom became flimsy, swaying as if caught in a gentle breeze. The ceiling then folded in on itself, allowing fine green mist to drift into the room. In seconds, it coated everything: fixtures; lights; the stall doors and walls. Everything then melted to the floor; the plane upon which Jerry stood having transformed into an oozing slop.

And in the center of the maelstrom, Jerry stood. His eyes were closed; the change would be smoother if he saw nothing.

Jerry felt the green light submerge his feet. He felt the things within it coil and writhe around his ankles. And then he felt something else, something much larger than the things that swam about his shins. A leg brushed against his chest. It was warm and rubbery, and probed and prodded his body like a toddler exploring its surroundings.

Jerry's eyes sprung open and were greeted by his nightmare.

It was all there: the huge cracks spewing green flames; the enormous peaks rising into a distorted sky; indescribable forms dancing to inhuman music. And most of all; a solitary creature, part spider, part oozing jelly, standing before him on shivering legs… two of which were busy tapping his midsection.

Any reasonable person would've passed out from terror or fled for their life. But not Jerry; he felt right at home.

Reaching out to the spider-thing, Jerry felt it ooze forward and adhere against his body. And in an instant, they became one.

****

Aaron looked over at his two buddies. Both shook their heads. He stifled a laugh. He was glad Jerry was late for class. "What a loser," he mumbled under his breath.

"Has anyone seen Mr. Costello?" Ms. Ethan asked. "I'm sure I saw him in the hallway earlier today."

Aaron couldn't resist. "I did, Ms. Ethan. He's hiding in the boy's bathroom."

Ms. Ethan, a compassionate and patient woman, grew worried. "I'll be right back," she told her class, and scurried out of the room.

Aaron felt good with himself. With any luck, Jerry would get detention, or even expelled. He stretched his arms over his head and closed his eyes. He ignored the commotion all around him as he drifted into a light sleep.

****

Huge flames of green erupted in his mind's eye. They spewed out of enormous peaks that rose like swollen blemishes from the feral landscape. And within the turmoil, dark figures jostled back and forth as if dancing to some music he could not hear.

Aaron watched the chaos from his seemingly secure spot. He marveled at the sheer volume of the scene, and despite its frightening proportions, found himself mesmerized by its scope.

And then a lone figure emerged from a steaming lake. It crawled out of the dark red liquid and slowly made its way to where Aaron stood. It loosely resembled a spider, but with a gelatinous aspect to its form.

Aaron backed away from the beast. It wasn't the overall appearance of it that scared him the most, although he never liked spiders. It was the thing's face that he found most abhorrent. It reminded him of someone he knew.

Jerry?

And when the creature smiled at him, the shock was enough to send Aaron back to reality.

****

"You okay there, Aaron?"

Aaron came to at his desk. His hair was disheveled and his hands were shaking. He looked around. "What's going on?"

One of his friends came up to him. "I think you were having a bad dream."

Aaron nodded. "Yeah, I guess so." He rubbed his eyes but still couldn't shake the image of that horrible face grinning at him. "Just a dream. It was just a bad dream." But deep down inside, Aaron knew it wasn't. He also knew that eventually he'd have to go to sleep, and when he did, Jerry would be waiting for him.

34. CONDEMNED EXISTENCE BY ROBERT FRIEDRICH

Dusk falls upon the construction site of an unfinished mall. The workers left hours ago and the site is seemingly quiet, until loud moans shatter the veil of silence. Among all the equipment, dry wall and ceramic floor pieces, a woman is bent over a red barrel while a man is thrusting into her from the back.

Her moans grow louder as he grabs her by the hair and pulls. Both of them are enjoying this pervasive display of quick sex. As he is about to reach the pinnacle of his self-satisfaction, she reaches back to intensify the pleasure and scratches him with one of her nails on his thigh. This startles him for a second, but soon this little bloody scratch is forgotten. Finally he climaxes and the thrusting stops while their fading moans echo around them.

He pulls up his boxers and jeans, while she remains there, bent over the barrel. He ties his belt, takes out his wallet and throws some money notes at her back and smiles.

"I'll see you around babe," he says with a satisfied smirk on his face.

"Yes, Tony, you'll see me around," she mutters as she pulls up her panties and fixes her skirt.

Tony simply walks out of the construction area, gets into his car and drives away.

"Damn, I sure wish there were more chicks like that around the bar…"

His smirk does not leave his face even as clouds fill the night sky. He arrives at his apartment building and parks his car in the nearby lot. He enters the building and goes up a few flights of stairs before entering the corridor where his apartment is located.

His place is shabby and not much care has gone into it. *Cold and lifeless* best describes his dwelling. Slowly he undresses to nothing but his boxer shorts and jumps into bed. Nothing could bother him in this moment of satisfaction, and thus he falls asleep quite fast.

Uncovered and undisturbed he lies in his bed, and yet something strange transpires. The little wound he has forgotten about begins to bulge, as if something was under his skin, and begins to move. Slowly it moves there within him, undulating, as if whatever was beneath his tissue was looking for something.

Suddenly he becomes aroused again and his boxer shorts bulge with his erection. This time it bulges even more so, but is concealed by the boxer shorts as it moves around inside his phallus. The other bulge in his leg slowly begins to approach his groin; the closer it gets to the second distention, the faster it gets.

Obscured by the boxer shorts, the two bulges meet in his erection and seemingly combine before a feeble chittering-like sound resonates from within him. Tony awakens in confusion and pain. He looks at himself and sees his uncontrolled erection and the protruding bulge upon it. Dazed by his sleep, he tries to take a closer look but can't, for out of nowhere, severely sharp pain nearly paralyzes his body. He feels something strange within him but can barely scream. He is paralyzed from the neck down. The pain intensifies as he trembles in his bed, unable to move or see what is causing it. He looks once again and sees that the bulge beneath his boxer shorts continues to grow in size.

He crunches his teeth from the excruciating pain and is out of breath, when suddenly his boxer shorts and erection blow wide open. The pain is indescribable as his blood sprays all around. All he can do is look at the horror; from the remains of his penis a mechanical barbed- wire-like worm protrudes and wiggles around. Thin and long, it twists from within his flesh, with thin scalpel like appendages and something that resembles a head. But the head then partially opens and a red light shines from it, as if from an eye.

Tony is about to faint from the pain, while all he thinks about is the hope that all of this is just a dream. The worm wiggles and seemingly scans Tony. He tries to raise his arm and pass the paralysis, but in that moment the worm-like creature emits sharp scraping noises, and all the electronic devices in his apartment begin to turn off and on. Inexplicably the worm begins to draw electricity from the nearby electronics. Spark and bolts jump around wildly as the electricity is conducted straight to Tony's body, internally and externally.

He trembles and shakes violently in pain as the electricity races throughout his entire body. He lets out a final scream of agony before his heart simply gives up and stops beating. The worm stops to channel the electricity and slithers slowly from the wound, onto the electrocuted body. It reaches his chest and seemingly scans him again.

While it scans him, small electric discharges rattle the locks and knob of his door, unlocking it without a key. The door creaks as it slowly opens until the security chain prevents it from opening further.

The worm-like machine stops upon Tony's lifeless body and slowly cuts him open with its sharp appendages. After just a few precise cuts, his chest is open and the worm crawls half way inside. More blood sprays out of him as the worm exits his chest, carrying his lifeless heart with it. It crawls down from the bed onto the floor and towards the door, leaving a small trail of blood behind it. It exits the apartment, where the woman from the construction site is seemingly waiting. As it crawls onto her leg, she reaches down and the worm drops the heart into her palm. Small electric bolts are emitted silently from the heart as it touches her hand, and then fade gently away.

"Good boy," she mutters toward the worm.

Slowly the worm digs itself into her arm and disappears beneath her skin as she takes a bite of the heart, as if it was an apple. The lights in the corridor go dark and the building is swallowed up into obscurity…

35. LUST FOR LIFE BY SYDNEY LEIGH

If you can't feed a hundred people, then just feed one.
~ Mother Teresa

The words on the page didn't change. He willed them to move with desperate intensity, begged the letters to reassemble themselves like he used to in school to outplay dyslexia. Yet there they stayed, unmoving, typed with finite delicacy beneath the boilerplate salutation of the hospital's oncology department. *How could this be happening?*

There was no way he could tell Wendy. Not now; not in her condition. With four months to go, he could push back the surgery until after her delivery. What more could he do? It had already spread from one to the other. He would simply wait. After the birth of their first—and apparently last—child, he would tell his wife that he was losing both of his testicles to cancer.

***

Charles stared hard at the doctor.

"I don't get it. I mean, this is a mistake, right? Christ, it *has* to be!" The doctor's sigh implied otherwise. "But everything's been fine so far. Better than fine! We read all the books, went to all the classes, did everything we were supposed to. Right, Wendy?" His wife managed a listless nod.

"No." Charles rose and folded his arms as though his defiance would be enough to reject the reality. "No, this is a mistake. Now you're telling me she has this—this thing, this—what did you call it?"

"*Eclampsia.* This type of complication is not uncommon during first pregnancies in women your wife's age, Mr. Isaacs. And with—"

"*Eclampsia*? What the hell does that even *mean*?" He looked at his wife's new shroud-face, the pall cast by months of hope suddenly rescinded, aborted by mere words, foreign words presented to them in place of baskets stuffed with hooded towels and teddy bears—a birth announcement heralding the delivery of nothing but despair to tuck under zoo animal blankets and a moon-face mobile in a nursery filled only with the unwelcome sounds of repose. *Did Benjamin Moore have a color wheel for that?*

Charles turned to the doctor. "I just don't understand. I really don't. I mean, how the hell can Wendy *die* from something we didn't even know she *had*? You *did* actually say '*die*', didn't you, Dr.

McCauley?" His voice rose, bordered on frantic. "You did say my wife might *die*? As in *dead*? *DEAD?!*"

"Charles, please!" Wendy looked away and cradled her midsection with hands not yet maternal.

"Mr. Isaacs, try to calm down. I'm sure this must be extremely difficult. But as I tried to explain to you, your wife's condition went unnoticed because many of the symptoms of this disease are so common in pregnancy." The doctor sat beside the examination bed and threw his hands in the air. "You did nothing wrong. Swelling, nausea, headaches, indigestion, weight gain—one would naturally assume those were typical side effects during a first pregnancy. Pre-eclampsia often goes unreported for that very reason—and therefore, often undetected as well. With no history on her biological parents, we're left guessing about genetic predispositions. We simply couldn't predict whether her normally high blood pressure would increase as expected … or as swiftly and dangerously as it did." Charles paced the small room, shaking his head and muttering inaudibly, angrily.

"I just don't believe it. I just don't. This is ridiculous! I mean, one day she's fine, and the next, you're telling us she might *die*? This is insane!"

"You'll excuse my candor, Mr. Isaacs. Looking back won't yield answers in this case. Not the kind that can help us today, at least." The doctor placed his hands on his knees and fixed his gaze on Charles. "The real problem here is that you don't seem to understand that we need to induce labor and deliver your child immediately, or your wife will suffer from a variety of damaging—and yes, potentially deadly—convulsions. We don't have much time." Wendy buried her face in her hands and wept softly, bare feet dangling from the edge of the bed. *Were they that swollen before? Why hadn't she told him?*

"But the baby is only, what?" Charles countered. "Twenty weeks? That's too young!"

"I know. And as your wife's physician, I must inform you both that the survival rate of a baby that age is only around one percent." He shifted his gaze to Wendy and back to Charles again. "Look. I realize how this is difficult to hear. But it's highly unlikely the baby will be leaving the hospital with you and your wife. As you yourself could tell from listening to the fetal heart tone, it was almost non-existent. To be completely honest, Mr. Isaacs, I'm afraid your baby may expire before delivery."

"Expire?" Charles screamed. *"It's not a fucking credit card, you asshole!"*

"No." Charles dropped to his knees and pressed his face against Wendy's belly. *"Please, no."* The doctor placed his hand on Charles's shoulder.

"Once we've stabilized your wife, we can discuss the treatment options—even prevention methods you can pursue to avoid this happening during her next pregnancy. You can try again, Mr. Isaacs. In fact, there *are* methods of preventing this condition in a future pregnancy—though as I mentioned to Wendy earlier, they are rather unorthodox."

"He's right, honey," Wendy said. "I don't want this any more than you do. But if it's not meant to be, there's nothing we can do but try again. The baby can suffer long-term damage even if we do decide to wait—and that wouldn't be fair," she cried. "They can run some tests to see if there are underlying causes for this, treat them, and then we can do other things to help before we try again. Ok? *Ok, Charles*?"

"You don't understand," Charles whispered. "I can't. I just *can't*."

"Yes you can," Wendy urged. "And you will. *We* will. *Together*. You told me a long time ago that you wanted a child more than anything. That you would do whatever it took to have one." She wept freely now, imploring Charles to relent with a tender, desperate gaze. "And we *will* have one. Just not right now, Charles. It's not in the cards. I realize that now, and I hope you do, too." The doctor stepped closer.

"Listen, Mr. Isaacs. We really need to get your wife stabilized. The longer we wait, the more risks there are for her health. Her organs are all in danger of failing, and we need to get her blood pressure under control immediately." He covered Wendy's hand with his own. "But I'm asking your permission to go ahead and prepare her for surgery. I know it's not easy, but this is something we all need to agree is best… and move forward from there." Charles stood and faced Dr. McCauley, a gray, bespectacled man of slight frame.

"Let me just make sure I'm getting you, doc. You're asking my permission to remove our child from my wife's body and let it die? Just like that? If it hasn't already *'expired'*, we'll just… take it out and watch it die? That's what we're all agreeing on here?"

"Charles, please!" Wendy begged.

"No, Wendy. I'm sorry, but we are *not* going to let this happen! We need a second opinion—and that's what we'll get." He grabbed her shoes and worked her feet into them.

"Mr. Isaacs, I'm afraid there is no time for a second opinion," the doctor insisted, stepping closer and gesturing for Charles to stop. "This is of a most urgent matter, I assure you."

"Charles, what are you doing? Where will we go?" She clutched at her abdomen and rocked back on her heels. "I don't feel well, Charles."

"Anywhere but here, Wendy. That's where we'll go. This is nuts! My god, just think about it!" He pushed past the doctor, who attempted one last time to dissuade them from leaving.

"Mr. Isaacs, I must ask you to—"

"Fuck off!" Charles screamed, and flipped a stainless steel tray of medical instruments on his way out the door. "Stay the hell away from us," he warned. He grabbed a fetal stethoscope and shook it at the doctor. "We'll see how 'non-existent' my child's heartbeat is once we get away from here, you sick fuck."

***

The trees became a constant blur of shadows as they drove through the night.

"Charles, where are we going?" Wendy pressed her fingers against her temples and closed her eyes. "I'm not sure this is a good idea."

"Trust me, Wendy. Okay? I'm going to take care of this. We'll go to the lake house and I'll make some calls from there. I don't want them trying to find us at home." Moments later, he heard Wendy's shallow breath of sleep and reached for his unborn child in the darkness. "I won't let anything happen to you," he promised quietly, and turned onto the birch-lined dirt road.

***

The first seizure was the worst. It came after Charles checked for signs of life under his wife's thick, stretched skin and found nothing. He positioned the trumpeted end of the fetoscope over each and every inch of Wendy's stomach for hours on end until she insisted he stop.

"The baby is *dead*, Charles. *Dead*! And I'll probably be next!" She stumbled past him into the bathroom, where he heard her wretch and vomit. The next thing Charles knew, the irises of her eyes disappeared somewhere into the depths of her skull while her whole body jerked and twitched in a sickly dance. He made a makeshift bed on the floor and tended to her through the night. Mostly, though, he spoke to his

191

son begged for him to come back; invoked the powers that be to deliver his one and only child into his life—and into his arms.

In the morning, Wendy's color had turned sallow. He moved her to the bedroom.

***

"I don't feel well, Charles." Wendy grabbed at the sleeve of Charles' shirt and rolled her head back and forth, the pillow marked by a sweat-shadow beneath her.

"I know, sweetheart, I know. But the baby is getting stronger, Wendy. Isn't that amazing? Our baby, Wendy—*our son*. He's actually going to be okay!" Charles leaned in closer and smiled, whispered. "And do you want to know something else? I think I can hear his heartbeat." Wendy shook her head and spoke between short, shallow breaths.

"But … the baby is dead, Charles. The doctor told us … a baby so young wouldn't make it. It's not right, Charles … the baby … he can't survive … our baby's dead, Charles. Our baby's—" Another convulsion seized Wendy's body, a rag doll jerked and plucked by invisible savage strings. She languished for the remainder of the day, rising later only to vomit bile into a small pan Charles kept by her side.

***

Wendy's voice came creased with weakness. "Charles, please bring me to the hospital. I—I think I'm dying." Her cheeks fell into the downward slope of bone, and thin clumps of hair rested on the bed sheets beneath her.

"But Wendy, look how big he's getting. Here—put your hands here and feel your son." She pulled back in alarm as he rested her palms on the mound which had begun to eclipse her midsection.

"It's kicking," she murmured. "Moving. Twisting. It—it hurts." She trailed off, once more seized by a convulsion. Her teeth bit down hard on her tongue and bubbles of white foam surged from the corners of her mouth.

***

She looked less like his wife each day, and more like a spent receptacle for the rapidly growing child inside her. Skin strained tautly against muscle and bone, and she ceased to take in food, liquids, or excrete any waste. But still, the baby grew.

***

"Can you see at all?" Charles peered into the cloudy film covering his wife's amaurotic eyes. She moved her dry, colorless lips and barely formed the word.

"*Help.*"

He leaned in proudly and held his ear to the thriving swell which moved and shifted beneath him. And now, more than ever, it was evident that the steady rhythm he heard was not quite a beat, per se—but more like a crushing or grinding sound. Like chewing.

Wendy lasted just long enough for their son to finish her spleen before moving on to the apex of her heart, which pulsated every now and again until the last valve was devoured. Charles waited patiently while the baby ate his way out of his mother's chest.

Charles held his child and smiled. The first few days would be manageable, but he'd have to get creative once Wendy gave this hungry boy his last feeding.

36. THE LEGACY OF CLAN MAG AOIDH BY APRIL BULLARD

"You promised me the real story, Aunt Evelyn," begged Claire, her eager blue eyes reflecting the flames from the fireplace. The old woman sat in the rocking chair while the girl sat on the floor with her shoulders nestled between her aunt's knees. Both were dressed in soft flannel nightgowns leaving their bare feet exposed to the flickering heat from the hearth.

Evelyn continued their evening ritual, drawing the brush through Claire's thick auburn hair. "Why would a level-headed lass of fifteen years be interested in some old family tale?" she teased.

"Because I know there's more to it," Claire insisted.

Peat logs crackled in the fireplace. Heavy scented smoke curled and stretched up the chimney, adding its pungent aroma to the old polished wood and beeswax candles in the colonial log cabin.

"Ah, child," the old woman dropped the wooden handled brush in her lap and reached for her tea cup. "Let me have a sip before I begin." Aunt Evelyn's evening tea always held an extra tablespoon of rye whiskey instead of cream or sugar. She closed her eyes and let the stinging brew tingle all the way down to her belly, jostling memories into a single thread of thought.

"You're stalling," moaned Claire.

"Very well, child," she sighed. The cup clinked in its saucer and the brush began another round of gentle but firm strokes through the wavy, dark locks.

"Long, long ago, when our family lived in the old country, before the English built their stone castles on our riverbanks and even before the Norse began to land on our shores, our clan was known for having the finest, most sought after wolfhounds on the Emerald Isle. At that time Jerlath was chieftain of the clan Mag Aoidh. His prized line were the largest, strongest, and most fiercely loyal hounds with luxurious coats of silver white fur. Every nobleman and warrior wanted a hound of their own. Some to fight with them in war, some to protect their family and herds, and others wanted to be seen in the same light as legendary heroes like Finn Mac Caill and Cu Chulainn.

"Now, the youngest son of Jerlath was Madoc, of clan Mag Aoidh. He was tall and strong, with flaming red hair. Madoc married a dark haired beauty, named Niambh, from a northern clan. She bore him five fine sons with hair like their father and lastly a daughter with dark auburn hair, named Cliona.

"The child would not stay with Niambh when Madoc and the boys were training the hounds. Cliona seemed to have a special connection with the beasts. When she was but five years old, she would whistle and Madoc's two largest males would leave their master. Cliona would grip their shoulders with her tiny arms, hang between them and command the hounds to run. She seemed to fly like a dark haired spirit, hovering between the speeding silver hounds. Her little pink toes touched the ground once for every four of the dog's full strides. Laughter would echo over the river as the happy trio raced along the banks scattering ducks and dragonflies in their wake. Cliona's joyful whoops were carried on heather scented winds-"

"Just like me! I used to do that with your old hounds, Auntie!" Claire exclaimed, spinning around to look into her aunt's wistful blue eyes.

"Yes, my child, just like you," Aunt Evelyn agreed. The night wind whispered through the window casement as the last crimson hint of dusk disappeared. Lacy curtains swelled then shrank like ghosts playing hide and seek in the dark cottage. "Up now, child, into your chair."

Claire settled into the matching wooden rocker next to the small table with the old woman's tea. Floorboards creaked as Evelyn crossed to the hearth. A howl sounded from the front porch. "Quiet, my Angus. Not yet. Not yet," the old woman called. Nimble fingers snatched all traces of loose hair from the bristles of the brush. She tossed them into the fire before placing the brush on the mantle and returning to her rocking chair. Firelight danced in the wavy gray tresses that hung to Aunt Evelyn's waist, giving a hint of the auburn haired beauty she once was.

"Angus, your black hound, seems anxious tonight, Auntie," suggested Claire.

"Don't worry, child. That old wolf always gets testy around a full moon. Now, where was I?" Evelyn took another sip of tea. "Ah, yes. On her 10th birthday, Madoc gave his beloved daughter three black pups. Two males and a female, to raise by herself provided her household chores were not neglected. Cliona loved the pups as if they were her own children, naming them Lorcan, Lugh and Fidelma. She trained them to guard, to hunt, to herd and to play. She groomed the hounds before brushing her own hair each night. Lorcan, Lugh and

Fidelma faithfully slept on the floor around her bed. She embroidered special collars for them and a matching girdle or what you would call a belt for herself. She even wove extra blankets for them, before making her own winter cloak.

"Three years later, Madoc allowed Cliona, now thirteen years of age, to bring Lorcan, Lugh and Fidelma to the spring tournament. As the games progressed, rumors flew around the camp of the dark lass that ran with the hounds. She entered all the contests, and was always one of the three in the winner's circle. Her wavy auburn locks fell to the black manes of her three hounds, and prize ribbons dangled from the girdle that matched their collars.

"On the last day of the gathering, at the evening feast, Jerlath, the chieftain of clan Mag Aoidh announced that King Niall's second son, Brendan, would wed at the summer solstice. Jerlath had selected the best two hounds from the gathering to be presented as a wedding gift from the clan. Teague, the magnificent white male from his own stock, and Cliona's black female, Fidelma."

"Wait a minute," interrupted Claire, "I thought the hounds were a birthday present for the prince, not a wedding present!"

"Now, child," Aunt Evelyn scolded, "Do you want the true story or the fairy tale?"

"The true story," came the timid reply.

Aunt Evelyn took a long swig from her tea cup before beginning again, "It was decided. The next morning Cliona and Fidelma left with her grandfather Jerlath's household, abiding there to prepare the hounds for the royal presentation."

Claire jerked her head towards the old woman, "But-"

"I know, child," Evelyn winked, "She made her father, Madoc promise to care for Lorcan and Lugh until her return." The girl settled back with a satisfied grin. "No more interruptions," snapped Aunt Evelyn. "The truth of this tale is especially important tonight.

"Life in the chieftain's household was busy. Cliona spent half her time training and grooming Teague and Fidelma under the watchful eye of her grandfather and the other half learning the formalities involved with the high wedding from her grandmother. During the evenings by the fire, she embroidered beautiful new collars for Teague and Fidelma and a matching belt, all adorned with the black, white and red knot-work pattern favored by her mother Niambh's clan.

"Two days before the wedding, the chieftain's entourage camped beside the Shannon River near the hill fort of King Niall.

Overwhelming crowds of people, noises and color swarmed over the makeshift city around the fort. The sights and smells dazzled the imagination, but Jerlath kept his granddaughter and the wolfhounds secluded in secrecy. He gave Cliona a soft, pearl white linen tunic and fine woolen crimson surcoat with black and white embroidered trim to wear for the presentation.

"In the middle of the feast, Jerlath strode into the center of the great hall. The mighty chieftain wore a pearl white tunic and surcoat of crimson with black and white embroidered trim, just like Cliona's. His striking image was adorned by a jeweled belt with the clan sword in its scabbard and an immense, black fur cloak. 'By your leave, my liege,' he bellowed. The hall fell silent and King Niall nodded. 'Prince Brendan and Princess Meredyth, it is the honor of Clan Mac Aoidh to gift you with our two finest wolfhounds, Teague the White and Fidelma the Black.' Jerlath bowed retreating out of sight.

"Then Cliona appeared with Teague and Fidelma on crimson leather leashes, one in each hand. They stopped in the middle of the hall. Cliona removed the leashes and tossed them behind her. The hounds stood on their hind legs with front paws on the other's shoulders creating an arch that she gracefully twirled through. The wolfhounds came apart, crossed behind, and suddenly leapt out in front of her, growling in a ferocious attack stance that made the bravest warriors in the audience flinch. Even King Niall pressed himself back in his throne while Prince Brendan stood, his hand ready on his dagger. Cliona set her arms akimbo and stuck out her tongue at the vicious dogs. They fell over and played dead to roars of relieved laughter from the crowd."

"I've seen you do that!" Claire piped in. "My brothers used to tease your hounds and get them growling mad. Then you'd come over and stick your tongue out and 'thbpbpthpt pfft' at the dogs and they would roll over and play dead."

"Yes, child," nodded Aunt Evelyn reaching for her tea, "And what happened to your brothers?"

"Grandpa took the boys by the ears and disappeared behind the barn. I don't think they sat down for two hours after that!" Claire giggled.

"Now, child, where was I? Ah yes, Cliona and the hounds gave an amazing display of acrobatics and dancing, the likes of which had never been seen, ending with Cliona between the wolfhounds in front of the head table." The old woman sipped from her cup before continuing, "Cliona removed her embroidered belt and the dogs laid down with their heads on their front paws. She showed the hounds the belt, then knelt and presented it to Prince Brendan. Even after all her practice and preparation, Cliona knew Fidelma was no longer hers. A single tear fell down her fair cheek.

"Though Prince Brendan had just been wed that very afternoon, he fell in love at first sight with the wondrous Hound Maiden kneeling at his feet, and was struck speechless. King Niall took charge of the awkward moment and granted her a boon. Cliona asked for the runt of Teague and Fidelma's first litter. King Niall was touched by the simplicity of her request and granted the boon with the added decree that Cliona should visit the hounds every summer solstice until the boon was met.

"Heartbroken to lose her Fidelma, but bolstered by the promise of one of Fidelma's pups and meeting the prince again, Cliona returned home to Madoc and Niambh. She bred Lorcan and Lugh on the condition she had first choice of one pup from each litter. By the time King Niall's messenger came the next year, with Cliona's invitation to the summer solstice celebration, she had five new pups in training.

"During that second summer solstice feast, Jerlath marched Cliona, now fourteen years old, to the high table and asked if the King's boon to his granddaughter was remembered. Cliona was wearing the same pearl white tunic and crimson surcoat she had worn the year before. In the torchlight her auburn hair caught the fire's glow while her ocean blue eyes glistened like sapphires. She had grown into womanhood and her shapely beauty could not be hidden. Prince Brendan and Cliona looked upon each other. The whole world paused for a moment, as it always does with the recognition of true love. Princess Meredyth's eyes burned with jealousy but she kept her voice polite, "We have been consumed with other royal matters. The hounds are well, but alas, we have no pups."

"And alas, no news of a royal heir, either," said King Niall, with a sly wink to Chieftain Jerlath. "The Hound Maiden of Clan Mac Aoidh will be the Royal Mistress of Hounds until the boon is fulfilled."

"And so it was that Cliona and all her hounds moved into the royal fortress. Cliona was given a chamber of her own, above the special stables for the wolfhounds."

"Whoa!" Claire burst out. "Meredyth was the wife, not the jealous old queen? That means Cliona and Brendan were set up! The King saw it! So did her grandfather, Jerlath!"

"Since when is it strange for royal families to work around a not so successful political marriage?" Aunt Evelyn's eyes twinkled. "Now let me finish, child, it's getting late. Prince Brendan found excuses to be with the Hound Maiden. Cliona tried not to, but she fell in love with Prince Brendan. Soon, they were meeting by moonlight in Cliona's chambers guarded by Lorcan and Lugh."

"By the time of the fall harvest, Fidelma was ripe with pups. Prince Brendan paid less and less attention to Meredyth. She became so jealous of the hounds that she decided to act. At midnight for three nights in a row, Princess Meredyth took sweet meats from her own plate and stuffed the centers with a little quicksilver. Then she ordered her maid to sneak down to the stables and feed them to Fidelma.

"On the third night, the maid saw Prince Brendan leaving Cliona's chamber and told the princess. Meredyth's jealousy grew to hatred of the Dog Maiden and her filthy wolves. On the fourth night, Princess Meredyth prepared a lethal dose of quicksilver, stole into the stables and fed the black hound herself.

"By morning, Fidelma was very sick. Everyone gathered in the stables. Cliona held the wolfhound's head as it gave birth to her pups. Four were gray and stillborn. The last was a tiny, squealing, red-haired female. Princess Meredyth declared the boon fulfilled, the Royal Mistress of the Hounds should take the pup and be relieved of her duties. Fidelma watched as Cliona gathered the red pup in her arms, 'I will love you, care for you and raise you as my own. You are named, Aideen, for the love that burns like fire in my heart.' Then Fidelma the Black died. Cliona wept, keeping little Aideen in her arms. Heartbroken and disgraced by the disastrous first litter, Cliona and her hounds were sent back to her father's household the next day.

"Over that long, cold winter Prince Brendan spent every full moon alone, hunting the wild woodlands, and the rest of the time in the stables with Teague the White. Princess Meredyth was left in the royal fortress alone, growing more desperate and bitter with each passing day.

"Meanwhile, Cliona kept to herself, raising her hounds and concentrating on household skills in preparation for marriage, as did every young maiden of her age in clan Mac Aoidh. Lorcan and Lugh fathered more pups. Aideen grew hearty and strong with a lustrous red coat. But every full moon, the little pup had frenzied fits, snarling and snapping at everyone but Cliona. Madoc wanted the dangerous pup killed. Cliona would not stand for it. She could not bear the loss of this last precious link to her Fidelma, so Cliona would take to the woods to train her hounds for the duration of the full moon. As fate would have it, she and her love met once again in the forest. Their rendezvous at Prince Brendan's camp became routine and soon Cliona found herself with child.

"At the spring equinox celebration, Princess Meredyth sat pale and thin, with an empty womb. Cliona, the Hound Maiden of Clan Mac Aoidh, stood cheerful, flush with glowing health and her own pack of thirteen hounds. Prince Brendan held secret council with his father, King Niall and Jerlath of Clan Mac Aoidh. Cliona and her hounds would be moved immediately to the royal hunting lodge, and guarded by two men of Clan Mac Aoidh. Once born, Prince Brendan would claim Cliona's babe. The King could dissolve the marriage to Princess Meredyth for being without child; only then Prince Brendan and Cliona could be wed.

"All summer, Prince Brendan continued his hunting trips during the full moon and Princess Meredyth noticed a change in the way she was treated in the royal household. She soon realized the urgency of providing the Prince an heir, or she could be sent home in shame. Try as she might, Prince Brendan was no longer interested in consummating their marriage.

"When the Prince insisted on his hunt during the harvest moon, Princess Meredyth ordered her maid to follow him. The loyal maid returned with news of the pregnant Hound Maiden in the royal hunting lodge visited by the prince. Princess Meredyth was enraged! She would not lose her crown and her place to a dog trainer!

"At the next full moon, Prince Brendan left to go hunting again. Meredyth went into action. She packed a special basket full of food and wine, all tainted with quicksilver. Princess Meredyth made herself as beautiful as she could be, then took the basket to the lodge herself. She could either poison her rival, or bed her ailing husband and beget his rightful heir, or perhaps both.

"The guards could not stop the princess from entering the royal hunting lodge. Luckily, Prince Brendan and Cliona were off in the woods. Princess Meredyth placed her basket on the main table, then went to the Prince's bedchamber and fell asleep waiting for his return.

"At sunset, the happy couple arrived. The guards warned them of the princess, and Prince Brendan went inside. He found the basket and the sleeping princess, and gave the basket to Cliona for her to hide in the stables with the hounds.

"Hungry from a full day in the woods, Cliona ate food and wine from the basket. She tried to feed the hounds as well, but Aideen started snarling and barking. The pup pounced, spilling the basket onto the stable floor. Lorcan, Lugh and Teague the White cornered the red-haired pup as Cliona began cleaning up the toppled basket.

"Suddenly, she fell to the floor screaming in pain. Lorcan, Lugh and her faithful hounds surrounded her, adding their blood curdling howls to her shrieks of agony. Teague kept Aideen the Red howling in the corner."

"Oh my god!" whispered Claire, "This isn't the way the story goes at all!"

"Do you know the truth of this tale or do I?" growled the old woman. "Do not interrupt me again! The fire is low and we don't have much time.

"Prince Brendan and the guards burst into the stables, followed by Princess Meredyth. The prince ran to his beloved's side. They held each other tight as Cliona gave premature birth to their baby girl. Princess Meredyth took the child in her arms. Traces of silver glimmered on Cliona's fingers as she reached for her baby. Prince Brendan noticed the food scraps gleaming with silver on the floor.

"Quicksilver! There was quicksilver in the royal stables! You poisoned Fidelma, my hound! You poisoned my love! Now you would poison my child as well?" Brendan roared, pointing at the babe in Meredyth's arms. The wolfhounds took his yell and pointed finger as a command of attack. They sprang on the princess. Aideen the Red leapt to the falling newborn, catching her forearm within her jaws, and guiding the child gently to the floor.

"By the time the guards got the hounds under control, Princess Meredyth was dead. Her body was ripped to shreds, lying in a pool of blood. Brendan cradled Cliona in his arms. The red-haired pup drug the newborn to Cliona and Brendan, as gently as it could. The Hound Maiden stroked Aideen's head and took the child in her arms, 'I saved you, child of Fidelma, and you saved my child. The circle is complete.' Cliona cleansed the bite marks on the babe's forearm with her tears and wrapped the wounds with the ribbon from her hair. With her dying breath, Cliona made Prince Brendan promise to guard Aideen and her child with his life.

"Brendan, broken with sorrow, renounced his royal duties and family ties. He remained a recluse in the woods with his auburn haired daughter and the wolfhounds. Stories are still whispered, in taverns along the banks of the river Shannon, of sorrowful wails heard only during the full moon and of an auburn haired beauty that assumes the form of a wolf and runs with the hounds."

Angus howled from the porch. Moonbeams shone through the lacy curtains and danced on the hardwood floor.

"Why did Cliona have to die? She couldn't help falling in love, could she?" asked Claire.

"Love, even true love, does not guarantee happily ever after, but there is more you must understand. We have no time. Give me your hands, child."

Claire held out her hands. Aunt Evelyn turned them palms up, exposing the scar on the girl's forearm and the matching scar on her own. A crescent shaped arch of dark spots, as if they both had been bitten by a dog. "There are those in our family that understand it is not a mere fairy tale, but a real piece of our family history, our ancestry, and our legacy. We are the children of Cliona. We carry the quicksilver tainted blood of the Hound Maiden of Clan Mac Aoidh. One girl child in every generation will be born with the scar. She will have blue eyes, auburn hair, a special affinity with the hounds and a curious allergy to silver. Just like me and just like you. When she reaches the age that Cliona died, she will run wild with rage as a wolfhound in the light of the full moon."

Claire tried to speak, but only a howl came out. Aunt Evelyn's eyes twinkled, then answered with her own blood-curdling howl. They joined Angus on the moonlit porch.

Three wolfhounds dashed into the woods. One black, one gray, and one with auburn hair.

I guess it was as I was sawing the little kid's arm off that I realized how far things had gone.

Before that it had mainly been fun – me and Clark sitting at the laptop screen, Greg holding that giant camera on us, all trying to outdo the other with what we could come up with.

"Let's put," Clark said, giggling, "I want to fuck a burns victim."

"You can't put that!" I said back to him. But I was giggling, too, and my fingers were hovering over the keyboard with a feverish desire to type something.

"Nah," Greg said. "That's no good."

"What do you mean?" Clark asked.

There was an undercurrent of anger to his voice.

Clark didn't like it when his suggestions were questioned.

"That's not enough," Greg said.

I looked at him.

I was often surprised he *could* speak, lugging that camera on his shoulder. You see, it wasn't one of the sleek new ones we used for our show. No, it was some huge monstrosity he had found in an antiquities shop, and had instantly fallen in love with. We used it for our private projects, to capture stuff we didn't necessarily want put on the screen yet.

"What's wrong with it?" Clark countered, a little bit of aggression joining the anger now.

"You should say you want to fuck a burns victim," Greg replied, "when she's still recovering in hospital."

The three of us laughed at that, the tension draining out of the room to be replaced by joy.

And typing.

Of course, it hadn't always been that way.

A few years ago, we'd all been puking into the gutter at the end of a long drinking session, wishing we hadn't spent our taxi money home on trying to get into the knickers of that woman with no bra and homemade tattoos and stretch marks and a "Mum" ring. Just another Friday night, in other words. But as I was still vomiting, regretting the choice of that microwave curry I'd eaten before leaving the house, Clark and Greg got into one of their usual *tete-a-tetes*.

They usually went something like this:

"Don't fucking touch me, man."

"Or what?"

Brief skirmish.

Then arms around each other.

"I fucking love you, man."

"I love you, too. Let's see if that lass fancies a three-way."

I hadn't realized that the man who had previously been puking alongside me was now watching my two friends with interest.

They were squabbling again, this time over whose shoes were the best, so they hadn't noticed.

"Incredible," the man said. He was old and had a beard, and I was fascinated to see that he had somehow managed to avoid getting any vomit caught up in the hairs. He looked at me. "Are they your friends?"

"Yeah," I replied, a little hesitantly.

"They're marvelous," he told me. "They're just what I'm looking for."

And he reached into the pocket of his – which I then noticed looked to be expensive, designer – and produced a business card and handed it over.

WALKER ELLISON, it said. TV PRODUCTION EXECUTIVE.

"You're going to let them on TV?" I said. "What about me?"

And I curled up into a ball and started simultaneously sobbing and soiling myself at the unfairness of it all.

"Don't worry," he said, and laid a hand on my convulsing shoulder. "You look perfect for it, too."

There wasn't really much to the show – just drinking, swearing, and trying to fuck each other's girlfriends.

Yet people loved it.

Men.

Women.

Kids.

But by series eighteen – four filmed every year – we were starting to get bored with our new lives of privilege.

Until we met Weasel.

He was this former child star who now, at the age of nineteen, was considered past it. His last few albums had flopped, and his record label had dropped him. Even the last resort home-filmed sex tape that he'd had 'accidentally' released to the media hadn't done much to boost his sales.

So when we met him backstage at an awards ceremony (where we won three, incidentally), we expected him to be a little jealous of us, resentful of our continued success when his own career seemed to be going down the toilet.

But instead he greeted us like old friends.

Invited us back to his place.

And showed us to a very special room that he called 'The Dungeon.'

"This is where I do it, guys," he said.

I looked around.

It really wasn't much of a dungeon.

It wasn't even much of a *room*.

There was only a table and a chair, a laptop sitting on the former.

Only Greg seemed impressed by the place. Looking around, an expression of awe on his face, I was betting he wished he'd brought his camera with him.

"Do what?" Clark asked.

"Do you ever wonder," Weasel said, sitting down on the chair, "how I keep getting invited to awards events, even though I haven't had a hit song in a year?"

That may not sound like much. But a year is a long time in modern show-business.

"How I keep myself in the papers?" he went on.

"No," I said, curious despite myself. "How?"

"Easy, guys," he said, and he moved the mouse on the laptop, bringing the screen to life. "I'm *controversial.*"

We looked at the screen.

"I say something offensive," Weasel continued. "On my own website or on social media. Something racist, something sexist. Then, a few days later, I apologise for it."

"That's it?" Greg wondered. "That's enough to keep people talking about you?"

"No, that's not *just* it," Weasel replied. "There's more. If whatever I say is racist, I reach out to whatever race I've slurred. We go on a voyage of discovery as we try to understand each other." He winked back at us. "And there's normally a camera crew that wants to get in on *that* action, believe me."

The images on the screen of the laptop verified his words – a scrapbook of media outrage, headlines like WEASEL DOES IT AGAIN, a new thing for which to apologise every six months or so.

"Why bother making music at all," Weasel asked, spinning around in his chair to face us, "when I can just have a career like this?"

"You just . . . say stuff?" Clark asked.

"That's right." Weasel grinned. "The more offensive the better."

"Wow," Greg said. "Wonder if *we* can get away with that?"

We did not want to copy Weasel completely, though.

We did not want his "offend-apologise-repeat" regime to actually *replace* our TV careers.

The three of us were just getting a little bored when the official cameras stopped rolling, and wanted to do something that would both keep us entertained and keep people talking about us.

So offence it was.

It was actually pretty easy – drop the N-word during an interview, make a joke about rape on the actual show itself. In fact, after a few months, it got so we could offend someone without even trying.

And each time we did, we made a full and frank apology.

Usually on TV.

Often live.

Walker Ellison loved it. He even got in on the act, inviting "representatives" from whatever group we had offended to come on air and accept our apologies. Although, as you may have guessed from those inverted commas, they were not representatives at all but were actually actors.

And that night, making the burns victim remark, I was already thinking that the makeup department would have a job on their hands faking *that* one.

The thought sent me to bed with a smile.

But then, a few hours later, I woke to find Greg standing over me.

"Greg," I said, rubbing my eyes, sitting up in bed. "What the hell you doing, man?"

"Can't sleep," he said.

And I noticed the camera was at his feet.

"Why?" I asked. "What's up?"

He sat down on the edge of my bed.

"It's not enough," he said.

"What isn't?"

"The things we're doing," he replied. "The things we're apologising for. It's just words. It's not doing it for me anymore."

Over his shoulder, I saw that Clark, too, had appeared in the doorway of my room.

Was nodding at Greg's words.

"We need to push this," Greg went on. "I want to see what *else* just saying sorry can get us out of."

I wish I could say that I disagreed with him. But even now, knowing what he was about to suggest and knowing what it led to, I can't. Truth is, I felt the same. I also wanted to take what we were doing deeper.

"Okay," I said, and now Clark actually *entered* the room, came to sit next to Greg at the edge of my bed. "So what did you have in mind?"

Greg smiled as he told us.

Ah, fan clubs . . .

Every star has 'em.

From what he had told me, Weasel's was much bigger now that he was a serial offender than it had ever been when he was just a singer.

A sub-department of Ellison's production company took care of all the details, of course. But it was easy enough for us to swing by, chat up the pretty girl on reception (we'd all fucked her in the arse one time, as part of our special, late night, X-rated edition *Cool Guys Get Tough*) and take a look at the database, find out a couple of things.

Like the address of our youngest fan.

As we piled into a car, the three of us, I found myself surprised that the company still kept people's physical addresses. I had expected everything to be digital. But Ellison sometimes ran competitions for the fans, for them to win signed merchandise and stuff. I suppose they needed a place to send this stuff when people actually won.

Along the way, Clark popped into a hardware shop to buy a saw and an axe.

Whistling as he went.

It was another hour before he came back out.

"Sorry," he said. "Stopped to sign a few autographs."

"Don't have to apologise to *us*," Greg said, and laughed.

I was driving, I should explain. Clark – now that the fucker was back – was in the passenger seat. And Greg, of course, was in the back, recording everything on that camera of his.

"Okay, folks," Clark said, holding the tools up, speaking for/to the camera. "I've just bought these." A mocking tone crept into his voice as he added, "and may I apologise in advance for how I am about to use them."

We all laughed.

Whilst before us, little Jimmy Usher's house came into view.

We didn't go straight inside, though.

We parked down the street and waited a few minutes.

Practising our repentant faces.

Knowing how many times we'd have to say "I'm sorry" to get out of this one.

But that was the challenge.

Right?

Finally ready, we exited the car and walked towards the front door of the Usher household.

I looked over at Clark, walking beside me.

"I don't know why *you* get the axe," I said, jealous.

"I have more upper body strength than you," he replied.

I wasn't sure if that made sense or not, so I said nothing.

Instead, I looked back to Greg.

"You sure you don't want in on this?" I asked him.

"Nah," he said. "I'm fine just filming."

I shrugged.

Then knocked at the door with one hand.

The saw was in the other, hidden behind my back. For now.

A pretty woman in her thirties answered.

"Yes?" she said.

We gasped.

"Hey," Greg said, shocked. "She doesn't recognise us!"

"She will," Clark said.

And punched her in the face.

She went sprawling back into the house and collapsed, and the three of us stepped in, closing the front door on the way.

That was when the little boy appeared at the top of the stairs.

He recognised us.

But I'm not sure it was recognition of our famous selves that made his eyes go wide, or the dark stain appear on the crotch of his pyjama bottoms.

"Get him!" Clark shouted, and we ran up the stairs towards him.

He screamed and bolted into his bedroom.

He had no lock on it, though, and we found him cowering beneath his bed when we entered the room.

We pulled him out.

And got to work.

We weren't bad men, though.

Honest.

It was never like we wanted to kill him.

We just wanted to see if another set of heartfelt apologies would get us out of something this extreme.

Of course, maybe letting Greg stay downstairs with the big cumbersome camera was a mistake.

He'd said it would be more fun this way, though. If he just caught the sound of the boy's screams on film. If he let the imagination of the audience fill in all the blanks.

We hadn't realized.

We thought Clark's punch had been a lot stronger than it actually was.

Greg must have been pretty shocked when her eyes popped open and she got to her feet.

And, wearing that big thing, he couldn't keep up with her as she ran up the stairs and into her bedroom.

All he could do was shout, "look out, you guys!"

But we didn't.

I was sawing and Clark was swing-swing-swinging with the hammer and we were just too enraptured with the sight of the boy's arm sliding off.

We didn't hear her enter the room until it was too late.

Or see the gun in her hand.

I felt the bullet punch its way through my guts.

And then I felt nothing at all.

I woke up in hospital.

Handcuffed to the bed.

Handcuffed.

Like some common criminal!

But I soon realized I had more pressing issues.

Like I couldn't feel my legs.

But I suppose I was maybe lucky to get off with just that.

Clark died of a gunshot to the throat. Or choked on his own blood following the shot. The medical examiner couldn't say for sure.

Greg's cause of death was easier to determine. It wasn't strictly from a gunshot, though. No, what happened was that as he'd reached the top of the stairs the woman had aimed low, had shot him through the leg. And he'd fallen down the stairs and hit the ground at the end of them – and then a few seconds later the huge camera had landed on the back of his head, pretty much crushing his face into the carpet.

Little Jimmy Usher survived, though.

Naturally.

Like I said – we never *meant* to kill him.

But the little shit had been naughty – watching our show when he wasn't supposed to. Signing up to our fan club without his mother's consent.

Considering that, you could make a case that all we were doing was giving him the punishment he deserved. Although my lawyer disagreed with that analysis.

Weasel distanced himself from us, the bastard – said he'd always thought there was "something off" about us. Then quickly changed the subject when the interviewer pointed out the similarity of our recent career trajectories.

And as for Jimmy's mother . . .

Thanks to her I'll be in a wheelchair the rest of my life. Pissing into a bag for the remainder of my no-longer-televised days.

At the trial I kept on looking at her. Kept on waiting. But the bitch never broke. Never said a word directly to me.

And you know the worst thing?

She never even once said sorry.

38. BOXES BY CHARLES DAVID BENNETT

She keeps her memories in boxes. Photographs and obituaries of loved ones, postcards—she had sent to herself—and souvenirs of holidays past: keepsakes from childhood, mementos and love letters/poems of failed relationships. She would decorate said boxes with colorful wrappings, inked art or oil paints. The boxes were the canvas of her life; in the ones she cherished the most she would place a fresh rose from her garden each day.

She was not an especially sad woman, although she did have the occasional bout of depression, as most loners do. Her name was, Rachel Gibson; a short petite woman of 5'4" with a slim, average build. Her long strawberry blonde hair framed a fine featured face and hard green eyes. Rachel was not wealthy, though she did have a tidy nest egg saved from the thirty plus years she worked as a surgical nurse. Now she held a part-time job doing research for a local law firm, but the job was slow and she spent most of her time tending her rose garden and boxes.

This morning—as always—she opens her mother's designated box first, the box is painted with flowers and rabbits. Rachel removes the old rose and sets it aside. She picks out and reads the obituary clipping that says her mother, Sara Gibson, passed away from an inoperable brain tumor. Sighing, she replaces the clipping, picks up her mother's photograph and regards it.

"I sure do miss you momma. I wish I could still confide in you." She says to the fading picture as a tear rolls down her cheek.

Rachel gently returns the photo and places a fresh rose in the box before replacing the lid. Next she turns to the plain white box which holds her father's pictures, and opens the lid. There is no rose in this box, and Rachel spits on his picture.

"Asshole!" she mumbles as she turns and walks across the room where she switches on the radio. The old device crackles to life and a country song begins to sing:

"Well I'm feeling a little bit lonely baby,
come and pick me up.
Now I just can't get enough of
your taste, my touch,
a little bit of love and a whole lot of lust!
Said I'm feeling a little bit lonely baby,

so come and pick me up…"

The tune suits her liking, so she cranks the volume and begins dancing playfully around the room. The song eventually fades and is replaced by local news. She turns the volume down, then sits at her computer desk.

"Computers are another kind of box," she says to her dog, who stares at her questioningly, "an electronic box that transports us to the magical world of cyberspace!"

She grins smugly and logs on to her favorite social media site: Lonelyhearts.com.

***

David McCarthy hadn't made many friends in the years since the tragic death of his beloved Angela. David did, however, manage to acquire a girlfriend for a short time. Mary left him after a year. She claimed he was "too needy" and that the only reason she stuck with him that long was that she felt sorry for him. (The truth of the matter was that she used him to make another man jealous. When the latter was accomplished, she dumped him.) Mary's hurtful words and actions sent David spiraling into a blackened pit of despair he could not circumvent.

This evening he could not sleep. There were too many things going bump in the night; too many ghosts of past mistakes in his head. David is haunted by worries, stalked by fear and hounded by anxiety. Indeed, his life has become nothing more than a trail of bitter tears; shattered dreams in a broken place, and like a church yard shadow, there was very little left of him. David made himself a good, stiff vodka drink.

"Beware nerves," he said to himself, "Doctor vodka is coming to calm you."

He took a long pull off the drink, winced, then padded over to his computer desk and logged on to Lonelyhearts.com. David found he had a friend request and a short personal message from a woman who called herself, 'Summer66'. He confirmed the friend request and went looking at her profile pictures.

"Pretty lady," he thought. He picked a favorite, then typed a short comment:

"Great picture!"

The reply was almost immediate: "Thanks, lol."

David sat and reread the message she had typed, and then with joy saw that she messaged again.

Summer66: "Your profile interests me and I'd like to get to know you better. Want to chat?"

David responded:

ScifiDave23: "Sure. What are you looking for?"

Summer66: "I'm seeking friendship at first—no game playing please—with someone who appreciates some of the same interests and temperaments I enjoy. That special someone is a man with integrity, who is spiritually compatible with me and having similar beliefs. A man who is responsible, intelligent, has a good sense of humor, who is positive and clean and neat in habit. A man who is romantic and passionate about living and loving. I would prefer this man show interest and be supportive in my interests. He should be financially secure and have a 'been there done that' attitude. An adventurous individual who likes to travel as much as he likes to stay home with his someone special. I would like to connect with someone like minded for friendship first, leaving the rest to the universe."

ScifiDave23: "I believe I can give you what you're looking for." He wasn't sure of the financially secure part. He ran his bank account pretty tight and didn't have a lot of extra cash. No matter, he decided. He'd wing that part and come clean to her about it later. 'Win her heart first,' he thought.

Summer66: "Lol. So is your name really ScifiDave23, or do you have a more realistic one?"

ScifiDave23: "Hahaha! My name is David McCarthy, but just call me Dave. And yours?"

David lit a smoke while awaiting her reply. He was almost finished with his cigarette and wondering if Summer66 was ever going to reply when the message came.

Summer66: "Sorry. I had to let my dog, Tailo, outside. He is old, if I have him another year I'll be doing good. My name is, Rachel Gibson. So where do you work?"

ScifiDave23: "I am a shift manager at a local fast food restaurant. It's not the most glamorous or high paying job, but it's all I need right now." David sent the message and grimaced. This was usually where they said that we're not a match.

Summer66: "No worries. We do what we need to, to get by. I've decided I don't want to be alone anymore and want someone to share my life with. What about you?"

ScifiDave23: "I am looking for the same thing. Just friends first, then see where it leads."

Summer66: "I'm in my bed now with my laptop while surfing cable channels, trying to find something good to watch; I may have to go to Netflicks to find a movie. Do you have a phone with unlimited texting?"

ScifiDave23: "Yes Mam."

Rachel gave him her number and told him to go ahead and text her if he'd like. Over the next several days they exchanged texts and a few voice calls and made a date for the coming Friday night. They agreed that she'd pick him up and David gave her directions to his apartment.

***

Friday evening Rachel phoned and said she was on her way. David turned on the porch light and sat outside, chain smoking and waiting impatiently. Finally, the white BMW pulled up to the curb across the street and David walked out to meet her.

"Hi!" Rachel said, looking just as excited as David felt.

"Greetings, Rachel!" David replied.

"You think my car will be alright here?" she asked.

"Oh, sure!" David beamed back.

He brought her into his apartment and gave her the grand tour while introducing himself. When they sat on the couch she sat very close to him—any closer and she would be in his lap. David put his arm around her, which made Rachel, uncomfortable, and she said as much.

David didn't really know why he did it, it just seemed the natural thing to do, but he apologized and asked what she'd like to do.

"Well," she said, eyes sparkling, "I thought maybe get something to eat and rent a movie?"

"Sounds good," David said and they went about doing just that. It was the start of a ritual that continued every weekend—as well as several surprise visits from Rachel during the work week—for several months.

One random Saturday Rachel canceled on him, to his great dismay. It was a lame excuse but David accepted it with grace, though, he was sure she had found someone else. 'And why not?' he thought, 'That's the way my luck always goes.'

The following Sunday, David took an opening shift to cover for a fellow co-worker. It began at four a.m. but he only had to stay till ten. He told the other manager, that he was going to do his outside walk around early and let himself out. He started for the trash bins at the rear of the parking lot and as he rounded the backside of the restaurant he heard some commotion from a stand of tall brush beyond the curb.

He turned and smiled but the smile faded quickly. There were two of them—masked gunmen with semi-automatic .9mm pistols. He knew he was in trouble, and the men wasted no time putting one of the guns to his head the other to the middle of his back.

"This is what's gonna happen," said the one holding the gun to his head. "You're gonna knock on that back door and they are gonna let us in."

"They won't," David squawked.

"You want to see your kids again?" the gunman hissed through his teeth.

David nodded yes.

"Then you'll make sure they do!" said the evil voice as the gunman in the rear shoved him to the door. Just as David was ready to pound on the door, the exterior lights came on and the huge road sign illuminated, signaling that they had opened for business. David's assailants hustled him off to the copse of bushes from which they came and commanded him to lay face down. They took off his shoes and used the laces to hog tie him. A gun pressed against the back of his head and the evil voice hissed:

"If you make any noise for fifteen minutes we'll come back and shoot you!" One of the gunmen shoved David's dirty sock in his mouth and left him lying in the dirt.

David heard the gunmen flee, spit out the sock and lay there silently crying and wanting nothing more than to be in the arms of Rachel. He was unsure how long he lay there, but the sun had come up and he could hear the drive through speaker. With renewed courage he began yelling for help. Eventually one of his co-workers came around the side of the bushes.

"Holy shit!" the kid exclaimed when he saw David, and turned to scurry away.

"GET YOUR ASS BACK HERE!" David screamed and the kid obeyed. "There is a Bic lighter in my right pants pocket, get it and burn the shoelaces."

After statements were taken by the police, David punched out and told them what to do with their job.

***

At home David gulped down three powerful vodka drinks but was still shaking violently. He made a fourth drink, then sat down to text

215

Rachel, but his nervousness and the tiny android keyboard made the task impossible. He called her instead.

"Hello?" Rachel said.

"Hi, Rachel. How's things?"

"Everything's fine on my end. Your voice sounds different, are you okay?" she asked.

"Not really, I quit my job today."

"Why?" she asked.

David broke into tears then and told her the story of the gunmen and the cops.

"Oh my god!" she said in amazement, "Why don't you pack some clothes and stay with me for a few days?"

"Okay," David agreed nervously. He heard an exasperated sigh come from her end of the phone.

"I'll pick you up in half an hour, be ready." Rachel's voice was firm, almost angry.

"Alright, I'll be ready, see you then," David said.

***

Rachel and David spent the next three days at her house, cooking meals, working in her garden together, watching movies and cuddling on the couch, making love, laughing and generally just having fun.

David awoke on the fourth morning and Rachel was not beside him in bed. He realized he hadn't thought of the attempted robbery or Angela or even that he smoked. He knew then that he was in love, that Rachel had become his world.

David got out of bed, dressed, and went into the kitchen. He helped himself to some coffee, then stood in the kitchen window watching Rachel in her garden and loving her. She turned and waved at him, and David smiled and waved back, but something seemed different about her. He was getting a second cup of coffee when she came in the back door.

"Morning, honey," David said with a smile.

"Morning!" Rachel's eyes were hard and had dark circles under them.

"Come down stairs, I want to show you something," Rachel said, opening the basement door.

"Okay," David said and started down the stairs.

David wasn't sure when he first got the idea that Rachel was intent on murdering him. 'Was it just paranoia from a nightmare?' he thought. There had been subliminal signs, little suspicions for the past month. They way her eyes stared daggers at him. The relationship was too calm, like a stretch of tropic water where monsters dwell just under the surface. David decided he couldn't go on like this and that he wouldn't try and stop her if she was intent on doing such a thing. They reached the basement and he looked at all the plastic drop cloths hung everywhere.

"Going to do some painting?" he asked.

"Yeah, I'm thinking about painting it red." And with that, Rachel struck him forcefully in the head. David went down hard, face first.

"Jesus!" he moaned. He slowly rolled over and saw her standing over him. She still had her latex gardening gloves on and had acquired a claw hammer from somewhere; the basement seemed surreal and floated around her in an effluvium of hysteria.

"Rachel, honey, what's the problem?" David said.

"I'M TERMINATING THIS RELATIONSHIP, YOU NEEDY BASTARD!" she yelled, and swung the hammer. David instinctively put his arm up in defense—the hammer connected with his forearm and broke it.

"AGRHHH! YOU DON'T HAVE TO DO THIS! LET ME GO AND I'LL SAY I FELL!" David screamed. He decided that he didn't really want to die after all.

"FUCK YOU! I HATE MEN!" she yelled as the claw end of the hammer connected with his right temple, removing his eye. David saw a white flash and unfeeling darkness mercifully came. Blood spurted everywhere and his body began flopping around in shock.

"QUIT JUMPING AROUND, YOU SPINELESS WORM!" Rachel screamed as she went into a blind rage. She kept slamming the hammer into David's head until it sounded like somebody hitting a pile of hamburger with a mallet, and his body ceased all movement. She then retrieved her surgical tools from a shelf, and dismembered him.

When she was finished she placed his body parts in boxes, and put each in one of her many freezers; in the one which held his heart she placed a rose.

"I told you we'd be together forever," she said as she spit in the box.

After cleaning up, she went upstairs and put on her favorite song: 'Teasing Tina' by The Swinging Doors.

"Well I'm feeling a little lonely baby,
come and pick me up.

Now I just can't get enough of
your taste, my touch,
a little bit of love and a whole lot of lust!
Said I'm feeling a little lonely baby,
so just come and pick me up…"

She sang along and smiled as she sat down at her computer box, logged onto Lonelyhearts.com and updated her status:

'The past is full of ghosts and there is nothing in the future because it hasn't happened yet. All we have is the here and now. Would some nice gentleman like to box it up with me?'

39. RETURN OF THE GREEN GUY BY JOHN ALFRED TAYLOR

Ed Seidel penciled the last panel, outlined Happy's speech balloon in blue, then took the stack of illustration board to Mike.

"Perfect as usual," Mike said, without bothering to compare the sheets to the thumbnails. "Bet you could draw Happy Hare in your sleep."

Mike stared when Ed muttered "Wish I could." Ed hated Happy Hare, Chirpy Chipmunk, all the inhabitants of the Tulgey Wood, even if talking animals were his bread and butter. Fun Incorporated was still going, when so many other comic houses had spiraled down into bankruptcy. *Happy Hare*, *Kanga Down Under*, and *Real Fact Comix* carried them through the bad time. But *Crimewave* and *Shock Stories* had to go, with Kefauver waving the E. C. cover with the blonde's decapitated head and *Seduction of the Innocent* a best seller, and schools and churches sponsoring comics auto-da-fé.

And when *Shock Stories* went, Scum went too. That really hurt, because Ed had invented the character with minimal input from Mike. Almost like losing a child. Ed hadn't even been able to do a last episode to kill the Green Guy off clean: he missed the walking haystack still.

"Do your fuzzy worst, "he told Tom when he handed the inker the stack of penciled pages. Ed didn't mean *worst*. The way Tom could hint at fur was amazing, and he'd done wonders with Ben Day screens to suggest Scum's boggy hide.

Now back to pencil the Myrtle the Turtle story—he and Tom had fun with the patterns on her shell—this time he'd try a flower in every scute.

Scum was trying to tell him something. Moans were all the creature could muster, and the wet green face leaned over him, mouth-hole narrowing and widening like a camera iris as it groaned again. Desperately Scum moaned louder, and Ed sat up, suddenly awake. The digital clock said 3:10.

Ed got back to sleep soon enough, but remembered the dream at breakfast. He stopped chewing for a second, wondering what the Green Guy had been trying to say, then shook his head. Crazy to let a dream bother him.

But it colored his mood all morning till Mike called him over to the corner that served as an office. Jeff the writer was already sitting by the desk. "Want to bounce some ideas off you two. I've been thinking we could use another superhero book. Mutaman's fine, but he's getting a little old—don't mean get rid of him, just go in another direction. Just noodling this new character, want your input to help flesh him out. His name is Copycat—we can figure out his real name later. He's Copycat because he can change his appearance to look like anybody."

Interesting possibilities, Ed thought. "So how's he do it?"

"Don't know," Mike said. "That's why I want your input."

"Maybe a radioactive spider bites him," ventured Jeff.

"Nah," Mike said. "Who'd believe that?"

Ed nodded. "How about a rare Tibetan drug."

"That's good. Tibetan is always good."

"And then he uses his gift to fight crime," said Jeff. "The standard option. But what's his motivation?"

"Revenge, like Batman. Though not because his parents get killed. We'll figure it out."

They decided Copycat's actual name would be Leo Bast, but weren't so sure how Bast's unmodified self should look. "We've named him after a cat." Ed pointed out. "So why shouldn't Leon have a feline look—I'm thinking Orson Welles—"

"Too fat," said Mike.

"You're thinking *Touch of Evil*. But I'm remembering Harry Lime and Welles as Borgia in *Prince of Foxes*." Mike still looked dubious, so Ed leaned over and snaked a sheet of paper off the clutter of the desk. "Let me show you," he said, sketching quickly. "And we give him a mustache like a cat's whiskers."

He exhibited the result to the others. Jeff nodded, and Mike said, "That's Leo Bast all right."

Mike dismissed them after telling Jeff to write up the beginning of a script. "We need backstory. How he gets his power, how he learns to control it, what crime or injustice he has to avenge." He turned to Ed. "You think about it too, because three heads are better than one, Let's get back together tomorrow morning, see what we have."

Ed returned to *Kanga Down Under* with new energy, though not for Kanga. Mike had been right about him being able to do funny animals in his sleep; now he was penciling the Merry Marsupial like an automaton while visions of Copycat danced in his head.

Copycat's special ability would make him a new kind of superhero. Others used disguise sometimes, but it was all Leo Bast had. With him guile trumps force. So plotting should emphasize intrigue, devious but clear to the reader—tricky, hard to do.

And what about that rare Tibetan drug? He'd said Tibetan off the top of his head, but how would their hero get hold of the stuff?

Next morning they were sitting around Mike's desk. "Still can't figure how Leo gets hold of the shape-shifting dope," Ed said.

"Leo's an anthropologist," Jeff said.

"Anthropologist? Then forget Tibet," Ed said. "Just my first thought. Make the Amazon the source—witch doctors, jungle boogie, curare, all that."

Jeff nodded. "Right. The Amazon for sure."

"So what drives Copycat once he learns what he can do?' asked Mike.

Jeff checked the scribbles in his notebook, "You said revenge. But not like Batman. Can't have young Leon's parents shot in front of him. But what if his father is driven to suicide—big banker, captain of industry, something like that, made the fall guy by his crooked partner?"

"Sounds good," Mike said.

"So Leo has to clear his father's name, get the goods on the partner," Jeff added.

Ed remembered what he'd decided yesterday: "And do it by trickery. Copycat uses disguise, not muscle. No BIFF, BAM, POW for him."

"Absolutely," Jeff said. "Stealth is it. And I can think of problems fists can't solve."

"For instance?" said Mike.

"What if he runs into the guy he's impersonating."

"Good twist. Write that into your script."

By the time Ed went back to Kanga and the Kooky Burra the Amazon Basin had flooded his imagination. Re-sharpening his blue pencil was sufficient to exorcize the vast image, though not the idea of green.

Mike ok'd the script for Copycat number one, and Ed and Jeff got to work. Collaborating with Jeff was always easy, because Jeff thought in pictures as he wrote the dialogue. Ed sketched panels one after another, figuring how they'd fit on the page:

The witch-doctor telling Leo a bad thing was happening in his faraway country, and that he must go back. Handing Leo the sealed gourd holding what he'll need when the time comes. Leo in the dugout seeing the city of Santarem round the bend. Leo sending the telegram and waiting for the answer. His mother's cryptic reply concerning his father's death—

No funny animals now, Ed thought as he expanded the thumbnails full-size. He was having fun drawing the villain. He had the perfect model for the father's crooked partner, this Bishop on TV with the sickly smile who told people life was worth living. When he was a boy Ed had played with soap sculpture and now imagined Bishop Sheen as carved from a huge block of Ivory with a light bulb inside to give him that holy glow.

This was what comics were meant to be: full of thrills and mystery, maybe a little scary. Like the Green Guy was.

The Green Guy—Ed's pencil stopped moving for a moment as he wondered. Nah. He shook his head, but couldn't suppress the thought. Just maybe. Once he finished the page he wandered over to Mike's corner.

"Something came to me," Ed said when Mike looked up.

"Yes?"

"Copycat can't make the whole book."

"Been thinking about that," Mike said.

"So why not bring back Scum?'

Mike grinned. "Your special green-haired boy. Might be fun, but it's only been a couple of years."

"Sure," Ed said. "We had to kill *Shock Stories* then, but things have calmed down since."

Mike shook his head. "We'll never get it past the Comics Code goons."

"Why not? Scum might look a little scary, but he never hurt anybody—too busy figuring out who he is and what to do about it. Besides, he fits right in with Copycat—they're both shape-shifters. Just that Scum can't do reverse."

"Maybe." Mike said. "Let me think about it."

Ed dreamed of Scum again that night. The shaggy green face was nearer, mouth open in a shape of woe, but no matter how loud he moaned and writhed, Ed couldn't understand what his creature was trying to say.

Mike gave him the green light the next day. "Bringing back Scum's worth a try. Write me a script, and we'll see. Better begin at the beginning again: the crash in the swamp and all that. People forget, or maybe never read *Shock Stories*—think of *Copycat* as a comic with a new audience."

That evening Ed rode back to Brooklyn with a grin on his face. On the walk home he picked up takeout Chinese and two bottles of cheap champagne. Tonight he'd celebrate, because he had the whole weekend to work on the script.

He sat at his kitchenette table afterwards, finishing the second bottle of champagne while he sketched Scum's beginnings over again. The millionaire playboy Jon Simmons having engine trouble over the Everglades—the plane augering in—Simmons' fierce denial of death as he was sucked under—messy, tentative drawings to get him in the mood. Tomorrow he'd be sober enough to tackle the script.

Ed woke alert and eager, but didn't hurry through breakfast— surprised he hadn't dreamt of Scum. Or maybe he had, and couldn't remember.

No point in getting dressed: he'd work in his bathrobe and slippers. Ed cleared the table, laid out a yellow legal pad, sketch paper and pens, then realized he needed something more.

Ed had created Scum from duckweed and moss, chlorella and spirolina and spirogyra, but needed something solider than imagination. He'd ended with a boxwood mannequin covered with shreds of sponge rubber, all spray-painted green. He'd never taken the figurine to work: it had been his secret, and he'd buried it in his closet at the end.

The carton wasn't easy to find, because it was in the back, hemmed in and hidden by bigger things. Ed stared at it for a second before going for a paring knife. The box reminded him of a tiny coffin. Sealing the mannequin up and hiding him in the closet had been a kind of funeral. Now it was resurrection time.

He dusted off the top as he leaned over. It had bulged over the years till it looked like a peaked roof. When he started to run the knife down the tape it split all the way to expose a line of virulent green. The flaps burst open, and Ed staggered back from a bubbling green column, a pillar roaring to the ceiling and spreading out above him. He stared up as it descended to blind him and fill his mouth before he could scream.

Next Wednesday Mike stood outside Ed's door while the super tried his pass key. Mike had dialed Ed's number repeatedly the last two days; he'd come and waited to be buzzed in before alerting the supervisor, and now they'd knocked with no response.

The super turned the knob, pushed, then shook his head. "Must be bolted on the inside."

"What now?" Mike said.

The super shrugged.

"We've got to break in," Mike insisted.

"Ruin the door?" asked the super.

"He might be sick or dying."

The super stepped aside to give Mike leeway. "Be my guest."

Mike backed across the hall, took a quick run, and slammed into the door, half-falling from the rebound, the only result being shaky legs and a sore shoulder. It looked easier in the movies. The super joined him in a second attempt. The door resisted them both. The super cursed and went in search of a tool. Returning with a crowbar, he drove the tip between the doorframe and the door, leaned back to get full leverage. Tortured wood creaked and splintered, a bolt ripped loose, and they were inside.

"Ed," Mike shouted, "Ed!" No answer. No one in the kitchen-living room, no one in the tiny bedroom, no one in the bathroom. Baffled, Mike looked around again, even examined the open closet. The place was a mess—there were green streaks on the ceiling and the rug, there was a cardboard box in the middle of the room half-full of green goo, but nothing else.

Mike dialed 911.

All they ever found of Ed was a slipper with a foot still in it near a disjointed posing mannequin.

40. THE MIND OF AN *ARTISTE* BY RAYMOND GATES

Where to begin?

The thought wanders through his mind as it has so many times before. A mental bloodhound, searching the creative centres of his brain, sniffing out the inspiration required to create his next masterpiece.

The commencement of a new piece is always the most exciting time. Certainly, the process of creation-though at times fraught with frustration, indecision and second thoughts-is not without excitement. The finale, the final reward for his efforts, is also exciting, though not always guaranteed. Too many times he completes his work, only to find the final product does not live up to his vision. The beginning, however, is unique. The thrill of starting something new. The anticipation of creating something to stun and amaze all who see it.

A shiver ripples through him as he gazes down at his tools, and his subject. This is how the painter, or the sculptor, must feel as they stare at the blank canvas, or the unmarked slab. Closing his eyes, he allows his hands to rest gently on his instruments, trusting his instincts to find the right one. His vision goes far beyond that of the dabbler in pigments, or stone-cutter. He is an *artiste*.

The cold steel is familiar and welcoming. He opens his eyes and grins. As he raises the scalpel and sees his reflection in the polished blade, his vision becomes clear.

The eyes. It always starts with the eyes.

He takes hold of the girl's face with his free hand. Though the industrial tape should keep her firmly in place, one always works better on a steady surface.

He has always been intrigued that all his subjects have the same response when he begins his work. The stark, wide-eyed look of terror he can understand, but it's the intense, pleading stare they give him. As if they believe with a single look they can hold him back, take away his inspiration, and destroy his vision. Like so many, they cannot see the world for what it is. They cannot see life for what it is. Their blindness repulses him, at times to the point of physical illness. In this moment, as the scalpel approaches their face, when the reality of the world should become clear, what do they do?

They squeeze their eyes shut. They maintain their blindness as long as they can.

During his first explorations, he felt nothing but anger and disgust at this futile effort. He takes it as a personal affront, an insult to his creative genius. Consequently, by his own admittance, his earlier works are not his best. Over time, as his methods and vision developed, he began to pity them. These sheep, blindly following the misguided flock. Taught to shut out reality and remain ignorant to the truth. They have never been given the opportunity, the guidance, to see things as they really are.

He leans in towards her face. Her screams do not make it past the rolled bandage stuffed in her mouth. Even now, she tries to resist his fingers drawing the lid up and away from the globe of her eye. The blade moves closer, catching the light and evoking her blink reflex. He almost loses his grip on the thin flap of flesh.

Almost.

With a deft movement, he runs the blade from the inside edge of her eyelid through to the outer edge, freeing it from her face. He discards it without a thought, and secures a small piece of gauze against the fresh incision. He uses a saline ampoule to wash the blood away from her eye. It would not do to have her metaphorical blindness become real, especially when he plans for her to be the first admirer of his greatest work ever.

Despite her efforts to break free, to plead with him, to deny by force of will alone what must happen next, the other eyelid comes away quick and easy. He pauses to admire his opening strokes. Her eyes are quite beautiful; a creamy shade of green, accented by their bloodshot appearance. All the more striking now that the veils have been lifted. He adjusts the medical lamp so the light doesn't fall directly onto her eyes, hoping that his thoughtfulness might still her protests.

"My dear, you are blind no more", he says. It does not seem to offer her any consolation. He's never understood this anguish. The procedure is no more traumatic than circumcision. His male subjects have expressed far more concern about that.

An image of removing her tongue with the soldering iron flashes through his mind, so intense that for a moment he is overwhelmed by the pungent scent of seared flesh. He dismisses the thought before it takes hold of him. There is merit in the task, and while it might make a bold statement in its own right, it does not fit with the vision unfolding in his mind. It is something a lesser artist might consider. A way of inspiring controversy and interest in their work. As an *artiste*, he is above such trivial ambitions. He creates his masterpieces not for the glory of others, not even for his own glory, but because they are there to be created. They need to be released, to be expressed, to come out of the darkness and into the light of day.

A smile creeps onto his lips. His eyes travel to her heaving breasts, her lungs in overdrive as terror and adrenaline course through her body. His hand settles between them, feeling the pounding of her over exerted heart. It thumps against her sternum as a prisoner might beat their fists against a wall. His own heart flutters. The purpose of this piece is revealed. Out of the darkness, into the light. He reaches behind him for the correct tool.

She turns every breath into an attempt to scream. Perhaps she believes the more breath she can force through her throat, the more likely she will be to dislodge the bandage. The pounding of her heart intensifies, as if trying to escape its bony cage. The pruning shears, curved like the upside-down beak of a predatory bird, settle upon her skin. The thumping in her chest becomes erratic. He waits for her to draw another breath to accommodate the next scream.

At the peak of inspiration, he tilts the shears and the point easily punctures the soft area just below her sternum. He is blessed with good fortune. The penetration catches her breath, freezing her in time. He squeezes the handles together, forcing the blades to bite through the flesh. Cartilage yields with a sound like dry twigs snapping.

A tremendous crash from behind draws his attention.

Armed, uniformed men burst into his sanctuary. The world explodes in a bright flash. The ceiling spins around him.

What's happened? His line of sight is now level with the floor. He hears movement and yelling all around him. It's like the background noise at a party, there and not there. His instinct is to get up, or at least to move, but his body won't obey. His left side feels completely absent, though he appears to be intact. He rolls his eyes to search the room, and analyze his predicament.

Then he sees it.

On the cream coloured wall, there is now a large, wet, crimson splatter. Amongst the red wash he sees an assortment of gore: pieces of flesh, tiny bone fragments, tufts of hair, and a pinkish-grey matter he does not recognise. It is exquisite in its randomness. Chaos given order. Transfixed, he barely feels the fingers pressing against his throat.

Joy wells up inside him. This is what he's been searching for, what he's been trying to express, trying to show the world. Who created such brilliance? Who has been able to release the vision he's tried to unleash all these years?

A shrill, ear-splitting wail jolts him. What could have happened to cause such a heart-wrenching sound? Concentrating, he shifts his weight and frees his right hand. He manages to lift it towards his head. He finds a small opening in his forehead that should not be there. He reaches around to the back of his skull, his fingers tentative in their exploration. They touch the ragged border of another opening, much larger than the other.

He reaches into the newly formed cavity. Blood drips from his hand as he brings it into his field of vision. His fingers hold a soft, almost gelatinous piece of pinkish-grey tissue.

Out of the darkness, into the light.

Half of his mouth smiles. A tear trails along the crease of his nose. Scurrying hands roll him onto his back and tear at his shirt. A shudder, his body's best attempt at a laugh, racks through him and he allows his eyes to close.

"It's beautiful," he whispers. There is no indication if those surrounding him hear or understand him. They tear his shirt off and shine a bright light into his eyes. The light is receding from him, as if disappearing down a long, dark tunnel.

He thinks of his masterpiece. The light winks out.

41. TO HELL AND GONE BY MARK SLADE

Fat, stinking bitch fell off top of me and squealed as she rolled out of the bed, landing on her fat fucking ass. I reached over to the bottle of wild turkey that was on the nightstand beside me. I gulped it down and let it burn to make sure I wasn't dreaming again.

She popped up, resting her oversized head on the bed. She giggled, her curly blond hair bobbed up and down. "Was it good for you, baby?" She smiled, her out stretched rubber lips crossing one side of her round rosy cheeks to bridge together the other side of her face. Her makeup has run together, reminding me of those fucked up paintings of clowns by John Wayne Gacy.

I nearly puked in my mouth.

"For fuck's sake," I moaned, looked away.

"What's wrong, Mr. Sour pants?" She climbed on the bed and the mattress sank in. She crawled towards me, making kissy noises. "You didn't get off, baby?"

Wrong fucking thing to say to me.

I grasped the bottle's long neck and slammed the flat side across her fat fucking head. The bottle exploded. Shards of glass and liquid mixed together like a pornographic rainstorm.

She wailed. Blood streamed out from under that horrible bleached blond scalp, dribbled in her eyes at an alarming speed. She pleaded for an answer to a question I am mother fucking tired of being asked. She backed away from me on the bed, moving to the foot.

"Why? What—what did I say, baby?"

"You opened your fat fucking mouth, piggy!" I screamed through gritting teeth.

I grabbed at her hair. It came off in my hands. I was surprised by it, a bloody blond curly spider nest bounced in my hands, and I dropped it on the bed.

She was bald. Even scarier than before, the hoop earrings she was wearing were now even larger than before. Blood was still pouring out. I could see the wound was actually an inch from where the wig sat on that pinhead.

She was cowering in a corner behind the bed. Begging me to stop, waving her hands wildly, asking again that same mother fucking question. I tossed the mattress out of my way, knocking the lamp from the nightstand.

She started to pray to her God. I cursed her God, inching toward her.

The first punch caught her in the nose, breaking it. The second one turned that pug nose into mush. The third punch caused her nose to sink in. The fourth punch forced her cheekbones to sag. The fifth punch was the clincher. Her eyes rolled into the back of her head. She slumped down, limp, her mouth parted just slightly, and I got a horrible fucked up idea—but I fought the urge bringing my underwear back over my waist.

I picked up the mattress and placed it back on the cheap bed springs. It creaked and moaned when I sat down. I looked down and found a loose cigarette on the floor. I scooped it up in between my fingers and found my lighter curled in the blanket on the floor. I lit the cancer stick with quiet passion.

"Yeah, baby," I said to the dead fat fucking hooker poised for God's grace in a dark corner. "I got off—just then."

The phone rang. I scrambled to find it, realizing I had moved it to the window ledge. I answered it on the last ring, kicking empty bottles of vodka and Jack Daniels out of my way. It was Nelly on the other end, my agent.

"Where the fuck are you?" she screamed in my ear. "You have a reading at two-thirty! It's noon now!"

"Ease your conscience, darling," I greased my tongue into her small mind. "I'm on my way. Just waiting for a taxi." I brain fucked her and this wasn't the first time.

"A fucking taxi? I hired that creepy bellhop from Oklahoma so you wouldn't have to wait for fucking taxis! Where the fuck is he?"

"Well, darling, we were at the bar last night—"

"Oh no," Nelly said dimly. "Sam promised me he wouldn't take you to bars again. It's a struggle as it is to book you for readings at these uptight bookstores and colleges. The last time in L.A. —do you remember that? The publicity?"

"Well, darling, Rolling Stone thought it was funny," I soothed.

"I didn't!" Nelly bellowed. She began to a sob.

"Everything will be fine, Nelly. I can see you're still angry at me for that little piece of chicken in the last town."

"You could hardly call her 'little'. My God, what is it with you and those kinds of women?"

I licked my lips, trying hard to find the right words. "Darling, Nell. You know I will always have you in my heart—"

"Don't," Nelly demanded.

"It's true, darling. I crave certain things, but I always come back to you." I told her.

"Don't...." she begged.

"My little Nell, always looking out for my wellbeing." I told her.

"Someone has to," Nelly cooed.

"And you do such a devastatingly grand job of it, my darling. When I get back, you better not be in your office with your skirt hiked up," I laughed and Nell laughed along with me.

"I'll make sure I am," she said with conviction.

At that point Sam poked his head in the door. He was still dressed in his bellhop uniform. I once asked him why he still wore it even though he no longer worked for that hotel in Oklahoma.

"You are who you are," Sam said. "Why not dress the part."

Most fucking certainly. Why not dress the part.

"Guess who just poked their head inside?" I said to Nell. "Sam! Well I must go and be on our merry way." I made kissy noises into the phone, then placed the receiver on the cradle.

Sam came in, smiling from ear to ear. "A grand time I can see," he screeched, as his pointed tail swished around. He showed his blackened broken teeth as he laughed. He looked around the room, stopped when he found the dead cunt behind the bed. "Oh. Yeah." He shot a look at me, his brown eyes turning the color of brimstone. "A great time as I can see. Its guys like you that make my job easy."

"Yes," I said, pulling a tropical shirt and slacks out of my suitcase. "I know Sam Hill. I know I make your job easy."

I turned my back on him as he fell to his knees slowly. I looked in the mirror, seeing my naked rotting body in the cracked image. I could hear him slurping, his face buried in her face.

I dressed quickly, sloppily. The slacks no longer fit me since the only nourishment I receive is any alcohol I can find. It's all my body can handle anymore.

"Come on, Sam Hill!" I called out to him, he stood, wiped his mouth, fixed his bellhop hat on his head. "Another town, another reading… another feeding."

42. SOMETHING'S WRONG WITH ETHAN BY DOUG ROBBINS

The moon, enshrouded in green mist, leered down at me like a rapist as I sat on the sofa watching television. My eyes fixed on the image of Michael Myers slashing Annie's Neck. "This movie's so cheesy," I thought. "Where's the blood?"

I felt a presence, staring at me. Out of my peripheral vision I noticed a slender figure, standing beside the sofa. I turned my head and saw a boy of about nine gawking at me. "Hello Ethan," I said. "Your mom and dad told me you were in bed. Can't you sleep?"

The boy said nothing. His pajamas were blue and appeared to be made of cotton. His blue eyes, cold and wet, looked like he had been crying. "Are you ok, sweetheart?" I asked.

No reply. "Would a warm glass of milk help you sleep?"

Ethan just looked at me. I shifted in my seat. His gaze, unyielding made me blink. The television started flashing on and off. "Wonder what's wrong with the television?"

The telephone rang, and I answered it. "Hello," I said.

No answer.

"Hello," I repeated, this time, putting more bass into my voice.

Nothing.

I sort of slammed the phone, and then heard footsteps stamping over-head. "Is someone else here?"

The boy winced at this question. I shuddered. "*Weird fucking kid,*" I thought.

The television continued to flicker and then the lights began flickering as well. Unseen finger nails scratched at the window, piercing my ears like a thousand razor blades. I turned to Ethan and asked if his house was haunted. He smiled and said nothing.

I shuddered. Soon I began to hear what sounded faintly like organ music, coming from somewhere upstairs. The pictures on the walls started rattling. I felt my mouth get dryer and dryer. Ethan outstretched his arms and began levitating five feet off the ground. Slowly he started spinning in the air until his feet pointed toward the ceiling and his crown pointed toward the floor.

I grabbed the boy's wrists and tried pulling him down to the ground but he would not budge. I blinked my eyes, and heard a voice call to me from the stairs. I looked over and I saw Ethan's face staring at me. "How'd you get over there," I asked in shock.

"I've been upstairs the whole time, sleeping," Ethan replied.

My mouth hung open. The other Ethan was gone. "Who was that?" I asked.

"I don't know, but I'm glad I'm not the only one who has seen him now…" Ethan said, allowing his voice to trail off. "I guess he likes you," Ethan added. "And he told me he's looking for a new home…"

43. PALADIN BY AARON J. FRENCH

The Holy One: a beauty and a demoiselle. Lives in the house on the green hill, at the end of the road through rugged wilderness, full of clumping cypress and bushy spruce, where the crest of the hill appears to merge with the horizon; she stands on the balcony of her large wood-and-brick home, surveying the surrounding forests and the farther ocean beyond. Circles of black and white birds wheel in the sky. Her long reddish hair gets pulled by the wind.

The Paladin goes to her, for he has come from halls of loneliness, from city streets burned out with fires and poverty, where the living lie half-dead in alleys, and the somnambulistic souls who pursue a life not designed by them, but by something unseen, strive toward nothingness. His job and his heart and his career and his livelihood, once these stood before his ego as utter truths but have since fallen away, so that now he only passes through windows, openings in and out of the worlds. He peers into places where he should not look— where he should not *be able* to look.

Still, it is a race to leave himself. And so the Paladin is running. Running out of all things. But especially out of *time.*

He rides broad-chested and regal astride a fine red *equus* 2012 Ford Mustang, with a front splitter and a pair of blocked-off fog lamp openings and boomerang striping along the body-sides. He is dressed in the leather tux of his father, and his father's father. He is shouldering the burden of his lineage. A bloodline thrums in his veins. As the steed picks its way along the road leading to The Holy One, the Paladin looks out among the foliage and the tempered sky overhead, his mood something doleful, like a piece has been taken away.

Part of him misses that old life. But truly he despised it, and is glad to be free. It is only this *transitioning* period that finds him saturnine— that wears upon his soul, as a hammer melds lead into steel. For he is mourning the death of parts—singular parts—of his individuality.

He is becoming that which he was not.

So when he talks to her in the wind, they are flying side-by-side, through cloud and sun. She smiles at him. That smile which heaves him forth into a new being. Out of pain, loneliness, death. The same happens again as they comb the bottommost regions of the seafloor. She raises her hands from where they were digging in the shells and rocks, and touches his face. It reminds him of the lonely life he left behind. The life before he met her, living alone in the dregs of his past experiences, clicking through the Internet in search of something more—until now—now her—now *this*.

The Holy One. That which he has always wanted. She is everything. She is perfect. And now she is his.

Standing fully upright, she is under six feet tall. Her long reddish hair, with a streak of brown toward the ends, glimmers radiantly. She is accustomed to wearing long white skirts and a blue blouse, her handbag and her iPhone, constantly changing positions.

There is an air of nobility about her—that would suggest she came from royalty, or at the very least from aristocratic bloodlines, above the commons herds who flock the streets amid fog. Her face—pale, chiseled, Grecian, smooth face of stone—is illuminated in the upper half by twin globes of greenish blue, which look upon the world in endless fascination. Her pupils are portals, he knows; they are entryways into forests of magic.

"I once spoke to a maple tree," she says, as they sit in the dark, redwood dining room of her home. She has prepared peppermint tea and dispenses it in a pair of porcelain cups. She tells him of her life.

As she joins him at the table, sitting in one fluid motion which seems extended somehow, elongated, she hands him his tea. He replies, "What does it mean, spoken to a tree?"

"Exactly what it says. You can learn a lot from trees. Their inner voice is a causeway to gods. Their voice echoes deep within the elements of all human beings. Listen and practice will allow you to hear them, too. Come, I will show you."

She gets up from the table.

He has slept dreamlessly after she is gone, after the murderer has taken her. He remains alone in the upper rooms of the house, alone in the bed, staring out the window, where a bulbous moon and a parade of stars meet his gaze. He thinks of The Holy One and he tosses and turns, for he cannot sleep. He cycles through the television stations, but they are all blind. There is a small bronze bust of Goethe on the night stand, and lying beside it, a shaving razor, and beside that a hand mirror. The Paladin is afraid to touch any one of these. The razor, especially. Things have souls. Things can *kill* you.

…kill her, kill you, kill me…

Yes.

Morning light streams into the room. The bust of Goethe turns, is animated and talkative. The old poet remarks to him, "You know, I once was so lonely and miserable that I thought of committing suicide. Over a woman—yes, of course, partially—but over a host of additional, more existential reasons also. The hand with the knife pierced my navel but stopped soon after. I wrote a book. *The Sorrows of Young Werther*. Ever heard of it?"

"I don't speak German," the Paladin replies.

He gets out of bed and goes out into the world to find her.

The body of The Holy One is pinned up between two trees, lashed to the branches, arms spread to either side. A bloodless corpse. Hanging, still prettily, still a radiant, physical organism now devoid of personality and life, but a treasure nonetheless. Still holy. Still *pure.*

He cuts her down with his father's dagger and carries her into the woods. Tears follow. The trees speak quietly to him, whispering words of solace, which permeate his being. He carries her farther to the crest of the green hill, where a clearing of grass lies open beneath a gray bowstring sky. A single, tabletop of stone has been erected in the center of the field. He places her on it, sprawled on her back, arms dangling over the sides, as clouds gather in the heavens.

Lightning. Thunder. The Paladin raises the dagger… It rains.

"I'll tell you what I'm gonna do," I said plugging in both my grills. "I'm gonna cook my lunch. God knows you've eaten enough of the ones I left in the refrigerator."

"I'm ssssorry," George said, snot bubbling out of his nose and the chains around his ankles and forearms rattling against the wood as he struggled against the handcuffs I'd put on him. He fought the metal bonds but couldn't escape.

For once, I owned him.

"It's okay. Instead of you eating my lunch and me starving, I thought that maybe today we'd eat lunch together and try and talk through our differences."

I could already feel heat rising from my grills. I'd gotten so sick of George making me take the late lunch period only to get there and see him finishing off the final crumbs of my lunch.

He'd smack his lips, grin and say "What was this today? Your wife makes a great sandwich. Such a wide variety too. Tell her to keep it up."

The guy was twice my size and dumber than a bucket of shit, but for some reason popular with everyone. The crew flocked to eat with him as he devoured my lunch, knowing full well the prick was eating my fucking lunch but never saying a word about it to him. Although they never hesitated to point and laugh at me.

I didn't really care about them and I would've called George on it, but he was also the foreman on my line. He monitored everything. From someone showing up wearing open-toed shoes to clocking his buddies out a couple hours early on Fridays, he watched over it all. Like choosing who had to come in on Saturdays, and if they got paid for the overtime. At least he wasn't there to eat my lunch on Saturdays.

I don't know why he targeted me. He probably saw me as weak, which I guess was a fair assessment considering how long I'd tolerated his bullying.

Before I dragged him in here and restrained him, I'd laid out my smorgasbord on the break room counter. My creamy tomato soup was already in the microwave and I went about using both my grills to cook up my lunch. I was starving and George had already eaten my day's lunch an hour ago.

Today I packed an extra cooler in my car and set about making myself a sandwich.

Peeling off a few slices of bologna, I tossed them on one of the grills. George's eyes widened and he started babbling when I pulled out a kitchen knife with at least an 8-inch blade. One of my favorites, and I loved the look of fear flickering on his face. I teased him a little bit, and then I buttered a bun and started toasting it on the second grill.

"My wife doesn't make sandwiches like this," I said. "This is my own creation. I call it fried bologna grilled cheese," I said and unwrapped a slice of cheddar and a slice of provolone.

"Somebody help me. You're fucking crazy," he screamed.

"The shift is already in full swing. You know how loud the shop is. Ain't nobody coming to save you, and all I want to do is have a meal with you. So instead of screaming, why don't you just talk to me. I'm cooking here, doing all the work. The least you can do is entertain me."

George just blinked at me, took a deep breath.

Then said, "Okay, Wendell, what do you want to talk about?"

"You don't have to be formal with me Georgie, you can call me what you always call me."

George shook his head.

"Do it!"

My bologna sizzled on the grill.

He sighed.

"Alright. What do you want to talk about, Wendy?" he asked.

"That's better. Now. I want to know why you always eat my lunch. I've asked you not to a million times and you still do it. Why?"

George closed his eyes. Opened them.

"You want the truth?"

"Yes, George, yes I do."

"Honestly? Because I could. Because you're the kind of guy that people walk all over. The kind of guy that always pays his overdraft charges and doesn't complain when he gets short-changed by a cashier. The kind of guy that doesn't get any pussy. The kind of guy who doesn't send back a shitty meal at a restaurant. The kind of guy who doesn't fight. That's who you are and I thought that's who you'd always be. I gotta say, Wendy I never expected this."

"You're right," I said and paused. "And I'll be honest right back with you. I usually do the right thing and I almost always avoid conflict, no matter how in the right I am. But I guess everyone has their breaking point. Am I right Georgie?"

"I… I guess so," George said. "Just look man, you made your point. Let me loose and I won't tell anyone and I'll never touch your lunch again. Hell, I'll bring you lunch every day for the rest of the year to make up for it."

"But George, you've been eating my lunch for the better part of three years now. And the ridicule and the Saturdays. And the list goes on and on."

"Fine, 3 years, forever, whatever, just end this shit and I'll make it right."

"I really wish I could trust you," I said and lifted the lids on both grills. I laid my cheese slices down and they began to melt.

"Smells good," George said.

"Well, this is one of my favorite meals. I came up with it in college. Never really outgrew it. Goes great when you dip it in tomato soup."

"I remember some of the crap I used to eat in…"

"Shut up George."

The microwave dinged. My soup was ready.

He shut up.

"Problem is," I said, and pointed the knife at him. "George the foreman. Got a nice ring to it, but I'm sure you've heard that one before. I like to think I'm a little more creative than that. But, these *are* George Foreman grills. Man, that guy sure knew how to trim the fat. Anyways, like I was saying, problem is, I only brought enough to make one sandwich."

George didn't say anything for a few moments.

"But I thought you said we were going to eat together," he stammered.

"Oh we are, and sorry to be rude, but for reasons you'll understand in about five seconds, I had to cook mine first."

"You could cut the sandwich in half," he tried.

"I don't think so. But I *do* think you brought something for lunch."

"It's gone, I already ate it. Yours too," he said and looked at the ground.

"I don't think you ate all you brought," I said, "but I think you're going to soon."

His eyes widened as I raised the knife. But I turned and used it to scoop my melty, crunchy sandwich off the George Foreman grill and put it on a paper plate. It smelled fantastic. Gooey cheese dripped down the browned edges of the bread.

"Can I tell you something George?"

"Uh, okay."

"I don't have a wife. You were right earlier, I do have trouble getting pussy," I spat.

George didn't answer.

"All the food you've ever eaten here was prepared by me. From the lobster macaroni and cheese to the cucumber chicken salad. I take my food very seriously, and I guess I'm glad someone got to enjoy it. But," I paused and slammed the knife down tip first into the wooden table. It stuck up like a crooked tooth.

"But what?" he asked.

"That person should've been me! Do you have any idea how long it takes to make cucumber chicken salad? And you fucking ate it right in front of me. And I'd bet my life that your palettes are too fucking ignorant to fully understand and interpret the flavor."

"You don't have to insult me," George said.

"Shut up. Now, it's time to prepare your meal. I've always wanted to try this," I said. "Ever since I got one of these grills back in college. Congratulations George, you've made that possible. Today is the day."

"What are you…"

"You know the best part about taking a semester at culinary school?" I interrupted.

"I can't say that I do."

"It's the cutlery," I said. "You gotta buy your own knives," I brandished my big blade. "This shit has to go through bone like hot butter. I don't splurge very often, but I've got the best cutlery the world has ever seen. Check it out," I said.

His mouth opened but I was already brining the blade down. First his right hand, then his left.

Lots of blood.

Lots of screams.

The hands fell free, with one slice apiece. I wasn't bluffing about the sharpness of my blades. His severed hands hit the linoleum of the break room floor with a pair of soft plops. The fingers quivered like legs on a dying spider.

"Hope you're hungry," I said and scooped both the squirming hands up and put each one on the table. After buttering each palm, I shook out a handful of spices. Garlic, cayenne, and onion powder with a pinch of salt and pepper.

"Sorry, but I don't think we have the time to try any marinade."

I tossed each hand on its own grill and shut the lids.

The meat cooked while George the Foreman screamed. The man and the machine. The aroma of cooking meat and spices made my mouth salivate as much as my fried bologna grilled cheese before it.

His screams tried to make words, but it wasn't quite happening yet. I walked back over to him and put my hands on his shoulders.

"Look George," I said. "I'm cooking your hands. You smell that? They smell pretty good. There should be some good meat on them too. I reckon fingers are kind of like ribs. Especially the pads of each. Sorry. I didn't have time to use a slow cooker, so they might not fall off the bone."

George squeezed his eyes shut.

"Listen, you're bleeding really bad. And I think your hands are about done. You've done such a great job, that I'm willing to give you a hand. Two actually, and you're going to eat them."

"No," he whimpered. "You're fucking crazy… I won't eat them."

"Yes, you will," I said. "I brought barbecue sauce, A1, and ketchup. That might help. Also, you're gonna bleed out if I don't help you. Tell you what, you eat just one of your hands, and I'll cauterize both your stumps. Stop the bleeding. Do we have a deal?"

He didn't answer right away. George's blood squirted like a Mortal Kombat fatality. I looked over to the grills and saw steam rising and thin rivers of fat trickle down from the grill into the George Foreman patented grease trap.

I went over and pulled the lids of both up. The blackened meat smelled delicious. Flakes of skin flew up, caught in the air stream from the vent, and danced through the room like ashes at a campfire.

I stabbed a burned palm with a meat fork, hoping that I hadn't overcooked his hands. Holding his skewered hand in one of my hands and my sandwich in the other, I sat in the chair across from him.

"Alright George. It smells great, let's eat," I said and took a big bite of my sandwich. It was still warm.

He just stared at me. Maybe he was going into shock.

"Oh right," I said, rolling my eyes, "I forgot, you need help." Then I put the fork that held the severed meat to his lips. He didn't even resist. He took a big bite, chewed, swallowed, and then took another.

After he finished his entire left hand, I kept good on my word and used the George Foreman grills to cauterize the stumps of his wrists. The meat pinkened and blackened just like his hands, but the blood stopped flowing.

George looked like he was going to pass out, but he fought it; his eyelids fluttered yet he somehow stayed conscious. I couldn't imagine the pain.

"Doesn't even need any sauce," he said.

I took a bite of my sandwich and considered tasting his other hand. Maybe it really was that good.

Just as I started to reach for it, he started to move. He screamed in pain but since he no longer had hands, he was able to slip the burned stumps of his arms out of his restraints. His legs were still attached to the chair legs, but his forearms were free.

I didn't even think about his arms getting loose this way, but what he did once he had them free really blew my mind.

"It's good," George said and reached his crusty stumps out and pushed them together and picked up his other hand. He went at it like a bird and had the meat picked from the bones within a minute or so.

"Damn Wendy, you are a good cook," he said. "I ate so much I'm getting sleepy. Can I just go to sleep now?" he asked.

"One more thing, and then we're done," I said.

"What's…" George's pasty, bloodless face could barely get the single word out.

"I need you to tell me if your feet taste any better."

Snake season is not like any other season. It's not like winter or summer; although the heat of summer, the parched grass and the even harsher dryness you feel on your skin and lips as the sun beats down, begging you to slosh water all over, is a good hint that the snakes are around.

Snake season begins when the first person in the neighbourhood calls "Snake!" and the word spreads around quickly. As a kid I wasn't certain how the pieces fit together, but I always knew that it worked. Some time in summer, Mum would tell me, "It's snake season."

Mum told me everything about looking out for snakes. How they camouflaged well in the grass and the dirt. The brown ones were the ones you watched out for – in a bad way. If you ever see a snake, don't aggravate it. Just call for your mother. Don't beat it with a stick. Don't try to catch it. That's for the professional snake catcher. Did you hear the one about the boy who tried to catch a snake by himself? Children who try to catch snakes come to nasty ends.

"No," I said. "Tell me what happened? Was it poisonous? Did he die? Did he scream? Did his skin go black? Did his eyeballs pop out? Did his whole body go all crusty? Did his tongue stick out, that's what I heard? Did he froth at the mouth? Did his fingers fall off?"

"Children who ask too many questions also meet nasty ends," said Mum. "Just stand still. The snake won't bother you if you're calm and level-headed."

Dad grunted. He wasn't used to snakes the way she was, and he called her advice "damn nonsense". "I wouldn't let any snake, brown or green or any colour get the better of me! I'd hunt it down and stamp it out!"

"You try that and you're dead," Mum replied, and Dad went red and yelled more.

I saw a snake in the house when I was nine years old. I was pulling out some boxes in the storeroom and there it was, a glistening green-brown thing curled up on the tile floor.

Was it green or brown? Green-brown. I wasn't taking any chances. I stood very still and then I called my mother.

Both my parents ran for me, but the snake hesitated only a second and slithered away.

"It was there. I saw it," I whispered. "A snake! It's the season."

Mum's hand rested on my shoulder. "That it is. Next time we see the snake, we'll inform the snake catcher. You did well. Just as I would have done."

A ripple of pride went through me. I had always admired how Mum seemed to know everything about dealing with snakes, and everything else on the land around us. Perhaps some of it would rub off on me.

But Dad went berserk. "Where did the little blighter go? I want it. I'm not letting some stupid reptile fool me! Where's the snake?"

"It's not going to show itself with you carrying on in that manner," said Mum serenely. "It's gone now. Let it be."

"Let it be! Shut your face woman! Let a snake loose in the house? Are you a fool? No, I'm after it. I'll hunt it down if it's the last thing I do. Snake! Snake!"

Dad moved into the storeroom, yelling as he tossed boxes and packages behind him. Mum held me close. I didn't like to think of the snake then. I knew the most important rule, never agitate a snake.

It could be anywhere. It would lie low and hoard up its resentment till it finally decided to make its move. I could feel the tiniest quiver in Mum's hand as it held my shoulder, but she didn't say anything. She just watched as Dad tore up the place.

"The snake's moved. I bet he's gone for the kitchen. Dirty bugger." Mum and I followed Dad and stood at the kitchen entrance as he went on the prowl.

Dad yanked open the kitchen drawer and inspected the two biggest knives. Then he dropped them both and smiled when he found the meat chopper. He turned it over and admired its weight, how large and sharp it looked.

"This'll get the snake," he said. "I'll hack him into tiny pieces. Where is he? Was that him?!" Dad brought the chopper down on the floor with a thwack, but there was no sign of the snake. Thwack! Thwack! Dad whirled and went for it.

I knew I didn't have to watch, but this performance from Dad was mesmerising. His body seemed to be in more than two places at once as he dived, jumped, ripped drawers out of the cabinets and swept crockery off the shelves, roaring at the snake to come out. Meet him like a man. And then the next moment he'd be singing, "Snake, snake, come out, wherever you are! I've got something for you! Here comes the chopper to chop off your head!" and cackling.

"Get out of the way," whispered Mum. "He's mad. He's got snakes on the brain." But she could not stop watching herself. I squeezed her hand.

The cupboard received two hefty blows. Dad was landing that chopper on every surface he could, shouting that the snake would pay. I kept thinking how close it sometimes landed to his toes, and how I hoped he did not miss. But Dad didn't seem to care.

Then, the chopper came down and caught a scaly strand as it fell. The snake.

Dad hooted in triumph. He seemed surprised himself to see the snake caught. There were two pieces of snake in front of him, still wriggling, as he brought down the chopper again and again.

"I said I'd have you in pieces and I'll bloody well do it!"

I ran over. Little pieces of the magnificent brown-green snake were still quaking and the head looked up at Dad reproachfully. He was staring at it.

You can't chop me away and expect me to leave. We're in the house. We're everywhere. It's snake season!

Dad shook his head. "No!" he said. "I killed the snake. I win!"

"You don't win against the snakes," said Mum. "You just learn to live with them."

Dad kept staring at it, and muttering, "No! No! I killed the goddamn snake!"

For days afterwards, Dad walked around obsessed. He'd look in the mirror, reminding himself that he'd killed the snake, and then burst out "Go away!" but at what, I didn't know. He walked around whispering, "snake, snake, snake! I've got you! I'm gonna get you!"

He did not speak to Mum or to me. I'd look at him and think how good it was that Mum thought I was taking after her. Dad was crazy. Thank God I wasn't showing any inclination towards this.

He'd go to the kitchen drawer, pull out the meat chopper, and turn it over and over. "It's a snake killer. Me and it, we're snake killers."

"Pull yourself together," said Mum tersely one day. "You've got snakes in your head. You do nothing but wander around and look at that chopper. The car needs washing. The shed needs painting. You do nothing around here."

Dad looked up. "I killed the goddamn snake. I won."

"You never win against the snakes. Not in snake season."

"You goddamn bitch! Didn't you see what I did? Are you with the snakes? Are you a goddamn snake? Snake!"

Mum looked at him calmly. "You don't know anything about snakes."

Dad raised the chopper. "I know about killing a snake."

Mum moved then. She did not scream, she just ran. She moved faster than I had ever seen a snake move. I clambered to my bedroom.

Dad howled. "Where did you go, snake? I'll find you! No snake beats me!" His face was swollen and red and his chopper came down, everywhere.

"Mum!" I screamed. But I stood in my bedroom. *Keep very still.* What did Mum say about not moving if there was a snake on the loose?

I could hear Dad next door, and he was yelling, "Snake!"

"You're crazy, you're out of your mind," I heard Mum say. She did not sound hysterical, but dismissive, cool, unruffled. As I had always known my mother.

"I know a goddamn snake when I see one," answered my Dad. "Snake! No bloody snakes in my house. I'll get every last snake and I'll rip it out. I'll make them pay. I'll show them who's boss!"

The chopper came down, and I heard the shrill yelps and the moan. My legs crumpled. Mum, oh mum! My arms shook.

I waited till I could control my shaking arms and opened my bedroom door a crack. Dad was bending over Mum's body – the pieces of it strewn in the bloody mess on the floor. The little pieces of her limbs. They were still twitching. Dad was looking at Mum's face.

I can wait. I'm always in the house. You can't just chop me away.

"No!" yelled Dad "I killed the snake! I got rid of it!" He grabbed the meat chopper, and bent his knees ready to hunt again.

You never win against the snakes. Our kind, we're all around you.

Dad gave her a long stare, and then her eyes closed. He cocked his head as if he was listening for something. But not for long. He was on his feet, his eyes blazing.

I closed the door to my bedroom. I looked around. What's best? Under the bed, out the window? My legs were frozen. I wasn't calm and clever like Mum. I didn't know about the land, I didn't have her instincts. Not yet, but I'm growing like her. And I'm what's left.

I could hear Dad screaming, "Where's the bloody snake? Where are you? I'll hunt it down! No more snakes in my house!" Then the sound of the chopper against the door.

46. WALK A MILE BY SHENOA CARROLL-BRADD

Bella sat cross-legged on the rug in her family's cabin, playing with a boot while her mother made supper. Dry mud caked the sole, and the left lace was so badly frayed it looked like dandelion fluff, ready to be scattered with a breath. Bella walked the boot back and forth on the braided rug, then glanced over her shoulder to where her mother stood, humming and stirring the stew pot. "Mama," she asked. "Why do we keep the shoes?"

Her mother rapped the wooden spoon against the pot rim to shake it dry, then set it aside. "Well, let's just think about that for a second," she replied in her "teachable moment" voice. "Just about everything has a chance at a second life. Clothes can always be washed and re-worn, or altered to fit, unless they're too damaged or stained."

"Then they can get turned into other stuff." Bella ran her fingers along the bumpy rug beneath her, braided together with plaid and denim, and a few streaks of lilac fabric she liked the best.

"Exactly." Her mother came over and knelt beside her. "Nearly everything has its use, but unless the shoes fit one of us, they're harder to re-purpose." She gently took the boot from her daughter and turned it in her hands, as if appraising an ancient artifact. "Some can be sold, but not as easily as jewelry and purses. Shoes make people suspicious. They ask questions, and what do questions cause?"

"Trouble."

"Exactly." Her mother turned the boot upside down so its open mouth gaped at the floor. "On top of that, people outside the family often hide who they are. They lead entire lives built on deception and lies. But their shoes tell you the truth, if you know how to read them. Shoes show the true measure of a man." She pointed to the dirty sole, indicating the inside arch. "See how it's more worn here? He shifted his weight to the inside when walking and running, which indicates weak ankles. Not a good runner. And, even though some wear is expected on work boots, this condition goes far beyond normal. The leather's wearing through in several places, so we can safely assume he was a hard worker, but not well-paid, and spent his wages on something other than his clothes and appearance. Maybe he had a family to support." She shrugged and handed the boot back to Bella. "Or perhaps he was a booze-hound. I guess we'll never know." She wiped her hands clean on her apron and stood. "It's time for supper, baby. Go wash up and call your pa."

Bella sprang up and put the work boot back with its brethren on the dirty, but still impressive, mountain of shoes in their front hall. She wiped grit from her hands and raced to the heavy door of the cellar where she wasn't allowed. Bella tugged the door open enough to hear her daddy working down there with his screaming tools, where the air always smelled like dirty pennies and outhouse. She clapped a hand over her nose before calling, "Daddy! Supper's ready!"

The shrill saw shut off, and heavy footsteps approached the stairs. "Thanks, darlin'. Tell your ma I'll be right up."

Bella washed her hands in the kitchen sink, then seated herself at the table. She heard her father come up the stairs, but he turned toward the bathroom instead of coming straight to the kitchen. *Probably washing his hands too.* Bella kicked her little legs under the table as she waited, head propped in her hands, lower lip protruding with thought.

At last, her daddy came to the table. He ruffled her hair with a big, wet hand. "What's up, buttercup? You look like you're gonna pop a gasket if you think any harder."

"We were just discussing the shoes," her mother said, ladling up bowls of stew. "I still think they belong down in the cellar, with everything else."

He gave a lazy shrug and dropped into his chair. "Why, butterfly? Are they scaring off your vibrant social life?"

Her mother scowled, but said nothing else as she set out bread and butter before taking her seat. The family joined hands and bowed their heads to say grace.

"Holy father," Bella's daddy began, "we thank you for your bounty, and for continuing to shine your blessings upon this family. We thank you for the lost hikers, the lack of cell phone service 'round here, and the washed out roads, for your ways are mysterious and great. We are, and shall always remain, your humble, hungry servants. Amen."

"Amen," Bella and her mother echoed.

Her daddy squeezed her hand, then released it, and they began their meal in silence.

Bella ate slower than usual, letting each spoonful settle across her tongue before she swallowed. When she swished it around like mouthwash and put her head to the side, her daddy looked up.

"Whatcha thinkin', stinker?"

She swallowed quick. "Mama said you could tell a measure of a man by his shoes." She stirred the stew, fishing out a new spoonful. "I was just tryin' to see if I could guess what shoes supper wore."

Her mother dabbed a napkin to her lips. "It's a clever idea, pumpkin, but I don't think you'll have much luck. And remember, we don't talk about the shoes outside this house, right? That's family business."

Bella nodded slowly and went back to her stew. Her mama was right, of course.

The work boots were an old addition, added to the pile months ago, and the man who had worn them, be he booze-hound or caring father, was long since gone. But still, she swished each bite around before swallowing, sure that she could taste hints of leather and earth mixed in with the vegetables, savoring the essence of a hard-working man.

Running along the boards behind the wall, the pack moves as silent as the grave, stopping when the house settles from the harsh winds of the oncoming storm. Looking back at his four fellows, he flashed a feral grin and used his long bony fingers to make hand signals, telling them to get ready to move into the room.

Tonight they would dine on fresh child.

The family that lived in the house had given birth to a new little girl three days ago, something the Gyrmkin could sniff out from miles away, and had brought this pack crawling. It would be a matter of days before the child was too old for their tastes, and the family had been so observant of the old ways used for keeping the Gyrmkin away… salt in a circle around the crib, a silver cross under the child's pillow and red wax candles all helped to hold them at bay.

But tonight the mother had been tired, and had retreated to bed early. The father had put the child down in her crib after softening her up with a pacifier dipped in sweet rum, allowing the farmer to go to bed for a good night of undisturbed sleep. They'd taken the precautions, but he could smell something different in the dank walls of the child's bedroom. Something… inviting.

Sliding down the stud, the Gyrmkin leader, wielding his two pronged iron fork, moved up to the base boards, tapping on them with his long fingers, looking for loose wood. Smiling a smile full of black gums and broken brown teeth, the pointy eared creature blinked owlishly at his compatriots before hissing an order. Quickly two of the smallest of the band set about prying the baseboard open, using their own implements as tools to loosen the board enough for the group to slip through.

With a pop, a single slate of baseboard fell to the ground, the solitary rusty nail pointing skyward at an odd angle. The small opening was more than enough for the not-so-merry band to see the room in the low light of the infernal red candle. Hissing at its baleful glow, the leader pulled a small leather skein of water from his side, tossing it to the smallest of their group. Barking and pointing, he commanded the youngling to go and extinguish the flames.

The youngling juggled the water skein about as he struggled to catch it, before running off across the floor, giving the ring of salt a wide berth, towards the dresser where the candle sat. The leader and his second-in-command, a snaggletooth creature with one good eye holding a long bit of wood with an iron nail jutting from the end, stood and watched as the youngling scrambled up the side of the dresser. The creature squeaked as it tried to find handholds to pull itself up, his rat-like tail holding the skein away from his yellow furred, mange covered hide.

The leader surveyed the room, staring at the thin granules of salt poured in a circle around the babe's resting place… golden eyes roamed the entire circle until he spied it: a thin spot amidst the trail. Not enough for a human to perceive, but for creatures of their size, the Gyrmkin could spot a thin spread of salt with ease. Barking quickly to his last two younglings, one with great floppy ears and the other with a longer snout, he nodded towards the thin spot and gave the hand signals for them to approach the salt and to clear a path.

Long-snout, leaning heavily on a sharpened butter knife, gave him a glare and growled his refusal. Using his hands, he said that he wasn't about to get burned for the likes of anyone in this band. Floppy-ears sulked behind Long-snout, holding a metal nutcracker as his implement of war in his long arms.

The leader quickly turned on Long-snout, leaping upon him with a savage cry, instigating a melee of vicious biting and scratching of each other. One-eye watched impassively, moving forward to try and get into a good position should he need to help his leader. Floppy-ears skulked up behind the brawling duo and slung his nutcracker into the mix, slipping the crushing metal around the throat of one of the Grymkin and squeezing, just enough to offer a threat.

Long-snout, breathing heavily and sweating now that iron was pressed against his patchy fur lined neck, winced as the leader took an extra moment to break one of his long fingers as punishment for this little rebellion. Standing up and spitting down onto the prone form of Long-snout, the leader pointed toward the circle of salt with a wavering finger, growling low in his throat a warning that promised far more dire consequences should it not be followed.

Long-snout, sniffling, got up from the dusty floor before giving Floppy-ears an evil glare. Together, the two moved out into the room to deal with the thin spot in the salt, both taking deep gulps of air before approaching, to try and not breathe in the painful mineral. The light in the room began to flicker as the agonized squeaks of the young Grymkin echoed throughout the room, until finally the flame was extinguished.

A dull thud followed by the scampering of paws on bare board was the only warning that the youngling was now down from the dresser, running across the room with the empty skein in his tail, charred black skin crackling away to reveal corded muscle, and bubbling streams of melted fat dribbling from between the jagged fault lines in the creatures skin. Portions of the face and neck were burned in the fashion, and he whimpered as he drew closer to the leader.

The leader walked up to the burnt youngling, sniffing along his body carefully. The scent of burnt flesh and blessed smoke sat heavily on the burnt one's fur. Burnt-skin whimpered when the leader's long tongue licked at the wound; the larger Gyrmkin obviously enjoying the taste of the dribbling fat, or perhaps just the flavor of one of his own in pain. Either way, the foul creature snatched the skein from Burnt-flesh, tucking the leather bound gourd into a ragged belt wrapped around his waist.

One-eye sucked in a breath, catching the leader's attention; the older creature was pointing up at the crib, where the child rested. His long finger pointed out the silver cross poking out from beneath the pillow, a glimmer of shining metal in the darkened room. The leader hissed, shoving Burnt-flesh away, kicking at his bent tail as he marched closer to Floppy-ears and Long-snout to see how they were handling the weak link in the ring of salt.

The answer was not well. Already Long-snout, with his bruised neck and finger bent at an odd angle, was working slowly at scooting the salt away with his knife, pressing forward with held breath as he kicked up miniscule granules of the harmful mineral. Floppy-ears used his longer reach and a rag from his belt to wipe away at the area Long-snout cleared, cleaning it of any residue that might burn their paws when they crossed over.

Seeing that the path was half way forged, the leader moved up and hopped over the remainder of the ring, holding his breath so as not to burn his lungs, and then proceeded towards one of the wooden legs of the crib. Slinging his own tool over his shoulder, the leader clambered up the wooden leg, long nails scraping into the lacquer for purchase as the Gyrmkin ascended toward the infant. Climbing over the lip of the barred wall, the leader stood over the child watching it sleep the sleep of the innocent, before hopping down onto the soft goose-down pillowing. Moving closer to the child, the leader ran a lone claw along the child's foot, causing it to whimper and pull back. But the leader's eyes weren't on the child.

They were on the cross.

Sniffing the air, he could smell the scent of silver heavy in the air, along with the sweat and grime of the unbaptized child. Smiling viciously, he turned to look through the bars and whistled to the others, motioning for them to climb as he had. Turning back to the silver cross, he pulled out the water skin from his belt and walked towards the head of the bed. Looking with a sinister eye, the leader grabbed the edge of the silver, using the water skin as a glove, and pulled it out from beneath the pillow slowly until the full cross was out for all to see. Dragging it to the edge of the bed, the leader used his tail to buffet it over the edge, wincing at both the loud clattering noise it made as it struck the wood and the burns that had swelled up on his bulbous tail from where he'd touched the holy icon.

Looking behind him, he saw his band of merry misfits gathered near the head of the child, their watery eyes all peering at him, waiting. He moved into position between One-eye and Burnt-flesh, holding his claw over the child's chest. The Gyrmkins, their long fingertips overlapping, slowly but surely pulled the child's soul from its body, dividing the energy between them all. Burnt-flesh's scorched wounds quickly began to ripple and stretch over each other, the skin and fur slowly devouring the scarred flesh until nothing but smooth pink remained. Long-snout's finger popped back into place with a tiny crackle. One-eye's missing orb slowly filled in; an iris growing from the quickly ballooning white orb. Even the leader, with his numerous scars and wounds from battles past, smiled as his body grew young and whole again.

This continued on until finally, the child's chest stopped rising and falling, the life ebbing from its fragile form. And with the stealth that the Gyrmkin had used to enter the room, the newly regenerated squad of rat-like creatures clambered down the crib and spirited away, sniggering with one another as they felt the renewed energy of youth pulsing through their emaciated frames.

48. THEODORE BY WILLIAM HOLDEN

A chill crept down Justin's spine as he turned off the bathroom light and made his way down the hallway. It had been four years since he had slept in his parent's home, four years of living alone on campus, yet as he walked into his old bedroom, the fears from his childhood lurked in every darkened corner, as if they had been waiting for him to come home.

He turned off the overhead light, undressed down to his boxers then slipped under the covers. He looked out across the room and noticed that the moon was peeking out through the clouds. The moon's radiance filtered through the window and chased away some of the shadowy corners. He smiled, thankful that the light would keep the creatures of the night from coming out from their hiding places while he slept. He pulled the covers up over his shoulders and snuggled his head against the pillow. The moon's shimmering light began to fade as it played an insidious game of peek-a-boo through the clouds. Justin, all too familiar with what came out once the light died, closed his eyes to the dimming light, and prayed that he would be asleep before his room became an eternal black hole.

The hardwood floor in the hallway creaked bringing Justin out of sleep. He opened his eyes. The moon was buried in the clouds, yet his room had not fallen into complete darkness. The floor creaked again, it sounded closer, more distinct. He peered over the covers. A cold chill crept down his spine as he noticed the hallway light shining in from underneath the door.

Didn't you turn the light off? his mind questioned. It responded with a terrifying, *yes.*

"Mom? Dad?" he called out knowing all too well that his parents would not be back until morning. As his voice faded away, another sound broke through the silence of the house – footsteps, and they were getting closer. The footsteps stopped. A shadow swayed against the light that drifted under the door. Justin's heart raced in his chest. The drumming in his ears was deafening. "Hello?" His voice trembled with fear. He tried to reason with himself as he waited for a response, but the childhood terrors would not give in. They gripped his heart and seized his breath until he thought they would suffocate him. Panic exploded in his fractured mind, as two gentle knocks came to the door.

His mind returned to the nights as a child when his mom would rap on the door, a secret, unspoken signal to let him know that she was there. After a moment, she would open the door, smile at him, and tell him that the monsters were gone for the night. He waited to hear those reassuring words. The doorknob turned. The lock disengaged, and yet his mother's comforting words never came. He pulled the covers over his head to hide himself from the unwelcomed visitor. The light in the hallway flickered out. He lay in complete darkness as the door creaked open.

A nervous sweat broke out across Justin's body. The smell mingled with the growing heat under the covers. His body's odor stung his nose. He held his breath as he listened to the footsteps moving closer. They stopped at the foot of his bed. He waited in the unending silence for its next move.

The floorboards groaned, yet there were no footsteps. A breeze passed over his bed causing his sheets to ripple over him. Justin tried to look through the thickness of the covers, hoping for any sign of what was happening in his room. It was then that he felt something cold, something with form or mass hovering over his bed. A soft, wispy sigh permeated the silence. He listened more carefully. Silence fell around him. He knew he could no longer trust if the sounds he was hearing were an instrument of his imagination, or something much more sinister.

He continued to stare into the sheets knowing that something was on the other side. He felt it watching him, lingering just above his covered body. Fear gripped his chest like a block of ice. It burned and ached bringing tears to his eyes. He knew he could not hold out much longer. He needed to breathe fresh, cool air. He needed to get out of his room, but in order to do that he would have to face what was on the other side. He gathered a fist full of the dampened sheets. He took a deep breath. He said a silent prayer and with a sudden movement, he pulled the sheets from over his head.

Justin screamed as he sat up in his bed hoping his sudden movement and loud voice would chase away the intruder. He let out a nervous laugh as the scream lingered in his throat. He put his hand to his mouth to stifle another scream as he peered over the edge of the bed. There were no shadows moving about or boogeyman waiting in the darkness. He looked out across the room. The door was shut. The hallway light extinguished. He fell back into the bed. A deep, heavy sigh tumbled from his lips. As he shifted in the bed, he felt something brush against the inside of his thigh. A moment of fear rushed through his body. He peered under the sheets. His childhood teddy bear was lying between his legs.

"Theodore?" he questioned as he pulled it from underneath the covers. "I thought mom got rid of you when I went to college?" The bear stared back at him with its dead plastic eyes. He kissed its cool nose then wrapped his arms around the bear as he curled into a fetal position. He closed his eyes to the shadows knowing that Theodore would be standing guard. As he began to drift off to sleep, he felt something tug at the bear's paw as a breathy voice whispered, "Mine."

49. THE PROTÉGÉ by Arran McDermott

"I know who you are."

Samuel looked at the boy (he was probably actually in his early twenties, but everyone under the age of forty looked like a kid to him) with confusion. He had never seen this grubby, greasy-haired individual before in his life and had no idea what he was doing on his doorstep now.

"Excuse me?"

"I said I know who you are, Dr. Samuel Wentworth. I know all about what you did. You're the Springfield Ripper."

"I have no idea what you're talking about. You must have the wrong house."

Samuel started to close the door, but the stranger stuck his foot in the way.

"Please remove your foot," he said, his voice calm, "or I shall call the police."

"Call them," the boy replied, smiling. "Then I can tell them where the bodies are. The ones they never found."

The boy stared at him, unblinking. Samuel sighed. "Come inside."

The unexpected visitor walked in without hesitation. Samuel waved at a couch in the living room and the young man sat down. Samuel sat in a chair facing him. There was silence for a moment as the guest looked around the room, taking in the large bookcase overflowing with shelves, the expensive looking paintings and sculptures and the lack of a television. He picked up an expensive paperweight on the coffee table and studied it for a moment before putting it down.

"Nice place," he said.

"Who are you?" asked Samuel. "You know me, so it's only fair I know your name."

"I'm Jeff." He offered his hand, but Samuel ignored it.

"How did you find me?"

Jeff leaned forward and clasped his hands together.

"Wasn't that hard, actually. I like to read up on old serial killings. I find that shit fascinating. I know the police interviewed you as a potential suspect back in '07 – one of many. You were present at or near the scene of the last few Ripper killings, had a detailed knowledge of anatomy and you had no alibi. But then a few days later

they found that sap Gregson with a bullet in his brain and a note saying
he was sorry for what he'd done. DNA evidence in his flat tying him
to several of the victims. Everything wrapped up in a neat little bow.
Too perfect, if you ask me."

Samuel rubbed his chin, thoughtfully.

"I'm sorry, I don't quite follow. Are you saying I killed Gregson
and framed him for the murders I committed?"

"That's exactly what I'm saying."

"And you have proof of this, or is it just a hunch?"

"Well, let's just say I know the right people. I have enough
evidence to make things very uncomfortable for you. Phone records
that tie you to Gregson. CCTV footage that shows you leaving his flat
the day before his body was found. Stuff that nobody ever bothered to
look for because they thought the killer was already dead."

"What about these other bodies you claim to know about?"

Jeff look ashamed. "That part I lied about. Sorry. I had to get in the
door so you'd listen."

"I see. And what do you want from me? Money?"

Jeff laughed – a high-pitched, grating sound. "Hell no. I don't give
a shit about money. What I want is your time."

"My . . . time?"

"I want to learn from you. I want you to teach me how to do what
you do."

Now it was Samuel's turn to laugh. "You're either joking, or
insane."

"None of the above."

Samuel stood up. "I need a drink. You want something?"

"Just water."

Samuel poured water into two glasses while Jeff watched him like
a hawk. He handed the younger man a glass but he just stared at it until
Samuel drank from his own. Jeff took a tiny sip and smiled.

"So you want to be a serial killer?" Samuel asked him.

"All my life. I've practiced on some animals, but I want to move
on to the next level. I need guidance."

"Why do you want to do this? There must be some reason."

"I want to be someone. I want to make people fear me."

"Then why don't you just buy a gun and take it somewhere with
lots of people? That seems to be the thing kids like to do these days."

"Fuck that shit. There's no art in shooting a whole bunch of
people. Anyone can do that. I wanna be like one of the greats – Jack

the Ripper, Gacy, Lecter. I wanna bring back the old school stalking and slashing. Everyone wants the quick fix now. The terrorist bombing, the mass killing. Where's the heart?"

"Well, you're a determined young man and I wish you luck."

Samuel stood up and offered his hand.

"That's it? You're not gonna help me?"

"I believe we're done here."

Jeff stood, his face twisted in anger and disbelief.

"You're a coward. I expected better of you. You were my hero, man!"

Samuel turned away.

"Don't turn your back on me!" Jeff roared.

Samuel removed something from a desk drawer and then turned back. It was a slim black object with prongs.

"What is that?"

Samuel fired the tazer. Jeff's body convulsed and he fell on the floor. His crotch darkened and spit flew from his mouth.

"A word of advice," Samuel said. "Never trust your heroes."

He set to work.

***

Jeff awoke to find himself naked and strapped to a table in what appeared to be the basement. His mouth was gagged and there was an IV drip in one arm. Samuel stood beside him.

"Welcome back. I'll begin my work in a moment. I wanted to make sure you were fully awake so you could appreciate it. But first, let me clear up a little misconception."

Samuel leant over him. There was a scalpel in his gloved hand. Jeff tried to shout 'Let me go!' but all that came out were grunts. Sweat poured down his face.

"You were right about me being at the scene of the last few Ripper murders, but you reached the wrong conclusion. I wasn't the killer. I was tracking Gregson. Hunting him, if you will. I found his cell phone number from a victim who got away. She was too scared to talk to the police but I convinced her I could help. I called him a few times, as you know, but it was to scare him off. He wouldn't listen. I had figured out his pattern, yet he always managed to stay one step ahead of me. I would arrive just after he had fled the crime scene. But on the night of one murder, the last murder, I got lucky. I tailed him back to his apartment and waited till he fell asleep. I broke in and he woke up to find me sitting on his bed with a gun pointed at him. I told him that if didn't grab a pen and paper and write down exactly what I told him, I would kill him right there. Do you know, the son of a bitch actually smiled? He wrote down his confession without any prompting from me. He wanted to be caught."

Samuel paused, rubbing a hand over Jeff's torso as if testing the firmness of a cut of meat.

"I saw his glee at becoming the next celebrity killer and all the attention that came with it and I knew what I had to do. I put a bullet in his head and left the gun in his hand. I removed all evidence I had been there. I half-expected the police to track me down anyway, but they never did. I realized I had found my calling in life. Hunting the most dangerous prey of all. Usually I have to work hard to find psychopaths that are worthy of my attention. What a pleasant surprise it is to have one actually come to me."

Samuel pressed the scalpel to the right side of Jeff's abdomen, over McBurney's point. The boy screamed behind the gag.

"This will hurt quite a bit, I'm afraid. But the upside is that you will most definitely be cured of your anti-social tendencies when this is over. Oh, I'm sorry, did you want to say something before I begin?"

Jeff nodded frantically. Samuel lowered the gag.

"Stop, you crazy fuck!" the boy shouted with all his might. "I was just joking. I don't want to be a killer. Please. Stop." Tears ran down his cheeks.

"I'm afraid it's too late for that. Now please be still. I don't want to sever an artery by mistake."

He replaced the gag and went back to work. He hand moved fast. The scalpel cut deep and clean. Once the incision was made, Samuel reached in and carefully peeled back the layers of the abdominal wall. His fingers broke through the membrane and found the base of the appendix. He worked to remove it with precision from the cecum. By now not even the gag could drown out the screams of the writhing man below him. Luckily the room was quite well soundproofed. He carved out the bloody mass and dropped it in a metal dish. He lifted it up so his reluctant patient could see it.

"Beautiful, isn't it? I shall focus on your non-essential organs to begin with. Don't worry, I have a generous supply of your blood type available to replace what you lose. We shall be here for some time."

Samuel removed the kidneys, pancreas, intestine and part of the liver, putting each organ aside carefully. The patient lapsed in and out of consciousness during this time, but Samuel continued to monitor his life signs. It was over five hours after his initial incision before he finally called it a day.

50. THE CHANGE BY R.L. UGOLINI

Wanda married Albert Fenske for his health insurance. Albert married Wanda Pugh for her breasts. Theirs was not a love match.

All her life, Wanda had felt destined for something greater than what she always got. The feeling ate away at her like a hunger for something never tasted. In her youth, the idea excited her, but at fifty-three, it only made her want a nap. Whatever the missing something was, she'd given up looking.

And then she found Albert.

Albert was a pack rat with a pot belly and wide feet. When he ate, his mouth opened so wide under that wiry soup-strainer of his, he reminded Wanda of a baleen whale trolling for krill. At times, sitting across from him at their cluttered kitchen table and watching him eat his eggs she feared being sucked into his gaping maw. Other times, the idea intrigued, no, titillated her. Call her Ishmael – she was just that kind of girl. One who could, she prided herself, overlook quite a lot – his cathode ray tube collection, his Star Trek memorabilia, and those damn meteorites he kept all over the house and never let her touch. Some things, however, were beyond what she felt she needed to put up with.

***

Albert felt the same about her.

"Have I ever told you about how in the '50s, the government started secretly adding atropine to chicken feed?"

In fact, Wanda did know. She knew Albert was an old gas bag with a fondness for the rattle and smack of his own phlegm-thickened voice. He was also a genuine-article conspiracy theorist.

Wanda rolled her eyes. "Stressed-out chickens. You've told me a million times, Albert."

"That's right. Stress can do funny things. Those cages got the birds packed in so tight, all they can move are their heads. So they peck at the bars until their skulls crack open."

"I'm trying to eat here, Albert."

"And in the next cage and the next and the next, there's yet another hen, crammed into its cage that's been doing the same damn thing. But then it starts doing something different. You know what that is, Wanda?"

Wanda knew there was no stopping him once he got going. "It

starts eating its neighbor's brains through the bars of the cage."

"Two points to you, wife. It's a feeding frenzy in there. At the end of the day, if you want more than a warehouse full of shit and feathers, you got to calm them down. Thus, the atropine."

Albert set down his fork and reached idly for the emptied out margarine tub he used to contain a half dozen or so walnut-sized ironites. His fingers stirred the collection until he found Pip. The heavy little nodule – worn smooth and kept rust-free by frequent handling – was one of his favorites.

In fact, it was second only to the one he called the Jammer. That one, weighing in at six pounds four ounces, was the shape and size of a walrus dong. Albert kept *that one* on his nightstand. Just for show, of course. He didn't truck with toys in the bedroom. Took away from the more animal pleasures. And besides, something about meteorites and women didn't sit right with him. He supposed it hearkened back to his and every other red-blooded American boy's childhood belief in girl-cooties. Elementary, perhaps, but where there's smoke... Women had all those *hormones*. NASA knew this – that's why they delayed so long before giving Sally a ride on the shuttle, making her the first woman in outer fucking space. True, the Soviets claimed this "first" years earlier, but Albert had never been convinced that *that* little Ruskie hadn't smuggled a Y chromosome into low-orbit.

"But, see," he continued, rolling Pip between his fingers, "you do that and atropine starts showing up in the eggs, Wanda. And then breakfast is no longer such a rise and shine affair, is it? More and more, ignorant working stiffs start reaching for a second and a third cup o' joe just to make it through the day. And that's when, instead of regulating the chemicals going into the feed in the first place, the good ol' boys at the FDA struck a nefarious bargain with the South American coffee growers. Our own government convinced Juan Valdez down there that it was to their benefit to subsidize the American pharmaceutical companies, bringing down the price of Buffalo wings for the average American – good for us – while at the same time, driving the cost of beans through the roof – good for them. And *that*, Wanda, is why Colombia and Bolivia now have the controlling interest in the United States poultry industry."

***

"Oh, for God's sake."

All that lip-wagging only served to remind Wanda that he was still there. He was extremely hard to ignore. As was her growling stomach.

264

After Albert's verbal diarrhea du jour, however, the eggs she'd prepared were out of the question. Instead, she flipped through her outstanding orders for nursery stock.

After Albert left for work, she'd prepare cuttings of *Fusspot, Mini-Me*, and *Blush* to ship FedEx and then maybe head to the mall. Wanda ran her own mail-order business, selling rare African Violets throughout the tri-state area. And as the sole owner and employee of *Saintpaulias Stock and Supply*, Wanda knew there were times to reap and times to sow. Considering the scrambled eggs now cold and curdled on her plate, she also knew there were times to Cinnabon. Being her own boss almost made up for the lack of a company health plan.

"Speaking of which," Albert said, yawning as he tossed Pip back in the tub, "is there any more coffee?"

***

He couldn't stand Wanda's snot-clotted, atropine-laced huevos bland-cheros. But his ulcer, chronic over their three-year Jerry Springer *Prime Time Special* of a marriage, had become a constant companion and welcome distraction from Wanda's increasingly moody presence. He'd never been a gourmand. At least, not the culinary kind.

Wanda was hell-bitch prickly, but damn, if she wasn't finger-licking good. When she wasn't griping about something else he'd done, which wasn't often, Albert couldn't keep his hands off her. Her attitude only bothered him when he was sober. After a couple beers, Albert imagined he could see Wanda's gentle side show through. But only when she didn't know he was watching her.

He watched her all the time.

***

"Would you stop staring at me – I feel like an animal in a zoo." Like one of those shit-hucking monkeys. Not that he had driven her to that. Yet.

Wanda thought Albert needed a hobby. One that didn't involve flea markets or Sci-Fi conventions, anyway. And she needed her space. She hated the heavy feeling of his constant attention. She hated how his peppery scent lingered in a room long after he'd left. She hated his masculine bulk and she hated listening to him breathe. But what Wanda hated most about Albert was that he was the best fuck she'd ever had.

So when Albert didn't come home with the usual Friday dinner of a bucket of extra crispy KFC and a bottle of four-dollar wine, at first

Wanda was ambivalent, then annoyed, and then, as usual, hungry, horny, and sober. Albert, dog that he was, disappeared like this on occasion. But he always dragged his mangy hide home, sniffing her out like she was an open can of oil-packed tuna that had sat out too long.

***

Albert couldn't get enough of the way Wanda smelled.

She wasn't like any other woman he'd ever known – and she didn't smell like any of them either. He figured it had to do with her selling those overpriced leaf cuttings to dowdy housewives and emasculated husbands. Or, at least, that was how Albert saw her business model. Plants you couldn't eat or smoke had no reason for being. In fact, Albert suspected many of the hybrids Wanda sold originated as offshoots of a black op genetic cloning initiative funded by the Reagan administration. One of the varieties was even named "Jelly Bean." The proof was right there, in plain sight, growing in racks on his back porch. But Wanda remained skeptical, if not openly mocking, of the evidence. His insistence seemed to only drive her to work harder. And her work, such that it was, left her sweaty and covered in dirt.

Beads of moisture pooled between her breasts, marinating her flesh in salt. The residue, when dry, gave her cleavage the pungent scent of cheese popcorn. Fertile, fungal soil caked her fingernails and hinted at wild things, beastly and feral. But the smell of her wanting him was the crème de la crème. He went to work with her dried, musky essence crusted in his love-stache, and breathed deeply all day, whetting his appetite for more.

And so, Albert was somewhat surprised to have completely forgotten about Wanda during the entire three and a half minutes he was giving it to Goldie Rasmussen in the ShopCo break room.

Goldie was a pudding-faced flat-chested junior college sophomore. The ambitious B-cups of her dingy padded bra caved in on her insufficient breasts, but Albert overlooked her shortcomings by bending her over a chair. He was a problem solver and a man who could see any cup as half-full. The commercial break was just long enough to finish his business and tuck himself back in his ShopKo slacks without missing a single bit of *The O'Reilly Factor*.

Albert checked his watch – he had nine minutes left on his break. He slumped onto the vinyl couch to catch the rest of the show, but out of the corner of his eye he watched Goldie, hoping she'd go back to her register.

But then, there she was, in front of him, blocking his view. Her grungy fingers held out the larger half of a deli sub she'd swiped from the communal fridge. "I think it's, like, salami, which isn't my favorite, but it's got, like, other stuff in it? Tomato, some kind of cheese. Onion. Lettuce. Lettuce is good. Do you, like, want to split this with me?"

Geoff Putzer had written his name and "This is not your sandwich! This means YOU!" on the wax paper wrapper. Which just about begged anyone other than the "Putz" to eat it. Albert slid over and patted the cushion beside him. "Step into my office. Let's see how good that lettuce is. Did I ever tell you about how iridium from meteorites is in all the fresh produce we eat?"

"Iridi-what?"

"Or how César Chavez really died of cancer after being exposed to iridium isotope dust kicked up by his fellow migratory workers?"

"Chad, my, like, cousin, saw him box in Vegas one time."

Albert prayed to the prostate gods that he would not piss his pants with excitement. Young as she was, Goldie had been around the block a time or two. But her mind was a blank slate – completely untouched, and his for the taking.

"Have I got a story for you, Goldie-girl." As he ate, he considered the irony, or whatever you'd call it, that fat girls had the best breasts. Case in point, Wanda. That woman had more rolls than a bakery. Goldie, on the other hand, was almost scrawny. And flat as a knotty two-by-four.

And yet, he liked her.

Goldie was a good kid. Friendly. She always seemed interested in learning from his experience, too. Unlike that shrew at home. And a man liked to feel appreciated.

***

Around eleven-thirty that evening, Wanda drove west on Rural Route 12, heading for town. She had the windows of the pickup rolled down, and every few miles, she tossed a Star Trek action figure into the drainage ditch running parallel to the road. By the time the glow of the main drag flooded the cab with light, the only remaining member of the away team was Mr. Spock. Wanda hefted him high over the chain link fence surrounding the county fairgrounds and wondered, briefly, how logical he'd find 400-pound pumpkins and floppy-eared rabbits.

She steered Albert's hand-me down pick 'em up truck through the

Taco Bell drive-thru and then to the Dairy Queen next door, blowing her last twenty on a dollar menu free for all. Salty then sweet, wash, rinse, repeat. She finished all but one burrito on the way home, took a handful of Bean-O and a Lactaid, and went to bed gut-busting full but still hungry.

***

Monday morning, Wanda stood barefoot in the chilly kitchen dressed only in Albert's favorite Star Wars T-shirt, black with yellow lettering reading "Look at the *size* of that thing!" A frozen waffle had jammed in the toaster and she was in the process of prying it loose when Albert traipsed in, smelling like lunchmeat gone bad.

"It's about time you showed up. One more day and I'd have given you up for dead. I suppose you'll be wanting breakfast." She didn't want to know where he'd been. And she didn't want an apology. She was aiming for a fight. The ol' grudgefuck was even better than make up sex.

But instead of reaching for her, her rat-fink husband held out a manila envelope, marked with several greasy finger prints. Inside, Wanda found a stack of neatly bound legal documents from the office of Schneidelman & Cox suing for a no-fault dissolution of marriage.

That stupid, stupid man.

Divorce papers, effectively ending her blue-collar fairy tale of a double-wide dream home, a husband hung like a porn star, and in-network $20 copays.

Her life, such as it was, was over.

At first, she hadn't even realized.

***

Screw the five or seven or however many stages of grief Oprah and her minions went on about. Only one of them seemed to matter to Wanda, and that was anger. Or to put it more precisely, outrage. She always thought that if anyone were going to do the leaving, it would be her waving sayonara to his sorry ass, not the other way around. How dare he. He obviously didn't realize just how good he had it.

But now, everything would change. They were upside down on the mobile home, behind on car payments, and maxed out on their credit cards. Thoughts of bankruptcy ate away at her already clouded mind.

She couldn't think. She'd been having trouble focusing since Albert left. Something was wrong. Something big – Lyme Disease big. Hanta Virus big. Black Death big. Wanda wondered if Albert had gone and given her a venereal disease as the ultimate parting gift – thank you for playing. And yet she didn't have the cash or the credit to get herself checked out – ShopKo had already dropped her from Albert's medical plan.

She'd have to go on COBRA, if that were even possible, because right now, she was dealing with some fairly serious pre-existing conditions.

To start with, she had an overwhelming and unexplainable paranoia about chickens, but this may have only been the stress, which was making her hair fall out. No matter how she brushed or teased, angry pink patches of scalp caught the light and winked at her in the bathroom mirror. Meanwhile, her complexion had turned the waxy yellow-green color of a fresh bruise.

And she was bloated. Her arms and legs bent with difficulty and her fingers had swollen until they resembled uncooked bratwurst. She was a fat, balding, senile old broad. It was enough to make her cry, but her tears had dried up days ago. Her eyes were so swollen and crusty it hurt to blink.

But even all that wasn't the worst of her problems.

Despite everything – despite her marriage death roll, despite her Chapter 11 cliffhanger, and even despite the mutiny her body and mind were waging with one another – Wanda was still hungry, horny, and sober.

And not for lack of trying.

Migraines as relentless and hulking as her ex-husband had settled in right behind her eyes. The constant throbbing, drilling, vise-like pain kept her awake, and she found herself up at 3 a.m., watching plastic ladies on the shopping channel sell tanzanite baubles. The flickering light of the TV soothed her as she mindlessly ate and drank her way through the remains of the fridge, only for everything to come back up again in multi-colored half-digested chunks. The shag carpeting down the hall to the bathroom alternately squished and crunched underfoot from interrupted trips to the latrine.

Her jaws ached from all that chewing and her throat weeped blood and puss from stomach acid burns. When the high-gloss television spokeswomen transitioned from jewelry to hair care products, Wanda dialed the toll-free number on the screen. But her tongue had swollen in her mouth, making the words "follicle stimulator" impossible. Despite her vomit-enforced sobriety, her speech came out slurred. The operator had been polite and determined to make a sale, but after several failed attempts to understand what Wanda was saying, blamed a bad connection and asked her to call back on another line.

Sitting alone in her darkened living room, sweating into the velvet plush of her La-Z-Boy, she shifted her attention from the products on display to the women selling them. Some focus group must have been at work. Not one woman was under forty-five – and most had to have been well into their fifties. Women of a certain age. Professional, informed, savvy. But women, by mere chance being born female, had expiration dates, and all these bottle-tanned, derma-peeled, lip-waxing women were past theirs. If life were a journey, these travelers had long since shambled off the main road to decompose quietly in the underbrush. She wondered if they'd come across Kirk or Bones. A thought came to Wanda and she began to count back.

Counting anything lately was difficult enough. But remembering the last time she'd been on the rag was more than she could manage. She couldn't do it. It'd been too long. Her tears weren't the only thing that had dried up. Wanda recognized a new stage of grief – depression – as she became convinced of the reason behind her health problems. She didn't have the plague after all. No, it was worse than that. She was becoming one of those rotting women.

She was going through The Change.

***

When Albert didn't come back for his shit, Wanda sold it on Ebay, starting with those inexplicable tubes of glass – his cathode ray collection. Who knew garbage could be so valuable? Proved the old saying about one woman's trash being some idiot's treasure. She might be a dragon with hot flashes, but she was squatting in a trailer park lair of old fool's gold. Just the one from what turned out to be a 1954 black and white General Electric cabinet television brought in a serious wad of modern-day cash. More than enough to get the works at the La Petit Beau Monde salon in the mall – especially now that Wanda had stopped buying booze and fast food. She couldn't remember the last time she'd eaten much of anything. In fact, the way Wanda did the math, she'd lost 287 pounds – that 245 of them had belonged to Albert was beside the point. *She* was down three dress sizes.

And her hair looked fabulous – she'd purchased it off a rack and had the extensions woven into what little of her own she had left, which grew from her scalp in tufts like chicken down. But no one needed to know that. She was a redhead now.

She'd baked the jaundiced look out of her skin in one extra long session in a tanning bed, and now instead of looking like death

270

warmed over, she was golden brown and delicious. A mani-pedi took care of her nails – they'd taken on a crazy-long hermit-in-the-woods appearance lately – and makeup smoothed out the new crepe paper wrinkles in her cheeks.

After the salon, Wanda shopped the sale racks at Macy's, finally deciding on a leopard print sundress and a pair of black stiletto sling backs, and told the salesgirl she'd like to wear the clothes out of the store. She left her old T-shirt, jeans and sneakers in the changing room.

The dress fit perfectly as long as she kept her bat wings at her sides but the shoes were too tight – she had both wide and long feet and a half size larger would have fit two times better. But at 70% off, the price was right, so Wanda had jammed her toes into the straining leather and decided to make the best of it.

Feeling like a new woman, she took herself down the length of the mall in what she preferred to think of as a carefree window-shopping pace, but was really a slow, aching shamble that had surprisingly nothing to do with her feet. The deep tissue massage she'd had after the mud bath and mineral water rinse hadn't eased the soreness in her muscles. Rather, it may have caused more harm than good – Wanda was almost sure she could still see indentations in her calves from where the girl's forceful fingers had kneaded and squeezed. And her left leg was strangely numb without the pins and needles assurance that it was just asleep.

She hobbled past the food court with the Cinnabon to a bench midway down the concourse. From there, she could trawl the Abercrombie & Fitch clientele for emo-addled 20-somethings with more testosterone than they knew what to do with, but not so much that she couldn't help them out. Wanda needed sex.

Which was much easier said than done. Willing partner aside, her hoo-ha was as dry as Great-grandma's Thanksgiving turkey. But that was a minor detail. On her way to the mall, she'd stopped at Ritz Pharmacy and bought out the entire shelf of personal lubricants. She was good to go.

She waited until she thought no one was looking and then scooped up her useless left leg, settling it across her right and tucking under the excess skin that pooled around her thighs.

The mall was just starting to get busy. With each moment, the crowd seemed to grow, but few, if any, of the passersby were men.

Next door to Abercrombie & Fitch, single 40-somethings popped into the Pottery Barn Kids to buy baby shower gifts. Years ago, Wanda had been one of them, paying ridiculous amounts of money for wooden alphabet blocks in the hope that by doing so the karmic universe would allow her own biological clock to keep ticking a little while longer.

But then, she met Albert. That gene pool, thankfully, had dried up years before she met him. Or rather, Albert had gotten himself snipped, saying something about the government employing female agents to procure DNA specimens for a global genetic database. Whatever his crackpot reason, she couldn't say she was disappointed. However, there was, as she was discovering, a big difference in not particularly wanting kids and not being able to have them at all.

Of course, this wasn't a concern for everyone out shopping that morning. Wanda suspected that the harried young mothers she watched walk by might have welcomed The Change – any change. They pushed tandem-strollers with screaming infants and squirming preschoolers past both Pottery Barn Kids and Abercrombie & Fitch, their tired, nervous gazes darting across the way to Pea in a Pod Maternity Wear.

Meanwhile, way down at the Cinnabon, a bouncy, giggling swarm of preteen girls formed and reformed as they wove through crowds of slower shoppers. Usually, 'tweens were only that excited when there were boys in sight. Wanda craned her neck, feeling like the four bells' watch, high in the crows' nest, looking for flocks of seagulls to find schools of anchovies. Or Moby Dicks. Or whatever. She wasn't picky – she'd take almost anything. There were some exceptions, of course – she vetoed anyone who wasn't old enough to buy his own beer. Which, when she finally found the object of the girls' distraction, was the problem. That long-haired, skinny-jeans, lily-white creature couldn't have been more than fifteen. If he were even male. Wanda couldn't be sure.

While she waited for the tide, and her luck, to turn, she flipped open last month's *Cosmo*, but the words swam on the page. The storefronts dipped and swayed before her and suddenly lightheaded, Wanda reached out to steady herself, thankful she was seated. When the nausea passed, she gave up on *How to Hook 'Em* and instead, used the magazine to fan herself.

And then there he was. A golden man-child in a Chico State hoodie, faded plaid shorts and flip-flops. She caught his eye as he and his buddy, an unfortunate acne-scarred pear-shaped lead-eater, left the

Apple Store. As they walked toward her, Wanda smiled, congratulating herself for finding the perfect fishing hole. The shabby chic Adonis passed within three feet of her bench, his eyes never leaving her until he turned into Abercrombie & Fitch. As they entered, he asked his friend a question, which Wanda didn't hear. But she did catch part of the friend's reply – "...reeks. Like something vomited death."

Wanda sniffed. He was right. Something smelled foul. Like the fridge ever since the time she found that frothy green slick oozing from deli paper marked "lunch meat." She was glad to hear someone else had noticed it too. She'd been wondering if it were just her.

Wanda considered making some excuse to follow Chico State into the store, but couldn't find the energy to stand. Where did these people get so much stamina? And if she were to corner that college kid between racks of boxer shorts and distressed tees, what then? How would she ever relate to someone so much younger than she was? Yet, what choice did she have? Men her own age only seemed interested in women half of theirs. And men older than she was were dead.

As if to prove her point, over at the Pea in a Pod, a moon-faced coed guided some doddering old fart out of the store. She loaded her purchases into his arms and left him standing there, a clueless, potbellied boulder in a stream of shoppers.

***

To Albert, the mall was a giant midway of hucksters and confidence men. But in her own special pseudo-Pig Latin way of hers that passed for speech, Goldie had convinced him to go – and he went, if only so she'd stop talking about it. Silence, he'd learned, was one of the many perks of what he now thought of as the sweet release of death. "Like, I need those jeans – you know, the ones that, like, stretch in front for when I get, like, fat and stuff. And, like, you should come with. We could like, hang out together."

Albert had learned "together" included not only him but also all his so-called buddies – Hamilton, Jefferson, and Franklin. Apparently, the little twink fancied herself a gold-digger. This amused Albert more than the concept of manufacturer's mail-in warranty cards. Everyone knew those things were shipped off to minimum security prisons for low-cost data entry. The last thing he wanted to do was to inform soon-to-be-released convicts of his latest big screen TV purchase. Not that he could afford one.

Especially since he hadn't enjoyed the pleasure of folding money in weeks. The only thing getting him by these days was the Amex, the one piece of plastic Wanda had never known about. The credit limit was shit, but he figured it'd be good for another hundred or so before some assistant sales manager got crazy with scissors.

He watched Goldie scamper into Abercrombie & Fitch. Before she took off, she'd dumped her pregger pants with him and mumbled "flip-flops are, like, BOGO." He had no idea what that meant, but he was sure as hell not following her in to find out. The pansy-ass cologne wafting from the store was enough to emasculate a man. Fruity, was what it was.

Albert sucked in another breath of the thick mall air, trying to clear his lungs, but this time, he detected something beside the pretension of youth.

She was here.

Wanda.

He could smell her. Musky and fleshy and more woman than he'd remembered, and that said a lot.

Like a blue cheese set to age in a dark, moist cave, her scent had evolved to one so sharp, so bold, so reminiscent of faraway places people lied about having visited. Pungent with lustful regret and the militant, unwashed apathy of an Iron Curtain house frau. It reminded him of his time stationed in Stuttgart, three-day passes, and one mind-blowing ménage à trois. And of the stories, not necessarily true, he told of his liaisons there.

But he was almost right on her before he recognized his ex.

Wanda was a changed woman. She'd lost weight in all the right places, but by the look of her, there was still plenty to hang on to, and her breasts, offered up for display in a low V-cut neckline, were still the best he'd ever seen. And she'd become a redhead. He wondered if she was red everywhere.

She'd aged, he could see that. But she also looked better, if that were possible. Like older women he sometimes noticed – the ones who had all their shit together – and knew it, too. As if in his leaving her, Wanda had found something better. Something of her own. There was a confidence there that was new and exciting.

Still, one thing Albert could spot from a dozen paces was a woman on the prowl. The animal print of her dress and the intense tunnel vision in her eyes made him feel hunted – not in the sought-after way he was familiar with, but in an overpowering testicle-eating sort of way. He almost turned around. Almost. Because, in the end, he had never met a she-cat he couldn't get to purring.

Albert walked over and took a seat. "Have I ever told you how much you look like Nefer-titty?"

***

"The gazillion year old mummy?"

Albert rolled his shoulder in a half-shrug that Wanda had come to recognize as a gesture of mild surrender.

"Before the embalming. You look good, Wanda. A far sight better than you should, all things considered. Hot, even."

"You look like crap, Albert. Like a man who's been eating bat shit and calling it funnel cake."

"At least I can see what I'm eating. What's going on with your eyes? They're all cloudy."

"Your mere presence is getting me all tearful."

"I knew you missed me."

"Like a hole in the head."

"I wasn't going to say anything, Wanda, but it's hard not to stare."

"Stuff it, Albert."

"Glad to. What do you say we go check out the far back changing room in the Big & Tall? For old times' sake."

She wasn't that desperate. Yet.

What had she seen in him? "Your girlfriend doesn't look very pregnant."

"Nevertheless. She showed me the pee stick."

"You old fool."

"I know you know it's not mine. But Goldie doesn't know *anything*, poor kid. She doesn't have that much guile. She's a fifteen watt bulb, Wanda. Her master plan is focused entirely on how to get my money."

Wanda snorted and the sudden force of air rushing out of her nostrils ripped loose a piece of her septum, which fell into her lap. She flicked it onto the floor.

"And I also know you know how pointless that is," Albert said. "But Goldie? Well..."

"You thinking of raising it?" she asked.

"Hell, Wanda. Do I seem like a daddy to you?"

"Well, then?"

"Just loving the one I'm with. And by 'with,'" Albert said, leaning toward her, "I mean I'm keeping my options open, Wanda."

Since he'd sat down, Wanda hadn't seen another eligible young man. And, to be honest, the college kid hadn't been all that interested

275

or he'd have stopped to say 'hello.' No, the only man she'd managed to attract was her ex-husband. What had seemed like such fertile ground had turned into slim pickin's. With effort, Wanda rose from the bench. "It's time I go, Albert."

He scribbled a number on the back of small piece of paper and handed it to her. "Call me if you change your mind."

***

Wanda slumped into her La-Z-Boy, noticing, as she did so, how the exposed skin of her forearms left dusky shadows on the beige plush fabric. She turned on the television, and as she flipped through the channels, she idly swabbed her gums with her tongue, tasting blood. Not fresh, iron-rich, life-giving blood, but thick, coagulated ropes sloughing like fruit leather. She worked a piece between her teeth until she felt the suck of a molar pop loose. Pausing momentarily, Wanda tensed in anticipation of some sort of gag reflex and recalled a time when losing a tooth would have been cause for great concern. But all she felt now was resignation.

She swallowed the mouthful, tooth and all, and leaned over to remove her shoes. As she kicked off the left one, she heard a crinkling sound like old cellophane and when she looked, she noticed her little toe was missing. Or rather, the wrinkly gray Cheeto wasn't missing as much as it was simply not attached to her foot any longer. Wanda dumped the toe onto the shag carpet and slid the shoe back on. She no longer sweated the small stuff. In fact, she no longer sweated at all – one of the many perks, she supposed, of going through The Change. Other benefits included brand new shoes that happened to fit perfectly on a foot with only four toes. Just to prove her point, she reached down and, what the hell, snapped off the right pinkie toe, too. Congratulations were in order – these were obviously unnecessary appendages and she had just evolved past them. Still, she had half a mind to add calcium supplements to her grocery list.

That was if she had half a mind at all. Her mental confusion had worsened, but she'd found it took no thought at all to think like a man. Men were problem solvers. Albert certainly was one, anyhow. And Wanda had a problem that needed to be fixed.

She rummaged through her purse until she found the paper Albert had given her – a carbon copy Amex receipt from Pea in a Pod. She dialed her cell and braced herself for the inevitable smug drawl of a tomcat that had known all along he'd get the cream.

"Alright, fine," she said into the phone. "Just this once."

276

***

Albert sped down Rural Route 12, feeling like a one-man stampede to water. 'Once,' as Wanda had insisted, wasn't nearly enough, but it was a start. Albert knew exactly how to have his lady-cake and eat it too. A thing like this was not to be rushed. A starving man who ate too fast would find no satisfaction. And he had worked up one fucker of an appetite.

He and Goldie had spent spring break naked on the Rent-A-Center sofa bed in his studio apartment, absentmindedly diddling each other with sticky fingers and talking back to Judge Judy on the boob tube. But that had been weeks ago. Lately, the only bulge in his pants that got Goldie excited was his wallet.

On his way, Albert bought a box of Merlot and swung by KFC, but when he got to Wanda's, she ignored the peace offering. She greeted him at the door, reaching for his belt and pulling him inside. The living room was sour and moist and dark.

"What's with the flies?"

"They showed up...a while ago," Wanda said. "The violets...powdery mildew...crown rot. Lost all my stock. Must be from that."

A cloud of tiny gnats swarmed Wanda's head like electrons sputtering inside a degassed cathode ray tube. Their frenzy was mesmerizing – until Albert noticed the ants marching from the corner of her mouth to her ear canal.

The old broad was batshit insane.

Still... he'd done worse. Best just to get what he came for and get out. "Never liked the plants, anyway. Are we going to do this or what?"

That was the last thing he remembered saying. Wanda wasn't in a talking mood, and after suffering Goldie's non-stop chatter, he was grateful for the silence. And besides, in no time at all he couldn't have formed words if he'd tried. His tongue was too chalky – a dried up plowboy in the furrows of Wanda's Dust Bowl.

***

Wanda rolled out of bed and stood. Her left leg dangled freely from where her femur had popped loose from its ball joint. The full force of Albert's weight on her had strained the skin across her pelvis, creating tiny tears, like runs in pantyhose. She wondered if he'd noticed.

She looked at the man sleeping in her bed. His naked, hairy bulk lay like a yearling calf, dead from natural causes and bloating in the

277

sun. Except that his gut continued to rise and fall rhythmically as he dreamed, completely secure in his right to her bed.

There was a Shroud of Turin look to the sheets from where her skin had ground into the cotton weave. And around Albert, curly black hairs lay like hirsute fallout from a B-list horror-porn nuclear winter flick. He'd shed all over her brand new linens and left his salty sweat and peppery musk on the pillows.

But for once, his scent didn't repel her. Instead, it made her think, in some fuzzy, muddled way, of the savory wholesome satisfaction of eleven herbs and spices. She bent over him and sniffed his chest hair, then his Adam's apple, his brow ridge, and then her nose pushed through the fringe of his receding hairline.

He roused a little at this last bit. Once he woke up, he'd start talking and ruin everything. Or worse, he'd leave. The delicious, intoxicating scent...aroma...would be gone. Forever. For Wanda knew he would never come sniffing around her place again.

Her gaze fell on the Jammer. The smooth hard metal beckoned her. She reached across to his nightstand, careful not to bump him.

"Chickens, Wanda!"

Wanda wrenched her arm back and looked at Albert, fearing he'd caught her about to touch one of his precious meteorites. He'd have a fit when he discovered she'd done far worse than that – she'd sold every one of them but the Jammer.

But he'd just been talking in his sleep. Wanda knew he didn't have to be awake to shoot the shit. She leaned over again and grabbed the heavy nodule. Kneeling over Albert now, she hefted the meteorite, feeling the weight of it in her palm. But it was too much for her atrophied muscles and gravity, yes, *gravity*, she told herself, pulled the meteorite down in one forceful blow, leaving an impact crater in Albert's forehead. He grunted, twitched, and was still.

She'd killed him.

She'd killed the rat-fink bastard. She'd killed her husband. Ex-husband, rather. Not that he hadn't had it coming. She looked at the Jammer, now bloodied. Hadn't he always told her not to touch his damn meteorites? Perhaps this was destiny. Perhaps, this was *her* destiny.

Wanda sucked in a breath and felt a sudden rush of air. She lifted her free hand to her neck and felt a rip in the skin at her throat. Her lungs crackled and popped with the increased pressure. She couldn't remember the last time she took a breath.

But she felt good. Really good. As if she finally found her purpose. Perhaps it wasn't menopause at all. Perhaps, it was only a midlife crisis – men had them all the time. Albert had had three.

She strained to lift the Jammer again, guiding it to the same spot as before. Again and again she pounded until his skull cracked. Like peeling a hard-boiled egg, she picked bits of bone and hair from the bloody mess, chipping away at the ragged edge with further strikes, until finally, the shiny, kinky pink of her ex-husband's brain glistened before her.

"What do you know? You got one after all."

Wanda poked a boney finger into the braincase and threaded out a long strand of neo-cortex. The tissue was rubbery and resistant, like uncooked sausage. She'd heard that a typical brain was sixty percent fat. But considering how Albert had used his, she expected to find a mouth-watering amount of marbling. She crammed a handful in between her remaining teeth and bit down. Chewy. Succulent. She closed her eyes and concentrated on the gourmet sensuality of the experience. A smile cracked the thin, dry skin of her cheeks, separating her mandible from her skull. Blood ran down her throat, wetting the silty walls of her esophagus and gumming in crevices. It should itch, but it didn't.

He tasted delicious, in a gamey, road kill sort of way. Those secret nuggets, those gems of trivia and minutia Albert had cultured all those years had imparted a rich, exotic, almost erotic flavor that hit the spot like nothing else.

Her headache, constant these past weeks, had completely disappeared. In fact, she felt better than she had in years. Nothing ached, nothing pained. It was as if she had no sensation at all, except for a sudden insatiable hunger for her dear, departed ex-husband.

Wanda wondered about this sudden change of heart. She'd married Albert for his health insurance coverage, but that no longer seemed to matter. Perhaps, she really did care for him more than she realized – maybe, she even loved him for his mind.

Key was waiting for Hester when his new flat first began to sound like home. The couple upstairs had gone out for a while, and they'd remembered to turn their television off. He paced through his rooms in the welcome silence, floorboards creaking faintly underfoot, and as the kitchen door swung shut behind him, he recognised the sound. For the first time the flat seemed genuinely warm, not just with central heating. But he was in the midst of making coffee when he wondered which home the flat sounded like.

The doorbell rang, softly since he'd muffled the sounding bowl. He went back through the living-room, past the bookcases and shelves of records, and down the short hall to admit Hester. Her full lips brushed his cheek, her long eyelashes touched his eyelid like the promise of another kiss. "Sorry I'm late. Had to record the mayor," she murmured. "Are you about ready to roll?"

"I've just made coffee," he said, meaning yes.

"I'll get the tray."

"I can do it," he protested, immediately regretting his petulance. So this peevishness was what growing old was like. He felt both dismayed and amused by himself for snapping at Hester after she'd taken the trouble to come to his home to record him. "Take no notice of the old grouch," he muttered, and was rewarded with a touch of her long cool fingers on his lips.

He sat in the March sunlight that welled and clouded and welled again through the window, and reviewed the records he'd listened to this month, deplored the acoustic of the Brahms recordings, praised the clarity of the Tallis. Back at the radio station, Hester would illustrate his reviews with extracts from the records. "Another impeccable unscripted monologue," she said. "Are we going to the film theatre this week?"

"If you like. Yes, of course. Forgive me for not being more sociable," he said, reaching for an excuse. "Must be my second childhood creeping up on me."

"So long as it keeps you young."

He laughed at that and patted her hand, yet suddenly he was anxious for her to leave, so that he could think. Had he told himself the truth without meaning to? Surely that should gladden him: he'd had a happy childhood, he didn't need to think of the aftermath in that house. As soon as Hester drove away he hurried to the kitchen, closed the door again and again, listening intently. The more he listened, the less sure he was how much it sounded like a door in the house where he'd spent his childhood.

He crossed the kitchen, which he'd scrubbed and polished that morning, to the back door. As he unlocked it he thought he heard a dog scratching at it, but there was no dog outside. Wind swept across the muddy fields and through the creaking trees at the end of the short garden, bringing him scents of early spring and a faceful of rain. From the back door of his childhood home he'd been able to see the graveyard, but it hadn't bothered him then; he'd made up stories to scare his friends. Now the open fields were reassuring. The smell of damp wood that seeped into the kitchen must have to do with the weather. He locked the door and read Sherlock Holmes for a while, until his hands began to shake. Just tired, he told himself.

Soon the couple upstairs came home. Key heard them dump their purchases in their kitchen, and then footsteps hurried to the television. In a minute they were chattering above the sounds of a gunfight in Abilene or Dodge City or at some corral, as if they weren't aware that spectators were expected to stay off the street or at least keep their voices down. At dinnertime they sat down overhead to eat almost when Key did, and the double image of the sounds of cutlery made him feel as if he were in their kitchen as well as in his own. Perhaps theirs wouldn't smell furtively of damp wood under the linoleum.

After dinner he donned headphones and put a Bruckner symphony on the compact disc player. Mountainous shapes of music rose out of the dark. At the end he was ready for bed, and yet once there he couldn't sleep. The bedroom door had sounded suddenly very much more familiar. If it reminded him of the door of his old bedroom, what was wrong with that? The revival of memories was part of growing old. But his eyes opened reluctantly and stared at the murk, for he'd realized that the layout of his rooms was the same as the ground floor of his childhood home.

It might have been odder if they were laid out differently. No wonder he'd felt vulnerable for years as a young man after he'd been so close to death. All the same, he found he was listening for sounds he would rather not hear, and so when he slept at last he dreamed of the day the war had come to him.

It had been early in the blitz, which had almost passed the town by. He'd been growing impatient with hiding under the stairs whenever the siren howled, with waiting for his call-up papers so that he could help fight the Nazis. That day he'd emerged from shelter as soon as the All Clear had begun to sound. He'd gone out of the back of the house and gazed at the clear blue sky, and he'd been engrossed in that peaceful clarity when the stray bomber had droned overhead and dropped a bomb that must have been meant for the shipyard up the river.

He'd seemed unable to move until the siren had shrieked belatedly. At the last moment he'd thrown himself flat, crushing his father's flowerbed, regretting that even in the midst of his panic. The bomb had struck the graveyard. Key saw the graves heave up, heard the kitchen window shatter behind him. A tidal wave composed of earth and headstones and fragments of a coffin and whatever else had been upheaved rushed at him, blotting out the sky, the searing light. It took him a long time to struggle awake in his flat, longer to persuade himself that he wasn't still buried in the dream.

He spent the day in appraising records and waiting for Hester. He kept thinking he heard scratching at the back door, but perhaps that was static from the television upstairs, which sounded more distant today. Hester said she'd seen no animals near the flats, but she sniffed sharply as Key put on his coat. "I should tackle your landlord about the damp."

The film theatre, a converted warehouse near the shipyard, was showing *Citizen Kane*. The film had been made the year the bomb had fallen, and he'd been looking forward to seeing it then. Now, for the first time in his life, he felt that a film contained too much talk. He kept remembering the upheaval of the graveyard, eager to engulf him.

Then there was the aftermath. While his parents had been taking him to the hospital, a neighbour had boarded up the smashed window. Home again, Key had overheard his parents arguing about the window. Lying there almost helplessly in bed, he'd realized they weren't sure where the wood that was nailed across the frame had come from.

Their neighbour had sworn it was left over from work he'd been doing in his house. The wood seemed new enough; the faint smell might be trickling in from the graveyard. All the same, Key had given a piano recital as soon as he could, so as to have money to buy a new pane. But even after the glass had been replaced the kitchen had persisted in smelling slyly of rotten wood.

Perhaps that had had to do with the upheaval of the graveyard, though that had been tidied up by then, but weren't there too many perhapses? The loquacity of *Citizen Kane* gave way at last to music. Key drank with Hester in the bar until closing time, and then he realized that he didn't want to be alone with his gathering memories. Inviting Hester into his flat for coffee only postponed them, but he couldn't expect more of her, not at his age.

"Look after yourself," she said at the door, holding his face in her cool hands and gazing at him. He could still taste her lips as she drove away. He didn't feel like going to bed until he was calmer. He poured himself a large Scotch.

The Debussy preludes might have calmed him, except that the headphones couldn't keep out the noise from upstairs. Planes zoomed, guns chattered, and then someone dropped a bomb. The explosion made Key shudder. He pulled off the headphones and threw away their tiny piano, and was about to storm upstairs to complain when he heard another sound. The kitchen door was opening.

Perhaps the impact of the bomb had jarred it, he thought distractedly. He went quickly to the door. He was reaching for the doorknob when the stench of rotten wood welled out at him, and he glimpsed the kitchen—his parents' kitchen, the replaced pane above the old stone sink, the cracked back door at which he thought he heard a scratching. He slammed the kitchen door, whose sound was inescapably familiar, and stumbled to his bed, the only refuge he could think of.

He lay trying to stop himself and his sense of reality from trembling. Now, when the television might have helped convince him where he was, someone upstairs had switched it off. He couldn't have seen what he'd thought he'd seen, he told himself. The smell and the scratching might be there, but what of it? Was he going to let himself slip back into the way he'd felt after his return from hospital, terrified of venturing into a room in his own home, terrified of what might be waiting there for him? He needn't get up to prove that he wasn't, so long as he felt that he could. Nothing would happen while he lay there. That growing conviction allowed him eventually to fall asleep.

The sound of scratching woke him. He hadn't closed his bedroom door, he realised blurrily, and the kitchen door must have opened again, otherwise he wouldn't be able to hear the impatient clawing. He shoved himself angrily into a sitting position, as if his anger might send him to slam the doors before he had time to feel uneasy. Then his eyes opened gummily, and he froze, his breath sticking in his throat. He was in his bedroom—the one he
hadn't seen for almost fifty years.

He gazed at it—at the low slanted ceiling, the unequal lengths of flowered curtain, the comer where the new wallpaper didn't quite cover the old—with a kind of paralysed awe, as if to breathe would make it vanish. The breathless silence was broken by the scratching, growing louder, more urgent. The thought of seeing whatever was making the sound terrified him, and he grabbed for the phone next to his bed. If he had company—Hester—surely the sight of the wrong room would go away. But there had been no phone in his old room, and there wasn't one now.

He shrank against the pillow, smothering with panic, then he threw himself forward. He'd refused to let himself be cowed all those years ago and by God, he wouldn't let himself be now. He strode across the bedroom, into the main room.

It was still his parents' house. Sagging chairs huddled around the fireplace. The crinkling ashes flared, and he glimpsed his face in the mirror above the mantel. He'd never seen himself so old. "Life in the old dog yet," he snarled, and flung open the kitchen door, stalked past the blackened range and the stone sink to confront the scratching.

The key that had always been in the back door seared his palm with its chill. He twisted it, and then his fingers stiffened, grew clumsy with fear. His awe had blotted out his memory, but now he remembered what he'd had to ignore until he and his parents had moved away after the war. The scratching wasn't at the door at all. It was behind him, under the floor.

He twisted the key so violently that the shaft snapped in half. He was trapped. He'd only heard the scratching all those years ago, but now he would see what it was. The urgent clawing gave way to the sound of splintering wood. He made himself turn on his shivering legs, so that at least he wouldn't be seized from behind.

The worn linoleum had split like rotten fruit, a split as long as he was tall, from which broken planks bulged jaggedly. The stench of earth and rot rose toward him, and so did a dim shape—a hand, or just enough of one to hold together and beckon jerkily. "Come to us," whispered a voice from a mouth that sounded clogged with mud. "We've been waiting for you."

Key staggered forward, in the grip of the trance that had held him ever since he'd wakened. Then he flung himself aside, away from the yawning pit. If he had to die, it wouldn't be like this. He fled through the main room, almost tripping over a Braille novel, and dragged at the front door, lurched into the open. The night air seemed to shatter like ice into his face. A high sound filled his ears, speeding closer. He thought it was the siren, the All Clear. He was blind again, as he had been ever since the bomb had fallen. He didn't know it was a lorry until he stumbled into its path. In the moment before it struck him he was wishing that just once, while his sight was restored, he had seen Hester's face.

THE END

To be continued in…

**Demonic Visions
50 Horror Tales
Book 5**